Huckleberry Finn in Love and War

The Lost Journals

Dan Walker

PublishAmerica
Baltimore

First printing

ISBN: 1-4241-9476-8
PUBLISHED BY PUBLISHAMERICA, LLLP
www.publishamerica.com
Baltimore

Printed in the United States of America

Dedication

To my wife, Mary DeGroote Walker

And my mother, Mary Catherine Moore Walker

Author's Note

Even contemplating a sequel to Sam Clemens's immortal *Huck* requires some chutzpah—although it's been attempted before, notably by Clemens himself, who gave up after a half-hearted sixty pages or so. For myself, I certainly wanted to spin a good yarn—or, if you will, to spin the yarn Clemens himself might have spun had he followed his heroes where logic would have led them: to the cataclysmic events of 1861-1865. Perhaps he sensed that and shied away—perhaps those events required other voices, like that of my narrator, with which he felt less familiar.

Whatever the case, I reject old Sam's gambit, in the original, of calling attention to possible "morals" by denying them. There are morals here. I am, after all, a teacher, and it was the encouragement (and occasional gibes) of my students who led me to this presumptuous effort. Why disregard (they wondered) Clemens's own sixty-or-so pages, however half-hearted? Because he himself disregarded them, of course, as he had every right to do. But it seemed to me that his characters had attained lives of their own that could not so easily be cut off. They belonged, if not to me, at least to the ages.

Where would they be when History called? What choices would they make? For the boy who once said, "All right then, I'll go to Hell," what might that mean when his duty was to abandon the love of his life? To kill or capture close friends on the other side?

Hell might be preferable.

Prologue

Beside my bed is one of those glass bubbles with a winter scene inside it. You know, with a little house and a sleigh and a forest of fir trees, and when you shake it, it's full of snow. It's the latest thing. My wife gave it to me to calm my nerves, and there is something pacifying about it, to imagine yourself inside that glass with a little warm shack right ahead under the trees, and all around you is snow, and you're riding home in a red sleigh, and everything's made of water and glass, or whatever it is they're making these things out of nowadays, and home is right there when the snow settles, and your duty is just to be there—right there—and how hard can that be?

The trouble is the whole thing just reminds me of another little bubble inside my head, and there's a forest in that one, too, but instead of a house there is a row of fresh graves, three of them, each with a sword thrust into it—two with little pieces of paper tied to their hilts, the third topped with a riding boot and a black slouch hat. It's dusk in that jar, and when it shakes, instead of snow I see smoke streaked with moonlight, and off in the woods I hear axes and the sound of guns.

What it takes to give that jar a good shake is what happened the other day: my neighbor, a Mr. Chiang, told me a reporter had talked to him about a topic that might concern me:

"He seem interested in what happen to somebody name of Huckleberry Finn."

Just tosses it off, like mentioning the weather. "But why now?" I wonder. "Why in blazes now?"

"Don't know why in blazes. But this your field, so I tell him talk to you."

Well. Whoever it was, and whatever he might already know, I knew he was missing a crucial piece of evidence—and it's not in any jar, but in a drawer of my dresser. That night I took it out and looked at it: Huck's journal, a thick stack of paper sewn between cardboard, which once, at least, was impressively marbled. It's much faded now, except for a monarch butterfly pressed inside it in a wax envelope. Her wings are still black and gold. (How is that possible, I wonder?)

So it is time to think about preservation.

One way, of course, is just to tell the story myself, since I already know more of it than any reporter is likely to find out. But how can I do that? I'm old. It's getting late for this.

Chiang thinks I'm making too big an issue of it: "Have some student type, and you edit, then publish. Simple."

"But there's my part, you know," I point out. "And there are other sources, too. What about those? So I'll tell it." I smile at him brightly. "Readers will like me, don't you think?"

"You?" He shakes his head sadly. "You are a cynical old man."

"Well, maybe, but what about that reporter? He's going to want to know all the mysteries—find out every—"

"Get scoop on reporter!" he harrumphs. Then he leans over my table, scoops up a page with the trowel-like blade on the stump of his left wrist. "Look like you already start. Your book about Love and War, *you say?"*

"Well, Yin and Yang, you know." I hesitate: this isn't my field. "They can attract, can't they?"

"Yes—" He taps the manuscript gently with his blade. "Yes—if they not explode each other first."

Part 1

...So there ain't nothing more to write about, and I am rotten glad of it, because if I'd a knowed what a trouble it was to make a book I wouldn't a tackled it and ain't a-going to no more. But I reckon I got to light out for the Territory ahead of the rest, because Aunt Sally she's going to adopt me and sivilize me and I can't stand it. I been there before.

~Conclusion of *The Adventures of Huckleberry Finn* by Mark Twain

1. Born Again

It's dark in the barrel and hot and sticky, but there are cracks between the staves, and he can breathe just fine. The jouncing when they carry him to the wharf is all right, too; he can stand that well enough with the cushion of pork fat, and even the rolling up the plank, that's kind of exciting, you know, and then they put out to sea, and *that* rolling is no problem either—nothing worse than what a river does to a raft in a rough breeze. The ride on the little steamer is pretty slow, though, and he's getting itchy and uncomfortable, but he has to stay put till they're out to the fleet and under sail.

And finally they're aboard and re-stacking the barrels aft before stowing them below, and as they roll him along he's starting to think about when to pull his escape latch with the thumb loop, but—hey! They've stacked him topside down! And that means his latch is pinned on the deck.

He hadn't considered that possibility.

And sure enough, he soon feels the soft lard moving up his neck—or down, rather—and minute by minute the strong, ripe gobs of fat are around his chin, then his cheeks, his ears, his hair, his mouth, the hairs of his nose, cutting off the sound and the light—the air—and with his last good breath comes a tang of salt. He cries aloud, or tries to. But then, "All goods below!" He hears the command ring out, its noise covering his own, and the men start at the end—the other end!—at least an hour away from his own barrel. A potentially fatal hour.

The last thing he can hear is the cry of a gull.

The sergeant guarding the operation on deck moves back along the line, counting them off, and now he puts his ear down next to a barrel at the end of the bottom row. He has to grip the rail to keep from banging his head. It's a raw day for south Texas, and even in the bay there's a good chop. They are far enough out now that the line of gulls patrolling the shore seems to bob up and down, above and below the horizon. Not a good day for loading at all, but the officers are in a hurry, and…what *is* that?

"Lieutenant!" he calls out, "I think there's something in here. Lieutenant?"

An officer sticks his head up from the hold.

"Why, of course there is, Prescott. There's a couple hundred pound of salt pork."

"Yessir, but I hear something like scratching and then like a choking or something. If there's nothing but pig bellies in there, sir, they ain't all dead yet!"

"Choking? Probably some animal's got itself—"

"There it is again, Sir! Lord, it sounds human!"

"All right, Sergeant, get a crowbar or something. A bayonet might work. Let's see if we've got a stowaway. And keep that musket handy."

And soon he stands on deck, in nothing but a pair of torn-away knickers, shivering in sweat and pork grease in the raw breeze, and suffering the laughter of soldiers and sailors and the cool gaze of an American captain, plus a few other officers, and a couple of muskets leveled at his chest. So he can tell he's in trouble, that his fat (so to speak) is in the fire. Not that that's anything new for him.

"Well, sir," says the captain, with a bit of a smile, "that's a strange outfit in which to put to sea, runaway or no. And what are you running from, you say? A father who whipped you, but who's dead now, and a nice Christian family who wants to adopt you, and—a friend named Tom whose *games* you're afraid of?"

"Yessir."

"And the cavalry—you ran away from *that*?"

"Yessir. I was just a stable boy."

"But not because General Taylor mistreated you—"

"No, sir. I liked him fine. But I wanted to see a battle, sir, and I wanted to see real Mexican soldiers—and see the elephants—"

And that gets a laugh, of course, from the men on deck. *See the elephant! He wants to see the elephant!* But the captain doesn't laugh. He looks over at an officer seated on one of the barrels, portly and bewhiskered, but with alert eyes. "Well, General Scott?" says the captain. "Shall we heave to and put him ashore? That will take time."

"Not like *that,* certainly." The general chuckles. "We'd at least have to dress him and feed him first—and *clean* him. But even then—well he can't be more than fourteen or fifteen."

"Eighteen, sir!"

"Well, I doubt that. And be glad I *do* doubt it, young man, because if I thought it were *true*, I'd throw you overboard and let the sharks deal with you." The laughter stops. "Whatever it is, we're south of the line by now. We can't just go straight to shore. General Worth, can your troop ship take a cabin boy? If well supervised? If we promise to get him off your hands when we come ashore."

Worth, leaning against a mast, harrumphs. "If you say so, General. I'll give him to Totten to run errands when he's got the dropsy."

Colonel Totten, seated, looks as pale and un-seaworthy as advertised. A gull on the mizzen behind him picks curiously at his shoulder strap. "Fine," he says, then to the captain: "He's all yours, Captain. Teach him to pray. That's what we'll all be doing soon enough, I'll warrant."

The captain is hard to read when he turns to the boy—is he pleased or not? "Well, sir. What did you say your name was?"

"Huckleberry, sir. Huckleberry Finn."

Yes, that's Our Boy. But of course the captain to whom he is assigned wants to know more about his ward than the runaway-orphan story, assuming that's true. And Huck, for his own part, is thrilled at being billeted with an officer, though the man's patient questions make the boy nervous, and he prays a bit more than Huck finds comfortable. The good captain, however, does have enough sense not to "come at me," says Huck, with salvation in mind. Also he is patient with Huck's own questions and treats him not like a waif, but like a soldier. "You, sir, are part of a military expedition," he tells him, gesturing with a sea biscuit as he sits on the box it came from, holding a wind-blown chart down with the other hand, "and you must earn your rations like the rest."

One duty assigned is to keep a journal, but Our Boy also learns how to scrub a deck and oil a capstan and break down a box for kindling and do other jobs, and it turns out he has pretty good sea legs—unlike the captain, who, ironically for an excellent military horseman, throws up a lot. This is early March after all—a stormy time along the north Mexican coast in 1848. Huck has a light foot in the rigging, and a sharp eye on the mast-head—spotting a

Mexican mortar on a rail car behind a clump of chaparral several hundred yards inland, for example, in time to keep the ship out of range. And at night in the ship's claustrophobic officers' mess, where everybody but Huck has to stoop till seated, he gets to listen to soldiers with names like McClellan, Hooker, Johnston, and Grant—names you have heard—but they talk a lot more about rail-heads and swamp-dredging and the inanities of peace-time fort life than they do about Indian fighting and outlaw-hunting, which would have interested Huck. After a few evenings, he writes:

I was board [*sic*] as a pine plank. If I had to hear another story about building canals and such, I allowed I'd climb back into my barrel and strike out for shore, sharks or no sharks!

He should have gone to the enlisted men's mess with the regulars in Worth's division, the Sixth Infantry, say. They'd at least have taught him to curse and play cards.

As usual, of course, Huck's instincts are right: most of these officers were egregious bores, no matter what the subject. I got to meet many of them myself, years later, after they had much more than swamp-dredging to be interesting about, had they been able. If you don't believe me, read their memoirs. Self-promotion, mostly. Except for Grant's, maybe, which are brisk and interesting. He was dying of cancer at the time, which may put things in perspective. And he had, I admit, a capable editor: Sam Clemens himself! Huck's captain was a larger figure, for better or worse, and *he* knew how to use words. But he died before he could write his own story. How strange, then, that this captain should have insisted Huck himself keep a journal. Perhaps for its presumed educational value? It's lucky for us, though, because in it he answers the captain's questions about what he has been up to. One promise Our Boy did keep, of course, was to light out. And he tells Captain Robert E. Lee—Scott's chief of engineers—all about it.

2. Lighting Out

It was a cold night, with a pebbly snow and a thin wind. Pebbles was good, though, and with a little packed snow they wouldn't clatter much on the rebound off the pane and roust the neighbors.

I was looking up at the light in the second-floor window. I knowed[1] he was awake and likely reading of a book because he don't use a candle to say prayers, on account of a candle shadow is the Devil's tongue when it flickers, and that hurts the prayer. Why it don't hurt the Baron Von Trenk or none of them other heroes, he don't explain. And I was just about to make my toss, going for a bounce off the sill, which would make less of a racket, when I stopped and thought, as I watched that flickering: did I really want to be worrying with all the nonsense in Tom Sawyer's head, when there was like to be enough of the real kind where I was headed? Elephants and A-rabs! Why they probably has *real* elephants in the Territory. Huck Finn, I says to myself, ain't you learned by now that pretend foolishness and real foolishness is a dangerous brew? Ain't you learned nothing? And I decided I'd learned one thing, right enough: people that stands out in the cold making up their minds can't complain when their thoughts is froze over. So I snuck back into the widow's and allowed I'd strike out by myself—and I'd do it soon, before spring even. Tom Sawyer, I knowed, could *smell* adventure like a dog could smell a dead skunk. I wanted to be far enough downwind to be safe.

But then, just a few days later, after church, there was this note stuck in the little testament the widow makes me carry, to "preserve my soul" she says, if only I'll clutch it to my breast when I feel the "wonder lust" coming on, she says. Well, I knowed by the writing on the paper whose wonder lust this was all about! The note says:

Huck—I'm coming with you! We'll head out Easter morning on account of the egg hunt will give us cover, and maybe Becky will come, though she says she won't and the judge would [disinherit?] her, but I think she likes me enough. At the hunt I'll leave you a note about where to meet—in the purple egg with the white circle.

Tom

But, my lord, I didn't know which was worse: to have Tom Sawyer and his nonsense along, or Becky Thatcher and *her* nonsense. Anyways I knowed sure as shootin' that having them *both* along was a horrible fate! I almost druther be adopted.

****

Lee looks up. "You didn't like Becky?"

"Well, sure, I guess so. But she's a *girl,* you know. And girls are trouble."

"I see."

"Most girls. Leastwise, that's my experience."

"Well—when *did* you leave, then?"

In February, as Huck tells it, while it was still cold, he had left his money with Judge Thatcher, except for twenty dollars with which he had secretly hopped a stage for Topeka. The stage got nearly there before breaking an axle in a wash-out and being captured and robbed by the notorious Loftus Gang. Before the Loftuses could decide what to do—they had actually been bounty-hunting for runaway Negroes—they in turn were attacked by renegade Kiowa, who robbed and scalped the Loftuses and would have liked to scalp Huck and the passengers—one of whom was Buck Grangerford, who, as it happens, had not died in the infamous feud after all, but survived with a romantically consumptive lung and a determination to work on his uncle's newspaper in California. And it's lucky for us because Buck later turns out to be a good source—or at least a vivid one. Lives a long time, too, for a consumptive.

Well, it seems the boys convinced the Kiowa that they were acolytes of some sect or other and were Seekers with magical powers. Just to be safe, the Indians decided to send the two off into the prairie in search of Truth. Instead of Truth (which would have saved us all a lot of trouble) they found a troop of U.S. cavalry, who took the boys to the fort and then went back after the renegades and their hostages. Lee's first reaction to the tale is amusement:

The captain laughed hard and allowed he could "sense some real 'stretchers' here, as you would put it."

But I swore it was all true. "See, Buck was a lot like Tom, Captain," I says, "and I guess I been with Tom long enough that it rubbed off on me, too." Then I told about the fort and how Buck allowed he'd still head West as he planned, and Miss Nancy, she'd go on, too.

The captain wanted to know who Miss Nancy was, and I says all I knowed was she was the niece of some Secretary of Something or Other in California, and she was very pretty and awful proud and brave when the Indians and outlaws had us. The captain asked if I was sweet on her, and when I didn't say nothing he laughs and says: "Well, you're turning a bit red, Mister. But that's to your credit."

Then he leans over the rail—we'd been sitting at the bench on the poop deck—and he looked down at the foam coming up from the stern, and the smell of salt spray was strong, and I was afraid he was going to upchuck, but he didn't.

Instead he says—and he warn't smiling now, "Huckleberry, do you know what you have chosen here?" he says, and he picks up a half biscuit somebody had dropped and sails it out over the wake, and a couple of gulls dove right down and went to tussling over it. They looked like one big bird flapping around. "The Mexicans will not let us march right up to their capital and parade down the street. We will have to fight our way. Men will die." He looked down at me. "Some of them very young."

"Yessir, I know that." Then I says, "I seen folks shot down with my own eyes back in Arkansas, while I was spittin' distance away. And I been shot at myself. I won't run from a fight."

"That's not what I'm afraid of," he says, and looks away again. "I'm afraid you'll run the other way—*toward* one. Instead of following orders. Do you get my meaning, mister? What it means to be a soldier?"

I said I thought I did—but how I could do *anything* disobedient on this ship was a mystery to me! Then I told the captain about the fort and

how I wanted to join the cavalry right there on the spot and claimed to be eighteen, but nobody'd believe me. But they'd sign me on as a stable boy if I could get a "parent or garden" to "a-test" I was at least 16, and I told Miss Nancy that if she really wanted to show appreciation for rescuing her, like she said, she could 'dopt me till I enlisted and then let the cavalry sivilize me. Well, she thought about it a bit, and finally she signed for me as my older sister. She allowed it was better than just leaving me to shift for myself. She looked at me when we said goodbye and took my face between her hands and I was afraid she was going to kiss me. But she just give a sigh and says, "Some day you'll have a sweetheart, Huck Finn," and she smiles and says she wanted me to promise her I wouldn't tell that girl a pack of lies and go off into the desert. So I said I promised. What else could I do with her smooth, pretty face right up to my freckly one like that, and THEN she done it, she kissed me real soft right on the lips, and she smiled and said she had to do that, being as she was my sister, and then she turns and walks back to the coach, and I wondered if I'd ever see her again.

Well, now I was a member of B Troop, and then—and if this ain't luck, frogs don't eat flies!—on the very day Buck and the others headed out west, B Troop gets orders to help cover a wagon train going to General Taylor's army on the Rio Grande, because floods and ice floes had done choked off the river traffic.

The captain didn't say nothing about that kiss, but he said he was surprised I didn't enjoy the cavalry and asked how come I still run away. Well, I allowed the cavalry was fine as far as it went. But it turns out stable hands don't see much outlaws or Injuns, but they see *lots* of manure. By the time we got to Texas I ain't seen a Injun yet, except the drunk one that cooked for us and spit in the gravy to give it a "French kiss," as he put it, but I seen lots of turds, from horse's asses of *all* kinds, and it was my job to shovel them all. The officers said things was quiet, partly because it was peaceful country along there anyhow, and partly because we was "a military train," and there was enough of us to scare off anything smarter'n a wood tick. So I made up my mind that Mexico was where the fun was.

And so, one morning the men stowing supplies on one of Winfield Scott's troop ships at the mouth of the Rio Grande get the surprise we have described. The experience yields some fun later when it turns out that the engineers Huck is with can sleep in the bug-ridden Mexican low country only if they slather themselves with pork fat and sleep under shields made from the barrels it came from: Huck has been there and can give clever advice. But, sea legs or no, Huck is a landlubber. He wants to get to shore. To see Mexico.

And finally he does. Scott makes up his mind to come ashore in the sand hills, which offer some cover, and it's a great wide blue-sky day with a mild chop, and the boats lower away, with General Worth in his own launch looking every inch the soldier (and looks matter in war, as they do in everything else) with his guidon fluttering on the prow, and the Sixth is in the lead, sergeants and boatswains hollering at the oarsmen to make time, and Huck watches from his launch with the engineers as the men of the Sixth splash onto the beach and form in a hurry—the defenders will open any second!—and they rush the sand ridge with a cheer—and take it! No defenders! Someone has blundered: the Mexicans have sent no force to contest the landing. It's a relief to Worth's regulars, of course, but a disappointment to Huck, who was hoping to See the elephant. For Our Boy, it doesn't come today.

But it will come.

3. The Head Can Save the Heart from Some Tight Spots

Next day, as Lee and a naval ensign supervise the unloading, Huck is given a camp stool and told to play checkers on the beach with a soldier who had given his knee a bad sprain while disembarking. The fellow, a young sergeant named Prescott, is not a bit pleased about his lay-off since it means missing out on various details to go into town—to buy supplies and hire wagons and maybe stop by a local "'stablishment." Huck, however, enjoys watching and is impressed by the military precision on display.

It warn't nothing like the river steamers I seen back home. The soldiers and sailors sung songs to keep time, and I'd heard some of that at home on the river, but here there was no slouching and loafing nor dragging things and stuffing them ever which way and shaving off tops and shorting bales and barrels to make them lighter. No, sir, everything here was weighed and counted, before and after, by a officer with a clipboard, and everything tied off all regular, and tight as a tick in canvas or barrel or board box, and *clean* canvas, too. And all numbered and stamped with USA or USN.

Mexican folks from the town had come to the shore to watch—and some maybe hoping to get hired. They was in a holiday sort of mood, just like folks at home, except that when a flag come ashore nobody uncovered and there warn't no cheering. It was a pretty ornery lot, except for one old white-haired feller, which everybody seemed to look up to. They had a blanket spread out for him up on a sand hill with a good view and a wood chair to sit on, but I don't think he enjoyed it, because he didn't smile nor nothing. There was a couple of girls with him with dark hair who looked pretty and had a little more interest. The young one would run down toward the beach and holler in Mexican at

us, then run back up. I smiled and waved. I wondered was she talking to me or the sergeant, and when I asked him if he spoke any Mexican, the sergeant said, "She called you a boy-man and a boy-soldier, both of which you are, so don't pay her no mind. Didn't you hear the captain? Now make your move."

Well, when she run back to where the old man set, the older girl spoke pretty stern to her. The older one was very pretty, too. I didn't pay no more attention, but I do wonder what kind of a fight a country can put up that sends girls and old folks to meet the enemy on its shores. And they calls *me* a boy-man!

A few days later, during the brief siege of Vera Cruz, Lee and a lieutenant (pork-greased or not, we are not informed) are making their way beyond the flank of the siege line to locate a battery placement. It needs to be undetectable till the moment of truth. They locate it, all right—Lee has an uncanny eye—but returning through heavy brush they sound a bit too much like a Mexican patrol.

I weren't supposed to be there but when the captain seen I'd come, he allowed I might as well make myself useful and so I carried the maps back in the big tube-case they kept them in. It was dark by the time we was through climbing around the hills and I was one big 'skeeter bite, greased or not. On the way back I was behind the injun-ears *[sic!]*, and it's a good thing because there was a mess of those saw bushes in the way, and the soldiers could whack them with their swords, so it was easier for me.

We got to camp a bit quicker than the officers thought, I think, or else the pickets had been pushed out further, because we was challenged when not expecting it. We shouted out the pass sign well enough, but something about it didn't strike the guard right, and he levels his pistol right at the captain, who stops in his tracks so sudden that I launch into him from behind with the map-case. The captain pinned it under his arm to keep it from falling but he was thrown forward off balance, and the guard corporal fired his musket from a crouch, and the captain dropped to his knees—all in the blink of an eye. I yelled and so did the lieutenant, and we was recognized and all right

now—there warn't no more shooting—but I was sure the captain was hurt. He opened his jacket to see what the damage was and seen the ball had gone between his arm and chest and straight through the length of the map case. It had a hole through the first of its ends, which was heavy tin, and a big dent in the other. Capt. Lee shook the case and out come a lead ball, and he laughed.

"You see, Mr. Huckleberry, you can't place all your faith in maps, but you cannot live without a sturdy map *case*." He clapped me on the shoulder and dropped the ball into my hand. It was still warm. "It's helpful to have some luck, too! Perhaps this may bring you some."

The corporal who shot at us turned out to be part of a new battery, and we heard that their officer of the day—a Lieutenant Jackson—had the man put under arrest for firing without finishing the challenge first and nearly killing an American officer. All think that was pretty strict and that such an officer will never be able to motivate troops.

This brush with hot lead reacquaints Huck with thoughts that have not occurred to him since covering up the face of his friend Buck Grangerford, who he had thought was dead, more than a year ago. As he and Lee sit near the surf on a couple of camp stools while the army unloads for the move inland, Huck brings it up:

I asked him what happened if a soldier died while he was trying to kill a fellow in the other army—would he go to Heaven?—and the captain sort of grunted and said, well, the Lord knew what it meant to do your duty, and he knew what was in your heart, too, and if you didn't have the heart of a murderer that was what counted.

But you see I was thinking about Buck—who was shot in a feud he didn't know no more about than a goose did, and shooting at good folks on the other side. Buck like to died that day—but he didn't. What did that mean? Did he say some prayer at the last minute, or did somebody just flip a coin? I asked the captain what *he* thought happens when somebody dies.

And he looks at me, then he looks back at the sea and says, "Judgment!"

And I says, "You mean like Heaven or Hell?" and he says it all depends on whether a body done his duty or not, but that didn't quite

answer—did the Shepherdsons and Grangerfords *both* get to go to Heaven? So I says, "Duty to who?

And he says right off, "To God and country."

Well, I studied about that a minute and then I asked what if God and country was on different sides? He didn't say nothing for a while, and when he give an answer it warn't that it just couldn't never happen, which is what I was expecting. Instead, he says, "In that case, Huckleberry, you will have to choose the Lord—and hope your country follows." He was looking out at the ocean. "And if I ever have to make such a choice—and I make it wrong—I hope I do not survive the issue."

I says I wished the same for me, but I warn't smart enough to make any such choice, and he says, "That answer doesn't come from the head, Huckleberry; it comes from the heart. Still," and he turned and smiled at me, "the head can save the heart from some tight spots. So learn as much as you can, young man. Learn as much as you can!"

And it's funny—he hadn't said nothing at all about prayer.

Vera Cruz surrenders after a couple of shellings—with little heart or head required. Scott loads up with supplies and reinforcements and heads up the road to the capital city. As the ground rises, the vegetation goes from palm and sawgrass to juniper, oak, and pine. The air gets higher and cleaner, the campfires brighter, and for a time the Mexicans get mostly out-snookered or outfought. Still, there are moments when things might have gone differently, and perhaps it's the luck of Our Boy. But his luck is about to change. For we now approach a crucial moment: the first appearance of the Butterfly. After that, things will never be the same.

4. Cerro Gordo: Being a Aide Ain't So Bad After All

Cerro Gordo is a mountain—a rocky outcrop north of the Mexican "National Road." This is the route Scott and the Americans are taking up into Mexico. It's well built—has a good, American, turnpike-style feel to it, even in the passes. Today, even motor cars have no trouble with its gentle grade and macadamized surface. The heights to its north are fortified, of course—the Mexicans have several batteries on Cerro Gordo and another mountain beyond that—and so are the ridges between the mountain and the Rio del Plan, which is not fordable there. It is a damned strong position. I've walked the ground myself, and I don't see how any determined force stronger than a deacon board could be dislodged from it—no matter how many attackers there were—and Scott has only about twelve thousand, same as the Mexicans. I guess "determined" is the key word. Did Santa Anna poll his troops to see how many were (A) totally determined to do or die for the Mexican Republic, (B) somewhat determined, C) slightly determined, or (D) not at all determined? Perhaps he should have.

At any rate, Scott has to attack soon. Coffee's running short, and Washington's summer round of obligée dinner parties and croquet teas will soon begin. But Scott is no fool: it is a strong position. Is there a way to flank it? Can he deal with the guns on the mountain without walking right up the road under their mouths? He sends Lee, his expert on ways and means, to find out. Huck wants to go, of course, as before, but Lee points out that this is far more dangerous than slogging around Vera Cruz, which, Huck will recall, nearly got them both killed. Huck must stick close to General Twiggs and function as an aide-de-camp. It sounds important, so Huck is mollified. He goes right away to ask his friend Sergeant Prescott what exactly an "aidycamp" is and finds that Jack's outfit, a pioneer company, has been transferred temporarily to Twiggs's division.

Huck finds the sergeant while carrying water to a work group leveling a gun site, which is choked with nettle and riddled with chiggers and fire ants. When the men take a break, Huck sees a soldier whip off his blue cap and mop his brow with a red bandana, his friend's trademark, and Huck shouts to him. The two sit on a stack of rails, munching crackers and dipping water out of the buckets Huck has been hauling.

Huck has already found that his high-sounding staff job is mainly to carry things and otherwise stay out of the way, but now he has other questions on his mind—about that "ball" Lee gave him, and about what is going to happen eventually up the road ahead.

I took the ball out and showed it to him. I asked the sergeant was it a bullet, and he said sure it was, and it was from a rifled musket. Most of the men have smooth-bores, he said, but they give rifles like this to some—specially scouts and pickets. You could tell because of the scars from the barrel grooves, which were there so when the ball was fired it expanded and could fit the grooves, which would make it spin.

"Why does it want to do that?" I asked.

"Why, because then it curves, and you can shoot around corners."

When my eyes got wide, he laughed and told me it was so the ball could sort of tunnel through the air better. Course, I'd used buckshot myself hunting with Pap, and I'd seen rifle bullets, but I never really studied them with the thought of being hit by one. The lead felt heavy, but also sort of soft, like gold. You could scratch it with your fingernail easy.

"That's cause it's lead. Lead is soft. Plus it's a lot cheaper than gold."

"That's so," I said, "but not near as pretty." Tom and I had once had the idea of scratching our initials in the gold coins we found in the cave so's we could spot them quick if robbers got their hands on them. When I told Jack I'd already carved my initials into the bullet with a pen knife, he jumped like I'd said I had smallpox.

"Damnation, Huck! Why'd you do that? Every soldier's afraid there's a ball with his name on it, and you go and *put* yours on one." He studied about it for a minute. Then he brightened a little and said, "Well, maybe it's okay. See, there's one with your name on it now, but

you've got it, not somebody else. You just got to hold onto it, by God, and you're safe. Maybe I ought to do the same thing."

"But wouldn't it be too soft to do no damage?" I said.

Before he could answer, one of the others—a tall soldier with a bit of gray in his beard—spoke up. "Huck, you want to see some 'damage,' looky here." And he pulled up his jacket, which was so full of sweat and dust you almost couldn't tell it had ever been blue. I could see a big round scar about the size of a half-dollar on his right side below his ribs. It looked twice the size of my bullet.

"Made by a ball no bigger than yourn," he says. Then he turned around, so I could see his back. There was two huge, ugly white scars on his back, like somebody had ripped him with a tomahawk and a scalping knife at the same time. I could see the side of his face and his chin whiskers as he looked back at me.

"You can touch 'em if you want. They don't hurt much no more."

I reached out an sort of lightly run my finger over one of them. It felt smoother than a man's skin normally would, almost like ridged glass, and cooler than you'd think hot lead would of left it. "I was shot by a Mexican in Texas a year ago," he says. "The doctors laid me out for dead, but I screamed so much they had to either shoot me or try to do something for me, so they give me enough whiskey to get a ox drunk, and when I passed out they just washed me out and sewed me up. They said they could shoot a stream of water clean through me. The bullet hit a bone in the hip and split into two pieces, and then those two went their separate ways an' out the back. The doctors said one barely missed a spleen and some other high-point targets, and the other missed the livers and took a bite of kidney with it as a souvenir on the way out. I was passed out for a week from losing blood, and then I got the influx and the outflux, and then the pleurusy or somethin', and then the sweats, and then one day I just sort of woke up and said, 'Damn, that hurts!' And later that year I was back in the ranks.

"Well, the camp surgeon said I was the luckiest single son of a bitch he ever seen. Plenty weren't that lucky. In that fight in south Texas the Mexicans had a twelve-pounder cannon on our right, and our color sergeant got his head blowed clean off by a solid shot. He stood straight up in line for a solid minute with no head and the blood

pumpin' up onto the flag, which was still in his fists. One of the boys that was killed had—" But I didn't wait to hear what that boy had. I went on about my business toting water. Maybe being a *aide* ain't so bad after all.

Despite such tales, Huck's lust for action survives, and later that day he figures out where the captain has probably gone. It's easy to see Cerro Gordo, and even the careful Lee has left clear marks through the brush and sand by the road and a trail up toward the high ground. Plus, both are on foot, and Our Boy is fifteen and rested, whereas Lee is forty or so and carrying twenty pounds of gear.

The upshot is that after a two-hour hike Huck catches up with Lee, who has been staking out a watering hole below the summit with clear signs of recent use. Lee hears a movement behind him and knows that to be taken prisoner here would mean loss of the element of surprise—and possibly his life. So he must capture—or kill silently—whoever is approaching. There are real trees up here in the mountains, so it is easy to lie in wait. And thus, Huck, creeping up the trail, is suddenly pinned from behind by a muscular arm around his chest and another over his mouth. Somehow he also feels a bayonet against his neck, although that would seem to require a third hand. He hears a gruff whisper:

"Struggle and I shall break your neck! Silencio!" Lee is not sure if that's the right word. Not for the last time, he regrets all those hours of French at the Point without a word of Spanish. It is instantly clear, however, who is his captive, and soon Huck is grinning sheepishly while Lee wonders if the boy has led the whole Mexican army onto him. And soon enough they hear much clearer sounds of approaching enemies. Lee ducks to the left of the trail, Huck to the right, and a squad of uniformed Mexican cavalrymen comes down to the spring to fill canteens and let the horses drink at the pool below. The Mexicans sit, drink, eat, come and go, in various numbers, for a long time. It looks as if there's never going to be a chance for the two Americans to reunite.

At one point, from Huck's side of the trail, there's a shout and what sounds to Lee like a scuffle. The engineer, who has covered himself with brush as best he can, is sure Huck has been captured and is only hoping the boy seems young enough to escape imprisonment or worse. The thought of what "worse" might be almost leads him to attempt a daring one-against-ten rescue, but his commitment to the mission keeps him quiet.

All afternoon the Mexicans come and go, and Lee maintains his position, almost in their midst. Fleas, spiders—who knows what?—all have their way with Lee, who moves not a muscle while desperately fighting off sleep. Finally, just after dark, the Mexicans leave and Lee takes the chance to look around and call softly for Huck. But there's no sign. Our Boy—prisoner or not—seems to be gone. Lee, however, has found the saddle between Cerro Gordo and the summit to its north, Atalaya. He can see and hear the Mexicans, in the moonlight, moving guns up the latter summit, which actually seems higher. He has calculated the best approach. Now he must return. In the dark it takes him most of the night. Scott, delighted to see Lee safe and sound, respects the engineer's judgment and makes plans quickly. Lee, going on fifty hours without sleep, is sent to lead Twiggs's division, nearly four thousand foot, plus a couple of light artillery batteries and a small regiment of horse, to the point of attack—which will sweep over a small swale and a meadow, up and over Atalaya and whatever is there, taking Cerro Gordo from behind, and then on across the road to cut off the main Mexican line. All this while Worth and Pillow are keeping Santa Anna excited about his right and front, near the river. At least that is the plan. Twiggs's signal to Scott that the waltz is starting will be a single cannon shot.

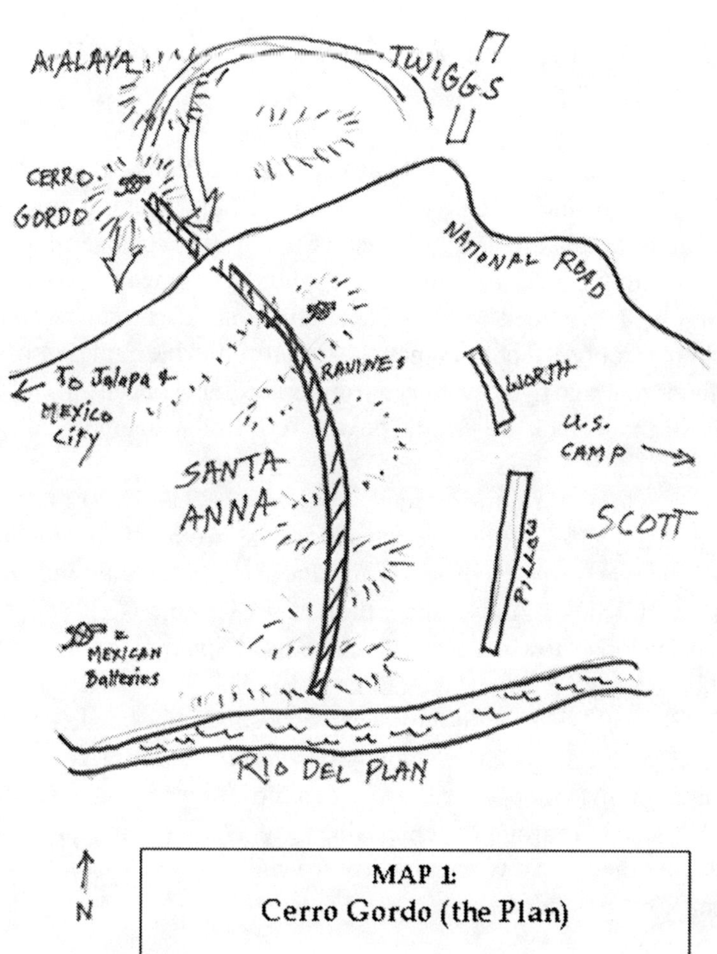

N

MAP 1:
Cerro Gordo (the Plan)

5. Charge Them to Hell, Captain!

And where is Our Boy? As it happens, he is not captured. Huck knows how to hide and does so very well. So well, in fact, that unlike Lee he does go to sleep. Early next morning he wakes, feeling a hand shaking him. As he comes around, he feels another hand over his mouth and a voice shushing him, but these are not the hand and voice of a captain of engineers or a Mexican *commandante*. No, indeed, they are both soft, the softest he can remember, and thus remarkably effective. When the face responsible comes into view, Huck is found and held by a new force. In this case it's a Mexican girl, as lovely as a *señorita* about Huck's age could be when covered with pine needles and stick-tights.

Huck lies there for some moments with her soft hand over his mouth, listening to her gentle breathing as she looks away around their laurel bush, watching her breast rise and fall beside him, the barely perceptible pulse in her neck, a small ant moving down under the cotton of her blouse.

Then she looks down at him and whispers in Spanish, smiles when he shakes his head and shrugs, then she tries English. "Who are you?" and something in Huck's eyes spills the beans, because now she laughs softly and says "Si, si! Where are you live? You with *soldados* at Vera Cruz, *sí*? I see you near *los navíos*. You are American boy-*hombre, no?* Checker-*soldado?*" She is thoroughly entertained by Huck's lame pretense at deafness—or idiocy. "*Si!* Where you live from?"

Huck now remembers her.

I recollected her—she was the girl yelled at us on the beach! Well, I knowed the jig was up with the deef and dumb act, so I said, "Missouri," and she put her finger up—Sh!—and said I should whisper. "You learn to whisper in school, si? Where es this Missouri? No!—no tell! I will think." Then she rolls over on her back and looks

straight up like the answer was somewhere in the laurel bush, and says, "Es in middle-west, no?" I nods my head and she smiles like she's right pleased with herself and asks me where I think she's from. I says I guess Mexico, and she looks at me like I'm the pitifulest school boy ever seen.

Then she whispers, "You no es smart as I am!"

Well, she asks me why I was with the *soldados*, and I says I was a aide, which is important, and I says I bet that was a better reason than *she* had. Well, that got her, and when she didn't answer right off I ask her why *she* was hiding.

She rolled back over close to me and says, "You must whisper…now, my father-uncle Hidalgo, es with these army for…how you say help him, keep bad away from…"

"Take care of him? Protect him?"

"Protect! Si—*Commandante*—General Santa Anna protect. But Father-Uncle say to me: 'No go out with *soldados*.' But I go, for I can ride—and what will hurt, si? But he may come—Sh!"

There was noises back up the trail, and she listened for a bit. Then she asks without turning, "What es your name, boy *soldado*?"

And I says, "Huckleberry," as quiet as I can.

And she looks back at me. "You name some kind of berry? This a baby-name, si? You no smell like berry, you smell like bad fat meat." And she laughed. "What es real name?" And I says it was as real as anything else about me, and as for the pig fat it kept off the skeeters, and then I told her how I got onto the ship. Well, she laughed out loud at that, then slapped her hand over her own mouth and looked stern—like she done disobeyed her own orders to shush and was mad at herself.

When she decided the coast was clear—it wasn't her "father-uncle" after all—she rolls out of the bushes and took my hand and led me over to the Mexican soldiers. There was a officer there on horseback with big moustaches, but behind them he looked pretty young and nervous and every now and then he'd shoot a look back up the trail like he was afraid of something. He reach down to the girl and says something sharp to her in Mexican and got down off his horse. He didn't seem that interested in me, only in her, but when he says

something to me in Mexican I knowed I had to try the deef-and-dumb act again or be found out for an American, and then they'd find Captain Lee, too. I just hoped the girl would go along. So I made signs like I couldn't hear and then I started drawing out a map in the dirt showing our army over near the river about to attack like *so*, right *there*, on the *other* end of the line—and I was doing pretty good, and all the while the girl was trying to 'translate' for him, but she was laughing the whole time, and I knowed she would give me up sooner or later, so when the Mexican turn to say something to the girl I turn and run off down the slope through the trees. The officer yells out something in Mexican, and I heard sounds that I knowed well was weapons being cocked to fire. I was making enough noise in the bushes that I'd be as easy to hit as a deer in a brush pit, but I heard the girl holler something back and then run a little way after me, but when the officer hollered at her something that sounded like "merry-possa" she stopped and let me go, and there warn't no shooting. So I guess she sort of liked me and didn't want me shot.

But why should she care if he's *caught*? My guess is that a commotion about the boy risks her own discovery—especially if, as implied, her uncle is a Mexican official traveling with Santa Anna and she is off on a lark to see the lines against his instructions. As for the girl's behavior, I suspect that the young officer, her guide on the lark, has been trying to show off for her and that, when they hear a commanding voice back up the trail and fear discovery, her *caballero* lets her hide. So, when the girl finds that her laurel clump contains a sleeping boy—that boy-*soldado*, no less—she realizes he must wake without noise. The girl has a cool head. As for why she should have remembered him in the first place, after having seen him only briefly near the coast—well, it is my experience that young ladies remember what they want to remember. And so do young men.

On his way back, Our Boy encounters American troops being led up the trail to the Mexican flank by the sleepless and disheveled but ramrod-straight Lee.

The captain was glad to see me, but he didn't want to talk none about what I done, more about what I seen. Well, I certainly seen more beauty than a body has a right to see, but the captain's interest warn't in señoritas. He wanted to know was there still Mexican cavalry thereabouts? Sure there was, says I, and some foot soldiers later on. How many? Well, I don't know, maybe a company of each kind but I couldn't see very far. Was they entrenching? I didn't know that neither, but they had cleared some trees and brush and they had axes on a wagon. He asked about cannon, but I hadn't seen none of those.

And finally I got a chance to ask a question of my own. "What does *merry-possa* mean?" I says. "Is it Mexican?"

But the captain didn't know, and then he give his report to General Twiggs—and it warn't about Mexican words, neither, but all about "rapidity of movement" and whatnot. At first they was in a sweat that the Mexicans had *let* me escape to gull us. But they was tickled when I told them about my map-drawing, and finally they reckoned it had worked. They judged the Mexicans still thought we'd attack on their right alongst the river, not on their left and rear up in the hills.

Lee and Twiggs are wrong, though. The Mexicans are now alert. The cavalryman reports the presence of a deaf-mute boy, possibly lost from the American supply train, and only driven by curiosity. The officer's superior, however, is interested by the dirt-drawn map and thinks the boy should have been brought in for more questioning—in sign language, if necessary. The officer's youth and social standing are probably all that save him from big trouble.

In any case, the Mexicans decide to strengthen their left with a regiment of foot and a battery of light artillery. As a result, by the time the American assault is launched, it is no surprise.

I got to be with General Twiggs and his staff during the "engagement," as they called it, though it didn't seem to me nothing like courting and getting engaged. There was Mexican cannon over there on the hill, right enough, and they was soon 'courting' us right smart. One round went off right near us, in the row of trees where our boys was lining up and sent pieces of shell whistling around us and a

hot wind that nearly blowed me over. Well, I dove for cover behind a rock, and so did the sergeant next to me, but General Twiggs just set on his horse as calm as you please, and damned the Mexicans for making him work so hard to keep his pipe lit. He was the steadiest fellow I ever seen in a fight.

When the men was all lined up and ready, one of the officers in the leading line—he warn't much older than me, his voice was still high and breaking up—he looks over and calls out, "How far should we charge them, General?"

And Twiggs leans over and spits and says, "Charge them to Hell, Captain. Charge them to Hell."

Well, the bugler at the end of the first rank blew the charge, and then the next one down the line takes it up like a echo and the whole line launches itself ahead. There was a little valley betwixt the hill we was on, and the Mexicans, with a little open meadow, maybe two hundred yards, and the Mexicans' line which was in front of some trees on the hill. It didn't look very far to run, but our boys was just walking, so as to stay in line, I guess, and about half way acrosst I seen flashes along the Mexican line like a hundred little sparklers and then smoke bloomed up, and I started counting in my head like you do when you see a lightning flash, "One Mississippi, two—" and I heard a crash, and a bunch of our boys had dropped down out of the line, but the file closers come right into the gaps from behind and then I seen our lines break into a trot and lower their bayonets toward the front, and *my,* warn't that bully, to do that just like on a drill field and while they was under fire, and then there went up a cheer and one flag lunged forward and the others, too, and then the first line disappears into the smoke. I seen the general lean down and cup his hands and holler to one of his aides, and the man spun his horse and galloped off down the line of trees, and it warn't long before I seen our second line come out and halt and fix bayonets and then move forward, and I tell you it was just a ripping sight. Finally the smoke cleared a bit, and I seen our colors swing up over the line of dirt piles the Mexicans built, and I hear another cheer, and it warn't long before I could tell the Mexicans was skedaddling.

I hollered at General Twiggs did he think we had won, and he looks down at me and takes his pipe out, and he was smiling a little through his beard. "It's a tolerable start, my boy. A tolerable start."

Well, if this warn't bully I don't know what is, and I did wish just this once that Tom was here. I tell you if I don't get to be in a battle soon, I'll just bust. And I'd a been in this one if there hadn't been a corporal right there looking to see I didn't do any sech thing.

So the assault succeeds, not due to any surprise, but mostly to the Americans' élan and discipline and to the size of the flanking force. Many Mexicans are taken prisoner. The rest flee up the National Road toward the capital. Lee is made a brevet Major on the spot for his work, and, we should note, he has seen the advantage of a flank attack.

Later that night, Huck looks up the Spanish-speaking Sergeant Prescott and again asks his burning question.

"*Mariposa?*" says Jack. "Oh, that's 'butterfly,' I think. Why?"

"Oh," I says, "I just heard somebody say it, is all."

But I could hardly keep my hat on now, because I knowed something important. If this was what that Mexican soldier hollered at the girl to get her to come back, the word for *butterfly* sure wouldn't a done it, if that's all it was. So the only other thing it could a been was her name: *Mariposa.* It's got to be.

For all the good that's like to do me.

6. Huckleberry's Charge

So Huck now has something besides war to wonder about. He wonders, for example, about the Mexican lieutenant.

I seen how he looked at her. And I bet he didn't cotton to the idea of some river rat like me holding her hand. He was handsome in his uniform, though he looked pretty young, too, even with the big moustaches. From his collar and buttons, Sergeant Jack says he's most likely a cavalry lieutenant. Maybe I can find out if there was anybody like that captured in the battle. I expect she's not his wife, because she's awful young and seemed too a-feared of getting caught. And "Mariposa" don't seem like somebody's last name. Maybe he's her big brother.

But eventually there is enough action to distract Huck from such speculation. Scott fights his way fort by fort along the Causeway into the city. At one point, Lee and his engineers have to build a road through the Pedregal—a lava field as inhospitable to heavy wagons and guns as the surface of the moon.[2] Scott has to wait through August for his siege equipment, and Huck again has time to muse upon his experience at Cerro Gordo, and to "bust" about seeing battle himself. Perhaps because of this wish, he becomes quieter and *less* erratic in his duties. So earnest and reliable is he in his water-fetching and potato-peeling and horse-grooming and dispatch-carrying that Lee and Twiggs begin to treat him as just another (very young) orderly and member of their little solar system, forgetting that he is little more than a captured asteroid in an unstable orbit.

In fact, Our Boy is made a regular bugler—no doubt so that Lee and Twiggs can be rid of him—and is put in Sergeant Jack's company to learn the trade. Jack Prescott himself, twenty or so by now, had begun as a bugler at sixteen. But what Huck learns most about is another instrument: the guitar. Jack has a banjo on the tool wagon, which he has taken out and played once in a while, but on the campaign he has acquired a rather classy Spanish guitar from a Mexican peddler—for the price of a good pipe and a pound each of coffee and tobacco—and Huck is dazzled to hear him play it. It is strung with a kind of coiled metal string Huck has never seen on the banjos and box fiddles he has heard all his life. This does not twang. It sings. When Jack plays by the campfire his sad ballads and colorful tunes from south Texas, Huck is mesmerized. This is something he must learn! Jack is willing to teach him when there is time—which there is for the next week or so. Prescott learned some music in the chapel in San Antonio, where he was raised and served as a hospital orderly, and he passes on a good deal about the names and fingering of chords to the avid Huck.

As for the fighting at Chapultepec, Huck does not get to see everything—for example, to watch Lieutenant Jackson jerk his two guns into place by hand, under fire and the approving eye of Major Lee, who has told him just where to put them (here's a man who follows orders to the letter!), nor to watch young Lieutenant Pickett lead his men to the parapet and vault it gallantly, sword swinging, blue cap off and golden curls flying. But on the way Huck does finally get into a battle, one of the bloodiest of the campaign, which occurs in and around a church.

On the way from Melino del Rey, the Mexicans had made a fort out of a convent, which is a place for nuns, with a church and some other little houses and garden buildings and one thing and another, and the generals had decided they had to get through there to take the route they wanted to take. It didn't take much work to make it a fort because there was already a wall around the whole place, which was acres and acres. I got to blow a passable To the Colors and then the Charge, and when the regiment rushed the wall, which was about breast high, the Mexicans didn't fight much there, but fired off a volley and run back toward the church and buildings. Jack's company, which I was with them as the bugler, made a fine charge and didn't take no casualties at all on that part of the battle, but when we swung over the wall and seen what was on the other side, we seen right away why the Mexicans pulled back. There was a big flat courtyard a couple hundred yards

across and twice as wide, covered with dust and wire grass, and then a couple rows of graves, and then a breastwork the Mexicans had built with logs and clay bricks and whatnot, and there was sharpshooters in the little church itself on the bottom floor and the top. Plus they had batteries on either end of the breastwork. Well, I *wanted* to see a battle, and I guess I got one. But it was about as strong a fort as I ever seen.

Almost impregnable—its only flaw being the gravestones. The Catholic Mexicans can't bring themselves to level them, but the American footsoldiers will be only too happy to collapse there and take cover as best they can while they fire off a volley and reload for the final rush. One American officer later reports that he and his men had felt strange huddling among graves:

I guessed it was as fitting a place to die as any. According to my stone, the Spaniard under it had been dead only a year—exactly a year to the day. I thought that an infernally bad omen.

Huck himself, while not entirely losing his lust for battle, knows enough now about the mechanics of killing to think about it like a veteran:

The brigade formed up again with our regiment in the center. When I took my place at the right of the line, Jack hollered back, "Look there!" and pointed off to the left where one of the Mexican batteries was ramming in barrel loads. "That's canister," he says, and that made my stomach do a flipflop. You see, what canister is, is a load of about a gallon of lead shot (or horseshoe nails, or whatever's hard and handy), packed into a can and then into the muzzle of a cannon and fired out, like a shotgun. If you want a idea of what that does at close range, take a box or two of dog treats and stand them up in close order like toy soldiers, and then call your dog. It'll help if the dog ain't had much to eat lately. I did wonder if there warn't some way to get around this place, stead of going straight through it, but I guess the generals knowed what they was about, because there warn't no hesitation.

Well, I wondered if I should pray, but the lieutenant looks over like he could read my mind and points at me with his sword. "Finn!"

he hollers. "After you blow the charge, you lay low, you hear? Along there!" and then he points at the ditch that run along the base of the wall—to drain, I guess, though there warn't no water in it now.

Well, I blowed the charge, and the regiment launch forward with a cheer and I run over to the ditch. There warn't nobody there next to the wall now, and pretty soon I decided I could stay at the ditch if I run *along* it and kept up with the line, more or less—and I could stay "low," too, as the lieutenant said, just by keeping my head down. So I run out that way to the right, soon as the firing started to get hot and nobody paying no attention to me—the captain and Lieutenant Pickett being up with the line now and lost in the smoke. Well, it's a good job I *did* keep my head down because shot and shell and I don't know what all was whizzing over me as I run, all around the wall to the right, till I got to the side of the little church. I drawed out the big cavalry pistol Jack had got for me and it warn't easy to keep it up straight. I judged I might jump through a window when the regiment come over the breastworks, and if there was Mexicans shooting from the doors or windows in there, I allowed I might bag one or two.

When I seen our boys drop down amongst the graves, it give me a funny feeling to see it, because I knowed some of them boys probably *was* dead. But when I got to the side of the chapel, I knowed it was time to make my move. I was betwixt the inner and outer walls—it was just lucky the Mexicans hadn't covered the gap—but then I stopped when it come to crashing through the window. They was all colored glass with angels and baby Jesuses and little trees and all kinds of Bible scenes more beautiful than I ever seen, and I guess they hadn't been shot through because the firing was at the front not the sides.

(The glass, as it happens, is actually American, recently imported from a specialty glassworks in Cleveland, and, in one of those lovely coincidences of war, had entered the Mississippi River at the port of Cairo precisely on the evening when Huck and Jim had lost each other in the fog!)

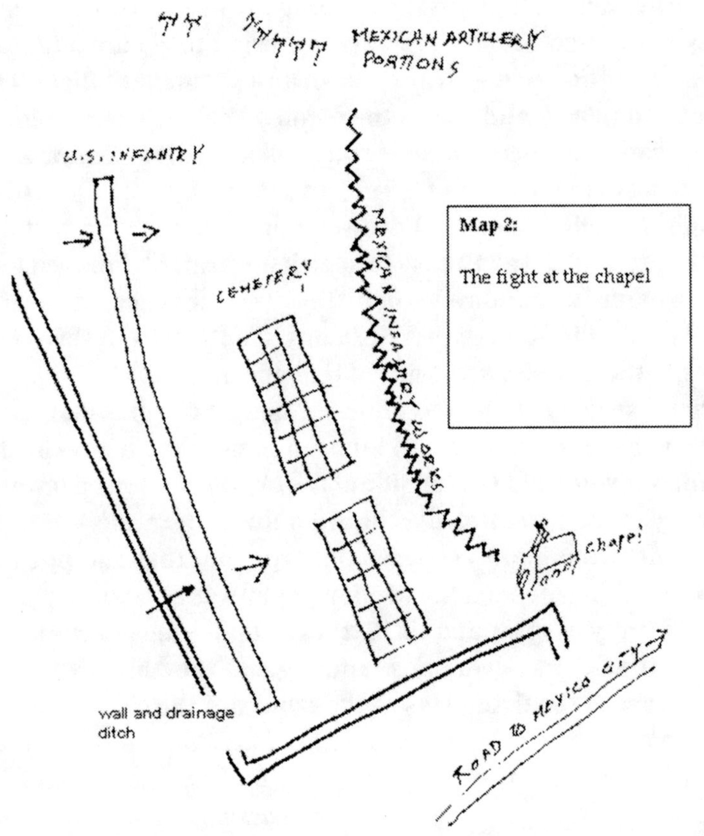

Map 2:

The fight at the chapel

Well, I was sort of covered, but not very well, by a pedestal or bird bath contraption made of clay brick. Balls was taking chips off that thing and the wall next to me—American bullets, too, and I'd sure hate to be killed by my own friends. And I was wearing blue now, so I couldn't play nothing on the Mexicans, neither. I needed to get in. Well, there was a little dent in the wall, a place where it curved out and then in about five yards further on, so when the next lull come in the firing[3], I made a run for it, and luckily there was a little door there. I leaned against it to figure how to break in without much noise, but it swung open!

There was a little loft in the back of the church with some robes and things hanging up and some church benches kind of raised up, like maybe the choir would sit there. In spite of the battle and noise outside, everything was all cool and moist and church-smelling in there and I felt almost like I should take off my cap and behave myself. But I soon seen I warn't alone. I could look down to the other end and see two Mexican soldiers at the crack where the big doors come together. Beyond the doors I couldn't see much for the smoke, which was also coming into the church, but I could sure *hear* the battle—crashes of muskets, and bullets thudding into the clay bricks and the big wood posts and rafters, and a lot of screaming and shouting in Mexican.

Now I was close enough for a couple of shots if I wanted to take them, but I held my fire, because I could see a little feller huddled on the floor behind one of the benches, too near the soldiers to trust my aim. I wondered if I could get the child's attention—or get to a better angle?

But right then a whole bunch of things happened all at once. First, one of the riflemen yells out and grabs his wrist, which I seen was bloody now, and the other, a corporal, he yells, too, and pulls a handkerchief out of his jacket and wraps it around the other's wrist as he leans against the door jamb, teeth all clinched up. And next that little feller behind the bench goes for his chance and bolts for the rear of the church where I am, and dives right into the same long bench where I'm hiding, and I had to reach my arm around and cover his mouth because I was afraid the little cuss would scream out.

But when each of us seen the other's face, we was both surprised! Because the mouth I had my hand over was one I knowed very well!

I raise my finger to my lips—sh!—and then I let go her mouth and, just to make sure, I whispers, "Mariposa?" And she was plenty surprised, too, but she just nods. I pegged her right the first time. She is a cool customer.[4] She was about to whisper something back but then the doors bust open and a squad of our soldiers piles through and takes the Mexicans prisoner, and then fans out into the church.

We stood up then, but the girl was really shooken up and held my hand like she was drowning. The solders was all covered in sweat and dirt and black powder, and some of them a bit bloody, and I allow they was plenty surprised to find me there. And then before anybody can say nothing, the girl runs down the aisle hollering something like "Señor Heedalgo! Señor Heedalgo!" and she darts behind one of the benches and tries to pull out a old white-haired feller in the clothes of a ordinary citizen—and he had blood on him, too.

I tried to smile and says, "Well, we whipped 'em didn't we?" but nobody says nothing, and the muskets pointed my way stays pointed—they wasn't interested in the girl: just me. Then a lieutenant steps forward that I didn't recognize, but I guess he was from our regiment because I seen Jimmy there with him. He had sandy hair a little lighter than mine. He had a sword in one hand and a pistol in the other, pointed up and cocked. The sword was in his left hand, not the right, so I wondered if maybe he was left-handed. He was dusty and sweaty as the rest, but he sounded just as all-business and military as Major Lee does. He says, "Is this the young man, the bugler?" looking right at me but not talking to me.

And Jimmy answers up, "Yessir, that's Huck," and says, "Huck what d'you think you're doing here?" But before I can answer, the lieutenant says, "Don't answer that, young man. You are under arrest. Corporal, conduct this fellow to the provost." Well, the corporal taken my pistol and marched me back down the aisle and across the yard like there warn't a battle still going on, and it begun to dawn on me that nobody here had called me a boy, only "young man" and "bugler," and it give my stomach the flipflops to think about what it meant to be a grownup in trouble, 'stead of a boy.

I give a quick look back for the girl, but she and that "Señor" was already out of sight at the back of the church.

In fact, as Huck realizes, he is indeed in "grownup trouble." He has: (1) left his assigned post during battle, (2) defied orders to lie low, and above all (3) apparently abandoned any military duties, bugling or otherwise, in favor of an interlude with a civilian girl from a high-ranking foreign family. As Huck says:

When you put it this way, it sounded like at least one hanging, maybe two. Again I couldn't help but think of Tom. How he would have loved all the trouble and danger and romance of it all!

Yes, but what about the justice of it all—the about-damned-time justice? The Bad-Little-Boy-Who-Finally-Comes-to-Grief *justice*? How many times have we seen Our Boy slip the noose with some cock-eyed story? We work our fingers to the bone all our lives, most of us, and who stumbles onto a pile of easy gold one night in a graveyard—remember that? *We* study hard and keep our word and come home at night, and who winds up eating on the same cracker box as the sainted Lee? We use good judgment and play by the rules. And who gets to have the most beautiful women in the world fall into the pews with him? (And I don't mean just this señorita, either.)

Justice indeed. If I'd been in command, I'd have flogged the little bastard.

Mean-spirited, perhaps. Especially since my own judgment, as we'll see, is not beyond question.

But it shows, I imagine, what the tale does to the teller. So I'll let it stand.

7. Let's Get Him Under Ground

Well, as the Americans consolidate their position and clean up the mess in the convent grounds—and a mess it is, with Huck's regiment losing over thirty percent killed and wounded—Huck waits on the divisional officers' baggage wagon, guarded by a grimy and uncommunicative corporal from the Texas Volunteers, who is "worn out as a fly on a bronc's ass," he says, and none too happy to be guarding "deserters" when there is probably good salvage among the church buildings—communion wine, for example. Our Boy thus has time to write.

I wondered where the deserters" was, but I soon figured out he meant me. I didn't like the sound of it, because it made me seem like a coward. It seemed to me I hadn't *acted* like a coward, but I see now that I also hadn't acted like a soldier neither. Maybe that church was as dangerous a spot as there was that day, but it weren't where I was suppose to be. I wished I could see Major Lee to tell him how low I felt for letting him down. But they wouldn't let me see nobody. All I got to do was talk right quick to a Lieutenant Maclernan [McClellan actually] who said he had orders to be my "counsel," but he didn't ask me many questions. He said I hadn't "nothing much to worry about," that there was "several serious counts" they could charge me with, but "charges haven't even yet been preferred."

Then he talked about hisself for a while—he was getting a "brevet captaincy" and was all excited to write his wife about it. I asked about Major Lee and said how bad I felt, and he said the major was probably pretty busy, and anyway was likely to be on my "panel," so he can't have nothing to do with me till the "hearing" even if he wants to.

He got up off the buckboard where he'd been sitting, pulled down his blouse, and turned to leave, but then he turned back and pointed

down at this journal. He says he seen me writing in it, and ask if I been showing it to Major Lee. I says I had—it was the major's own idea and he was helping we with my writing—but he sort of grunts and says, "I'd advise against it, Private, for the time being. As your counsel, I advise against showing it to anyone." He thought for a second, then he says. "You *could* show it to me, I suppose, but—no, don't show it to anyone. In fact, I'd advise you to keep it secret. Put it away and don't even write in it yourself."

"Why not?" I says.

"It's evidence!" he says. "It could be used against you. Well, good day, Private." And he touches his cap and twitches his moustache and give me a snappy little salute. Why he saluted *me* I don't know—and went on off toward the tents.

I studied over what he said—seems like a lot of worry if I ain't even been charged. And how come he calls me Private, since as far as I knowed I hadn't no rank at all. I also wonder about that girl, Mariposa. Why was she up on the mountain with the Mexican army anyhow? And how come she was in the church—which was not a safe place, I can tell you, and with a old man, a *señor* of some kind, if he warn't her father? Was she a nun? But she warn't dressed like one; they was both dressed almost as raggedy as I used to be. Well, it's a mystery.

I also looked around at all the truck the officers brung with them. There was file chests, strong boxes with locks, cigar boxes, hat boxes, writing desks with little holes where you could put ink wells like school desks but short so they fit over your legs, and testaments and little books of poems—one was called, *The Soldier's Songster*, and little cameo lockets like Emmeline Grangerford had, and shaving kits, and locked testaments, and letter files with strings around them (to hold letters from home, I judged), and picture albums, and bags of extra shirts and socks, and sewing kits, and even what looked like a painting easel with a couple of rolls of canvas, and some tins of—I reckoned—paints. I wondered how hard it was to paint, and who in the world could have time in a war to do it. I could draw a little—and I started to think about giving it a try—But now they're hitching up to move the wagons so I reckon I won't have time to get in any *more* trouble! And I guess if the lieutenant's right, I better be careful who sees me write this now.

Huck could well be confused about his own circumstances, too. As is often the case in legal matters, different wheels are grinding along different tracks. First, there is the wheel of combat command—Conduct in the Presence of the Enemy—which might already have stood him against the chapel wall and shot him. Then there is the Code of Military Justice, the court-martial wheel, used mostly for officers—which, having arrested someone, wants to grind along through elaborate proceedings. Lee's likely being on the "panel" is prophetic: after this war he will serve on court after court, to his great frustration—he wants field command—but he is so diligent and fair that everyone wants him as a juror.

McClellan is part of this, the court-martial "wheel." He is well cast. Although not a lawyer, he is in his element here: administrative detail. He has Huck out from under the above two wheels in short order, and under a third: Unit Discipline, designed mainly for misbehaving (but otherwise brave and loyal) men in the ranks. There is never any real chance, of course, that men like Lee and Twiggs are going to shoot an underage camp follower. They conclude, however, that Huck has to be taught a lesson. The roughest lesson on the Discipline Track would be flogging. But no one wants to flog a fifteen-year-old (if that's what he is). So they give him the next roughest: burial detail.

For this work, Huck is assigned, not to the crisp, young blue-eyed lieutenant who arrested him, but to Pickett—another blonde, who is in remarkably good spirits despite the grim work ahead. He delights in referring to Huck's sneak attack on the chapel choir as "Huckleberry's Charge"—because of the double meaning made possible by whatever crime the army might decide to "charge" the boy with (desertion? looting?) and what McClellan's billing "charge" would be if he were Huck's counsel. Amusing. If Pickett said anything about his own, we are not informed.

And speaking of the remarkable, Dear Reader—if you're clucking over how many later celebrities are here, conveniently close to our story, I admit there are an awful lot of (later) heroes and fools in this crew. But it's a small army, compared to later ones. And that's the way the universe is, you know: not smooth, like a good hollandaise, but clumpy, like bad milk. Look up at the stars, or into a drop of pond water. Things stick together: whether or not the center holds, there is a huddling of things, of matter, like sheep in a fog maybe—

but together nonetheless. And if you're wondering whether I was there, too—no, I was not—except in some metaphysical sense.

Anyhow, at work with the others on the field in front of the chapel, Huck soon realizes how wrong he was to think his own danger as great anyone else's during the fight for the convent. In fact, a strange thing—but not uncommon—is that during the action itself Huck was *not* afraid. It is only *after* the engagement that he feels his knees weaken and his insides churn. Huck may have been in harm's way, but the men in greatest danger were those who crossed that stretch of open ground in front of the Mexican works. Almost two hundred of those now lie on ten acres or less. This is the first clear view Huck has had of it. After all, he ducked into a chapel alcove during the worst of the action.

The field looked blue. You could walk all the way from the gate right up to shake hands with the priest, if there was one, without stepping on nothing but dead Americans. And I could hear screams coming from over the chapel wall, where they was sawing off arms and legs and tossing them over into the pits on this side. Jack calls them the "arm pits." Most of the wounded officers had been took away already, so the boys left here on the field was mostly privates. To see a drummer that warn't no older than me give me the fantods.

The ones we knowed right off had little pieces of paper on their breast weighted down with rocks—pins being in short supply, but rocks is plentiful—showing their name and home state and town, whatever was knowed. My job was to look for things that would show who they was—personal effects, as they was called—letters, family Bibles, and such. And collect any weapons, cartridges, and "accoutrements," that could be saved. It was tough work, you bet. Everything was blood-soaked—clothes, papers, and what-all—and hot, too. By noon, bodies and faces was all swelled up and stinking. They give me a handkerchief soaked in *tequila*, but it didn't help much, only made me woozier. Bottle flies was everywhere. Even with my jacket off I was dripping sweat.

They give the job of digging the long grave pits to the pioneer company—which looked considerable under-strength after the battle—so I was hoping to see Sergeant Jack.

Well, I got my wish.

About mid-field, I seen a soldier with a sergeant's stripes face down with his arm all splintered, and white bone showing through the sleeve, and thrown back over his head, the brown hair all mashed up with blood and bone. But when I seen a red handkerchief clutched in the hand...Well, my breath caught and I gagged and nearly fell flat out.

Then I hear a voice from behind me. "That ain't me, Huck. Looks like me, though, don't he?" Well, I jumped and turned around—and there was Sergeant Jack! And I tell you I never was so happy to see somebody that was prob'ly a ghost.

Jack was shaking his head. "I give him my handkerchief to bind up his hurt hand, and then just like that...well, it goes to show, Huck, what I said about writing your name on that ball. Some things is meant for you, and some ain't, and it weren't right to go switching them around by taking something of mine. Don't turn him over. I got his things. Let's get him under ground."

Huck's duty seems to cure him—if not of disobedience—at least of the urge to see battle. This is nothing like watching a feud from a tree, and even at the shooting of poor Boggs Huck was in back of a crowd, and whatever he did see was nothing compared to this. Huck will get over it, but it will take a while. For the time being, Our Boy wants to study war no more. What he does want to study is Mariposa.

8. The Place of the Butterflies

I can't sleep for dreaming, and I can't dream for seeing her face and hearing her voice, and I can't wake for sighing that she ain't really there. I don't know if this is what they call "love," but if it is I sure don't know how a body stands it long enough for it to carry the weight of the world, like the widow says it does. Looks to me like the world would run right off the road in short order with a busted single-tree.

Once we was in the City of Mexico I got new duties where General Scott "holds court," as he puts it, for the "dignitaries," and I can be on a "tighter leash," as he says. I'm a regular Aidycamp now with Colonel Totten. I got a ink well and a nibbed pen and blotters and stamp pads and everything. The stamp pads have the colonel's name signed on them backwards, but when you stamps them it comes out the opposite like a mirror, which the colonel says is the way the army works anyway—backwards. General Scott says I couldn't be trusted to stamp a general's name, but he reckoned I was good enough for a colonel. I had to stamp an order for a "disciplinary detail" once, and it made me smile to remember how somebody must of stamped my own papers then. But hadn't nobody forgot about all that because it come up at one of these "hearings."

When they calls me up to headquarters, I run up to the guard station, still in my bugler's blues and plenty worried. But it turns out I wasn't going to be charged with nothing, just questioned about some set-to that come up between the local folks, and General Scott was none too pleased about any of it. Well, my heart really started to pound when I seen who the folks was.

That Mariposa girl was there, and her family, too. One of them was that uncle she calls "*Señor Hidalgo*." And all the other folks treat him

very polite. They wanted to know all about what happen in the church. Well, some of the others had accused me of "defiling" the church and maybe her, too, but I made it seem like I'd seen the girl and her father was in trouble and had come to rescue them, which warn't quite the case, but was sure better than the other, and I could see it made a hit with the girl. And it helped that I didn't fire at the Mexican soldiers from the back, though I don't see why that mattered, they being the enemy and all. Anyhow, they wanted me to say what both the girl and her uncle was dressed like and what they was doing, and I told what I remembered and that was that; they didn't want to hear no more—like why I was out of position against orders, nor nothing. Well, I was pretty glad about that, but I still don't know much more about the family or what happened to them that day.

The testimony of the officer Mariposa was with on Cerro Gordo might have complicated matters, but he was conveniently missing in action—captured, in fact—and, were Huck as good a sleuth as I am, he could have found him. As for *why* the family was where it was, well the politics are quite tangled, and Huck gets to witness some of the internecine strife when the family leaves.

Later that day I seen the family troop back through a crowd of townsfolk. The family theirselves was guarded by dirt-farmers and Indians, and it's a good job they was, for the crowds was yelling and cussing and throwing tomatoes and rocks. The old man just walks straight and military, looking right ahead, but the girl, she hollers right back at them, and the other men has to hold her back from taking a run at one of the town boys. She went at him with a riding crop and a heavy bucket—and if they hadn't stopped her he'd of been as still as a saddle pad and about that flat, too. I don't know if I *should* try to see more of her, or stay clear, like Jack says.

I asked Major Lee about it, and he says the family is Santa Anna's relations or something, and they been told they'd be safe in a convent, and once the fighting started they *still* judged they'd be safer there than somewhere's else because even though we *yanquis* was known defilers, they allowed even we wouldn't kill ornery citizens in a church.

I says *they* looked pretty ornery, too, and the major says they probably judged they best not look like "the nobility" and be lynched by the "revolutionaries." But I thought Santa Anna *was* a revolutionary. I guess I got a lot to learn about politics.

He does. But just when Huck has given up on seeing the girl again, he gets his chance. Once the Americans are firmly in charge, pending a treaty, the family feels safe enough to return to their estate. Huck and Pickett and perhaps another officer or two are invited to accompany them for a brief visit. Nothing official about it—they just happen to be present and are swept up in a general, high-spirited invitation, in which Huck instantly includes himself. If the offer was *pro forma*, it is now too late to retract it!

Another guest, it develops, is a Mexican lieutenant of cavalry. After a prisoner exchange, he appears with a left arm badly enough wounded to ward off charges of cowardice—a bond you might think he'd share with Huck now. But Huck instantly does not like him.

I seen right away that the family all liked him. They talked respectful around him and made over his bandaged arm. The girl smiled at him, too, and once when he joked with her in Mexican she was all giggly and shy, and I tell you it hurt to see. That's because I think he is sweet on her, even though he's a lot older and an officer and all—and educated to beat the band. It come to me what a mud-rat I am and what a fool I'd been, thinking of myself like some knight or musketeer riding to the rescue. But I allow I'll be at that party even if I *did* invite my own self.

The visit matters little to the Americans (except for Huck), but the family surely sees the visiting *yanquis* as some assurance against both invaders and revolutionaries. As for the family's "estate," the word is misleading. The uncle's rank likely exceeds his wealth. *Hidalgo,* of course, is not his name, but an honorific. In addition to land—and there is admittedly a lot of that, in an upland valley a day's ride north of the city—there is a single-story, seven-or-eight-room hacienda made from adobe brick, with exposed log rafters, plus a few out-buildings. There is a slate roof and an indoor kitchen, matters of some pride. And, Huck notes, there are "real windows, with glass and everything," unlike most of the others he's seen in the countryside, which are just openings with wooden or cloth shutters. The family grows coffee as a cash crop, plus other beans, as well as tomatoes (though it's a bit high for them here) and other vegetables. Some of these others, by the way, are peppers—more about these later.

There's also goats, and sheep, and chickens, sorted out on the hillsides in little squares, like pieces of a quilt. They's also a few farmers on the property with a bit lighter skin and fellows that does different kinds of jobs working for the family, and some "dark ones," which maybe are half-Indian, who live in little shacks and work on the land. Could be slaves maybe, except they was armed that day I seen them in town, and I never seen slaves allowed with weapons.

One of these, an older man but tall for an Indian, would look to Huck more like one of the Cherokee or the southern Sioux and Comanche he has seen in the Territory and in north Texas—even wears an eagle feather in his cap. He has a clay cottage behind the blacksmith's, prestigiously close to the house, but seems to keep his distance. Huck wonders what his trade is, till Mariposa takes him and Pickett out to the place one day and shows them: clay pots of fantastic artistry, mostly thrown from a wheel. Now the location near the forge makes sense. It turns out the man has made much of what the family uses. There are also baskets and tapestries made with straw and beads and feathers and shells and bones and...well, Huck would love to have more of a look around than he is able to get on his guided tour.

I wondered why things was so dark in his shop. I couldn't see much at all, but the girl she just says, "Eyes grow custom to dark, and he no need to see much, work by finger, by touch. Light do more bad than good to color of *las piedras,*" which means "rocks." One thing I *don't* wonder at is that the further you gets from the house and the closer to field work, the darker the skin gets. When I seen that, I felt right at home.

The first night we was at the ranch, they had a big party, with story-telling and smoking and lots of drinks. Some of the stories was told in English because the lieutenant and the sergeant was there. I was

surprised that some of the stories sounded like ones I'd heard myself, but instead of being about snakes or apples they was about coyotes and cactuses. And stead of fighting and rip-roaring and hog-rassling and such, to settle a argument they et these little peppers. Two men would take turns chewing up a pepper, and then having a swaller of beer, and then taking another pepper. I never seen what was so brave or manly about any of that, the peppers looked little and harmless to me, but the lieutenant he thought it was bully, and while they was all at that, the girl come and taken me by the hand and drug me over to a corner near the kitchen where there was a window and it warn't so close and smoky.

There was a table there with a top colored like a checkerboard. She set me down on one side and her on the other and then she pulled out a box with little pieces in it. But the box warn't full of checkers but lots of little toy people, all different kinds. They was two or three inches high, and most of them had little *sombreros*, but a couple had robes with little crosses carved on them and tall hats and shepherd crooks like pictures of priests I seen at school, and a few had little crowns on their heads like kings. A few more was on little horses. They was all painted up gaudy with a lot of little touches—moustaches and gun belts and *serapes* and even strings of beads. Any fool could see somebody taken a lot of care in it, and I asks where she got them:

"I make them," she says, and smiles. She was real proud of herself. She says she "fired" them from clay in the forge I seen—with the help of "Old Man," as she calls him. The fire must be the way they got so shiny. Some was a little cracked, but hard and metal-looking.

"Now," she says, putting the pieces out. "We play. But you must be *careful!* You play chest?"

I says no I don't, far as I knowed. She says that warn't no problem, she'd teach me; she was going to be a teacher some day. And so when we got all the pieces laid out, she says I can be white and take the first move. The two rows on the one side had darker hats, and the other side lighter ones, and she says they was supposed to represent armies with kings and castles and everything.

Well, it turns out that after I got to move one of my row of little *sombrero* folks out one square, *she* got to jump one of her *caballeros* on horseback all the way *over* her first line, and right there I seen how it was going to be, and I allow she was a match for Tom Sawyer at making rules up as they was needed. I could see how maybe a horse might jump over some poor fellow fighting on foot, but that rider could be whipped by a "bishop" with nothing but a shepherd crook! And you'll never guess who the powerfullest fighter of them all was: the Queen! That's right—she got to sashay all over the board taking prisoners and whole castles all by herself with no weapon a body could see, and the sad old King has to set off in the corner and can only move one square at a time, and if he gets so much as boxed in, the jig was up!

I told her it was lucky there warn't no dukes, because *they'd* get to make up their *own* moves—and change into other pieces if they need to. That made her laugh, and she ask where I got the idea, and I says it was a long story. "When we finish you will tell me," she says, and we was finished pretty soon. It turned out her little *sombrero* fellows *could* turn into other pieces if they got to the other end of the board—which I reckon I gave her the idea for that!—*and* it turned out her castles could pick up and switch places with kings in mid-air! I should of just expected it.

So then she got me to tell a bit about what happened to Jim and me on the raft, and when I got to the part about Jim getting turned in by the Duke and King, and about Tom helping to steal him away with all the nonsense he got from books, I figured she would think that was just bully—all that stuff that Tom had us play on them—but instead it made her kind of quiet and thoughtful.

"That was wrong, Huckleberry," she says, as she put the pieces away.

"About stealing Jim?"

"No, about Jim have to buy back his childrens. Why you don't go to work and steal those, too? All who force to do against their wish should be steal away. *All.*"

And she slams the drawer shut. But before I can ask what the trouble was—I knowed there was *something* wrong, and I wanted more than anything to make her smile—she smiles anyhow and says, "*Vene*, I teach you to eat." But I seen what eating those folks did, and it did look like a worse danger than the fighting I seen. Lord knows what these people do when they's *really* in a feud. So I just watched.

I have no doubt that what Huck decided to "just watch" involved peppers. Some of these, Dear Reader, are *not* what you think of as peppers. They don't have that nice plump, pumpkin-like shape. After a few days drying in the sun they look like shriveled little goat's heads, like the Devil's face complete with horns. One is even called the *diablo*. Indeed, the smaller, stringier, and drier they are, the more they are prized. In fact, it seems that the highest test of manhood among the locals, Spaniard or Indian, is not a shoot-out, which any fool might blunder through, but a pepper-eating duel—which only the strong survive.

Years later I was able to witness one. The whole pepper was chewed and swallowed at once, followed by a quick gulp of something alcoholic. The chewing of the fruit was an important part of the ritual. I have never seen such symptoms. From the sweating and labored breathing, I would have thought the two men—who were friends, I was told, with nothing really against each other—were in the midst of a poisoning. Yet they were just working up to the most potent morsels, which the loser wisely refused and which sent the winner into convulsions.

Later, I myself was presented with a dish of peppers that were, I was told, of "medium" spiciness. Just to be convivial, I selected a single small blue-black fruit, called, I was told, a *patilla negra* (meaning "black sideburn," which should have warned me). I swallowed it at once, of course, without the chewing, which I knew to be life-threatening. The locals applauded indulgently.

It was a week before the lining of my mouth recovered. Within seconds, my tongue and cheek took on so much fluid that I momentarily could not breathe. Hives broke out on my neck and lips. Attempts to inhale caused my entire chest cavity to swell with flame. Water poured from my eyes. My scalp seemed to separate from my skull and fill with liquid. I staggered from the room to sink my head in a bucket of well water waiting to be heated for steaming *tortillas*. I am sure I left it hot enough for the task. My hosts were delighted, and I have no doubt the story is still told. So let those who complain about the blandness of army fare be careful what they wish for!

At any rate, after a day or two of touring the farm under the strict eye of the family, Huck manages to get away for a while with the girl. Or rather, she gets away with him. This is a feat, since she has received the nearly undivided attentions of that *caballero.*

One morning early there is a pebble at his window (just like the old days!) and, when he is sure Lieutenant Pickett has not awakened, Huck looks out to see Mariposa behind a hedge, in a blouse and military jodhpurs, her black hair tied back under a kerchief, smiling shyly and motioning for him to be quiet and come out. Then she heads for the stable. Huck is used to horses by now, and the Spanish tack, though with unfamiliar markings and ornamentation, looks designed for work (there are pommels, for example, and latches for lariats), but the girl wants to arouse no suspicions by taking two horses. Her own horse is to be off at the smith's quarters today, being shod, and she has permission to go retrieve him. She has gone and returned early, so if they ride the same animal, it will be long before she is missed. Huck's absence is more of a problem. Luckily (or did she know?), Huck has talked of fishing today at a place known to the family, so that a note left on his bed may be enough of a diversion.

She is the better equestrian, so he mounts behind her on a rump seat designed for children and pets. Huck is small enough that it works. Where are they going, he wants to know?

"*Los montes*," she says, gesturing to several high points a couple of hours' ride behind the ranch. As mountains, they look only middling, but since the plateau where the farm is located is itself more than a mile high, they have plenty of elevation. In fact, there is snow up there in the winter, even so far south. "There is place named for me," she continues. "*Lugar de la Mariposa* is called. 'Place of Mariposa.' Is high up. Come, we go fast. Put hands here, *si?*" And so they gallop, Huck with his arms around her to grasp the pommel, his face by her sweet-smelling neck and hair. Huck knows, of course, that her name—or at least her nickname—also means "butterfly," so the place might not really be named for her, but he wonders what is so special about it.

The truth is beyond anything he could have imagined.

We rode till noon nearabouts, on a trail that come into a canyon with some of the tallest trees I ever seen, with short little needles like Christmas trees. I seen some back home, but I knowed they was planted or brung back from the mountains, and these was borned here. The trail clumb up steady, and crossed the crick back and forth, then come out on a high flat, and when we turned and looked back down the draw you could see all across the valley where the farms was. And that valley was already high, so I tell you we was way up. I felt a little light

in the head like you feel at the top of a flag pole in the wind. I ain't never seen real mountains before, I know that now. And we was still below the gap between the two mountain tops which was about half a mile further.

All along, there was huge forests. Right at the top they wasn't as tall, though they was still straight, like little flags because the limbs only growed out one side, away from the wind, because the other sides was bitten off by storms in the winter. But some of the trees on the slopes away from the wind was so tall you almost couldn't see to the top—I bet some was two hundred foot or more, and you didn't even see branches till half that high. The girl said some of these trees was alive when the white men first come here, so they couldn't speak nothing but Indian. Now what sense did that make? I did believe her when she said there was frost up here sometimes, even in summer. It turned out she had brung a short jacket for each of us in her saddle roll, and I was glad of it.

To get up over the gap, which was rocky and steep, we dismounted and led the horse. At the top there was a windy meadow with wildflowers and little green trees no more than bushes. Finally we went down a draw and into the gorge on the other side where the crick was broader and there was a flat on each side and a mountain cliff on each side above that. It was afternoon, and the mountains had a sort of golden look, from the sunshine I reckoned. Well, now she stops and points at the peaks.

"See," she says, "they are golden."

Now I seen it warn't just the light. It was most like fall in the oak-hickory woods on Jackson's Island—except that there ain't no red here, just gold. We picketed the horse near enough to the crick that he could drink and she says, "Come," and she taken me by the hand, and we trotted the last bit down the trail, over pine needles now, and into the gorge between the peaks.

Well, it most took my breath away. It was level for a ways there, like a little valley with the stream down the middle and pine needles all over the banks under the trees and cliffs on either side. The trees on the flat was tall as ship masts, but not green. They was all glimmering, and fluttering with little golden leaves or blossoms. They

was just sagging with gold. The girl run around under the trees with her arms up, laughing, and I was laughing, too, with her. And then as I watched her it seemed like some of the gold started to fall and flutter down around her, some on the ground amongst the needles and cones, and some on the hands she held out, and then she calls, "Come, Huckleberry! *Vene!*" and holds out her hand with a little fluttering blossom on it, and one settled right on top of her head and she laugh out loud, and as I come up she points at my shoulder and all at once I seen what the gold was: butterflies.

The two on my shoulder was monarchs, I'd know that kind anywhere, and so was the one in her hand. The whole forest, the whole mountain, was covered with them—must have been millions and millions. Not a breeze stirred where we was, but the trees was fluttering and alive—and all golden.

"They are beautiful, yes?" she says.

"Oh, my, yes," I says. "I never seen anything so fine." And then I *could* of said—SHOULD of said, "except maybe you," but I didn't.

And then *she* says, "Except maybe me?" But she says it so shy that a body couldn't blame her. And then she says: "Come, Huckleberry. Es lunch." And we et what she brung for us.

There was some things which I recognize, like the big soft corn-flour *tortillas* rolled up around tomatoes and green peppers and onions and goat cheeses. There was also some sour, fruity things in there that tasted a bit like grapes but warn't. We also had some apples and pears and little strings of pickled beef and chicken. We sliced and buttered them up with some sauce that was green and soft and rich. It was fine and satisfying, except I wished we had brought more water up from the stream. Everything these folks eat has peppers in it.

She told me a bit more about the butterflies, too. She says her uncle told her they come every summer, from all over the world, right to this spot. They're late this season because of the late summer. I didn't see how they could find their way from all over the world to the same spot, but she says, "We did, no? You and I? What chance of this, no?" Well, that didn't make no sense, and it was just like a girl to say so.

After we et and cleaned up, the girl jumps up and says "Oh! I forget! Wait!" and went running back down to where the horse was. I

run after her, and I seen her bring out from her saddle basket a little guitar, lot smaller than Sergeant Jack's. She'd heard us play, and now she hands it to me and says: "You will play for me. Come." She sat on the blanket and said, "Make a song about me."

Well, I didn't know what to do—there was only four strings, not six, and they warn't tuned the right way—but I strummed out a little of "Froggy Went A-Courtin," except I made it about a butterfly. She thought that was funny, but now she says, "Make one for new—for me." So I studied a bit and worked on some simple chords A-minor/ C-major /A-minor/ G-major—with a F-major change stead of the G on the second time around. Pretty simple. And I started out:

Mariposa, Mariposa,
Your name is gold and green.
Your face is prettier than the butterfly
And anything else I seen...

Not much, for sure, but right off the top like that, it pleased her. She clapped and smiles a huge smile. I said that's all I could do without some time to think, and then she says, "Yes, you must think. But now I show you what I write for *you*."

Then she up and run to the far end of the gap to a stand of fir saplings up against a cliff face where some water trickled down. They was all covered with butterflies like the others, of course, and she tiptoed so as to not step on any of them, and then she picked up a dead branch and reach out with it like it was a paint brush, and brung it up against one of the fir trees. It made the butterflies flutter up in the air leaving a spot of green where she'd brushed them off. She moved the branch up twice and then across once, and I looked and seen a sort of a green "H" across the stand of little trees—where they was all gold before. Right soon the butterflies started settling back down, but she moved on down the cliff, brushing up a big U and then a C and then a K. By the time she done them all, the first letters was nearly covered in monarchs again. It was like having your name writ with disappearing ink. That was a strange feeling. But it was so pretty. I told her it was, and she came to me and says, "I like you, Huck Finn." Then she put

her arms around me and held on tight, and says, into my neck, "You remember that. What...whatever does come, Huck Finn." Then she was silent for a second, still holding on, and whispered in Mexican a little, like to herself. I hadn't no idea what she meant, but then she pulls away and turns back toward the trees and points.

They was all gold again with the butterflies, and she says "You remember, Huck Finn—whatever come—that on the mountain is gold and that under gold is your name, all green. And you will come to me here." And she turned back, and I seen her brown eyes shining like there was tears there, and I hadn't no idea what was wrong, but the girl she smiles anyhow, and then come forward again and put her face up and kissed me right on the mouth. And then she said I wasn't doing it right, she said it was just one more thing she'd have to learn me to do. And I allow she did her best.

We talked a bit then, about one thing and another, about her uncle and the ranch and school in the city—she was going to have to go back soon and then, "Who knows what?" but it didn't seem like nothing so sad. And then we kissed some more, and she asked me if I ever went to school and I said, "Some—once."

And she says, "You will again. You will study the music," and nods like it was all settled. And then we rode back down along the *rio* to try to catch some fish for an excuse for being out, but we couldn't catch a thing, so we rode on home and waited to get caught, but nobody never said nothing about it.

Well, what are we to make of this? You will have noticed, first, that for a country girl this Mariposa speaks pretty good *Inglés*. Clearly *she* has had some schooling. Second, Huck becomes much less specific after their kiss. There's a perfunctory quality there—a quick closing of the *cortina*. Does this vagueness hide a thorough sexual initiation? After all, here are two adolescents, alone and clearly attracted to each other. Still—Our Boy, whatever else I may have held against him, is a natural gentleman, a Green Knight, if you will. And the girl is a princess of good family.

And yet—Huck has been kissed, chastely or not (that, "She did her best," entitles us to wonder, doesn't it?) And another thing: the girl's foreboding about "whatever comes." We have our theories about this, and we will get to them.

But the most perplexing thing about this entry is that it's the last one—for a long time, more than five years. I have learned a few things and guessed a few more about the coming "gap," but there's no more about it in the journal.

The business about the monarchs, by the way, is true. They do migrate to this one place, once a year, from all over the world—by the billions. Someone should do a paper.

When I saw the place myself, years later, after the ignominious pepper experience, it was near sunset as I approached the twin summits—on foot, with only a cane. The green and gold fluttered back and forth, and there was a great undercurrent—from the whirring of a billion little wings. It was like the wind over the waves of some feverish sea in an opium revery. But as the sun set, the gold turned to red, and a gray fog settled in the valley, leaving the foothills humped like the backs of whales, like burial mounds, and the jar inside me was shaken, and I saw it all again, heard it, smelled it—the woods filled with smoke, the guns in the distance, the axes in tree trunks, the graves before me with the three swords—and as the red deepened, it was if the stain of some awful sacrifice deep under those waves had surfaced—to save or damn us all.

I, too, would have done what she asked, God help me. What anyone asked really. But as usual I was alone.

Well, that seems awfully florid, doesn't it? But I'll let it stand. It shows, if nothing else, what the tale does to the teller. I find it ever more difficult to mock this boy—and he is still a boy. And *he* still has his voice, does he not? I may have undertaken a task to which I am unequal. You must understand that I have lived my life mostly in other people's stories. I may not be up to telling my own. And yet I must, if the tale is to mean anything—if only to myself, never mind any reporters.

But I must keep some distance. I must look at my own part—which will come slithering along in its own good time—with a cold eye. I must reveal things not all at once, but as they might emerge in a dispassionate inquiry. The reader must forgive me, then, for avoiding the Big Picture, while I tunnel into my sources, as it were, and turn my facts up one by one, like artifacts, the gleanings of a dig. As I tell my students, something well-built reveals what it is, whether the builder calls it by its name or not.

For the time being then: down with Truth! Long live Accuracy!

Part 2

All you need to know on earth, sir, is your God and your duty. God can take care of himself. Your concern is duty. Duty. Duty. Duty.

—R. E. Lee

Duty be damned!

—Sid Sawyer

9. Time out of Mind

So Huck falls off the earth—or at least off the page—for about five years. He seems never to have developed a real interest in Mexico, except for its precious "Butterfly." He does seem to have been influenced by its music, but that is something he could take with him. He could not, unfortunately, take Mariposa. He must have soon realized that she was, if not beyond his reach, at least beyond his grasp. It is likely she was already promised to the young cavalryman. Although the parish records are good, and her family were certainly Catholic, no marriages are recorded involving a "Hidalgo" or a "Mariposa." Both names, of course, were probably pet names. Still, a determined investigator can add one thing and another and get two.

Thing one: the parish records of *Iglesia de la Concepcion* show for later that year and all the next only three marriages involving women young enough to have been Mariposa. Two of the grooms are listed as farmers, both in their thirties, one a widower and the other a de-frocked priest. (That last fact is not in the record, but a few gringo dollars can be excellent confessors.) The third is a twenty-three-year-old Mexican cavalry lieutenant named La Plata, his bride a sixteen-year-old named Maria Poseta Del Plan. Maria Poseta: Mariposa? Close enough!

Thing two: there is a christening—a son—eight months after the union. Quick work. Maybe too quick? But a month after that there is a burial: the cavalryman, dead of "accidental wounding." Strange: one thinks of a man killing himself while cleaning a pistol. In fact, though, I am told that in the Valley of Mexico the term was often a euphemism for a suicide or a dueling death. Full rites are recorded, so I rule out suicide. My immediate vision then: the arrogant young officer gets himself into an Affair of Honor—illegal by then, even in Mexico, but not unheard of. It is easy to imagine: Our Girl's natural vivacity, a furtive glance, a rash accusation, and our cavalryman—well, he cannot strike *her*, so he strikes someone it is an even worse mistake to strike, then finds his family can't buy him off, and Our Girl cannot bring herself (perhaps does not want to bring herself) to say the words of relief.

So: pistols at dawn, perhaps even sabers. He is a cavalryman, after all. And he leaves behind a son and—we like to think—a widow whose tears dry rather quickly.

Then what? There are no more marriages (or deaths) in the province under her name, maiden or widowed, and she would almost certainly have kept the officer's surname. And no title transfers either. What then? The Sisterhood? There are a number of likely postulants in central Mexico that year, at least three named "Maria." But that tells us little since it is not uncommon to take holy vows under a new name. So we lose track of Mariposa, as well as Huck. Of course, there are no military records from the period, since he never officially enlisted.

But, although we are not sure *when* Huck leaves Mexico, we do know more or less why: he gets a letter from home—and from, of all people, Becky Thatcher. We know about this letter, and a good deal more, thanks to a young Negro named Joe Taylor, in whose own diary, more than six years later, Huck resurfaces. Joe, at the time his journal begins (late 1855), is a former slave, likely a runaway, some sixteen or seventeen years of age, now legally free (he says) and living in Lexington, Virginia, where he works for a local teacher whom he calls "the professor." This whole Lexington episode is difficult to reconstruct, even though there are several sources, partly because no one concerned with Huck makes much effort to leave a usable record (and those who do are little concerned with Huck). Most of Joe's entries at least have dates, but Our Timeless Boy does not record such details.

Huck, of course, knows all about runaway slaves. But Joe is not Jim, his famous partner on the immortal Raft. For one thing, Joe Taylor is at least three years younger than Huck (who is twenty or so by now), whereas Miss Watson's Jim, you will recall, was more than twenty years *older* than Our Boy. As for looks, Joe is about the same height and build as Huck, who is short and slender and always looks younger than he is—an advantage for a confidence man. All we have to go on in Joe's case is Huck's famous Cactus-Juice sketch. More about this later, but for now I will note that it shows Joe's face dark enough, but lacking the full African nose and mouth. More "handsome" than Huck's, I'd say, although darker. In fact, a colleague of mine, looking at the sketch, pronounced the look, "Striking, Caribbean, possibly Jamaican," and allowed that she wouldn't be surprised to find "some European or even Arab blood in there somewhere." Like Huck he has a disarming smile and carries himself easily, like an athlete. We should not be surprised if it turns out he can ride.

Joe is also ambitious and determined to better himself. By this time he has learned his letters well enough, in an informal "Negro Sunday School," run by the Virginia Military Institute professor for whom he works, to keep a journal of sorts himself—a real journal, too. You'll recall the pretend one Tom Sawyer infamously has poor Jim "write" in his own blood as part of the adventure of setting him free. "In the books," you see, the prisoner always keeps a journal—whether or not he can write.

Hilarious, yes, but damned demeaning, and a strong mark against Tom.

As it happens, Joe's journal is actually Huck's idea. The school's founder, Joe's teacher-employer, is plenty busy and happy to let Huck help. In nice weather they sit on the grass patch in front of the professor's house and read to each other. Our Boy, though rather untutored himself, proves to have a gift with beginning readers. And, as we might expect, teaching seems to improve his own control of language. And since he has to practice what he preaches, Our Boy—*mirabile dictu!*—begins to write again. And pretty well, too:

To get my scholars to see what a word was I took a basket of crab apples and put one down on the ground when I said a word, and when there was a whole row of them I had Joe or one of the others pick the apple up when I called out its name. After a while I carved the letters of the word on the apple with a pen knife and let the fellow have it when he called out the letters right. We didn't have hornbooks, but there was a dusty patch next to the street where we could draw letters and then erase them.

Once his "scholars" have the sense of what a "*word*" is and know their letters well enough to invent spellings, Huck has them keeping diaries and writing letters to each other.

Young Joe's diary, however, even when dated, is of limited use in its early stages—difficult to make out and really no more than a log-book for weeks at a time:

boght kinlin an tuk wagon to smithes then tu de collige,

and so on. But. especially as his skill improves, Joe's entries are often more interesting than Huck's own, which are now strangely unrevealing about his motives and especially about his past. Here is the entry from Joe's journal in which Huck resurfaces. After more than a year of study, you will notice the improvement! I have, of course, corrected some spelling and punctuation:

Sept. 16, 1855

I learned the right way how to make my last name today: TAYLOR. I done spelt it wrong to now, with a E. I shown it to a friend of the professor. He real nice but quiet. His name Hucklberry [sic]. This is funny. When I met him I tells him I was BERRY happy to have such a friend, and he laugh at that. I don't know [how] to spell laugh. He want me to teach him the [banjo?] but I don't know nothing but strumming no picking. He's Huck to most folks, Huck Lee. I tell him his last name so high and mighty, but so easy to spell, he should go to the college. He smile. He say he been to college already, and he seen all he want to see of it. He tell funny stories which I don't know if I believes them. He seen the professor in Mexico, he say, and I will have to tell you some of the stories he tell about it. He say there's things about war he won't tell and if I knowed what they were I wouldn't want to know them neither. I tell him I don't want to know nothing I don't want to know. That make him laugh.

He been learning me letters and figures. I need the letters for to read the papers and the figures for counting stove sticks and kindling sticks, for the professor say he going to let me keep the records of that and pay me. One thing he didn't learn much of wherever he got his schooling was figures, which he say I'm right, he don't, so I tell him he should go to College with the professor, to learn them. I going to tell you more about Hucklberry later.

He does, too, and it's a good thing, because we find out that Our Boy has been odd-jobbing around Lexington for some time—having arrived in a snow storm the day after Christmas 1854. Why he should be in Virginia at all, let alone Lexington—and passing himself off as a Lee, no less—is not explained. But we can fill in some blanks.

First the Letter From Home. Joe has been helping Huck pack to move into new quarters at the Virginia Military Institute, where the plan is to make him a caretaker. (We'd love to know *whose* plan, wouldn't we?) At any rate, in a canvas satchel containing a roll of maps and blank pages and some pens, pencils, and jars of what looks like ink, Joe notices a bundle of letters and is proud to be able to read off the name on the top one:

BECKY it say on the bottom, and I ask was that his sweetheart and Huck say no I shouldn't even think such a thing, and I say why is you turning red then, and he say cause it make him think of Mexico. I say did he get the letter there, and he say yes, years ago and it's how come he left. I ask did he get bad news or something, and he say well in a way yes and a way no. He talk like that a lot. I just look at him like, "Well?" and he say the letter tell him Judge Thatcher done died, and I say well, who he, and he show me the return name spell out Becky Thatcher, and so I can guess: he her father? And he nod his head, and I say, laws a me! but I asks him why that make him come back if she ain't that important. He just smile. I ask him about the other truck in the sack and he turn and close it up and say it ain't no matter, just stuff he brought back from the war. He say that kind of thing when he don't want to talk about nothing. Then he turn back and smile again and say let's work on the banjo. He always do that, too. When he don't want to talk, we work on the banjo. We getting lots of practice.

So Huck goes home from Mexico to do—what? Comfort Becky Thatcher? A classy girl who wouldn't have given him the time of day a few years earlier? We don't have that letter, nor do we know how Becky knew where he was, but we can guess some things: in the *Adventures*, you may recall, Huck "gives" Judge Thatcher his money to keep it away from his own Pap. So it's reasonable to think the letter says something about the disposition of funds. But now, a bit about this teacher for whom Joe works.

10. Learning Our Letters

"The professor" Huck mentions is a rather eccentric teacher of math and artillery tactics at the Virginia Military Institute. In connection with his duties (lamp-lighting, fire-stoking, etc), Huck gets to listen in on some classes.

While I was sweeping the fireplace, the major was lecturing about functions and turned to do a demonstration on the chalk board. I could hear the chalk scratching as he talked, but also some shuffling and wood scraping on the floor. I looked up and saw Isaac McGarvey on the front row reach out his ruler and jab the pulpit [a lectern?] till it rocked and the water glass spilled. It got the notes all soaked, and I was ready to grab the little cuss, but the major he turned around and seen the papers was unreadable, and, I swear, he just started the lecture all over again, right from the top. I never saw anything like it. He had it by heart and didn't need the notes, but he had to say it all straight through from the first. He told them all to start their papers again and they would stay till he'd finished and take the time out in extra drill. Well, there was a groan all around, and I reckoned that would do it for Master McGarvey when the boys got a chance at him. There were other times like that, too, but it didn't seem to make any difference to the major's style of teaching.

By now you've guessed that this Major (his old brevet rank) is none other than Thomas J. (later "Stonewall") Jackson, the very officer whose pickets almost shot Lee and his young map-bearer that humid night near Vera Cruz. Huck likes Jackson, but not with the reverence he feels for Lee. To Huck, Jackson is more like an eccentric uncle—whom he respects, but whose ways provide some amusement. In fact, the man was known to his students, at least at first, as "Fool Tom" (not to his face, of course). They must respect his war record, but they hate his inflexibility in class.

Jackson's very first appearance at the Institute, two years earlier, should have been fair warning to anyone who heard about it. As Joe recounts it much later (after beginning his own journal), he had been assigned to meet Jackson, collect his baggage, take him to his quarters, and then show him to the office of the superintendent, a Colonel Francis Smith. When they run into Smith out on the green, the colonel tells Jackson to go up to his office and wait for him while he runs a quick errand—which takes longer than expected:

I showed the new professor where the office was and said I'd go take his things to his rooms. When I done that I waits a while to see did he need anything else, but the professor never come, so I judged they was going to take a long time at the office. I leaves the key on the desk in his room and the door open, and gone off about my chores.

In the morning I goes to the office to sweep out as I usually done, and I run into the colonel on the steps. He say good morning, and then I ask him did he and the new Professor talk all night, and the colonel slap his head and say, "Oh, my! I forgot all about the man!"

He ask me did Jackson get settled in all right, and I say, I don't know, I had to leave before he got there.

"Well, I must go and apologize!" he say, and off he go towards the faculty rooms. So I goes on up to the office but the door already open. And there sets the new Professor. I ask him why he back so early, and he say he never left. He look tired, but sit straight up like a soldier, and he say he was told to come here and wait, and so he done as he was ordered. Well, I went about my business of sweeping up and then left, but I run into the colonel coming up the steps. He was all in a sweat—he been to Jackson's quarters and he say, "Lord, the man done left us!"

I say "No, he ain't; he upstairs. Still a-waiting like you tole him—been there all night."

And he say, "Good God!" and then he hurry up to the office.

I always wonder how long the professor would of stayed there and waited—say if he had to do the call of nature or something. Then the colonel tell me, as part of my duty he want me to "look out for" the man. I say he need looking out for, that for sure! The colonel he laugh and say not to talk like that about my betters. And I thinks, when I see some of those around here I'll take his advice. But I don't say that.

Joe is a pistol, isn't he?

On the drill field, of course, Jackson's not such a joke. Still, there's a feeling that he is out of place. And he is. What he needs is a war.

How Jackson *did* come to be here is the subject of a conversation Huck reports in his journal. Jackson has been on the faculty for three terms by the time Huck himself shows up in Lexington. At the time we're talking about—after Huck's own arrival, but before his taking quarters at the Institute—Huck is staying with another local professor, Daniel Harvey Hill—not the illustrious A. P., although Harvey does become a Confederate general. Hill teaches philosophy and mathematics at Washington College, also in Lexington, and Huck finds him fascinating: a logical-minded Presbyterian, but (unlike Jackson) with a sense of humor. Hill and Jackson go back a long way: both served in Mexico, and both are West Pointers. Hill helps Jackson become a committed Presbyterian and encourages his Sunday School idea. By the way, so far as I know, Jackson never objected to slavery, if he ever thought about it. But the Negroes were persons to him, and persons have souls, and a Christian must study the Bible, and to do that he has to *read*. Where that logic might have led the man is an interesting speculation.

Anyhow, one night Jackson is over for dinner at the Hills', and Huck is doing the cooking—another interest he has picked up. Here is how Huck reports the conversation:

After looking over the teaching plans, Professor Hill looks up at the major and says, "Well, these notes look fine. What concerns you?"

And the major says, "I wanted to know the completeness—of the demonstrations."

"But Thomas, this is very elementary stuff."

"Yes, I know. But it was long ago, at the Point. I was amazed even to pass the entrance test there."

And Hill laughs at that. "Well, that test is a joke! I heard one boy asked to do a couple of products and sums and then read a paragraph from the *Declaration*, and boom! He's in! What did they make you do?"

And the major says well his uncles got him in, that was all he knew. Professor Hill nodded and said, "Well, yes, but you worked your way up, didn't you? You were near the bottom of the class at first."

The major thought about that and then said, yes, he was at first, but not in math; he was five above the bottom there. Then he seemed to pull himself up proudly, and says: "But I rose to the middle—and above the middle in math. Seven above."

Hill shook his head—at the idea that Jackson had remembered all that for so long! Then Hill asks him what the trouble was with the army anyhow, and the major smiles and sets up even straighter, and I thought: here it comes, something he thinks is a joke.

"You tell me, Harvey," he says. "You left the army, too. Our troubles probably knew each other by first name, sir!"

For the major, that'll answer for a joke.

The long and short of it is that Jackson, tired of Florida fort duty and squabbling with superiors, resigns his Army commission to take the VMI post on the recommendation of a former superior whom he *does* respect—Robert E. Lee. And that must also be what brought Our Boy to Lexington: Lee must have suggested it. But why? Has Lee sought to further the boy's prospects by installing him at another military college, at least in some role? Did he try to hand off the parental role to Jackson? Maybe, though buck-passing is not in Lee's nature. At any rate, for Huck, a suggestion from Lee is an order.

As for what went on in the five years after Mexico, the Letter From Becky is surely a clue. We actually know (or think we know) a bit more about it than he tells Joe, because there are a couple of other sources. One of these is Harvey Hill, who, lucky for us, writes letters. And through one of these we learn that Huck is in the room on another evening when Jackson asks his hosts their opinion of a lady he has met. Jackson is struggling to clarify his feelings and even has doubts about his own health. Hill has no trouble at all explaining things:

"You are in love, Thomas!" he laughs. "That's your problem!"

Hill's diagnosis is correct, but Old Jack needs a prescription: how does one propose, he wants to know? And when the talk gets around to fatherly permissions, Jackson notes that he is an orphan. At this point, Huck interjects that he himself has had no shortage of fathers. Well, that gets everyone's attention, so Huck explains that after his Pap had died, Judge Thatcher, before *he* died, had "gone to court" to adopt him. So: that could have been in the letter. It's the kind of thing the good-hearted Judge might have done, and that

Becky—good-hearted or not, but a stickler for propriety—would have had to reveal. It would probably nail down Huck's title to any found money and, with Mrs. Thatcher already dead, make him and Becky the Judge's heirs. Either way, Becky is by now clearly the head of the family. She is, in her own way, as much a force of Nature as Our Boy himself.

But then, says Huck, he "got another father" when a Colonel Lee adopted him—"out West." Surely *that* turned some heads. Hill reports no more of the conversation, but showing up in Virginia with such a tale is like showing up at the Court of St. James's with a high coat of arms: it had better not be a scam. If it *is* a scam—well, that's Our Boy, isn't it? It helps to remember that Lee, at this time, though from an illustrious family, does not yet have his own shrine on Olympus. Such a claim now would merely raise eyebrows, not (as it would ten years later) get him arrested and his picture in the Richmond *Examiner*!

We have to wonder what a certain señorita would think of this new father if she knew about him, don't we? But maybe she does.

11. Daughter of Gold Will Wait

During the 1855-56 term, as in the previous year, Huck spends most of his winter days around the College performing odd jobs, and the early evenings at the Hills' or at Jackson's—sometimes in the yard, when the weather's good, with his group of scholars. They read mostly what Huck calls "Sunday School stories" but also, interestingly, a couple of illustrated paper-bound books called *Tales from the Bard*—stories from Shakespeare and a similar collection of Greek myths—both hilariously rewritten to avoid scandal. (A goddess's sexual union with a bull, for example, becomes marriage to a rocking horse.) He has also been taking overnight hiking trips into the mountains with Joe, on which Huck usually takes his guitar and his canvas satchel. In spite of a Christmas snow, it's a mild winter. They report exploring the Blue Ridge and singing a lot around campfires. But of all this local color, the most striking appears in this journal entry:

That afternoon we hiked to Stone-Face Mountain and found the cave Joe told me about. I wanted to see it because he had told me the last "free Injuns" in the state had used it for a long time and might still. The town boys say there were pirates up there but I just smiled. Made me wish Tom was around. Still, Joe seemed all in a sweat to get there, and when we come around the last switchback under the cliff face, he pulled me back and shushed me. We stood there a while listening. There was a wind now that the sun was setting, and it was cold up here on the mountain, with little frozen rivers of ice coming out of the rock and crevices over the trail and big icicles hanging off the cliffs, and some leftover snow crusted in the cracks and under the trees on the north slopes. The mountain sort of sounded like the old man it was named after, huffing and puffing his breath out through his long stringy ice-hair.

And then I noticed the mountain had eyes, too! Red eyes, two of them, under the caves up ahead. And they were blinking. Joe says under his breath "One, two, three.... One...two! That's it, Huck, it's them. Come on." And he led me to where there was eight or ten dark forms at the mouth of the cave, two with lanterns which they covered up now. They looked like black folks, though, not Indians, and were dressed decent, not like they were on a work trip. They all introduced theirselves to Joe. Now we'd met coloreds before on our trips in these hills, though not many, and Joe had called most of them by their proper slave names: Sally's Jim and Mr. Carver's Joe and so on. Occasionally we'd meet freedmen, though there really weren't many Negroes in this part of the valley, slave or free, except on a few big farms, and even the ones with papers tried to stay clear of strangers, on account of they might be bounty hunters. But these had names like Tacitus and Socrates, and also Exodus and Leviticus. There was one called Sojourner Red, who was old and dressed like a preacher—had a black suit and white collar.

They didn't much want to take me into the caves, I reckon. Joe says they're pretty shy of charitable strangers now since a bunch of Methodists brought up fruits and pies for them, which was tasty but spoiled pretty soon, plus the Methodists had been followed by a posse of sheriffs which managed to arrest some of these folks—and some of the Methodists, too, after they assaulted the law officers with some disrespectful Bible verses. After that, these folks decided they'd just try and be Christians and leave the Church alone.

So Joe had to talk to them a bit in quiet. Maybe he told them about the reading school. Further back in the cave, there was even more of them. It was a bigger cave than I thought. Might have been fifty or so—some of them had little children with them. There was a campfire, and it smoked a bit, but there must have been a way out for the smoke because it wasn't so bad. I think they'd already had supper when we come up because there were tin plates with crumbs and leftovers stacked by the fire. They had stuck hunks of corn meal on sticks and roasted them over the fire, and then they dipped them in molasses and ginger sugar and offered us some, and boy didn't that taste good!

They could of been runaways, and that would of been a good place to hide, but why so many? Looks like that would draw attention. There

were little tied up bundles of, I guess, clothes and things, and some hand carts with bundles of what looked like books and papers. But I sure didn't see anything around that looked like "pirate" truck. They looked more like a bunch of Presbyterians at Sunday supper.

After a while, Joe and I went out to the mouth of the cave, where it was almost dark now and considerable colder and unrolled our blankets. We sat and wrapped up and watched the last light fade over the Alleghenies to the west and smoked a pipe. Joe looked real thoughtful, so I didn't say much. After a few minutes, the old one come out and sat down and put his hand out near me like he was feeling for me, and Joe said for me to put my hand out under it, and when the old man felt it he closed his warm fingers around my hand and I could see—or really feel—him smile. He turned a little toward me and I guess then I figured he *couldn't* see. I could see he did have a sort of white preacher's collar around his neck but hanging from it was not the usual two little flaps, but a couple of white feathers trimmed so they had that square kind of look. He talked in a quiet voice that didn't sound Southern or Yankee. But it sounded very proper and correct, except for a dropped word once in a while—like he was trying hard to be correct, but wasn't used to it, if you know what I mean.

"Mr. Huckleberry, I'm very pleased you are Joe's friend."

"Well…thank you. He's my friend, too." Then I added "And I'm pleased, too."

"You have been to Mexico—"

"Yes, sir, I was there with the Army during the war."

"Yes. I know. And you have seen Place of the Butterfly."

Every hair on my neck stood up. I had spoken of that day maybe once. Why on earth had Joe even remembered it, let alone said anything about it. Or had the old fellow found out some other way?

"I would like to see that," he went on. "My ancestors have spoken of it to me."

I had no idea what he meant by *that*—especially if he *couldn't* see—but I had to say something, so I says, "Well…your ancestors are right. It's sure worth the trip."

He nodded and smiled. Somehow I didn't like the idea of other people hanging around up there. It was sort of my place. Had my name

on it, as you might say. I added, "It's a long hike," and he chuckled at that.

"Oh, I can still walk, young man. Have you heard of Pike's Peak?" But then he changed the subject. "Tell me, Mr. Lee, you see my face?"

I noticed he'd called me Mr. Lee, which most folks don't around the town. But he didn't turn any more toward me, so I looked at him from the side and of course he wouldn't know the sun had set, so he was mostly a shadow now.

"Not much, sir," I said, "but there'll be a moon up soon and I could then. Or if you'll allow a lantern."

"No, Mr. Lee, that won't be necessary. We will wait for moon."

So we did and it was quiet for a while—and also pretty cold, and I tried to keep my hands warm under my arms in case he wanted me to draw. In about a half hour there was a moon up, not quite full but plenty bright under a low cloud bank. Very pretty, and what I'd come for. Finally I said I could see pretty well now, and he nodded. "So—Mr. Lee, I would like you to make a picture of me."

"Picture? You mean draw it?"

"Yes, with your pens and paints, sir. You do have 'em with you?"

Of course I had some pencils and char-sticks and pigments for watercolor, and a few lengths of foolscap and newsprint in my roll, but a portrait wants fuller light. Still—it was something to try, even though it was so cold I had to keep breathing on my hands. I'd done lots of landscapes in the moonlight before. But not a face. I asked him to move forward a little, and I gently turned his face out towards the valley, and then I saw it, looking past him and just a little up: the face in stone.

Good Lord, I said to myself. It's him. Chiseled into the rock. Now that I looked close, I could see: he had the nose and the cheekbone and the brow. His hair hung down, so I asked if I could pull it back, but he took and did it himself—pulled it back and pulled a little beaded band around it and hooked it. He was Indian all right. And the face was a dead ringer for the one on the mountain.

I was so goose-pimply—aside from being plenty cold anyhow and not getting any warmer—that I didn't know what to do first. How much did he want in the picture? He said, "I will trust you, Mr. Lee. As I trusted your father."

"My—"

"Your Great Father. He gave, and also he took. I want you to give back what you can." So he didn't mean the colonel? What did he mean? But he didn't seem to want to talk any more about that. He wanted a picture. So I drew—pen and charcoal—black on white—from the left looking West, the dark man's face in front of the darker mountain face, the lighter sky fading to dark above, and the line of low straight cloud lit beneath and behind, like an arrow into the forehead. Then the moon on the Alleghenies to the right, from behind, a soft sort of under-glow and it took a while because I couldn't see what I was doing very well and the only surface was the rock ledge.

After a while I told him I'd need to touch it up when we got home, add a bit of a wash, but he said he *was* home, and then he took it and rolled it up and thanked me. He said he would pay me in the morning. I said I didn't really want any payment, for I had enjoyed the experience and learnt from it, and he smiled and said I was wise. Well, I've been called all kinds of things, but never wise!

In the morning, though, he hadn't forgotten. We slept in the cave with the others, where it was warmer, and in the morning at sun up he came to rouse me and took me, feeling his way, out to the ledge again for my "gift." We walked back around the ledge to the east side where the trail came up, but we were still in shadow by the cliff, and it was hard to see him, and then he said, "How is this morning?"

I said there was a pretty sunrise; I wished he could see it. Then he said, "Now look up to your right, sir, where sun hits. You see back of stone man?" I said I did, and he said, "My gift to you is this, that if you watch, when sun comes over shoulder, face will change. Climb to top of ledge and above cave and you will see better. Go on." Then he added, "Take your arts."

I did as he said, and stood above the cave under a pine as the sun poured over the back of the head and back-lit it from the direction opposite of the setting moon, and I saw the mountain's "nose" soften a bit and the "cheek" sag, and he was right: it wasn't a Indian any more at all, but a white man.

When I climbed back down and showed what I'd drew to Joe and pointed out the change, the old man said, "You are right; it is not me any more. It is you." The old man asked if my picture would show trees, oaks and hickories moving up the mountain, and I said yes it would, and he said, "Those are your people. They move up mountain. My people are green—hemlock, white pine. Next moon, oak too will begin to green, and you will not see other kind from here. But we still hold summit. Up there, right at top, there is spruce!"

I told him that this was a fine gift and thanked him, but he said no, the real gift was a little farther away. He said if I went a little further down the ridge where I could see the waterfall under the face, I would have my real gift. I asked him what I would see there, and he said I would know when I saw it. I asked him if there was anything else I could do for him, and he said one thing: when I wrote to my white father, would I tell him what I had seen here. I asked did he mean the White Chief in Washington, and he smiled and said, "No, I mean *your* white father—in the Texas."

So—he did mean the colonel! "Is that where—you want me to tell him?"

"He will be there soon—as you know. Tell him you saw our people, and I, and our mountain. And tell him I thanked him, and blessed his son—and his daughter."

I was the "son," I guess. But which daughter would he mean? The colonel's own daughter—which I'd heard was sickly? Well, I didn't know what all this was about, but I told him I would tell the colonel. I tried to ask some more, but he just shook his head and raised his hand. "Daughter of gold will wait for you, sir," he said. "Daughter of gold will wait." Now *that* really give me goose bumps. He couldn't mean Mariposa, could he? How could he know about her? Then he smiled again and said, "Yes. You will find a way." Then he took out a little vial made out of the tip of some kind of horn—maybe from a deer or something—with a piece of leather tied across it, and he said there was "color" in it. "No color, by itself, but when color fades, this will give magic. Use very little." I wanted to look under that leather, but I didn't.

On the way down I said I wondered why, if the old fellow was blind, did he want a picture of himself? "Who told you he was blind?" Joe said. And I said, "Well, I just guessed...when he took my hand and...he always asked me what I saw."

"He see as well as you do, Huck. Better probably." And he laughed out loud.

"Well, how come he kept asking me questions about the morning and all?"

He said he didn't know; he guessed it was part of the mystery he liked to keep going. Then he told me what he knew about the group. He said they weren't runaways, although most folks thought they were, and so they stayed clear of white folks "down here." They were pilgrims, he said, and called themselves "Recorders." They believed in keeping a record of the people in their songs—and papers, too—and maybe that was why he wanted the picture.

Then I suddenly saw the real reason: he didn't want the drawing for himself at all. He wanted it for *me.* He wanted me to see the thing, and to draw it, and then to give it up. Why he wanted *that* is something I can't explain. Did he want to give it to somebody else? Maybe that Daughter of Gold? If *that's* who I think it is—well, I can't explain it. But I never been so joyful in my life as I was on the way down that mountain!

Nor can we explain it either—though, of course, we shall try.

12. Rank Speculation

So Our Boy, we may assume, has been committing Art all over the Blue Ridge on these jaunts, with and without Joe, who writes nothing about this adventure in his own journal, probably so as not to risk betraying Sojourner's folk. Huck's entry, in fact, is the first direct reference to his own art, and his promise to write Lee is reinforced by Professor Hill's report that Huck "borrows" ink and paper regularly and inquires about military addresses: for West Point, for Army posts in Louisville and St. Louis, for a Customs office in Galveston, and for an unnamed fort in the Indian Territory. He may well have written to Becky, but if he did, or to anyone else back in St. Petersburg (not to mention the Valley of Mexico) he wouldn't need to ask for addresses. But those he does ask for match up well with the movements of his newly claimed "father," Robert E. Lee.

Here's what we know about that: after various dissatisfying staff duties, and the less irksome but still unfulfilling life at West Point, the engineer finally gets his wish, a line command—then as now the best route to promotion—a lieutenant-colonelcy in the newly created 2nd United States Cavalry. Thus, in 1855 Lee begins the following odyssey—all on the record, and you can look it up:

1. From West Point to Washington, then by train to Louisville, arriving on 20 April, 1855, where he takes acting command of the 2nd Cavalry (whose full colonel is absent on—what else?—court martial duty.)

2. To Jefferson Barracks in St. Louis, to assume command.

3. To Galveston by steamer, (after a winter in Pennsylvania for more of the detested court martial duty) arriving on March 2, 1856.

4. To Fort Mason on the Bravos River in the Comanche Reserve to rejoin his command, arriving April 9, 1856.

Louisville, St. Louis, Galveston, and Fort Mason—right down Our Boy's address list! Clearly, Huck has heard from Lee about his itinerary or guessed it from other sources, perhaps from the old Indian—whose name, I will wager, is a corruption of something else. The records of the Indian Reserve on the Texas-Oklahoma border list an old Indian captured on a mountain in the Ozarks on June 3, 1849, not long after Our Boy's presumed exit from Mexico, with a mixed band of Sioux and Comanche, even though he claimed to be a Cherokee chief. On the report he is listed as "Sioux" (in spite his claim), followed by what is no doubt a pitiful rendering of the name's sound: "Chia-nu-red." *Sioux: Chia-nu-red.* Folks who didn't know the language and heard it said quickly might hear something like: *Sojourner Red.*

He is listed in 1849 as a prisoner, but not next year. So, if he's gone, where and why? And what could he have had to do with Huck's "Great Father"?

Like so much else, this Sojourner, too, falls off the earth for about five years, till he shows up (if I'm right about who he is) on the mountain that Huck sees as his likeness, to be drawn by that "son" of Our Colonel—whom the man seems improbably to have met, unless Huck's first instinct was right, and "Great Father" really is a metaphor for some white authority. And nothing in the official record indicates Lee was anywhere near him during the Great Five-Year Gap. After Mexico, it's straight home for Lee—and why not?—for some well-deserved leave, then some court-martial duty, then some bridge-building, then to West Point for three years, and then—and only then—back to the West. No assignments involving Indian horse thieves and mentalists. And nothing further on this Daughter of Gold.

But, as you might suspect, I have other evidence.

First, the circumstantial: Lee returns from Mexico to Washington in the spring of 1849, under sail to New Orleans, and thence by steam up the Mississippi and Ohio, eventually to Wheeling, where he takes the railroad the rest of the way—a straight trip, with no detours to the Ozarks. But the trip takes longer than it should: there is a layover for two weeks or more above Memphis while a steam-cylinder is repaired, and a cargo dispute is settled. But Lee, like any soldier with a family, must be anxious to get home. Other boats pass northward, with room for him, but does he take one? No, even though he is accompanied only by his horse and an orderly. He cools his heels for two weeks and arrives in Wheeling on the same steamer. Instead of taking new passage, he sends his orderly with the horse to a nearby stable and betakes himself, not to the comfortable inn near the docks, but instead by ferry to the US military post across the river, which is a mile wide there, almost as if he *assumes* he has at least a week or two, and isn't worried about missing the boat!

Now, we know all this only because the orderly, Sergeant Jim Connolly, bless him, takes the trouble to mention it in a letter dated June 6 to his sister in Maryland to advise of the delay. You soldiers, take note: write your loved ones, and keep those journals going, too. And *date* everything! Scholars will bless you for it.

So what was Lee up to? The interesting thing about the trip to the post is that there is no record of it—even though Sergeant Connolly says that is where Lee said he would be all week. So where was he? Two weeks is long enough to get to the Ozarks and back, maybe even Texas with a good horse—more than one, probably—if there's good reason, but what could that be? One clue is that when he returns to collect his horse and orderly, the sergeant says the major looks "beat"—tired and saddle-sore, not fit and rested, and in need of an hour or two to clean up before embarking. Connolly says the steamer is "reddy to go" when they arrive—almost as if they are stayed for. Has Lee paid the captain to arrange a long lay-over? Lee says nothing to the orderly, and the horse (Grace Darling) is not talking.

So we have to guess. And my guess is that Lee went to perform an adoption.

Yes. My theory is that Huck, distressed at the prospect of being part of Judge Thatcher's estate—even now, nobody believes he's eighteen!—somehow gets in touch with Lee and manages to meet him, maybe in St. Louis, to challenge things in court, or, more likely, on the edge of the Indian Territory, to arrange something through ritual that may be respected in court if it ever gets that far. So whatever goes on out there in the Ozarks—if I'm right—concerns and benefits this Sojourner Red without Huck's actually meeting him (unless he's disguised), and *perhaps,* somehow, benefits Mariposa, too. Who else, after all, could be that Daughter of Gold? And if it also benefits Lee and his country—well, then, so much the better.

13. Out Like a Lamb

Huck, at any rate, seems galvanized by the meeting with the old Indian. By mid-March, 1856, he has decided his sojourn in Lexington must end. "It's time to light out, for sure," he says. According to both him and Joe, Huck goes through a week or two of furious work at the Institute, as if trying to clear up a backlog of chores, and he rides out (as he rode in) under cover of storm, leaving this time in thunder and hail. But the accounts of the leave-taking itself differ.

According to Huck, he thanks the Hills, the Jacksons, the superintendent, says goodbye to Joe ("We shook hands and wished each other luck"), loads his canvas pack and guitar into a wagon he has hired to take him to the railroad, covers it all with an oil-cloth against the first drops of a spring storm, and heads down to the depot, where the storm really opens up, mixing the sound of hail with the sound of cinders from the engine's stacks hitting the roof as the cars begin to move. And that is that. Six weeks later, he recommences his journal with:

"Well, praise be, here I am in the territories again. And still got all my fingers."

(Whatever that means. Did he write something that is now lost?)

Taylor, however, tells the leave-taking a bit differently. According to Joe, he wants to go along, but Huck won't hear of it. Maybe Huck is reluctant to lead his young friend—free or not—down a dangerous road. After all, Joe has revealed little of his own background—no manumission papers, no talk of his parents, except vaguely as "slaves from the rice farms" who were "lost among the dealers." At any rate, he and Huck seem to have had it out the evening before Huck's departure. Here is Joe's version:

March 10, 1856: Cold & blustery. I taken the clothes down behind the officers' barracks on account of they wouldn't dry none today nohow and hung them up in the kitchen. I banked the fires so they wouldn't smoke, but I spec they will anyhow and I'll hear about it. Huck come by after supper and say he going to leave town soon but not to tell nobody because he don't want them to worry none. He say he'll tell me when if I promise to cover his tracks at the college the next morning to give him a good start, then tell the professor he done left on family business. I wonder how he judge he so important somebody going to come after him. But he say he taking no chances about "complications." I ask how he going to go, and he say he done saved enough to take the cars far as he need to. I ask if he going north or south, and he say better I didn't know, but I see he got his heavy blue army cloak and blanket roll, and I see the coat pocket got a B&O time card in it, so I expect he going north. I tell him whatever reason he got to go north I got a better one; why not let me come with him? He don't say nothing, so I say if he worried about people thinking I'm a runaway he can get papers from the professor and act like he my owner, till we gets to somewheres safe.

Well, he look at me like I a ghost or something. Then he look off and say, "I ain't gonna take nobody else down a fool's road."

And I say, "Who you calling a fool? You think I ain't better off in the north? You think I ain't saved some money, too? I's doing satisfactory here, but I been thinking of leaving for some time."

And he say, "Well, then what you need me for?"

And I say, "Well, I should a thought you might just like a friend along, or don't they let you have no niggers for friends where you going?"

And he just snap like a dry stick. "What you know about friends?" he say. "I had more *black* friends than you ever had, and had them in tighter spots. I been *shot* at alongside of them. And I may be again. And I don't know where I'll wind up, but I ain't a-going to be responsible for no boy!"

And that did it for me. "Who you calling a boy?" I wants to know, and I was so hot I took a swing at him, but he grab my arm before it got halfway there, and just stood there looking at me all clinched up, and

then his eyes turned, and he put my hand down and say, "I'm sorry, Joe, but I got to light out." And he say this the place for me, and the professor need me to help with the school and all—I was such a good reader now I could teach myself and the others, and probably half the teachers. He probably knew that'd make me laugh. He stop in the doorway and turn and say, "In fact, you know you should get 'em to admit you."

I was still mad, and short of breath, but that got my goat a bit, and I say get me to admit to what?

And he say, "Admit you to the *college*. Let you be a cadet and all. What a 'speriment *that* would make," he say. And he laugh—so I don't know if he serious or not—then he left. I 'llowed he'd be gone in the morning, and sho' 'nough he was. So I checks the railroad clerk at the College. He gone north all right. And if I wants to catch him, I could.

And maybe he does—because that is all there is of Joe's journal. Either he stops writing, or, more likely, he does light out, and whatever he wrote later is now lost—except for one mysterious and very important letter, now in my possession, which we will get to later.

But we are still left with the even greater mystery of the Five-Year Gap after Mexico. It is time now to divulge some of what I know about that time—beyond the hypothetical "adoption." And for some of it we must thank Buck Grangerford.

Grangerford's own memoirs will be worth the price, I assure you—a real newspaperman (with real sources) and apparently an occasional diplomatic courier for his elders. Meanwhile, he spins a good yarn if kept supplied with brandy and cigars. Of particular interest is his account of a meeting at a mission school with two Sisters representing the convent:

She was as fearsome as her reputation: I had no doubt the Army would have the Devil's own time trying to use the Mission for any purpose other than one she approved. Why they sent a youngster like me to face her, I can't imagine, unless they thought it would throw her off her guard. If that was their hope, they were mistaken!

My mission was to assure this Sister Agnes, the Mother Superior or whatever it is they call her, that my newspaper would not take sides

but would be happy to report her story to the public along with anything confidential she wished to convey to the authorities. Well, she brought out her spectacles and a sheaf of notepaper, cleared her throat, and commenced a disquisition. But I paid less attention to Sister Agnes than I did to her young companion. Now *she* was as pretty a little Mexican, sir, as you'll ever see, in spite of that nun's habit. She took care of the horses—no side-saddle for her, I noticed. And I swear she wore riding breeches—now that was a sight! There's something about high piety and cavalry pants that stirs the soul—made me think of Joan of Arc, you know. When they were ready to leave, she returned to the office alone and corrected several mistakes in Sister Agnes's notes. Pretty cheeky, I thought!—and then she asked me, "You were a friend of Huckleberry, yes?" Now, sir, how do you suppose she knew that? Well, I nodded, because of course what other Huckleberry could there be? And then she smiled and said, "You will tell him I remember his *musica*, and he must make more, many more *musicas*—for the child, you know—and he must come soon."

Now there isn't a young man anywhere who wouldn't do what she asked for one of *those* smiles. I'd heard Huck was at the Point, and I imagined I could write to him there—but before I could ask anything more, she took my hand and shook it, just like a man, and left. I supposed the child was Huck's—though, if you're right, it may not have been. I can see how he'd fallen for her; I was quite smitten myself. I never saw the child, though. Very strange. I thought nuns weren't allowed to have children. And that was the last I saw of her—though this older nun told me some things later when things settled down. "She once kill a man, you know."

And I said, "You mean the girl?

And she said, "Oh, yes, I hear from *familia*. Kill him—*se matado*! *Muerte*!" Not sure how to translate—might just as well mean, "killed himself," or even "*her*-self."

I wanted to know more, don't you see?—"*¿Verdad?"*

And she just said, "All done now—*terminado!"*

I asked was she still looking for Huckleberry—"young man?—boy *hombre*—?" and that rang a bell.

"Oh, *si*," she says, "*Si, si!—un joven!* Young one!" But I said wasn't this Maria a nun, and she said, "Oh, *si!* For *rato*—short time, I

think." and she laughed. So I asked was she looking for him, and she said, "Oh, *si*, Maria promise *encontrar*, to find him, win him *por Jesus.* Now what you think? What *she* mean win? Maybe not what *Jesus* mean, no?" And she laughed and clapped her hands at the thought, and that's all I got from her about Our Boy, but she complicated our lives for months, and if you'd like more about *that*....

For that we shall wait for the memoirs! But it's clear now, isn't it, that Our Boy and Our Girl have promises to keep? And as for the six months just *before* Huck's arrival in Lexington, I can account for that, too, thanks to still another source—which in this case is excellent, no brandy required.

14. Thin Grey Lines

West Point is a very beautiful place. Also a very cold place. That's a common association, as poets have observed. It's on a bank of the Hudson River. The wind pours down the river from the north during the cold months—its turbulence increased by the bluffs—and boils up from the river during the warm months, although it's not really a wind then, just a hot draft off the glassy surface. But at any time of day or year (I recommend sunset in autumn) the view across the river from above the parade ground is magnificent: the huge red oaks and maples near the point (if they're still there), the orange glow off the water up river—well, it takes one's breath away, if one has any breath left after drill, which is about all a cadet is allowed to do on the field besides "police" it. Should a cadet be on a mission by himself, he is expected to look straight ahead, at the mission, not the scenery. This place is about duty.

The term begins—during the time of our story, the early 1850s—in late August. All but the rising fourth-year men have already had more than a month of summer encampment. A good time for the new plebes to get a taste of the Point before classes begin, you would think, but that is not the Army way. Perhaps it might be too much of a taste—why scare off the new boys? It's too hot in July for the barracks, you know, so the cadets live in tents out on the parade ground. Camp is not about study. It's about drill, duties, and boredom. Pretty good practice for the military life, actually. Even in war, most of a soldier's time is spent not in combat, but drudgery. A few hours of heart-pounding, pants-wetting, life-altering excitement, preceded and followed (for the survivors) by weeks of drilling, marching, digging, guarding, and thumb-twiddling. Whoever can survive camp for four years is qualified to be an officer!

So, in late August the plebes arrive. Most of them show up at the rail depot on the Point the day before muster, either by railroad car or by steamer up the Hudson. It's quite an assortment to see—most between sixteen and eighteen years of age—still in their civvies, some with whole carriage loads of dry goods their sponsors and parents are sure they will need, some with little more than the clothes on their back. Some look like the urbane and self-assured products of prestigious New England (even European) prep schools, or of aristocratic Southern plantation tutors—while others look like the gawky and unsophisticated sons of Midwestern ranchers and sheriffs that they are. It is, and is intended to be, a melting pot. That's one reason the entrance examination is (or was) a joke: to prevent academic elitism. Congress, you see, is concerned that the officer corps be representative of The People. It's true: the idea is to ensure that ordinary numbskulls have a chance to be officers! A man of good character, after all, and good patronage, despite only marginal mental parts, might make a fine officer. He would, of course, have to pass his courses. Many do not. Still, you have to respect the democracy of the theory.

So let us follow in our imagination a young arrival: he stands on the platform in a suit with just a small valise and, let's say, a rather long cloth-covered roll or bundle of something under his arm. We are not surprised: many of the boys seem to arrive with some special thing, without which they are certain they cannot survive. Let's say his bundle is about three feet long, covered in muslin on the outside, tied with string around the middle and at both ends. (What's in there, we wonder—a sword? Something of religious significance? A baseball bat? A bassoon?…) The boy lines up with the others in front of the cadet adjutant assigned to check them in. When it's the boy's turn, he unties the end of the muslin and presents a piece of paper. The adjutant looks at it, frowns, then shrugs and points to a carriage ready to make a shuttle run down to the post with several other arrivals.

At the Institute, the boys dismount and are marched off through the pollen haze toward the underclass barracks, except for the boy we are following, who, when he shows his letter to the cadet officer, is handed a map and directed toward Thayer Hall. (How I wish I had that map!) At Thayer, the boy walks up the steps to the superintendent's office, where he takes a deep breath and opens the door. For the moment, we will leave him in the outer office.

Now we need to imagine ourselves inside with the superintendent. He looks handsome in his blue uniform with the gold buttons, braid, and insignia of a lieutenant colonel. With graying hair and moustache, but the tall bearing of a soldier, he exudes both reflection and command.

He's standing at the window, let's say, with a faculty member, who looks more professorial than military (although uniformed as a lieutenant)—shorter, balding, and full-whiskered, with a bit of a paunch. They are looking out across the post toward the collecting point where the plebes and their gear are arriving, cartload by cartload. We can imagine the superintendent smiling to think how much of that "truck" they will have to ship back. Even if there were room for it, cadets are not allowed to have much in the way of distraction. Not alcohol, of course, nor cards, nor tobacco. But not even musical instruments. No newspapers or magazines. No novels or plays—although poetry is allowed for some reason, maybe because the literature teacher wants the boys to memorize inspirational verse. The place really is appallingly boring.

But this superintendent is new—this is just his second year—and already he is thinking of some changes. Replacing French with Spanish, for one thing. And more English, too. Some of these young men can't handle their *native* tongue, much less a foreign one. But he has in mind still more compromises with the real world. He believes in order and tradition, yes, and his job is to make soldiers. But he knows they will also be citizens, and that most of them won't even stay in the army. The Academy already produces more officers than it takes to staff a peacetime military. Promotion, as he well knows, takes forever. So the ambitious often leave after a few frustrating years. A bit of law wouldn't hurt, and some *civil* engineering. In fact, adding a whole fifth year would be a good idea—slow down the pipeline, if nothing else. And why on earth do they forbid music, but teach dancing? Just for the occasional military ball!

Still, what he's about to do now, he knows, is a bit of a risk. Without turning, he addresses the man beside him, "Could you tell much about the boy's skills, Cadmus?"

"Well, he reads well enough, sir. I've doubts about his math and physical science" (shaking his head). "I've—sir, if I may speak frankly?—I must tell you I have doubts all around about this."

"Understood, Lieutenant" (nodding soberly, then turning and smiling), "but we've seen the like, you know."

"You mean Whistler, sir?"

"Jimmy Whistler!" (laughing out loud, now) "Our leader in the fields of drawing and of acquiring demerits! No, that's a different matter entirely—although they may share the interest in art. No, Mr. Willcox, I was thinking of someone else. Do you remember Jackson?"

"Tom Jackson, sir? What about him?"

"He came here straight from the mountains, you know. Near Harpers Ferry. Could just do sums, I hear."

"Yes, that is true, Colonel. When I—"

The mail slot on the office door slides open and a cadet's voice is heard. "Sir, there's a boy out here, with a letter that says—"

"Yes, I know. Tell him to wait just a moment."

The superintendent turns to a cadet who has been sitting in a straight chair on the other side of the office, by the desk—uncomfortably, because the boy, although instructed to sit, is trying to maintain a military posture. This boy's presence, by the way, is what allows us to paint the scene: he lives long enough to write memoirs.

"Young man." The boy rises to attention. "At ease, mister! At ease! We have a new cadet this term from your hometown. Possibly you would have been acquainted, possibly not. His last schooling, so far as I know, was in the fifth form."

"Fifth, sir?" Although officially *At Ease*, the boy looks anything but.

"Yes, fifth. Although he's a little older than you. Assuming your local schools were equivalent, how far would he have progressed, do you think, say, in mathematics?"

"Math? I don't know, sir. Not to algebra. Maybe long division. If he paid attention and was interested."

"Interested? Hm! I doubt that—at the time. But he seems to be now." The colonel looks out the window again. "Cadet, I'm going to offer you an important responsibility. I'm going to ask you to be his roommate, and to help him—to be successful here." Turning away from the window, he lifts a globe of the world from a shelf in the book case, twirls the Earth meditatively. "Help him *honestly* and *honorably*, of course."

The boy starts a bit, but maintains composure.

The globe stops twirling, and the colonel taps it gently—somewhere in the center of the continent—then looks up and smiles. "You are from the same area, so that should help, and your own record, I must say, is exemplary. Only one demerit. For...never mind, don't tell me. Lieutenant Willcox here recommends you; that is enough. Please understand, mister, that I want this to be successful...on its own terms, so I am not ordering you. I am *asking* if you are willing—and if at any time you wish a change made, or have something to report confidentially, you must feel free to approach me."

The cadet isn't used to being asked for his opinion by colonels, so he considers himself under orders.

"Yes, sir. I will do my best." But he can't resist. "May I ask who the new cadet is, sir?"

"Of course, you may. Allow me to introduce you. Lieutenant, would you show the boy in, please?"

When Willcox returns, followed by the nervous young man we left in the outer office, our perspective also reverses, and our imaginary view is over the new boy's shoulder toward the superintendent and the waiting cadet—on whose face the shock of recognition registers.

"My lord! Huckleberry Finn!" (We turn to see a similar shock on Huck's face.)

"Sid! My gosh, that *is* you, isn't it? Well, I never! I thought—"

"Well," says Lee, beaming. "I see you boys do know each other. That is excellent. I am sure we have chosen a fine…partnership. Tell me, Cadet Sawyer—Cadet, you *may* stand at ease—what do you think? Shall I entrust this plebe to your care for a while?"

Cadet Sid Sawyer (Tom's half-brother, you may recall) is not at all at ease, but he resigns himself to his duty and asks if there will be a new room assignment. His present room is a single—a matter of prestige for a third-year man—and the new upper-class barracks have indoor plumbing.

It turns out he will need to return to the underclass barracks—with some compensating privileges, of course. He will get to make life a bit more miserable than it would otherwise be early in the morning for a few plebes, who have been assigned to him for duties after reveille and before breakfast. Lots of policing can be done then. There is also opportunity for hazing. You cannot imagine, for example, the villainous ways in which chamber pots and latrines can be rigged by clever young engineering students. One of the milder ones is called the Leaning Tower of P. I leave the technical details to your imagination.

So, what we have here—do we not?—is a little social experiment. And Cadet Sawyer does not approve of it, not one bit. The principle itself is bad enough, quite aside from who is involved: the very idea that an untutored waif straight from the Territory, with no more preparation than he might get in a few years at a mission school, could arrive here as the superintendent's own protégé and be silver-spooned along…Oh, and if he *doesn't* happen to succeed—if he *doesn't* master, say, his trigonometric functions by Christmas, when he starts by knowing little more than his times tables—well then, it isn't the fault of the theory, or of the addle-brained administration that cooked it up—oh no! It'll be the fault of the poor cadet assigned to wet-nurse the fellow along! Sid's later memoir quotes a diary entry:

I'll be the goat; you just wait. It was always this way. Huck and Tom, Tom and Huck, damn them. Wherever Tom is now, I'm sure it's the same way there, too, for some other poor boy.

No, Sid is not happy. His only cheer comes from his realization that, even if he does his best, the experiment will almost certainly fail, and fail quickly, likely within the term, and that with a year to go, his fourth, Cadet Sawyer will be *owed*.

But Sid is a determined cadet, and devoted to duty. It is one reason he was picked for this. After all, there are other Missourians at the Point. So he grits his young teeth—a year younger than Huck's, in fact—and resolves to bear his burden. Actually, outbursts like the above are rare in his journals. Generally he can be seen looking on the bright side, reciting slogans and resolutions:

I know as Poor Richard said that there are no gains without pains, and if I can't take the heat I shouldn't rock the boat.

Well. All that survive now from these early diaries are what Sawyer himself saw fit to quote in his much later memoir, written while under arrest, fearing trial and execution—a condition that (like cancer) can affect one's perspective! But we'll get to all that. For now, it is enough that he has a very detailed memory.

And Our Boy, for his part, proves an avid, if unspectacular, scholar. He is interested in language (fortunately, since the transition from French to Spanish means there is an awkward semester when both are required) and in history and literature, although most of the latter is dreadfully boring. Huck tells Sid it reminds him of the tearful poems by Buck's deceased sister Emmeline, and he notes that at least those were short. Huck actually reads and writes better, Sid has to admit, than some of the grammar-school graduates. The boy is terrible, though—hysterically terrible—at dance and at drill (once accidentally bloodying a cadet corporal's backside with his bayonet). But so earnest and un-self-conscious is he about it all, that it is difficult to dislike him, much as his Sid tries. Especially since the boy works damnably hard on anything he thinks the colonel wants him to do, and the colonel checks on him regularly.

But then there's math.

Despite his prediction of doom, Cadet Sawyer takes a deep breath and pulls Our Boy up the steep slope of remediation. Without mathematics he cannot do the physical sciences or the scaled drawings in the engineering curriculum. Well, then, he will have to learn. In fact, it becomes a point of stubborn pride as Sid becomes identified with Huck's progress. "How's old Finn doing?" he hears, over the clinking pewter at the upperclassmen's mess. "With you teaching him, Sawyer, he's sure to be home for Christmas!" Well. Such ribbing engenders a competitive spirit. Sid will show them. His charge—hopeless as he is, damn him—will pass.

And he does, at least in his first two months' recitations. Once, in fact, after Huck has just stood up in Congreve's section room to rattle off the necessary steps in some proof, we get to hear the gravelly old prof comment: "Well, done, Saw—ah, I mean Finn! Sorry, I confused the apprentice with the master for a second." And everybody gets a chuckle.

Sawyer, of course, hears about it, as he is meant to, and doesn't know whether to laugh or cry. For he is the owner of a terrible knowledge: that simple geometry is one thing, but that complex quadratics and points in space—never mind integrations!—are another world entirely. Sid is like a driver who has towed a make-shift sled behind him well enough along the flat, but knows that once he heads up into the hills the ramshackle load behind him hasn't a prayer: on the first switchback it will plunge off into the gorge.

He'll flop. He has to. He can't do polynomials.

One would like, at this point, to show a little growing familiarity and warmth—or even heat—between Our Boy and his mentor. Perhaps a cathartic, bare-knuckled brawl, followed by a sodden reconciliation up at Sophie's, the tavern near the rail depot where one is generally allowed to buy an expensive drink or two before it is "discovered" that one is an underage cadet. Sid has been there, of course, trolling for plebes. The proprietor is Sophie's husband, Asa, who seems to be running the pub. So why the name, "Sophie's"? Most likely, Sid suspects, because services other than food and drink are available, for a price, and she is in charge of those.

The mentor, however, keeps a cordial but professional distance from his apprentice. Huck strikes up friendships, but they seem confined to the fringes of the class—James McNeil Whistler, for instance, who, whatever art talent he may have, is a misfit here, as Poe once was. Huck once comes in drunk and past taps, singing a song about a Spanish rose—in Spanish—and collapses in bed before Sid can say anything, facing the opposite wall in silence, apparently asleep. Sid watches quietly for a few minutes. Soon he sighs and begins to rise to prepare for bed himself, but just then Huck speaks, his voice muffled by the blanket. "Why do you hate me, Sid?"

Sid does not answer, and nothing more is said. Nor does Sid send Huck up for demerits: if the fellow goes down on Cadet Sawyer's watch, it will not be for missing curfew.

A more appropriate crisis comes, as expected, with a complex math problem. It takes about half a page to lay out and requires that one actually understand polynomial algebra. The work is, of course, pledged, as is all work, but Sid has been given permission to *coach* his charge to a considerable extent. Sid has requested this understanding be put in writing to protect him from the horrors of an honor charge. He has a copy of the order outlining the kinds of help he can give, and, in the soft glow of his oil lamp (plebes are only allowed candles), Sid glances over it while Huck sweats at the table on his side of the small room and asks the kind of questions that cannot be answered—and Sid knows they cannot—without at least another year of algebra. What really *is* an irrational root, after all? There can be a negative amount of something, of course, but how can there be a *square root* of something negative? Let alone the square root of something that is itself *imaginary*?

Huck is able to draw it in his mind, as it were, but not on the page, in proper form. The problem, of course, has a kind of shape—starting small at the top, then fattening out, spreading into two bowlegged limbs of calculations, then plopping down two feet, side by side, sort of on the right side of the page, balanced, as it were, on a one-line pedestal, in parentheses.

Then, as Sid watches over Our Boy's shoulder, he has an idea. *I suddenly saw it clearly—didn't want to see it at first—put it behind me. But if you put something far enough behind you, hard enough, it comes back around from the other side of the world.*

"Let me see," he says, "maybe I can explain it better."

Sid goes to his own desk, looks once again at his copy of the order: he may coach his charge toward a correct answer in pledged work, it says, as long as the charge, "*does the work, arriving at the answer himself,*" and that the charge is not allowed "*to hear the precise calculation, or to see the page upon which the tutor's own work appears.*"

Clear enough! He does the work himself, picks up his work sheet (which he will have to turn in, now that he has "helped"), and then stands, holding up his own work, reading by the light from his own desk, as he quietly and carefully explains the shape of the problem.

"I think I see," says Huck slowly, nodding up at his tutor, and reaches for his table of logarithms, to begin re-figuring. The pencil taps on the soft pine table top. "Thanks, Sid. I think I understand now."

Sid takes the paper back to his table, sits, leans back. "Thank you, sir, you mean."

Huck looks up. "Sorry, Sid," he smiles, "sir."

The die is cast. Huck will get this problem right, and perhaps others. Maybe he can bluff through a recitation. Eventually, of course, comes the exam. He will fail that comfortably. What will be the upshot, Sid is not sure. What has just gone on may seem innocent, but both boys know better than that. They know, in other words, where the light of truth shines.

And Sid knows that he has shot an arrow of treachery high in the air—so high, in fact, that it could blow back on the archer himself. He just hopes he has put enough distance into it.

15. Duty Be Damned!

Two weeks later, after Thanksgiving, the order comes: Cadet Sawyer is to report to the Napoleon Club after morning classes.

Sid feels his stomach tighten: he has been in that room. It serves as a lounge for faculty functions, often served by cadets, but also as the venue for serious proceedings. Located in the new Academic Building, it is impressively paneled and furnished—has the feel of a library, filled with books, portraits, and maps of the emperor's campaigns. Some of the framed maps on the wall, in fact, have been drawn by faculty—although on the most artistic drawings Sid notes the flamboyant signature of James McNeill Whistler—the very cadet who he has heard is about to be expelled for academic nonperformance. But how would that involve Sid himself?

There are several professors in the room—Congreve and Willcox, plus the underclass artillery master and a couple of others—and the superintendent, looking grave—sad almost. And Huck: in uniform, seated, but at attention. When Sid is announced, Lee looks up and (for some reason) smiles.

"Ah, Cadet Sawyer! It's good to see you," as if Sid has just chanced by! But he gets right to the point. "Do you recall helping this cadet with this particular problem?" He passes a piece of ruled paper to Sid, who, while trying to remain at attention, bends awkwardly to look at it. He doesn't touch it—as if it is poisonous. Yes, of course he does.

"No, sir, not directly. It looks like a number of solve-for-*x* simplifications we worked on. It looks like Huck's handwriting." (A nice touch, he thinks: sounds open and forthcoming.)

"It is, isn't it?" says Congreve to Huck.

"Yes, sir. I believe that was the hardest—"

"And Sawyer helped you how?"

"Well, sir, he...coached me. Reminded me of the steps."

"And you worked out the answer on your own?"

"Yes, sir, I was very pleased with myself, sir."

"Pleased." Congreve's bushy brows rise a bit as he looks back up at Lee over his spectacles. "Colonel, this work *must* have been copied."

Lee leans back behind the library table, hands propped up in a little isosceles triangle in front of him. "Go on, Professor."

"You see," Congreve continues, "the answer is correct" (pauses for dramatic effect), "but it could *not* have been correct. Look!" (stabbing at the center of the problem with a letter opener) "This negative figure plus-or-minus the radical. . .well, it wouldn't work. He could only have got the correct answer by copying it."

"Sir, I give you my word of honor—" (It's Sid, interrupting.)

"Yes, I know, Cadet. You did not show him your paper. Where were you standing when you, ah, *coached* him on this problem?"

He says he doesn't remember (although of course he does), but Huck, obligingly tells them, "Why, he stood right before my desk."

"But between his own desk and yours?"

"Well, yes."

"And you looked up at him?"

"Well, that's so, but he didn't show me—"

"And the light from his own lamp was behind him—"

Now the light, as it were, clicks on in Huck's mind. "Well, actually he—I think his body sort of blocked the light so's the paper and I was in his shadow. I always thought of myself as kind of in his shadow, you know." He tries a chuckle, but nobody responds.

"Your memory seems pretty exact now, mister, but you're inconsistent. You told us earlier he stood *before* you. The lamp would have shown full on—and through—his paper."

"But I didn't—"

"And you said you looked up at him."

"But he didn't show me the front of his paper."

It's quiet for a second or two. Sid holds his breath. Then Congreve, quietly, "Then you did look at it—at the back at least."

"Well, I may have glanced, but—"

"Colonel, the cadet copied Sawyer's paper by reading it from the reverse—by the lamplight. Look! [holding it up to the light] He was smart enough to know he had to transpose it to the other direction. But [looking over at Huck with one raised brow] not smart enough to know that the signs don't go in the opposite direction: negative four plus-or-minus eight, all over four, does not yield the same set of quotients as eight plus-or-minus negative four, over four. And if you look at the radical above...look at the direction! You see? The boy was able to copy from Mr. Sawyer's paper without Sawyer's even realizing it!"

Sid is stunned. His gambit has worked perfectly: Huck had taken the bait, and now Congreve has drawn the ideal conclusion: that Huck had copied the paper, but—crucially—that Sid did not realize it!

The board requires further convincing. Huck is required to solve a similar problem from scratch, with all watching. Several tongue-biting minutes later it is clear he cannot get past the crucial step—never knew how to do it—and is stuck. No quick story about Uncle Hornback and his niece stranded on a wreck will solve this. No bit of pig's blood and a few hairs left on the ax. No hiding Jim's hat. No, sir, this is something he can't fake.

And then Our Boy does something Sid never expected. He starts to cry.

Starts slowly with a bit of mouth-twisting and eye-reddening, then some lip-quivering, and tears begin to well from fluttering eyelids. Very convincing, thinks Sid—both disgusted and fascinated as he watches Huck rise unsteadily, like one of those little mechanical soldier dolls that stand jerkily to attention if you twist a key expanding the rods inside them. Lee rises, too, extends his hand to Huck's shoulder as if to draw the boy to him—but isn't sure how to do it—looks sadly over at Sid and then out the window over the boy's head, which is a foot shorter than his own, toward the parade ground where the corps is assembling by companies—in straight, gray lines—for artillery drill.

"Cadet," Sid realizes Lee is talking to him, "you have not had lunch."

"No, sir, but—"

"Report to mess, mister. See what they have left. In thirty minutes report to drill."

"Yes, sir."

Sid salutes and leaves. As he closes the big oak door, the tableau is still in place: Lee, with a tentative arm on the disconsolate-looking Huck—that charlatan!—the others standing or sitting awkwardly, looking at papers. Congreve staring at Whistler's map.

Cadet Sawyer goes nowhere near the mess hall. After drill, he walks to the point, below the rail head, watches a sloop shorten sail in the rising wind.

He waits till sunset, but clouds have begun to lower and there's little color. A bit of snow has begun to swirl around the docks under the swinging lamps. He hears some boatmen shout, sees a trail of white smoke over the bluff from a steamer, as if pumped out of the ground, hears a steam whistle over the wind, feels the cold bite through his cape. He tries for a while to hate himself, but can't. Just feels old. But not old like decay. More like...like wine. A dark, red wine. He's never liked wine—its complicated bitterness, its cynical parody of blood. Maybe he would now.

When he returns to the barracks, it is almost taps. He inspects his plebes for a while, for an excuse not to go to quarters. When he finally does, Huck and all his things are gone.

Two days later, a Saturday, Sid is preparing to serve tea to the faculty in the Napoleon Room—a bit of an honor, but of course this room, for Sid, contains the ghosts of his own villainy. So as not to disturb them, he quietly maneuvers his cloth-covered cart, loaded with tureens, roll-warmers, and place settings, down from the kitchen. Almost at the room, he hears something within and stops, listens...there it is again: suppressed laughter and hushed voices.

"—if they ever look, which I doubt."

It sounds like Jimmy Whistler—expelled last week. Sid had seen him earlier out in the lot with a one-horse trap, loading some belongings, but what's he doing now?

"Well, Curly, I think it's bully. Or if it ain't, there's no such thing."

More suppressed giggling, then after a minute or two, "My God, Huck. You've gone me one up, for sure. You're an inspired artist, my friend! I shall follow your career eagerly." More giggling.

"Well, it serves 'em right. You should a seen ol' Congreve's eyebrows go up and down."

"I heard *your* eyes were a sight, too, old fellow. Heard you got some tears going. What a tragedian you'd make. I doff my hat to you, sir." More giggling. "But listen; we must be gone. They'll be setting up tea any minute."

"Tea—wait a minute. Do you think they would notice—"

"No, Huck, no. We've done enough. Let's go over to Sophie's and drink a toast—to higher math!"

Sid ducks into a closet while they pass. No awkward good-byes, please! Alone in the room now, he looks around, checking for vandalism. But there's nothing obvious. The paintings seem un-defaced. He checks the sugar and cream: they seem all right, too. Very strange. Surely those two were up to something.

He finishes the tables and place settings, lights the oil and begins to boil water for tea. Then he sees it: Napoleon's portrait—the famous one, with some of his army in the background, his hand characteristically thrust into his vest. But the hand has. . .what? A sixth finger! He looks closer: yes! The paint is fresh. And the new finger wears a ring: a half-opal, Curly Whistler's prep-school signet. But what is Huck's contribution? And what can eyebrows have to do with it?

It is only after the tea, as he cleans up, that he notices it: in the middle distance, on the buckboard of a caisson, a soldier seems to sleep, hand suspended over a bottle on the ground, bespectacled face turned toward the viewer. The bushy brows leave no doubt: it's Congreve.

Sid never tells anyone, but he is not amused. In his mind, the moral order of the cosmos is now in question. For two days, he has been a tortured soul, a sinner, an adult. And what is he now? Whatever he flung onto Our Boy has rolled right off him, like water into the River.

It's not until he is about to leave that he notices the final touch. Yes, there's no doubt: curled under the caisson, licking the dropped hand of the drunken Congreve-soldier, is a little dog—with a face that is unmistakably Sid's.

As he leaves the room, he is seething with anger—not because of the prank itself, which he can't help but admire, even the inclusion of his own likeness, which, if ever noticed, will actually help free him of suspicion. Oh no. Worst of all is its skill. Huck is good.

Unforgivably good.

Sid is no longer among the saved, or the damned, but, worst of all, the mediocre.

That he can never forgive.

Whatever effect this episode has on Huck, it definitely affects young Sawyer—who, in his own way, is as much influenced by the illustrious Lee as is Our Boy. A darker, more introverted, but even more thoroughly disciplined cadet Sid becomes after this experience. Perhaps sensing danger, the superintendent calls him in near the end of the term.

Lee conducts small talk for a few minutes—while the cadet stands, embarrassed as ever—about careers, families—how are the parents? oh? so sorry to hear that, etc, etc.—without a word about Huck. Then, as Sid rises to be dismissed, Lee finally comes to it: "I want to thank you, Cadet, for your efforts this year."

Lee does not smile, but his voice conveys warmth. He extends his hand to clasp Sid's, and holds it for a moment, firmly, in both of his—as if to transmit a current. "Remember, all you need to know, sir, is your God and your duty. Your God can take care of Himself. *Your* job is duty [squeezing the hand now—jolting it in with every word] Duty. Duty. Duty. Never forget that."

And, for better or worse, he never does.

When he returns to his room before drill, he finds a postal card on the desk. It's the kind newly fashionable, with a picture on the front and a place on the back for writing, and the postage pre-paid. Shows a paddle-wheeled steamer—but who in the world—Likely for Huck, and a cadet doesn't read another cadet's mail, but Huck's gone and—well, the only way to identify it is to look at the back. So he does. He holds the card for a frozen moment, then curses, shoves it in his desk drawer, slams it shut, stares out the window, then curses again, grabs his rifle, slams the bayonet into its belt-loop, runs from the room and down the hall, then down the circular brick stairwell, where the acoustics are particularly nice, and shouts to an empty, echoing building, "Duty, my arse! Duty be *damned!*" with the echoes spiraling after—*damned...damned...*

And so ends the West Point episode—which immediately *precedes* Lexington, and I'm sorry to have placed it out of chronology. I did so because Huck skips it in *his* journal, which goes right from Mexico to Lexington. As to the post card, it is for Huck, but is otherwise mysterious: "My dear Huckleberry," it says. "What you feared has happened: there is a child. You must adapt your plan, and contact me soonest. Warmest regards, B." Various possibilities race through Sid's mind, but in each of them, the "B" can only be Becky. Beautiful Becky Thatcher.

16. Sanaco

Sanaco—it sounds less like an outlaw Indian chief than a modern petroleum company, doesn't it? Certainly the resemblance foreshadows what this poor countryside in the southern plains has to look forward to. We must go there, of course, because Our Boy does—after the stormy goodbye to Joe Taylor and Lexington—and so does his Colonel.

In the late 1850s the area we are concerned with—Texas north of Fort Mason and south of the Indian Territory—is home to grass, juniper, and scrub oak, with sycamore and cottonwood near the creeks, plus hyenas, rattlesnakes, a few ranchers, and (mostly) tame Indians. All of which practice their survival skills on any U.S. troopers exiled there. Is it pretty country? Well, it's not desert, or even pure prairie, like the lands farther west, which have an awful grandeur this cannot match. Still, on the edge of the Great Plains, it's a different country than the East, and has its own, more insidious beauties and dangers: there's green, for instance, but it's an unnatural sort, like some kind of makeup—comes and goes with the weather, and you can't take it for granted: when it rains things are green and muddy for a while, then dusty and yellow till it rains again. In the East you take it for granted that in the next ravine there'll be running water. You almost don't need to carry any, especially in the hills, if you're willing to boil it. Out here you learn to be aware of it all the time—how many miles to the nearest source? Is it salt or fresh? How reliable? What's the season been like? And when you find water, you drink it whether you're thirsty or not, if it's clean, and if not, you bottle it till you can boil it—because the trots you get from dysentery will kill you as quickly as thirst. In the 1850s, of course, we weren't as clear about some of this.

The reason any of this matters is that a renegade Comanche chief called Sanaco, with a war party of forty or so, is currently conducting raids on settlements and ranches along the forks of the Brazos, and it is the job of the commander at Fort Mason to stop him. When Lt. Colonel Lee arrives, he is in charge of operations because the top Colonel, Albert Sidney Johnston, is away on—what else?—court martial duty.

During two weeks at the Fort—March 6 to 20, 1856—Lee takes in the lay of the land, always crucial to him, and assesses the forces available for the inevitable expedition: two squadrons from Fort Chadbourne, one from Fort Mason, and one from Camp Cooper, on the Clear Fork of the Brazos, 170 miles further north—more than four hundred troopers, a big operation for those days. To find out if they are up to it, Lee will head north. But first he meets a group of six enlistees recently arrived from San Antonio to be mustered into the regiment. This is an interesting enough experience that Lee mentions it in a letter to his wife. Lee writes a lot to his wife—a praiseworthy trait in any husband, though perhaps not surprising, since there's little else to do. And in one of these, after a discussion of his meetings with Catumseh, an Indian dignitary from the Comanche Reserve—whose residents Lt. Col. Lee is supposed to try to "humanize" as he puts it—we find this:

After Catumseh and I muttered sententiously to each other for a couple of hours, it was time to move north. Three of the new troopers made the ride from Fort Mason with me. You may be interested to know that two of them were with me in Mexico and made an effort to re-enlist with us at the Fort—primarily, it seems, to renew our old association, and the regiment being under strength I gladly enrolled them. One of the three was in the infantry and has re-enlisted this time in the cavalry, which he tells me is reputed to have "a much better time." When I objected that the horse arm gets most of the rough work out here in the West, he rejoined, "That may be so, but with a horse he could at least get to and from work easier." He plays well on the guitar, and my aide and I enjoyed his company on the trail north. The other two are new enlistees and come with high recommendations from Virginia. One indeed, as a boy, was an aide and bugler in the Mexican campaign. I mention all this partly to show how small our peace-time army is, that those who have served once together are almost certain to cross paths again.

The former "aide and bugler" is, of course, Our Boy. And according to Huck, the guitarist is Jack Prescott, and the other is Joe Taylor. Assuming Joe has indeed enlisted, this is revolutionary. I am told that there were other Negroes and "half-breeds" enrolled in the frontier regiments even before the war of the Rebellion, but this is the first for which I have good evidence. Once again, Lee is a risk-taker.

Huck, though, is not on the surviving rosters. The 2nd U.S. Cavalry at the time lists 760 officers and men. Organized by Secretary of War Jefferson Davis himself, it contains some famous names, besides Colonel Johnston: Majors Hardy and Van Dorne, Captains Thomas and Stoneman, Lieutenant Hood…but no Finns, no Lees. Not even any Thatchers. If he's enrolled, we'd like to know what name he has picked, wouldn't we? About his status, Huck says:

I was assigned as "Assistant Regimental Adjutant"—a step up from "aide de camp," because I can read and write, the colonel says, better than some of the officers, and many of the other troopers can't at all. I told the colonel I could just take up where I left off at the Point and he could work me up in math if I promised not to cheat, but he didn't think that was very funny.

Such a post would normally be filled by a sergeant, not a new enlistee, but Huck says nothing about his rank *per se* during this period—about two years. He does keep up his journal, however, and it might make an interesting little monograph all by itself, full of the minutiae of cavalry life:

We sat around the fire while the lieutenant went to see about the time for the guard change because his watch had stopped. The ground was still warm from the hot day, and full of wide-awake bugs, and we asked Jack did he know any songs about chiggers. He said he only knew one about a Lady Bug, but his verses of that one and "Froggy Went A-Courtin'" sure weren't fit for the ears of any Lady I know!

There's also a bit about the north Texas flora and fauna, although Huck's vernacular would confuse anyone (like myself) unfamiliar with the area. What, in heaven's name, is a "pisser plant"? Perhaps a confusion with "pitcher," but one shudders to think!

The important entries concern the Sanaco operation.

It's a long one—takes about a month, from June 18 to July 16. I'll try to do a map, but it's not that important which river is where—and a good thing, too! Even maps created recently are often ambiguous. Lee's biographer, for example, refers vaguely to "the forks of the Brazos" as if everyone knew where they were. Historians have paid little attention to the expedition and the region, and reports that do exist often conflict. On some maps, for example, the Wichita and Ouachita Rivers are confused. But the expedition is important, so I'll do my best.

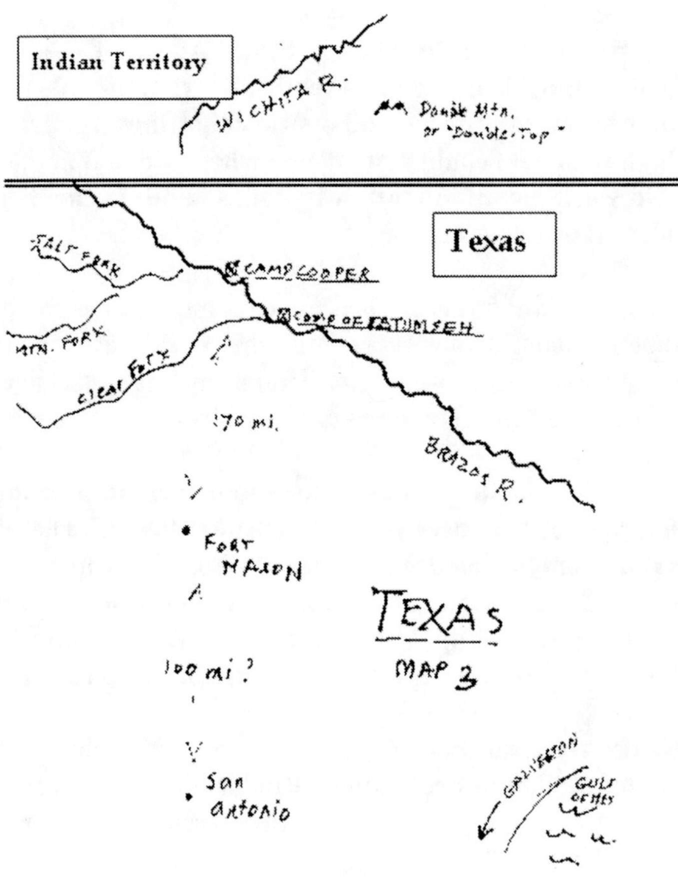

In a nutshell, Lee plans to send his squadrons out to the northwest of Fort Chadbourne, near the Brazos, in an arc around the area of Sanaco's depredations. As in later campaigns, he is hoping to surprise and confuse the enemy, cutting off retreat, and planning to improvise later, trusting his subordinates to know what to do. When they pass the headwaters of the Brazos near the border of the Indian Territory, they rendezvous near a low "mountain" called Double-Top, just over the border. Nothing is found except dust, snakes, coyotes, blistering heat, and (according to the Indian guides) cold trails. Four Indians are encountered; two are shot, and two escape, one apparently a female. According to Huck, Lee thinks about it for a half day, then, seeing smoke off toward Double-Top, he decides on his next move:

The colonel looked through his field glasses off toward the mountain, and above the haze we could see over the pass between the two hills.

"Well, Huckleberry," he says, handing me the glasses, "*is* it smoke, or just dust devils?" But he answered himself soon enough. "But even dust must be *raised* by something, a large herd, or a body of riders. Either way we should investigate. Still—"

He stopped so I finished where I thought he was going. "That's in the Territory, sir, isn't it? Can we go in there?"

He squinted away toward the hills. "Well, according to the Treaty we'd have to be in hot pursuit of an outlaw or renegade."

"Aren't we in pursuit of Sanaco?"

"Son, the government's always in pursuit of somebody. But 'hot' means you've witnessed the deed and have been in continuous contact on the chase. We haven't seen Sanaco or even a warm trail."

Then he seemed to make up his mind. He told me to go fetch Majors Van Dorne and Hardy and blow "Boots and Saddles." While the colonel drew a map in the dirt showing what he wanted them to do I hurried off to find the bugle and the map case and see if I couldn't stow some of my paint gear in one of the wagons. But I soon found out the colonel was sending the wagons back and issuing everybody seven days' rations. That caused groans all around because we knew what that meant: they'd get eaten up in a lot less time than that—otherwise they'd get wet or bug-eaten or something—and that meant there'd be

some pretty hungry and maybe thirsty days on the end of the trip. It also meant we'd have to be on the lookout for water.

Now, isn't it strange that Lee consults, not his senior officers, but Our Boy, a mere adjutant? Second, doesn't the reluctance to enter the Territory sound like a red herring? There is no record of the U.S. Government's paying much attention to such limitations—though this *would* explain why he didn't open the discussion to the aggressive Van Dorne.

At any rate, Lee splits his force again, this time four ways, sending Van Dorne and Hardy down the forks of the Brazos, and himself with a small company-sized party toward the main stream, which still has some water in it, figuring that if there is a raiding party loose they'll eventually make for that.

Here now, you may be thinking, haven't Indian fighters gotten themselves into trouble (George Custer comes to mind) by just such force-splitting in the face of an unknown enemy? But Lee will do this kind of thing again and again a few years later, in the face of an enemy he *knows* outnumbers him. Lee is one of the coolest gamblers ever. But here he faces, he thinks, at most fifty or so braves—some of whom are women, although old-timers say they'd rather be captured by Indian men than by their squaws—a force any of his columns could deal with. Except maybe his own, which almost looks like bait. Lee doesn't say anything about this to his men, though it occurs to Huck:

This Sanaco could have almost as many as we did [sixty-one], and we knew some of them had rifles they'd stolen. What if they took us by surprise? Every gulley or stand of cottonwood looked to me like a place they could be hiding. The colonel had sent the Indian scouts with the other columns, so Jack and a couple of his old friends from Mexico kept out on our flanks with ponies and field glasses and tried to make sure we weren't dry-gulched.

On the third evening we came closest to the mountain [Double-Top], and the colonel and Captain Smith spent an hour in late afternoon looking at the maps. Jack and Bill rode in from the left with news that they'd seen a fresh trail and found a couple of feathers on a rock near the boundary, a white one and a yellow, and there was some talk about what that meant. The colonel gave orders to bivouac for the night, even though there wasn't good water nearby, and then he went to have his tent put up, which also was not usually done on the trail.

When it was up, the colonel motioned me under the flap where he was sitting—it was making a good bit of noise in the wind, and he was trying to tie it down tighter while holding maps under his arm. I gave him a hand and asked if he hadn't better carry a map *case* in such dangerous country, and he laughed—he knew what I meant.

"Huck, sit down," he said and motioned to a cracker box like the one he was stooping beside, then he sat. He was dusty and red-faced, like we all were, but he seemed a bit more relaxed than you might expect. I asked him if he expected attack, but he waved it off.

"Do you see these feathers?" He stuck his head in the tent and came out with the yellow and white feathers and held them out while he squatted beside me. "These are all about talking," he said, "not fighting."

"Do you think he wants to parley, sir?"

He looked up at me and chuckled.

"Sanaco? I doubt these are from him, but I have full confidence in my men. If he makes trouble, it will be foolish because the other columns will come up in his rear." Then he was quiet for a second and picked up the feathers, stuffed them inside his blouse, then ran his hand through his hair. "No, these are from someone else—someone I *will* have to go talk to. Son, I need your help tonight. No, you're not coming with me—you hear me? That's a direct order. Look at me. Now I'm going on a patrol. I'm going to take a single scout with me, and a couple of fast ponies. Not my horse. You must look after her. Also—" and here he stopped to take a breath, "I'm going to ask you to help keep up a…an appearance that I am here all night and next morning. I will try to return to camp un-observed." He looked off toward the hills. "If that proves impossible, I shall be pleasantly surprised by the men's diligence, but I doubt it. We certainly weren't that efficient in Mexico."

"What'll I tell them?"

"Tell them I have a bit of dysentery, and need some privacy for a while, which is true, to an extent, and they'll believe that. Tell Major Hardy to act in my stead if anything comes up. I *should* be back soon. If I'm delayed, say whatever you think will work." And he winked at me. "Lieutenant Hood[5] may be able to help you. Now go off and take care of my mare."

As I rose to leave, so did he, and still stooping under the tent flap he reached for my hand and says, "If I *am* long delayed, Huckleberry, and Van Dorne comes up, he will assume command, and they may spend awhile in the brush, looking to find me vomiting my brains out, or worse. But eventually they will have to leave me behind. And one more thing…" If it's possible to be at attention while stooping and holding a tent flap, that's what it seemed like he was trying to do. "If they ask you direct questions about what I said, do not lie, sir. If they decide ultimately to follow me, say I advised against it, but do not lie. That is even worse than cheating."

Well, I wasn't sure what to make of *that*—or the secrecy: he was the commander and could go off wherever he liked and *order* the rest of us to stay here. Why the secrecy?

Why indeed? My theory, as you will see, is that there are things one does not want to explain to his fellow officers—especially if it means telling a "lie"—and the business about the treaty, red herring or not, would appeal to Lee. He would not want to converge on Double-Top unannounced with his whole force, even if he thinks his quarry is there. But if it's not Sanaco, who *is* it? Several hundred troopers is a lot to send out after such a rag-tag band.

Huck is curious, of course, about the mission and naturally thinks about following, but resists the idea, mostly because of that "direct order."

As the Col. suspected, there was no trouble about "intruders" during the night. I decided to let Lt. Hood in on the colonel's wishes, which I figured it would appeal to his sense of adventure, and I was right about that. There were flashes of heat lighting all night off to the north but no wind, and this morning it was Boots and Saddles at sun-up, already stifling hot, and we had to look sharp to get the morning reports copied and the colonel's horse watered and curried and my other chores done, and almost didn't get to eat anything. When I found a ground squirrel in my saddle bag I almost had me a better breakfast than the crackers and dried beef I had left.

The sun was well up now, and it wouldn't be long, I knew, till Van Dorne would come up, and I'd really have to "go to work," as you might say. First, I wanted to check with Jack, because I was sure he had to

of been that 'single scout' the colonel said he would take. I found him out at the branch where there was some run-off now that it had stormed in the hills. He was scrubbing his bedroll and underclothes to get the "varmints" out, he said. The water looked pretty muddy and probably had a lot of salt, but he said, "mud don't bite, Huck, and salt, you know, has medicinal qualities."

I wasn't sure how to ask him about last night without giving away the colonel's secret, so I asked him how he'd slept. He said not much at all from worrying about the Indians and standing lookout off and on with Bill and a corporal from A Troop. They wound up playing cards when they couldn't sleep for the chiggers. But his story checked out with the other two, and I could see his Peso hadn't been rode hard if at all.

Finally, just after lunch, the lookouts sang out Van Dorne coming up, and he would assume command if we didn't do nothing, so the lieutenant sent me to "check on" the tent. Lt. Hood and I were all set to collect the signs of the colonel's bad night of dysentery in his tent, and we had some real tricks planned, so we were kind of disappointed when the colonel himself came out—a bit raggedy looking, and mopping his brow and claiming to feel much, much better, and having learned his lesson about crick water. Right away, he give orders to use some of the horses' salt to purify 'all water on hand' *[which of course would not work]* and begun to ask about what we knew about Captain Thomas and all.

I was sure impressed that he could get in past us all without being spied—though I had to give him a leg up onto Grace Darling because he twisted his ankle the night before. I told him about how A Troop's color sergeant killed a snake down at the creek and cooked it, and tied the skin around the staff of his guidon like a totem. At that, he said, "Oh, I almost forgot. I have something for you." And he scrounged around in his bags and came out with a roll of paper and handed it to me. "I told one of the party I met that I would return it to you." When I saw the picture, my jaw nearly hit the ground. It was the picture I drew of that Sojourner Red fellow. He had asked me to tell the colonel he had "blessed his son," which I had done, and our meeting at the cave was long enough ago that the fellow could of got back here, but why had the

colonel gone to see him? All he'll say is that the "bearer" said I would know who it was from, and I guess I do, but I sure wish he would tell me something more about what happened.

As do we all! So the mysterious Sojourner has returned to the mountain—or at least someone has, bearing the famous sketch. But there must be more than art collection involved, to justify sending four hundred United States troopers on a merry chase. Were debts incurred in the Territory years ago, and now made good?

The merry chase, if that's what it's been, ends on the 16th. Lee sends his columns back down the three forks, and they return to their respective camps without even another warm trail to show for the ten additional days. If Sanaco is heard from again, we are not informed. And that is the sum total of Lee's experience as a field commander until 1860.

17. One Secret I Got to Keep

There is one more item of interest from Huck's Texas Cavalry Period—almost two years. Joe Taylor is not assigned to the headquarters troop as Huck is, and not at Fort Mason, but the two are together for a while as part of a detail escorting a visiting dignitary from San Antonio up to the forts—no less than War Department Secretary Jefferson Davis himself. (The two new regular cavalry regiments were Davis's idea, actually, and he is anxious to visit them.)

Joe is admiring Huck's picture again and notes that there is a bit of color in it—where Huck had sketched only in charcoal. Huck had put it down to weathering, but Joe notices the coloring is more or less appropriate—a green tint where there are trees, and so on—and suggests that the Indians might have added a bit of cactus-juice paint. This, Joe has heard, is made from the extract of certain cacti. Back at Fort Mason, though Huck is a bit put off by the Indians' cavalier attitude toward artistic ownership, he is curious enough to ask Jack about it. Prescott, their expert on things Southwestern, likes Joe's theory but says there aren't the right plants around here. An Indian guide at the fort, though, is familiar with the technique, and one day late in the fall he brings Huck a small pouch of pigments—powders to mix with water, or, in one case, the oil of some plant—linseed? All Huck has is hoof oil, but he gets Joe to sit for a portrait. While Joe sits and Huck sketches, the two discuss the season's events.

He didn't ask many questions about Sanaco—I figured he'd of been jealous of not getting to go, you know. But then I realized something that made shivers run up my spine, and I don't know why I didn't think of it before:

"Joe, you were on that Sanaco hunt after all, weren't you? It was *you* went with the colonel to Double-Top. You were the scout the colonel took with him."

He finally nodded his head and said, well, he guessed he could tell me that much since I'd guessed it anyhow. "But, Huck, I can't tell you no more about what went on there. That's a secret I got to keep."

And he never has told me, neither, so I just hope it didn't concern me.

As for why Huck didn't check with his friend sooner, remember that Joe was *not* assigned to the units selected for the mission. So Lee was able to take him along without Huck's knowledge. Why? Speculation is tempting: did Lee go to Double-Top to perform some service to Joe, or perhaps to his own nation? Lee is no free-lance warlord, after all. Was a treaty obligation settled there? Or did he perform another adoption, a *symbolic* one this time, a trading of God-fathers? Did Lee become Joe's and Sojourner become Huck's? Or...did Sojourner hand off responsibility, in some way, for a "daughter"? Or a daughter's son? That "Hidalgo" was only Mariposa's father-uncle after all. Was her real father Sojourner himself?

Yes, that is the rankest of speculations. But it helps explain why this Sojourner seemed to know Lee. Clearly, they had met somewhere after Mexico, and that could only have been during Lee's strange side trip on the way back, on which, if I'm right, Lee "adopted" Our Boy and incurred, in addition, a debt he has now repaid. And it will also help explain my final theory about Our Boy and his Butterfly. At any rate, speculation makes life more interesting. It is, you know, the only real defense we have against the Darkness.

We are now approaching another of the gaps in our story. Here's what we know: In late October of 1857 Lee leaves Texas. His two-year tour is not quite over, but when word comes that his father-in-law has died, he is granted enough leave to make up the difference. Lee's leave-taking from the regiment is reported to be sad but warm: his men like him. Huck makes a few desultory entries over the winter, but in the spring of 1858, he begins to get mail again from St. Petersburg, Missouri, his home town, although he says only a little about the contents.

A letter from Becky today—she's well, but has not heard from Tom since Christmas and is worried. I'll tell her not to fear; Tom can take care of himself, and loves mystery. Nothing to write about here, really.

That March Our Boy's own enlistment ends, and so does his journal—till late 1860, in fact, when he re-enlists, this time in a different cavalry unit, the 1st U.S., one squadron of which is assigned to guard Harpers Ferry in the early days of the war. And we know all this, not because he resumes keeping his journal like a good soldier, but because that same year he has another reunion—this time a fateful one—with his "great father," Robert E. Lee.

They have not forgotten each other.

****

Nor have I forgotten about that reporter. For example, what did he look like?

"I hear him on telephone," says the Chinaman, Mr. Chiang. "He sound like older man." He smiles. "Sound like you, if you ever learn to use phone."

"Well, he hasn't talked to me. What paper was he from?"

"He never say."

"Hm! For a teacher, you sure don't ask many questions."

"This your investigation, remember—you ask questions. You getting busy?"

"Yes. I'm getting busy."

Chiang has the only telephone nearby—ran the line himself from the switchboard at the college—and I'm afraid he'll get in trouble because his wire crosses the road at one point. So I borrowed his phone and checked the Washington area papers—they all have phones by now—and no one knew who might have talked to Chiang, but their people often developed their own ideas, and of course there were stringers and freelancers, etc., etc.

Free-lance. The word alone was enough to jiggle that jar. Within three days, I was willing to bet that whoever talked to Chiang was not a local reporter. Who could it be? To rule out one possibility, I will need to make another call. Long-distance, too. He'll have a phone, for sure. He has all the latest contraptions.

But first I need to talk to an old associate, now in California. It develops that the easiest way to do that is through the Western Union office near his hotel. As it happens, we could get a phone connection, but I still like the telegram. It enforces brevity—because of the cost, if for no other reason—and also it leaves a record.

My cable:

THANKS FOR AGREEING. IN ADDITION TO PERSONS OF INTEREST ALSO ANY INF ABOUT NOSY REPORTERS. BESIDES YRS TRULY.

His response, an hour later:

BESIDES S CLARA AND SF NO IDEAS YET. NICE WORKING FOR YOU. SHOE ON OTHER FOOT AS TWERE. WILL POST IN 30 DY.

Should have done that long ago.

Now the phone call. To make it long-distance I have to go to the college because otherwise I'd have to reverse the charges. And I can't just dial him directly, but must go through several operators. In fact, he has his own personal operator to take messages. The connection isn't clear either, and it gets worse unless I stop once in a while to generate current with the hand crank, as the college technician has shown me.

"No," the voice laughs. "It wasn't me. But I'm flattered, deeply flattered. Great idea—wonderful self-promotion, and I wish I'd thought of it. And I've no idea who. But it's not me."

"Well, I was pretty sure, but I had to make sure, you know—matter of principle."

The voice laughs again. "Principle! You know, I once had a couple of those, but—well, for all the use I got out of them, they just didn't seem to be worth the upkeep."

I laugh politely.

"No," he continues, "you go right ahead; you dug it up. I know you want to get into print first, and I'll allow it."

He'll allow it!

"Well, thank you, Sam. And if you hear anything about this reporter fellow, you'll get in touch?"

"Of course, of course!"

"Well, thanks again. And take care of yourself."

"I will—and you, too. We word-salesmen have to look out for each other."

"I'll try, Sam—even though that's not my line of work. Good-bye, now." Then, to the technician, "How do I get off this damn thing?"

"Salesmen," he says. "Good God! Is that what I am?"

Ten days later the Chinaman and I are sitting above a gorge high in the Blue Ridge. There is a rail fence for safety along the trail by the cave now—the work of a landowner who has given up preventing trespassers and is now trying to avoid liability. We have used it to tie the horses—rented from a lodge at the foot of the mountain when Chiang's auto gave out. Now we sit on a ledge far enough from the falls not to be soaked, but close enough that we have to speak up. It has been wet lately and there is plenty of water—a problem Huck evidently did not face.

"So you still think this Sojourner fellow know Our Boy already?"

"Sure, I think he was the artisan at the ranch in Mexico. He mentioned Lee, you know."

"But why Huck not recognize him here? He saw pot-maker, didn't he?"

"He did. But it was pretty dark, remember. Not as dark as that cave, of course. If I were a younger man I'd take a torch and climb all over the walls in there. I'm sure there must be some kind of message. He blessed Lee's 'son,' remember—and then 'his daughter.'"

"Hm! You jump too many conclusion! Most of this, you making it up, and for no reason. Maybe Huck not write about it because he not want people to know!"

"Well, maybe you're right. Anyhow, it's getting late, and I promised I'd show you the trees. Look up at the summit. The leaves are down up there now, and the sun's at a nice angle. Right on top. Here, use the binoculars."

"I see evergreen. Conifer—Pine—"

"Red spruce, Chiang."

He looks at me. "This far south—?"

"Yes. You see? Look at the cones. Here." I get out the collapsible tripod and set it on the rock in front of him. "Now you can hold it steady and zoom in. It's only an island of them, left from the Ice Age. To me, they stand for something—something that outlasts foolishness and betrayal and wars—for reason, for truth..."

"Ah! Truth and beauty—that what they stand for? Be quiet now, so I can study."

He looks quietly for several minutes, stopping to thumb through his field guide and grunting occasionally. Finally he unsnaps the glass and collapses the tripod, stands, scoops up the pack with the strap, and slings it over his shoulder. Then he looks at me and offers a hand up. When we're both standing, he looks back up at the summit, shading his eyes.

"You are right about red spruce. Balsam, too, I think. Also white pine—that maybe bad sign for spruce." Before I can ask why, he adds—patiently: "Alternate host—for blight. If younger, we climb up there, and I show you." He sighs. "You know—you like one of those trees. You not change at all. Ignore what around you and wait for Ice Age."

"Thank you, Chiang. I think that's a high compliment."

"Well—high or not—keep eyes low on way down hill. You slide with that cane, you be sorry. And scare horses, too."

But the horses are there and quiet—a bit bored, with nothing to eat but pine needles, and happy to be turning back to the lodge. As Chiang helps me mount, he says, "Thank you, my friend, for showing the trees. I wish them luck."

"At the lodge, you can read the rest of my story. You'll like it, I think—no conclusion-jumping at all. The sources are excellent."

As we start down the trail, I ask him if he thought the Sanaco episode was justified. He nods, but without much enthusiasm. "Well—have to be there. Have to show Lee go off to that mountain."

"And West Point—what about that? Does that show anything important?"

He thinks about it, then smiles. "Certainly. Show importance of mathematics!"

When we reach the Rapidan Road, the horses want to trot, and it's all we old men can do to restrain them, going downhill now under the brilliant reds and oranges.

Part 3

"What a small world it is."

18. Over the River and Through the Woods

There are bridges over the Rappahannock River where there ought not to be, right under the mouths of cannon (which anyone with half a brain would put on the bluffs right above), and not where they *should* be—that is, where there are fords. A ford tells you where anyone with a real need to cross, like farmers or soldiers, clearly prefers to do it. In wet weather, of course, these are often not fordable. So a bridge would be nice.

This is what a young blue-coated major is thinking as he waits in the cool gray dawn of April 29, 1863 near one of these fords above the town of Fredericksburg, Virginia. United States Ford, it's called. (What a good, loyal name for a ford!) Standing by a big sycamore, as if for cover should he need it, he is trying to see through the fog with his field glasses to the opposite bank. The foliage is out now, but the country is pretty open near the ford—with some woods and second growth right along the river, which become quickly denser on the other side in what is called the Wilderness. His sword belt lies behind the tree, lest it mark him as an officer, and thus a legitimate target. Enlisted men are normally in little danger here, by an unwritten code: yell before you shoot, and if you can't yell, shoot in the air first. When things are quiet, opposing pickets get to know each other. During the winter a thriving trade had gone on here—northern coffee, say, for southern tobacco—careful piles of black dirt crossing on little rafts made from cracker boxes. The major has even heard about, though not seen, a mock battle using snowballs in a nearby field between whole battalions from the opposing armies, with even some officers pitching in. Once, when the major had come down to investigate such goings-on, a Rebel soldier had called across to ask permission to cross and visit a friend from his hometown.

"I have no authority to give you that permission," he had called back.

"I know you don't, Major. I was just hoping you'd manage not to see me."

The major thought about it for a minute (that his rank had been detected was disconcerting), and when he spoke again, his awareness of universal proportions had evolved a bit. "I don't know how I *could* see you in all this fog," he called, then climbed back up the bank. Later, though, he went around to see the "friend," in case something could be learned.

But now there are no nonchalant, sociable pickets here. Now things are under way, and the enemy is alert and serious. The major thinks there is at least a brigade over there, plus a battery or two. There were a couple hundred enemy pontoon-builders at Germanna Ford, upstream on the Rapidan, a day earlier. Why? Surely the enemy wasn't thinking of *advancing* into the jaws about to close upon him? But the bridge-builders were surprised and mostly captured by the quick-moving blue columns. The campaign, he thinks, has begun well.

He thinks a lot, this major. It is his job. Right now he is thinking about what might turn up on the opposite bank instead of the person he is waiting for. From above and behind him on the bank, he hears a voice. "He should have been here by now, Major. We may have a problem."

It's a quiet voice, but louder than a whisper, which annoys the major. He frowns and motions down with his left hand (Sh!), then reaches with his right for his belts. Just then he hears a soft splash in the water about halfway across. He brings up the binoculars (could be anything—a turtle, a dead branch), and sees a little white bundle with a green ribbon floating in an eddy between two rocks. He takes a deep breath and moves toward the water, steps across, stone to stone where he can, wading a bit where he can't and hoping the grease keeps water out of his boots. Stretching between two rocks, he loses his balance, steps in up to his knee, well above the boot, feels the shock of the cold water, but snares the bundle, balances on the rock as he opens it—there's another bundle of tightly tied oil cloth inside the cotton—and scans the contents, a folded note with this on the outside: "Unfold this up on the bank. Meanwhile put newspapers in bag and re-tie. Leave it there." He takes a folded wad of newsprint from inside his blouse, stuffs it back in, re-ties the knot, leaves it on the rock, and picks his way back, squishing and sloshing.

Back on the bank he unfolds and scans the note, then immediately pulls his boot off before it can shrink, or the wool stockings swell, cutting off the circulation—which he knows can happen—and begins to wring out his trouser leg.

"Let the pants go, Major," says the voice behind him. "Let's see what you've got there."

The major swats away the gnats (seems awfully early for them), and clambers back up the bank, boot under one arm. At the top, he sets the boot down and extends the folded note to the officer waiting for him. The latter, a colonel, looks at the note and then turns and waves at a group of blue horsemen waiting further up in the fog by the road that twists down to the ford. One of them dismounts, hands his horse to an orderly, and walks toward them, removing his gloves.

When he joins them, the two waiting officers salute. He waves off the salute, reaches for the note, and reads it aloud: "One hour, upstream at the confluence. Look in a boat house by the trail. Be alone."

He looks up at the other two. "So. Do we know what's up at the confluence, George? That's only a mile or so."

"Likely nothing, General," says the colonel, "at least on our side. It's not fordable there now, and the banks are too low for a battery or a lookout."

"What trail do you suppose he means?"

But the major is impatient. "Sir, if I may…if we want to communicate anything here, we need to do so soon, or at least move out of view. The enemy is nearby in force, and we are providing—"

As if on cue, there come, in quick succession, the distant crack of a rifle, the snap of a branch near the general's head, a curse as he grabs his left ear, and a bit of commotion as the horsemen back up the road scramble to get out of range. The three officers on foot duck behind a row of cedars.

"Let me see, General. I have some—"

"No, it's nothing, Colonel….[and to the horsemen] Silence back there!" But he holds a reddening handkerchief up to his ear as he continues. "Well, I guess any such further business here is out of the question." He winces at the major. "I thought you said things were safe here—they shoot into the air first or something—"

"When things are quiet, sir. That was a month ago."

The colonel chuckles: "How do you know that *wasn't* a warning, General. He probably could have hit you *between* the ears if he'd wanted to. The major didn't tell them we'd be bringing a whole company down here, did you, Major?"

"No, sir."

"Well, that's still a damn lucky shot from that bank."

"He may not even be on that bank, General. We shouldn't have saluted you. My apologies. But listen. My man over there is worth a meeting or two.

Besides, the XIIth Corps will be across at Germanna soon enough, and that'll cut off anything upstream. What do we have to lose—except the major here? [Cheerfully elbowing the man next to him] You always say we have too many majors anyhow."

The general chuckles, though still holding his ear, then turns to the major—who is not chuckling. "All right. Major, this is your operation for, say, thirty-six hours—tomorrow night. We'll leave the colonel back at the Lacy house to—you know, read reports and put two and two together. Meantime—take a good horse and go up to the confluence. Follow this up. And let's have a report back, one way or another, by an hour after dusk tonight. At Ely's Ford."

"Ely's, sir?" This is the first the major has heard of that as a crossing point. "Which bank?"

"By then it shouldn't matter, but let's say the north. There's a farmhouse there at the top. General Meade will be around somewhere. Pay your respects, but don't tell him anything yet. If you come through in the dark, the challenge is *hammer,* countersign *anvil.* Remember it."

"Yes, sir. *Hammer* and *anvil*. But why Ely's, sir? Since the telegraph's here?"[6]

"Well, Ely's may have a line by then, but even if not, it's an easier spot for the colonel's people to get across if they have to. And listen. Don't take unnecessary chances. We *don't* have enough majors who can ford rivers with one boot." The colonel laughs. "And, Major—" but glancing at the colonel now, "we could use more *colonels*, if you know what I mean."

But the major, alone again, as he wrings out his sock, *isn't* sure what that had meant. Was it a hint of promotion or a dig at Colonel Sharpe—or a compliment to the man? Well, either way, he has work to do, and the sun is now up.

The road north of the ford has no likely turn-offs toward the confluence, where the Rapidan and Rappahannock meet. Nothing shows on his map, and he is reluctant to ask nearby farmers, likely secessionists all. But a quick scout back to the water shows a path along the river itself, nearly choked with greenbrier and honeysuckle and with some evidence of cows, but nothing fresh fortunately—a fine foot trail, but not much for a horse. Still—can he make it in an hour? He decides this may be the "trail" mentioned in the note, then remembers that the note itself is probably still on the ground by the road where General Patrick had dropped it. Cursing—how could *three* intelligence officers overlook a thing like that?—the major slips back up to the road and retrieves the paper. Before he sets out on the river trail, he ties his sword belt up in the tree, with a white ribbon around the hilt to signify intent to reclaim it, but keeps his pistol and field glasses. Later, as he picks his way along the trail in a place where there is more of a forest canopy and less brush, he takes the note out again and looks at it in the dappled light, with a mixture of anticipation and dread. Yes, the two printed c's are made with little crosses at the top—for luck. Very distinctive. It has been years, but the familiarity of the hand is striking. Well, if he's going on foot, he'd better move.

The sun is an hour high when the river widens and he sees a spur out in the middle—the peninsula dividing the streams?—and there is a boat shed on the left of the trail at the water's edge, with a peaked roof just high enough to stand under. Good, he was afraid he might miss it in the fog.

The shed has a water door—there are posts where it's over the water—also a land door. At the land door he says softly, "Hey in there!" then pushes, and when the door swings open to allow a little light he sees a row-boat at the water's edge and sticks his head in.

Instantly he is grabbed around the neck and tripped, his mouth covered with a hand, and he lies on his back at the edge of the water staring up into the face of his attacker—a familiar face, in spite of the rakish, light brown moustache and goatee. The attacker laughs and removes the hand.

"Sid Sawyer! You son of a bitch. I knew it'd be you!"

"Yeah, well, I figured it'd be you, too. Spying was always your line of work. You can get off me now."

His captor rises to a crouch, sticks his head out of the door and looks down the trail.

"Don't worry," says Sid. "I'm alone."

"You *think* you're alone, but who knows?" The other man picks up a rock, flings it out over the water, where it splashes. There is a second plop as something small drops into the water, then silence. "Well, I hope you're right. Did you double back once or twice to check the trail?"

"Check the trail?"

"Yes, for signs you were being followed. You know, fresh… Oh, never mind. You're a tenderfoot, all right."

When the man pulls his head back in, he faces the barrel of Sid's revolver.

"Empty your pockets, Tom."

"Oh, for Jesus'...Sid, what do you—"

"Empty them, Tom." Tom sighs and begins to pull his trouser pockets out.

"Coat pockets, too. Inside and out."

Tom wears a nondescript brown wool jacket over a lighter-colored vest and a white four-button shirt, buttoned to the collar, but with no tie, and looks like any of the dozens of horse dealers and dry-goods merchants Sid has seen among the camps. Tom pulls a handkerchief out of one vest pocket, a watch out of the other, then quickly shows the lack of side pockets in the coat, turns around, opens it to show both inside pockets and pats them—see? No weapons—then picks up his brown bowler hat and shakes it: see? Nothing inside.

He takes the coat off, starts to shake it, and before Sid can think, Tom whips the coat up and around the pistol and wrenches it from Sid's hand, pulling him forward almost into the water. Sid staggers but doesn't fall.

Tom scoops up the pistol, spins the cylinder, ejects the cartridges, stuffs them in his pocket, and hands the empty gun back.

"I'll give 'em back to you if there's need. Meanwhile, I judge you're too dangerous to allow with live rounds. Now sit down and talk to me."

Sid stands, seething, the empty weapon at his side. In the old days there would have been a brawl here, and, even now, Sid would love to tackle the fellow! But discipline tells. Also prudence. Clearly, Tom Sawyer knows how to defend himself.

"You think those are the only cartridges I have, Tom?" Sid says, trying for control. "Or the only weapon?"

Tom sighs, shakes his head. "No. And I didn't show you all my pockets, neither. Now look. We're on the same side here, Sid. We've got to trust each other a bit. We sure know each other well enough." His smile says: *I'm a winner, and you could be, too*. "What could be better than this, brother? Like old times, eh?"

What Sid remembers about old times with his half-brother doesn't engender trust, but he steps carefully into the boat, nearly loses his balance, then sits in the prow opposite Tom. "Well—all right, what do you have? Do we have to row out there?"

"To the point? Yes, unless you want to get out and push—and get *both* feet wet this time."

"You saw that, did you?"

"Hard to miss. The Rebs loved it. Grab an oar, will you?"

Sid rows, and it's tough work. There's a pretty good current at one spot—this isn't a ford—and they have to drag the little boat around some rocks or else miss the point—an island, actually, detached from the peninsula—and finally clamber over rocks and onto firmer ground. The area close to the bank is choked with river birch, but there's a grassy area under some sycamores with a couple of old campfire rings, each with a rusty bayonet stuck into the ground, holding what looks like a scorched corn cob in the muzzle loop—and the ubiquitous cow pies. Sid wonders how cows got out here.

"I'm not in danger in this uniform, am I? Are there Rebel troops near?"

"There's a regiment of Fitz Lee's cavalry around somewhere—help me drag this thing in, will you?—but they'll be watching the roads." They wedge the boat into a culvert under the house. "Still, you're a sight better off in that suit than out of it, if you're caught. In it, you're a prisoner of war. Out of it, you're hung for a spy. But I'd take that fancy cap off in case somebody *is* looking. Come over here." Sid follows, cap in hand, as Tom picks his way around the fire rings to a clump of sycamores on the other end of the island, under one of which there is another, smaller boat house.

He pulls out a carpet bag, unsnaps it, and describes the contents as he pulls them out: "Richmond papers—the whole month of April till last week. Those'll be interesting. And here: county land plots—Culpeper, Spotsylvania, Orange—shows landowners and boundaries, survey marks, roads. That's the main thing: roads. Right down to pig paths. Up to the '60 census. Got 'em right out of the court house, just walked in and asked to look at 'em. And looky here: a map I heisted from a saddle bag at a picket near Kelly's Ford. Funny thing, see, it's got nothing at all marked north of Chancellor. There's some business here—see these marks?—from Banks' Ford down to below the town—'A-N-D', it says—maybe that's Anderson's Division?—but they haven't the slightest notion, it looks like, of any danger to their flank. And I listened to enough talk to know that's so."

"So Stoneman's cavalry…" Sid stops, wondering if he has revealed too much.

But Tom takes it right up. "So the gallant General Stoneman has a clear shot at the Richmond railroads. He takes his—what?—eight or nine thousand?—right down to Trevillians, raises Hell on the Virginia Central, and by then the Rebs at Fredericksburg *have* to retreat. That's the plan, right? And if you look at these papers, you'll see the argument is over what's to be done about defenses *below* the town. They're worried about a *naval* assault, for God's sake. When they wake up, like as not, it'll be too late to do anything *but* pull back."

Sid thinks, scratches his clean-shaven neck. "You think that's what Lee will do? Just sit there and wait for us to cut him off? Or retreat? That's not his way, you know."

Tom nods. "No, it's not. But he doesn't know enough yet to do much else. What's Hooker sent across at Kelly's?"

It's sort of a nonchalant question, but Sid is wary. "Well, Stoneman, you know about."

"Oh, come on! At least a corps, I hope?"

Sid says nothing.

"Sid—I've given you enough to get me hanged if the Rebs find out about it. How can I help if I don't know where we are?"

"Well, let's just say, in twenty-four hours, if Lee stays where he is, he'll have more of us behind him than in front of him."

Tom whistles. "Well, I'll say. When old Joe throws the dice, he bets the table, doesn't he?"

Sid looks Tom over in what is now a bright, morning light. Tom is almost thirty now, and the hair is thinning a bit on top, as his father's did. But behind the goatee, the face is still smooth as river rock, the eyes sharp as mica.

"General Hooker has done well so far, yes. Look, Tom, what about you? What gets you through the lines? All I heard was that you were a 'citizen.'"

"Me?" (He grins, one hand on his lapel, the other on his hip.) "I, sir, am a reporter. An energetic and insightful—and patriotic—gentleman of the press. My card!" And he pulls a card from his vest pocket. *Thomas J. Sawyer, Correspondent*, *Richmond Examiner*, it says. "I also have one for the Washington *Herald*, but I don't carry it around over there, of course. That's why these little houses are useful, to store my identities. Now, looky-here." He winks and ducks into the house, comes out with a dripping bucket in which the necks of a couple of bottles are visible. "I also keep some nice cold military intelligence in here. Join me? It's Tennessee bourbon—honest injun! Don't ask where I got it."

Sid can't help but smile. But he drinks little of the whiskey. He prefers wine. Then he remembers something.

"Tom—you said the Rebels loved it when I stepped in. But if they could see me, why did they not shoot me, but then shoot at the general?"

Tom looks at Sid as if at a slow student. "Wouldn't you pass up a major for a shot at a general? But look here, Sid—they thought *you* were bringing information for *them*. They shot at that general because they thought you were about to get caught!"

"So they think—"

"They think we're on *their* side, yes. That's how this business works, Sid. It's damn complicated."

Sid thinks for a moment about complications. "But what brings you here anyhow, Tom—back East? When I saw you on Sharpe's list, I figured who it had to be—how many Thomas Sawyers could there be in this line of work?[7]—but—I hate to put it like this, but how do we know you're on the *right* side?"

Tom shakes his head slowly.

"Major, what did you give them? A three-day-old Baltimore *Sun*. Nothing they don't already have. Hell, Baltimore is practically secesh anyhow. You look at what I gave *you* and compare."

Sid nods, turning his shot glass slowly in the morning light. "We should have kept in better touch. What was wrong with the West anyhow?"

"Sid, this is where the excitement is now. The Rush is over out there, and—"

"And Becky? That's over, too, I guess? Where's she now?"

"Well—I haven't heard from her for over a year now. I guess you know that didn't work out. Last time I sent her something it was through a mission out there—where she was teaching. Look—" Tom sets his glass down on a stump and pulls out his watch. "I'd like to chew the fat longer, but it'll be halfway to noon before you can get back. What's next? What do we need to know?"

Sid looks at him, still unsure what to reveal. He himself doesn't know all the details of the federal plan. Yes, Hooker's reforms have helped morale—better rations, shiny new corps badges, and others you can look up (the origin of the slang term "hooker" being debatable). Sid's favorite is the new concern for security and intelligence. But that also means officers are told only what they need to know. So, if they blab over whiskey to the wrong reporter, there are only so many beans they can spill. (The opposite of Lee's practice, by the way: he wants all his generals to know the basic plan so that, even if they're out of touch, they *might* do the right thing.) Sid, of course, as an officer in the new Bureau of Military Information, knows more than most, but not everything.

"We need to know the location and movements of General Lee."

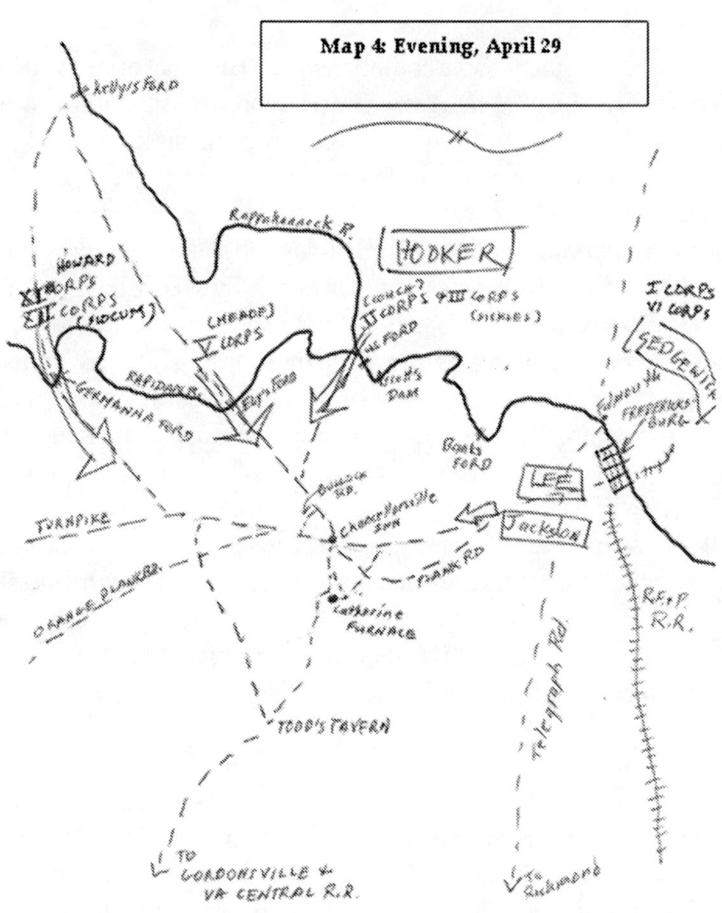

"Lee? Well, he's along the Rappahannock at Fredericksburg." Tom picks up a stick and draws a squiggly line in the dirt. "Jackson's on the right, below the town, and Longstreet's on the left, up to about Banks' Ford. Longstreet himself is still down at Suffolk, but two of his divisions are here now, Anderson and McLaws—you know all that. But Hood and Pickett have been ordered up on the R.F.& P., and I hear Hood's arriving already, or so Rebel prisoners say. There's plenty of action on the railhead at Hamilton's, so by tomorrow they could all be available."

Sid is quiet for a moment. Longstreet back from North Carolina? With at least fifteen thousand muskets! If true, that *is* valuable intelligence, certainly more valuable than the Richmond papers and a batch of land records. And "prisoners," he says—what prisoners? Still, it's not the key issue. If he asks too much, he may reveal too much. But there's really no other way.

"But that's not what I meant, Tom. I meant where is Lee himself? Where is his headquarters? What are his movements? Who is with him? How large is his company?"

Tom looks up, into Sid's face. He picks up his stick, holds an end in each hand, bending it, then unbending it, as he thinks. "Why would you need to know that, unless—"

"That's not something you need—"

"—Unless you're planning to *capture* him!" He laughs shortly. "Well, sir, that's a plan. You have to figure the great Lee is worth at least a corps. What a blow to the South that would be! I'll hand it to whoever thought this up." The stick suddenly snaps, and Tom tosses the pieces out over the water. "But it's a damn fool thing to plan, Sid. For one thing, it takes cavalry—lots of it—and Hooker has sent most of his off on a raid in the other direction. But even supposing I can find out for you by tonight where he is, and I probably can't, who says he'll be there an hour later? With him and Jackson, once the ball's under way, they'll be all over the dance floor."

Sid looks out to where the stick pieces whirl along in the current. A strong current. Fording Germanna will be difficult.

"He has to sleep, Tom, even if it's an hour. And couriers have to know where to find him. Find out when and where. By tonight—midnight. There'll be enough moon by then. Report to me at Ely's."

Tom nods slowly. "All right. I'll do what I can. Let's get you back over."

"Say," says Sid as they push off, "whatever happened to old Huck? Did he ever go West again?"

"Becky said he joined the cavalry, at least for a while. But it's been years, of course."

"The cavalry, you say?" Sid thinks about that. Then he looks down at Tom's card. "What's the J for? I thought you didn't *have* a middle name."

"That all depends. Up in Washington, it's Jefferson. Down in Richmond"—he winks—"it's Jackson."

"And your leg? How is that now?"

"Oh, you mean from the Great Escape! Shucks! It doesn't bother me much—aches a bit in cold weather and makes riding harder." He pulls out his watch and grins. "But I still like to see what time it is." He holds up the watch chain, and Sid sees—still dangling from it—the bullet taken from Tom's leg all those years ago after the failed attempt to spring Jim.

On the north side again at the boat house, Sid steps out—carefully—then reaches behind for his field glasses. There is a bad moment when Tom doesn't know what he's reaching for and startles, reaches for a paddle—as a possible weapon—but Sid freezes, turns slowly, shows the binocular case, and they both laugh nervously. Sid holds a hand up—Sh!—then, with the other, looks through the glasses at the now un-fogged north bank. Good. Empty.

Sid helps drag the boat out, then Tom steps in, thinks of something, and searches his pockets. He holds to the gunwale while extending the other palm with Sid's cartridges. "You might need these." He grins. "Just give me a fair start."

Sid doesn't smile, but he takes the cartridges. "Listen," he says, "we may be across at Ely's by tonight. So if you have to come through the pickets, be careful. The challenge is *hammer,* countersign *nail.*"

"Thanks," says Tom. "That is a sign of trust. *Hammer* and *nail*, it is."

"And here." Sid pulls an envelope out of his blouse and tosses it on the vacated seat. Tom looks at it.

"What's that?"

"Five hundred dollars, USA currency. Don't be insulted. You may need it." Then he smiles. "Especially if you forget the countersign."

19. My Goodness—
You Look Like Your Old Self, Sid!

When Major Sawyer again stands above a river, it's the Rapidan at Ely's Ford. It's just after dusk, the moon not yet up, as he waits at a fence gate in front of the farm house where the road drops down to the river. Things are a lot busier here than they were at U.S. Ford earlier. An entire corps is crossing in the gathering darkness, the Fifth, more than fifteen thousand strong. There are no fires, everything is wrapped, flags are furled, nothing shines except some of the Second Division's white Maltese crosses bobbing along on caps, as the men ford the stream with packs and bedrolls held aloft on bayonets. The water is cold and waist-deep, and some men have removed their trousers—a source of amusement if it were a daylight crossing and there were respectable observers nearby—but not now. A line of mounted staff officers and cavalry has been set up downstream for safety. The idea is to avoid noise, but in the darkness there are creaking wheels, labored breaths, muffled clanks, nickering horses, low curses, hushed commands, occasional splashes. It's like being next to a huge beast wallowing forward in the dark, trying not to alert its prey—a forlorn hope, probably, since the prey has excellent eyes and ears. But Sid knows that the prey, alert or not, is doomed if it sits and waits. Sid doesn't know everything, but he knows that either of the Union army's two wings by itself is large enough to do battle with Lee's whole force. If the prey is smart it will not sit, but run like Hell. But what if it does neither? What if—somehow—it attacks?

The major has had little time to think strategically, however. Since the meeting with his half-brother he has had a busy and mostly frustrating day, full of dashes up and down the Germanna Ford road, looking for units and officers who were not where expected, and who, when found, had little interest in cooperating with a boyish-looking intelligence officer. This is a sore point with

Sid. He is young—twenty-seven, and looks younger—but he's a West Pointer. His friend Frank Barlow—even younger, and a lawyer, of all things—is already a brigadier. And some in Sid's class at the Point are commanding divisions. As are mere politicians, like that Schurz blowhard in the XIth Corps. For real soldiers the way to promotion, as always, is through line command, because that's where men die and have to be replaced. Sid knew that, of course, when he accepted the post in the new Bureau of Military Information, leaving his engineer battalion. Still, it was hard to take sometimes.

"Sorry, Major," he'd hear from some frazzled adjutant, "but the general doesn't have this kind of information. Why don't you check with the quartermaster. We've got a war to fight here." And as he rode away, he might overhear something like, "Gee, Colonel, you could've offered him a cigar."

"Well, Sam, I could, but are you sure he's old enough?"

Ha ha.

The cavalry commander, General Pleasonton, might have been useful since what Sid envisioned might be possible with as little as one or two good mounted regiments, but Stoneman was off on his raid with most of the cavalry corps—whatever that was worth when Tom and every newspaper in Virginia seemed to know all about it. About mid-afternoon, Sid had decided to double back to U.S. Ford, where there was a telegraph post, to ask General Patrick to see if Washington could re-check the cavalry enlistment records for Huck. Perhaps Hooker's chief of staff General Butterfield could help. But that had meant bushwhacking through fields and fences along the river.

The horse had loved it—especially the fences. Sid didn't even know the animal's name; the colonel had given it to him. He'd rarely needed a mount in the engineers. Not for the first time, he wished he were a better horseman. Just his luck to get an enthusiastic jumper. He had been thrown once—an event that scared the horse so badly that it took the major several minutes to catch up and remount. As a result of that adventure, when Sid had later felt the need to relieve himself, he'd done so without even dismounting. (Such issues are seldom discussed in war histories, but are of great interest to soldiers.) Another time, he was almost shot when some XIIth Corps skirmishers mistook him for a Rebel scout.

Back at US Ford, he had used every resource available to get his messages through the signal corpsmen there—pulling rank, citing Butterfield, Hooker, the President, the Judgment of History. What actually worked was

Colonel Sharpe (another lawyer, and a hard-drinking one at that) who had stuck around to check the cable traffic before riding back to the headquarters at Lacy's. Sharpe cabled once, twice, and by five P.M. Sid had his answer: Averell's cavalry division, which he had been promised would be available, would not be back from Culpeper for twenty-four hours. A whole *day*! How could *that* have been allowed to lapse? Till then, the only available cavalry was Pleasonton's division, of which he and Sharpe might call upon one regiment of Pennsylvania cavalry assigned to Slocum, in command of the right wing—*if* he could find it—and a few troops of the 1st U.S. Cavalry, detailed to cover the fords, guard the wires, and run errands. That was it. And if he used any of those, he'd have to go to "the general commanding" (Hooker), through his chief of staff, Butterfield, and on down the chain, at least through corps. And by morning, the enemy might have made his move.

Tom's instinct was probably right: it was a hare-brained scheme. But it still bothered the major that the high command had seemed to lose interest. Lee worth "at least a corps"? Lee was the whole *army,* for God's sake. Sid himself had felt his influence. Lee was the South's morale, it's ideal, what it had convinced itself it stood for, besides enslavement. Lee was States' Rights. Lee was the Cause. Lee was the whole bloody *war*! How could they lose interest in *that?*

At six o'clock he had mounted his tired horse to head back toward Ely's and report to Patrick. There were two hours till sunset.

"Well, Sidney," Colonel Sharpe had said, watching him wince as he mounted, "at least you know the fences now."

"I guess so, sir." (*Or at least the horse does.*) "I'm hoping the horse is too tired this time. What's its name, if I may ask?"

"High Bar, I think."

"Sounds about right."

"He's young and spry. A hunter, Patrick says. Ran steeple-chase, too."

"I believe it. Well, come on, fellow. Let's go check on the rabbits."

"And Sidney—"

"Yes, sir?" Sid looked down, as Sharpe looked up and tilted his head, a grin showing under his moustache.

"Look, I know you don't approve of me."

"Sir, I'm sorry if I've ever given any cause to—"

"No, no," Sharpe waved his hand, "I understand. You're a professional soldier, and I'm not. But I *am* a professional investigator, and my instincts tell me that we make a pretty good team. I asked for you, you know. And I, uh—I have the highest regard for General Patrick, and I know he told you to report to him, but I'd like to consider you a member of—without violating—"

"I understand, sir. Rest assured that you'll receive any information." Then he had added, on an impulse, "And by the way, I share your concern. I thought what the general said slighted your position here. As far as I'm concerned, I report to you."

Sharpe had nodded. "Thank you, Sidney. And listen, I'm sorry I joshed you this morning. You showed a clear head there."

"Thank you, sir."

"Call me, George, Sidney."

"Yes, sir. George it is." Sid had turned his horse away, then turned back in the saddle. "Colonel—George—if I may ask, would you call me Sid? I hate Sidney. My mother called me that."

Sharpe laughed. "It's a deal, Major!"

All in all, though, it had been a disappointing day—even the exchange with Sharpe. Sid figured he would now be inducted into the colonel's drinking and card-playing binges. And his God-awful cigars. Was that how all these amateur soldiers cemented their friendships?

But then, about an hour before sunset, his luck had begun to change. Approaching Ely's from the north, with one of General Meade's couriers, he had seen the house—a nice frame farmhouse with two stories and a loft, four full chimneys—and expected to find Meade there. But as he and the courier had waited with the corps's lead brigade watching a cavalry squadron splash across to chase off some Rebel pickets, Sid had noticed a couple of ambulance wagons pull into the yard, followed by a carriage with two women and some men—rather well-dressed, the men carrying valises. Surgeons? (Please, let them not be dignitaries!) The women had gone to the rear of one of the ambulances and had begun giving directions to soldiers carrying chests into the house.

"Lieutenant," he had said to the courier. "Is that General Meade's headquarters?"

"No, Major," said the lieutenant, even younger than Sid, "or least-wise not yet. It's being fitted for a hospital. The general says he expects to be over the river and on the way to Richmond by daylight."

"Really? Where is he now?" Sid was still watching the house.

"Still back with General Griffin, I expect." The boy leaned over and spat—tobacco juice, from the looks of it. "I can take you to him."

"No that's all right. I need to wait for General Patrick." Then, unable to resist: "That's a nasty habit, Lieutenant. That chewing. A Southern habit."

"I'm not from the South or the North, sir. I'm from the West, and it's right common there." He spat with great care, hitting the gate post dead on. "I was born in Missouri. I was brought east for school when my father was re-assigned."

"Missouri? That's my home state."

"No fooling?"

It was no way to talk to a major, but the boy's glee was infectious.

"Yes. No fooling. We're both a long way from home, Lieutenant."

"You know, there's some in the ambulance corps from Missouri—women and men both. I saw it on their letters—you know, whatever it is they show to pass through and set up shop. They were from all the towns along the river. They signed up with the Sanitary Commission as volunteers to come East. Me, I came East with Pa when the government—"

"Lieutenant, if I wanted to find one of these Missourians, where would I look for him?"

"Why—I don't know, sir. I don't think that's them, there at the house, but they might know. I run into some back at The Lacy house, two of them. Look, Major," the boy had looked back down the road past the line of waiting infantry, where other couriers were galloping up and down the line in the waning sun. "I have to get back to report to the general."

"Fine. You're dismissed, Lieutenant." Then, as the boy turned his horse away. "Say! Lieutenant! What town are *you* from?"

He turned in his saddle. "Saint Lou! West of the Prospect! How about you?"

"St. Petersburg!"

The boy shook his head. "I don't know anybody there now." Then he turned away and waved. "I'll see you in Richmond, Major!"

Sid had watched the boy ride back along the line, ignoring the taunts from the veteran footsoldiers. He was probably used to them by now. They buzzed up like wasps at any fresh-cheeked staff officer with a horse and a clean uniform: "Lookit him charge, boys! Why I bet he could break the line at the Sunday school picnic!"

"Looky there, Sam! One of the nurses done stole her a uniform. Almost fits her, too!"

"Better hurry up, Sonny. Your ma'll be worried when the fightin' starts!"

The major felt sorry for him. But not too sorry. What those infantrymen faced was a lot worse.

Sid had tied his horse at the gate and approached the group unloading the wagons. In addition to the carriage-driver and a couple of orderlies—privates all—there was a civilian man, in shirt-sleeves and red suspenders (through which a substantial paunch protruded), with a broad, simple-looking face and monstrous red whiskers on either side of his chin—and a bit too jovial a mood for what was coming, Sid thought. The two women had seemed more businesslike. He had approached the closest, who was giving instructions to an orderly. Her figure had looked quite girlish from a distance; closer inspection showed her to be about his own age, but serious of face and no-nonsense of voice.

"Excuse me, madam. I am Major Sawyer from the—from General Butterfield's staff. Is this to be a hospital? Or will General Meade—"

The lady had turned, her lips tight. "Major, I will brook no further confusion here. I have letters to the effect that this will be a medical facility only, and not be used by commanders who may become targets. General Meade was perfectly clear—"

"Madam, please. You misunderstand me. I am only looking for information—urgent information—and I have little time."

"Major, I have little time either. There are six more corps hospitals to be set up before tomorrow evening."

"Then you must know more than I do if you expect a major engagement that soon."

"When the army crosses this river there is always a major engagement soon." But she extended a white-gloved hand. "How can I help you? I am Mary Carroll of the U.S. Sanitary Commission. And please remember; time is short."

"Believe me, I know," said Sid, taking the slender hand briefly—the grip was firm, almost manly. "Ma'am, I am told that some members of your…of this staff are from my home state of Missouri, and I was wondering if you knew, or perhaps the surgeon in charge would know—" he had looked over at the bewhiskered gentleman helping to wrestle a stack of cots off the wagon.

"I am in charge, Major," the lady had said evenly. She allowed a bit of a smile. (So she *could* smile!) "Are you taken aback?"

"No, no," said Sid, taken aback. "I apologize for any offense. I just didn't—"

"No offense taken, Major. But come—what about Missouri? I am from Connecticut, myself, although we have several volunteers from the West."

"You don't know their names, do you?"

"Off hand? No. But our most recent pass letter has a list. Only Commission members, though, and orderlies—no locals. We vouch for those as best we can. Who are you looking for?"

"In particular, an enlisted man, by the name of Finn. His first name is Huckleberry."

"No." She shook her head slowly. "No, and I think I would remember that one. But I'll show you the list. It's all I can do at this point."

Well, it was a longshot anyway. Sid thought it at least possible that Huck had rejoined the army after West Point. It was worth some digging, and Sid had spent a day in Washington back in March going through rosters of the regular US units. Tom's guess about the plan had been close to the mark. A quick cavalry strike *was* part of it—which included some misdirection, some feints by Stoneman's force, to draw off Stuart's cavalry, and then…well, at that point, the plans got a bit vague. But Averell's cavalry division was essential—because he could come in behind, from the west. "Play 'em as they lay," Sharpe liked to say. But if Huck *had* re-enlisted, his closeness to Lee might be very valuable. Very valuable indeed.

The regular U.S. rosters, though, showed no Finns—Huckleberry or otherwise. There were several Thatchers, and since the Judge's adoption *could* have gone through, Sid had checked them—all negative. If Huck had enlisted in any of the state volunteer units, those records would be all over the country in various state capitals and county seats. It had looked like a dead end.

Sid glanced briefly over the list: twenty or thirty names, from Belcher and Caldwell to Vendeman and Zapruder—but no Finns, no Huckleberrys, not even any *H*s. He handed it back.

"Thank you, Miss Carroll. Or is it—"

She smiled. "It's Miss, thank you."

"Just one thing—this 'R. Thatcher' here. Do you know the man?"

"Oh, you mean Rebecca? My, yes. She's invaluable—and do you know, come to think of it, she *is* from Missouri, I think, originally. She's at

Headquarters, I believe, at Falmouth, but she did speak of riding out with the reserve train. Do you know her?"

"Well," (Sid's chest had tightened) "if it's who I think, she—she may be an old friend."

Then a female voice had called from the porch. "Oh, Mary! I'm already here. I came out with the signalmen, because that way I could...who wants to see me?" She had come out, smiling and wiping her hands with a towel. Her hair was pulled back, but a few of the blonde strands had come loose and were hanging down over one eye. She brushed them back as she approached, looking tired and frazzled and impossibly beautiful.

"This officer—"

"Oh, my God. Sid Sawyer!" She is running down the steps, throwing her arms around him. "Oh my God!" (pulling back, looking into his face).

"Becky. I must—"

"My goodness, you look like your old self, Sid! How long has it been? I really did try to look you up here, but you're on some detail no one will tell me—"

"Becky, we need to talk—quickly. It's an hour till dusk, and that's all I have. Then I must meet with—Is there a room in the house?"

"Yes, yes, of course. Mary! I must leave things to you for a while. Come, Sid."

And she had taken his hand, led him up the porch steps, and into the dim interior.

Now, if you're bothered by the reunion of all these Missourians in the middle of a great war—well, it's not surprising Sid and Tom would reconnect, given their interest in spying. That Tom or Becky might be following the other around is also easy to figure, and cynical Sid suspects it right away. But also remember what we said about the lumpy-ness of the universe. Particles charged in certain ways are going to clump. That's just the way it is. Sid's own emotions, of course, are decidedly mixed. An operation that had once seemed a bit like a sharp game of chess now has the feel of stepping into a swamp—without any boots.

20. Huckleberry *What?*

"Oh, I do love Tom—always did love him, I suppose," Becky had said—but she hadn't seemed very happy about it—as she and the major had sat on a day bed in the reddening light of a study off the parlor, as orderlies and cargo moved through the halls into rooms downstairs and up—chests and cots and lamps and tin cups and plates and jars of ink and stacks of bedding and bedpans and bandaging and boxes full of scissors and sutures and corked bottles—all the paraphernalia of a military hospital and (but don't tell Miss Carroll!) a possible corps headquarters. "But it's Huck I guess you want to know about."

"Tom, too. How loyal is he?"

"Loyal? Tom? [a sharp laugh] Well, I'm sure I'm not the one to vouch for that! If you mean to the Union, I have no idea. But I'll say this: the nation will survive and prosper, I'm sure of it, with or without the South, and Tom's no fool: he'll know that, and he'll want to be on the prosperous side."

Sid had nodded. It was a strong argument. "And Huck? He's in the cavalry, you say?"

Becky had quickly confirmed this and Huck's reasons for leaving Mexico—and his feelings, when he wrote to her, about General Lee's possible role in the looming conflict. He was very concerned.

"Yes, I imagine so." There was a crash downstairs, and some vigorous cursing, loud footsteps on the porch. "Becky, I know it's late, but you passed over West Point. Did you write to him there?"

"West Point? When was he *there*, for goodness' sake?"

"Have you ever seen this?" Sid had laid on the table the postcard he had found on Huck's bed at the Point. Becky had looked at it, picked it up, turned it.

"Why, no. I don't think so. Who is 'B'? Oh, of course! I guess you thought it was me. But it must be Buck."

"Buck?"

"Buck Grangerford. An old friend of Huck's—from that summer with Jim. I suppose you wouldn't know him. Why was Huck at West Point? Surely not as a student?"

Sid had then summarized Lee's experiment, leaving out the details of his own role, and Becky shook her head.

"Well, it's amazing to me that he would even try such a thing. And of course he wouldn't if it weren't for Lee, and—oh, I see—you were hoping for information about General Lee."

"Is it that obvious? Tom thought it was obvious, too."

"Tom?" She looked genuinely surprised. "Tom's here? In *Virginia?"*

Sid frowned. He breached secrecy with every breath.

"I thought that's why *you* were here."

"Me? Goodness, no. I came East to be with Mary."

"But I thought she was from Connecticut."

"She is, originally. But we met in California. She had to come out there to practice her trade. She's a surgeon, and a fine one. They don't let women practice in Connecticut, but California doesn't mind. They're short of doctors."

"So you left California, to—"

"Well, certainly not to find Tom again. What a small world it is! He's not in the army, is he?"

"No, he—he does some newspaper work."

"Good gracious! I hope he's not following me. I do wish him well, and I'm not afraid of him, but.... Well, listen, Sid, I have duties here, but you should be able to find Huck on one of the cavalry rosters. He'd still be in the regular army, I should think, though I've not heard from him for months now. I pray he's all right. In a way I'm surprised he didn't leave to go with the South, as so many did. But in any case you're unlikely to get much from him. However loyal he is, I hardly think he'd betray his own father."

"His what?"

"Well, he *sees* Lee that way, Sid. That 'adoption' of Lee's was one of the things he wrote me about. It played havoc with Father's will."

"Adoption?"

"I don't know the details, but it stood up in court—and he signed as Huckleberry *Lee*, and—"

"Huckleberry *what?"*

"—And I thought that rather strange, in view of *my* father's attempts to make things right."

But Sid had heard all he needed. He had risen then, and so had she.

"Becky, thank you. I hope to see you again tomorrow morning, to—to confirm some things. You'll be staying here at the ford?"

"Why, yes, possibly in the loft, or in a tent, but what about Tom? You said—"

"I've said too much already, Becky. Please keep this confidential."

"Why, of course, but—oh! I nearly forgot! Here's something that came with the trains last week, for Huck, it seems—from out West. Heaven knows how long it's been floating back and forth. It would never get to him with *this* name on it. Perhaps if you find him?"

She had rummaged quickly through a valise, coming up with a worn envelope addressed to a "Huckleberry Thatcher"—from a Territorial post in California—and Sid had stuffed it inside his blouse.

"Thank you, Becky. I'll do my best." *Lee! Huckleberry Lee!*

Out on the steps he had turned to see her in the doorway. "And Becky. Please be careful. Your safety is important."

"*My* safety? To what?"

"To…to the Union."

Yes, he had said that—though he had certainly meant *more* than that. And probably Becky had sensed it, poor woman—her life just now getting refocused by this work, and here comes a convergence of three men from her past, two of whom she'd just as soon be rid of, Sid figures, counting himself as one of those two.

But now, an hour later, as he waits in the dark, while the Vth Corps fords the Rapidan, a word about Sid's own motives is in order. Sid is indeed out to get Lee, a legitimate target. In those days, though, the matter was less simple than it might seem now. Curious codes were involved. Certainly, sharpshooters on both sides tried to bring down commanders behind the lines, and capturing one was an allowable project. But sending a spy to sneak up in the night and snatch him (or worse) as he slept—that might seem less than sporting. Not that it wasn't done, but John Mosby, who specialized in that sort of thing, was considered a bit of an outlaw—and if caught, in or out of uniform, might have been shot on sight.

Sport is worth keeping in mind. Lee himself is reported to have said to General Longstreet, as the latter's troops were blasting brave Federal infantrymen to bits at Fredericksburg the previous December, "It is well war is so terrible, or we should grow too fond of it." And when a Confederate sergeant crept out from his position, under fire, to take water to the wounded, a Union officer is said to have ordered a cease-fire, saying, "That man is too brave to die!" Not too generous, mind you, or too harmless, but too *brave*.

What Sid has in mind is as un-sporting as can be. But his mind is clear: *Lee* is the traitor. He is in arms against the legitimate national government. The idea of one's loyalty to state and home outranking one's oath to the nation—well, it's illogical on its face, understandable in a boy perhaps, but not in a sworn officer, and a West Pointer at that—a *superintendent,* no less! Prisoners of war? It's a mystery to Sawyer why all such captives are not summarily shot. Death to them all!

But now, providentially, Sid is given the chance to provide Huck himself with a clarifying choice: on the one hand his country and on the other this sentimental loyalty to Lee—to some Natural connection that seems to outrank his duty as a soldier and citizen. Huck's *instincts* are so good, you see, and he is *drawn*, as it were, in the right direction—stealing Jim out of slavery just *felt* right, you know!—so that he doesn't have to actually *think,* but always somehow materializes in the right place morally, just sort of plops into it without any trouble. "All right, then, I'll *go* to Hell," and all that. As if only feelings were what counted. And the consequences just roll on down the River, for someone ordinary to deal with. Well, it just burns Sid up. But this—this!—will force the issue. Huck will have to—as he once said—"decide twixt two things," what is Natural, and what is Right. It's perfect. If there is a God, it's hard not to see His hand in this. Unless, as Becky herself had wondered, Huck *had* switched sides. That would present a different problem.

"I see the boots are dry now, Major. So you didn't get thrown in?"

Jolted from his reverie, Sid turns to see a shadow on horseback against the stars. For a second he wonders if the question is about Becky, then remembers the horse.

"Hello, Colonel. No, I think we understand each other now." He reaches up and scratches the roan behind the ears. Below, in the river, one of the white V^{th} Corps emblems bobs precariously in the near-darkness, and there is a splash as a mounted officer scrambles to give a hand. "Also he's pretty worn out. I thought you were going back to headquarters—to add two and two or something."

"Well, I can add as well here as anywhere, and I think we might compare figures before the general shows up—if he can, with that bloody ear of his. When we get our facts straight, we can wire him."

Sid hands up the papers given him by Tom and recounts the rest of the day including the conversation with Becky. As Sid reports, the colonel (who can't read the papers in the dark anyway) looks out over the river. There are much bigger splashes now, as the 2nd Division's artillery battalion begins to cross—horses staggering to pull the lighter wheeled guns over rocks, the heavier ones broken down and crated across in pontooned wagon beds, husky gunners guiding caulked caissons through the water and hoisting crew kits aloft. When Sid finishes, the colonel nods.

"So, what do you think, Sid?"

"I think we need a bridge here."

"You know what I mean. Do you think this fellow Huckleberry can be found in time to do us any good? And if we do find him, can we trust him? And if we can, what can he do, since Lee knows who he is and knows he's likely still with us? Seems quite a coincidence that this friend of yours just happens to be around, don't you think? Not to mention your Becky."

"She's not *my* Becky, Colonel." Sid thinks about coincidences as the moon begins to rise behind the woods to the east, and the river is flecked with silver. "*You* found Tom, Colonel, not me, remember? And you seem to trust him. Why is that?"

"Well, mainly because everything he's told us has proved out. And he could have betrayed one of my people in Jackson's camp and hasn't. Still, there are limits to what we'll tell anybody, you know."

"Yes, sir. But to answer your question, I think I'd trust Becky with my life, and I'm not sure about Tom, even if he is my brother. As for Huck—well, it's been a long time, and we won't know till we find him. At the very least we can check back through the rosters for Lees now. There is at least one regular cavalry unit around here."

"Yes, the First, or a couple companies[8] of it. I'll get on it. And they have the wire back up now. I wish I knew why we can't keep that thing up. You go on over and get back in touch with Tom, as promised. And you know what we need him for now."

"Yes, sir."

"I'll take care of the general."

The colonel leans down, holds out an offered cigar where Sid can see it in the dim light. "No thank you, sir."

Sharpe starts to turn his horse, then pauses. "He *is* your brother, you know. And this Huckleberry fellow's at least a friend. So you're all right with this?" Sid nods, but says nothing. "Damn. What a war this is."

"Yes, sir. It is."

Sharpe chuckles. "This 'George' thing just isn't going to work, is it?"

"Sir? Oh, I'm sorry, George, I just can't get used to it. I've always—"

"Sid, call me 'sir.'"

"Yes, sir!"

Then, without even checking to see if anyone is looking, Sid removes his boots, rolls up his trousers, mounts carefully, and heads down to the ford—stirrups crossed over the saddle, boots and socks held aloft—hoping High Bar's career as a hunter has taught him caution in the water.

21. What Do I Do, Arrest Him?

"Damn it, Sid, get these God-forsaken grave-clothes off me!" the captive splutters.

Sid is sitting on a camp stool outside his tent at Vth Corps's temporary headquarters. George Meade, the crusty little corps commander, was uninterested in Sid's business, and only too happy to get him off in a tent by himself.

The captive's guards—three privates and a lieutenant from the picket line—have him in a pontoon float that does look a bit like the bottom half of a coffin. His hands and legs are tied, but he's not gagged.

"*Nail,* you said! It was *anvil*! You gave me the wrong goddamn countersign, you son of a—"

"Shut up, Tom. I was doing you a favor."

"A favor!" Ejected from his bindings, he stands, glaring and rubbing his wrists in the firelight.

"Yes, a favor. This way, they bring you straight to me. If you have the regular countersign, they might just let you on through, and who knows where you'd wind up?"

Tom squints in the flickering light. "Who knows—You still don't trust me, do you? If you did, why didn't you just tell 'em to expect me?"

"I did. You had your own special countersign, Tom, and it *was* 'nail.' I told them to bring you straight here and make sure you didn't wander off. I didn't know they'd be this thorough. Thank you, Lieutenant. Good work. You'll be commended."

"Commended! He ought to be brought up on charges." He is still rubbing his wrists. "You're still burned about this morning, aren't you?"

The major smiles. "Let's just say we're even."

"Say, you don't have anything around here to drink, do you?"

"I can offer you some coffee. If you haven't eaten, there's some passable fatback and beans left."

Tom makes a face. "Well, I might take some coffee. But I'll pass on the beans."

"That's funny," Sid admits.

"I thought so."

Sid ladles out a tin cup of black coffee from the pot over the fire and offers it to the sergeant standing sentry by his tent, who accepts it with a nod instead of a salute since both hands are now occupied (Sid knows enough to be considerate of men in the ranks whenever he can), then passes another to Tom and motions him into the tent. They sit on stools at a little folding card table with an oil lamp suspended over it surrounded by a swarm of moths. Also on the table is a map, the roster of the 1st United States Cavalry, and another plain brown envelope.

"So—what do you know now, Tom?"

"Lee's in Fredericksburg tonight, if that's what you mean. Still at Yerby's, far as I can tell, and Jackson's there, too, but that's pretty hard to get at."

"And their dispositions?"

"Well, I didn't have time to get very far in, but there were a couple of Anderson's brigades at U.S. Ford earlier, like I said, but they've probably pulled back on the Chancellors' Inn by now. I hear reports of Jackson moving troops toward the turnpike—that wouldn't be a retreat. Though, if Longstreet's full strength is on hand—remember what I heard about Hood and Pickett—Lee's likely to pull Jackson back from below the town and send him up the turnpike right at you. Just a guess."

Sid takes a sip of coffee and considers the guesses. "My guess is you're right, whether Longstreet's up or not. What about Lee and Jackson, then? Where will they be tomorrow?"

"Well—tomorrow morning I reckon they'll ride out to look at the river front below the town. You've been doing a lot of demonstrating there and some of the VIth Corps have already crossed—you didn't know that?—but I expect they'll judge that's a bluff—it is, isn't it?—and then they'll ride up this direction. You *might* have a shot at Zoan Church or thereabouts tomorrow night, but I have to tell you, Sid, this is a hare-brained scheme." He shakes his head slowly at the map.

"Well, hare-brained or not, by tomorrow evening, say sunset, we very much want two things from you: first, bivouac plans for both Lee and Jackson. Troop dispositions, too, if you can, but that is not your main concern. Second—and even more important—help us find this man."

He pushes forward the roster of the 1st U.S. Cavalry and points to a circled name.

Tom looks, then leans back.

"Why him? Is he a relation of General Lee's or something?"

"Or something." Sid pauses. "Tom, the *H* stands for Huckleberry."

"Huckleberry! You don't mean Huckleberry *Finn?*"

"I think so, Tom. I think that's our mutual friend."

Tom whistles softly. "Well, I'll be damned." Then he leans back, pulls a cigar from his vest, flexes it between thumb and forefinger of each hand as if testing it for strength, and looks a question at Sid—does he mind?—then lights it in the oil flame, leans back, and takes a puff.

"You '*think*,' you say. How come you don't know?"

"Because we can't find him. One squadron of his regiment is directly under Pleasonton, but they're detailed to various headquarters. The order of battle shows K Troop in the XIIth Corps provost guard, but Slocum says they're out with the flankers—which takes in a lot of territory."

"But you say the *H* is for Huck. Why the 'Lee'?"

"Well, it's a long story. And some of it's pretty hard to believe."

"Try me. I just climbed out of a coffin. Nothing'll surprise me."

As Sid tells enough of the story to make the Lee connection, Tom takes a couple of puffs on his cigar, turns and blows a nice series of rings out the tent flap, but the smoke inside is still enough to cause Sid's eyes to water and his face to sweat.

"Well," says Tom finally, "I'll be damned. Do you reckon Becky knows he's here?"

"Becky? Why would she?"

"Well, she's his sister, after all—or at least she *said* the judge was going to adopt him before he died. I'm surprised he isn't listed as a Thatcher. He probably made up the business about Lee. How did you know he was in the cavalry?"

"Never mind, Tom. The point is—have you had any contact since he went west? Do you know how he thinks about things?"

"You mean about the war? Sounds like you know more about that than I do. My guess is he's a pretty strong Union man if he's re-enlisted and all. No, we never met out there. You know, I'd love to see old Huck again. And, you know, if that is our boy, and if he is on hand here..." Tom stubs out his cigar on the table edge, tamps it thoughtfully, rolls it in a piece of oil cloth and puts it carefully in a vest pocket. "And if he *is* that close to Lee—well, it's still a long shot, but it's a damn sight more interesting long shot now, that's for sure. But, see here, how do you want me to spend the day tomorrow? Looking for our boy, or following Southern generals around pretending to be an admirer? I can't do both, you know. Huck's on this side, and Lee's on the other, remember."

"You have a horse, I assume?"

"Yes, and a trap—unless you folks have pushed 'em into the river. I can get up to speed on the Pike, but I can't just trot up the road to town and back with Reb columns and our own all—"

"Look, here's what you do. First, get some sleep. Right here—there's a cot over there. I'll go see about your horse and carriage. Then at daybreak, head back toward town and tell the Rebels what you've seen. Tell them a huge force is about to fall on their flank, with even more coming from below the town. That's all true, and they probably know it already: *we* may be short of cavalry here, but they seem to have plenty. Give them a couple of corps names if it helps. Find out what you can about bivouacs and command posts and such. Then come back up the turnpike as far as you can and head up the US Ford road if you can get that far. We'll have cleared Chancellor's by then, I expect. One way or the other, about an hour before sunset, Colonel Sharpe or I will be waiting for you on the road to the ford. But on the way—and this is tricky—I want you to be alert for federal cavalry, or reports of it. Act lost, or whatever. You're looking for your cousin, Huck Lee, or something. If you really do get lost, try to find Second Corps headquarters. The trap is good: nobody will mistake you for a soldier in that thing."

Tom is silent for a moment, hard to read in the firelight. "Sid, in the first place, that sounds dangerous as all Hell."

"Well, yes. But when has that stopped you? Besides, you say they already think you're working for them. Why *do* they think that?"

Tom nods—acknowledging the points. "Well, they think *all* Richmond reporters ought to be working for them, and they think I am for the same reason you do—that I haven't sold them any three-legged calves. And you're right about the danger: it's not my main concern, and maybe that's because I'm too big a fool to know any better. And I guess you're right not to trust me much. So are they. I *could* be playing both sides. I haven't been very trustworthy in my life. Just ask Becky—though I expect you already have."

It's a shrewd guess. Sid doesn't answer, but thinks, *Here's at least some self-knowledge.*

Tom continues: "No, here are my real concerns: first, that's a long ride if I have to get all the way to town and back. I'll be late, even if I get lucky. Second, the Rebs don't really trust me any more than you do, and they don't advertise their camp sites like the Temperance Union. And there's Huck himself." He taps the roster sheet. "*If* this is our boy, and *if* I find him—and you're more likely to do that than I am—what do I do? Arrest him? Tell him he just won five hundred dollars? Tell him we need Lee's head on a stick in twenty-four hours or—"

"No, Tom. You give him this." Sid pushes forward the brown envelope. "Or his commanding officer, if you have to. He's a sergeant now. He may be the ranking man at his post."

Tom takes the envelope. "This isn't—"

"More money? No. Though there's more of that if you need it. *Don't* open it yourself—that way, if you're caught you can claim you found it in the road or something. Drive over it with the trap if that helps. It'll be all Huck needs to see, I think, but it wouldn't mean much to the Rebels, just a personal item or two. Now this is where it gets interesting, you'll like this part—"

22. I Should Run Him Through (8 A.M., June 30)

"He came to challenge the adoption, that's why," says Becky. "And he claimed *Lee's* adoption to get the ruling. I should have known Huck wouldn't like the idea, but Father was so set on making things right, and—well, he wasn't thinking very clearly near the end. But *I* should have...." and her voice trails off.

It's next morning, and the major is with Becky in the loft where she has spent the night. She is moving around, unfolding bedclothes and towels. Downstairs, the floor creaks as aides and orderlies get to work, and on the window itself, across from the day bed where they sit, a drizzle has begun to carve little rivulets in the glaze of pollen. There's not a lot of time, but the major needs to clarify points that came up with Tom, and also to find out about Becky's own feelings (for operational reasons, you know)—to the extent that he can—especially when she begins folding some of the same items she had just unfolded.

Why's she so upset? What's Huck to her—besides a stepbrother?

"I should have come back, Becky. They'd have given me a year's leave from the Academy. I could have—"

"That wouldn't change the facts, Sid. I was still in love with Tom, and you know what that does to one's judgment. At any rate—and you may not know this—I saw Huck twice after that, once in Virginia, and once in California. He arrived there shortly after I did—in '51, I think, or no, early '52. Huck said he had come to 'seek his fortune' but I really think he came looking for a girl he'd met years ago. I had gone to the mission there to start the school. By then Tom had left for the bay, so they may not have run into each other. The sisters there at the Villa were to help me. Tom was to send part of his profits...well, you can hear that from Buck if you're interested."

[Of course, we are interested, and here is what Grangerford says about it:

Tom? Yes, he came about a year later, and, soon enough, Becky. They were married already when I met him in Sacramento—and none of us a day over eighteen! But Uncle Will was happy to have Tom as a writer. He always had a way with words, you know. Uncle would send me out to get the story, and then he'd sit Tom down at that cherry-wood secretary, that very one over there, to write it up.

As you might expect, Tom had to "liven things up," as he put it, and the *Chronicle* got pretty tired of correcting the record. But Tom was popular, you know, so it wasn't long before he struck out on his own. To try to keep him settled, my family staked him to some property along the river—rich enough to get a strike or two before the real Bull-Rushers arrived later that summer. So when he sold out, he was into more money than I guess was good for him. He took Becky to San Francisco to "give the Muse a serious roll in the hay"—as he put it—but he cut a fine figure around town, and I allow he took more than the Muse off to the hay!

Now Tom loved Becky, no doubt about it, and she certainly loved him to put up with that, but I probably saw Tom more over the next two years than she did. He was always off "covering" something, while she worked on that school. Why, at least twice, he introduced himself, in my presence, as married to *another* lady—a "diplomatic cover" as he put it, to help him get stories. And he did get some! I don't know about their literary merit, but he was a pioneer in the production of shock and dismay. Indeed, he became disreputable and notorious and was quite pleased with himself. But just then, why, a couple of creditors began laying for him, and he disappeared. Say, is there any of that brandy left?...]

"Becky, you don't mean he *really* married other women?"

"Oh, yes, Tom enjoys marriage. He likes the romance, the ceremonies, the dowries, the—God only knows how many children he's had. Oh, Sid, I—"

"Becky—"

"I'll be all right. Just—oh, I'm sorry. I'm sorry."

"I should run him through, Becky. I should challenge his miserable—"

"No. No, Sid. I'll hear no such—Oh, I'm—I'm so sorry! What a mess I've made of your jacket. Your bars are all wet!"

"My bars are now consecrated. I'll never wash them again."

"Oh, Sid! Thank you for being funny. And—I'm sorry I threw myself at you. I'll get you a clean handkerchief."

"Becky—listen to me now—did you have any children by him? Or is the child mentioned in the card not yours, but—"

"I have no idea whose. I had no children by Tom. Just fortunate, I suppose."

"Fortunate for him, I'd say. Then there'd be somebody else to run him through."

"Sid, don't talk like that. Tom is Tom. And he's your brother. And it's over, and I'm committed to my work." Outside the loft window the drizzle has picked up again. She wipes her face. "What a dreary, drizzly morn."

"Yes." And if it kept up, it would slow down the columns—as well as Tom, that indispensable bastard. "So what did *Huck* do in California?"

"Well—he stayed at the mission for a while, trying to help with the school—and drawing, if you can believe that."

"I can believe it."

"I didn't see him again till we met in April of '61 near Harpers Ferry, at the railroad depot. Huck met me there. He was a corporal with a troop sent to change the locks at the armory." (She starts folding again.) "He was in agony, Sid. He was about to go see Colonel Lee at Arlington and—I think by then Lee must have made up his mind to leave the Army. So…"

"So the die was cast. And Huck still wanted to stay in the service?"

"Oh, yes. And he did, too. He promised to write to me at the Sanitary Commission, and I did receive a few letters. They are mostly about camp life, and the country he'd seen. Little about battles. I suppose he didn't want to worry me."

"But did he meet with Lee?"

"Yes, and he wrote me a long letter about it. You should read that one, if I can find it. I don't think he'd mind now."

Well, we have some of those letters, and they *wouldn't* worry anybody. Soldiers' letters often understate hardships, so as not to upset loved ones. But Becky is right: the one about Arlington is required reading.

23. Do You Know How to Pray, Huckleberry?

Dearest Becky: The day before yesterday[9] I went to see the colonel at his Arlington estate, and I have waited this long to write because I cannot tell which I am now—more miserable and wretched or resigned and settled. But I am still whipsawed like that even today, so I will just get this written, and maybe it will help.

I rode up the lane to Arlington House early in the afternoon. I could see the Potomac over the field behind the house, and I wish you could of seen the cherry trees, Becky. Everything was blooming, orchards and gardens, and it was hard to think of war coming, and of what that could mean for such peaceful scenes. I already saw what it could do to a church in Mexico.

I expected the hands would be out in the fields, but there was a good sight of activity around the house and grounds—I could see repairs to porch and roof and some painting going on. All in all, it looked a bit more run-down than I expected for such a grand plantation. I wondered if maybe none of the family was there. Rooney is gone and married now, and Custis is away at school.[10] Annie and Mildred, being sickly, I was told, were upstairs reading. But the colonel was "downstairs with his figures."

A boy who was trimming hedges took Butterfly to a post and tied her, then showed me in. I'd worn my uniform, in case it helped me get in. My excuse was that I had a message of sympathy from the regiment on the sickness of his wife, which we had heard about. That was kind of a stretch, since only K and L Troops are in the East now. The house servant at the door said he would announce me—but I looked up and there the colonel was. I hadn't seen him for a few years—he hadn't even joined the regiment yet, you see—but still he looked aged more than that. He wasn't in uniform, and that was strange, too, even though

I knew he was on leave, because I'd never seen him before without one. He wore a plain jacket, with no tie, and riding boots. He had his spectacles on and was holding a sheaf of papers. He looked like—well, like some shopkeeper or doctor, or just somebody's pap about to go on a business trip.

He looked tired, but he lit up a little when he saw me. He knew I had re-enlisted in the First, but he was on leave all that time. I saluted, but he shook his head and said, "No, Huckleberry. You can't do that any more." My heart dropped into my stomach at that, but he shook my hand and then took the letter. "The men are very kind," he said. "Please tell them my wife is feeling better, and that I thank them for their thoughts and prayers." Then he said, "I am afraid that I may not be joining them after all."

I asked if he'd gotten a promotion, and he said he'd been ordered to report to General Scott the next day. He said he thought there might be an offer. Then he said, "But I must tell you, son, that it is likely that…that instead I will have to resign from the service. In fact, I have already written the letter."

I was knocked over, Becky, as you can imagine. Nothing but the sun in the sky is more fixed than Colonel Lee in the United States Army. He probably regretted saying so much right out in the parlor and asked the servants to leave us alone for a while. Me telling you this is probably already a dishonor against him, but I have to tell someone, and my lips are sealed here in camp. Still, I don't doubt you will soon read about all this in the papers. He asked me to sit at the breakfast table by a window where we could look out the breezeway in back and see the river. He looked like he wasn't sure what to say, so I started it for him.

"You think General Scott's going to offer you a higher command, don't you?"

"That's likely enough," he answered, but he didn't look happy. He looked down at the papers in his hands, which looked like receipts[11]. I said I expected the general would offer him command of the whole army.

"That's why he wants to see you, I bet," I said.

And he said that was possible—and that it was his *fear*. "I am a Virginian, Huck." I think this was the first time he'd called me just Huck.

"A Virginian!" I said. "But you're an American. And an officer!"

"I will not draw my sword against my native state."

"But Virginia is still in the Union."

But the colonel said he couldn't count on that any more. "The legislature is meeting today," he says, "and I have no doubt they will secede rather than allow an invading army to pass through the state."

"Well—Colonel, I'm from Missouri," I said, "but if they leave the Union, they're the enemy."

And he says, "Huckleberry, Virginia can never be my enemy. My roots here are too deep. My family has a long tradition of service to our state."

And I threw in: "And to your nation!"

Now I know this was no way to talk to a commanding officer, or even a father. But, oh, Becky, this broke my heart, and that wasn't the worst. I asked what he would do then, if he resigned. I said "If you're the best there is, like everybody says, and I know General Scott thinks so—you don't think the whole country, North and South, are just going to let you go home and raise corn, do you?"

Well, instead of hitting me with the back of his hand like he probably should have, he looked out the window at the fields and said real quiet, almost to himself, "No, you are right. They won't. If war does come, I will have to defend my state."

Now Becky, I knew two things. First, I knew I couldn't go with him. I couldn't no more fight against the nation and flag that had made me their own than he could against Virginia. But that wasn't the worst—because if the colonel didn't "draw his sword" for the Union he would have to draw it for the South, and I have a two-year enlistment. That means, like as not, that we will have to fight *each other*. Well, I stood up then, and the colonel stood, too, and turned toward the window away from me—but of course I could see his reflection in the glass.

"I will tell you something, Huckleberry, and please do not repeat this. May I have your word on that?" I nodded, and so did my reflection in the window, and Becky, here I am repeating it, so please don't pass it any further. He said, "I have just received an offer of a brigadier general's commission from the Southern Confederacy."

Well, I was floored, and I said, "Surely you haven't accepted it?"

And he said, "Not yet—although I have thought of it. I may still have to carry a musket in defense of my home, if necessary. I cannot promise to do otherwise, but—"

"But you'll see General Scott?"

"Why should I do that, when I've already—"

"Sir, please promise me you will," I said, and then he turned and looked at me, and it was the saddest look I ever seen on a grown man.

And he says, "All right. All right. I will go to see General Scott and hear what he has to say. But I cannot promise to remain in the service of the Union, even in the West, if it means I might be forced someday to disobey an order that—that would violate my conscience. And when the general hears that, he may well place me under arrest—had you thought of that? I will also promise you this: that if I refuse an offer from General Scott—and we do not yet know that he will make one—I will also refuse offers of command from the Confederate States—including this commission. I will fight only for Virginia, and only if she is invaded."

I didn't know what to say. I wasn't sure what that meant. How can he fight for Virginia and not for the South? But I could tell it had been hard for him to say it, so I nodded and managed to say something like, "Thank you for your kindness, Colonel," and picked up my cap and gloves.

At the door he offered me his hand, and I took it. Then at the bottom of the steps I turned and saluted him. I said I was sorry, because he said not to do that, but I said he was going to be my leader forever, whether he liked it or not. But when I started to turn away he says, "Hold up there, mister!" And it was that kind of voice that you wouldn't dare to disobey, and I stopped and turned back and he was standing in the doorway.

"You are a soldier, Corporal," he says. "And as long as you *are* in the service, you will obey your lawful commanders and do your duty. Do you understand? And even when you are no longer a soldier, you will still have a duty, and you must do that also—as painful as it may be. Do you understand that?"

"Yes, sir," I said. Then he spoke more quiet.

"Your first duty right now is to pray—that war may be avoided."

"Yes, sir."

"Do you know how to pray, Huckleberry?" He stood on the top step, waiting.

"I don't know, sir. Not very well."

"Well, then learn, sir. Learn."

Well, there it is, Becky. You see, you *must* write to me now. You must teach me how to pray. And please pitch in yourself, too, for nothing I ever prayed for ever came true. And now I am ordered to pray for my poor country and all of our pitiful souls. That's a tall order, I think, even for you and the Widow.

With love and hope,

Yours ever,

Huck Finn

Dearest Becky... With love... Yours ever. The words thud into Sid's brain like bullets, their message achingly clear: why Becky keeps up with Huck and is so concerned for his safety. She is in love with him.

And he with her? Well, why not? That other girl was years ago, after all, and now here is this example of what seems to have been a long and intimate correspondence between Becky, a woman of beauty and breeding and accomplishment, and this...cutpurse, this freckle-faced truant! Now it all makes sense. After all, how many letters has she written to Sid? One to announce her father's death, one to congratulate him upon his graduation, another upon his captaincy. That last one did express a tender wish for his success and safety—as if those weren't contradictory hopes in this Army.

But Huck's command of language also amazes. Indeed, to Sid, it's as if a ragged moth that had flown into a cave nine years ago has re-emerged as a marvelous butterfly. The attachment to Lee is no surprise, but whence this attachment to the Army? To the Nation? To something larger than his Natural Self? Wherever that came from, is there hope in it?

"Sid," Becky's voice breaks in, "I doubt Huck would mind my revealing this, if it will help the Cause. But I can't believe he would be of much use to you against Lee. I hope you will not abuse my...my trust here. You will promise me that, won't you?"

Sid says nothing for a moment. He rises and looks past Becky at the window. The sky seems to be brightening. The green of the new leaves still seems startling, artificial, aggressive. Time *is* short. "Becky. I do appreciate your trust, and…I would rather not make promises I cannot keep. But it'll be easier for me not to know about a letter if I don't have it." He turns and hands the letter back.

"Oh, thank you. You're a friend, Sid."

"I'll always be that, Becky. But it may be impossible for me to prevent Huck's having to…perform difficult duties." He points to the letter. "Remember, Lee himself seems to have foreseen that. Huck is a soldier in our cause. And so am I. And who knows what that may require—of any of us?"

"Well, of course, that's always…" but she catches something in his eye, his voice. "Sid, you're not—you and this bureau—You *must* promise me you are not contemplating something truly dishonorable. You aren't, are you?"

Sid is silent for a moment, then, "Becky, I just said I cannot—"

"Sid Sawyer, promise me you're not planning to use our Huck as—as bait, or as—I swear, if you abuse your friendship so as to make my Huck—*our* Huck—hate himself, or his father—" (her eyes are dry now, her voice firm) "I swear I will never speak to you again. If that matters to you. Promise me." (If it matters!) "*Promise* me!"

But outside a horse whinnies, and a command is shouted, then a louder call—for a "Major" something—and Sid turns, throws up the sash, and sees a mounted officer looking up and hoisting a rolled-up sheet of paper, waving it at him. The rain has stopped.

"I'll be right down, Colonel," he shouts, gripping the window sill. *Damn!*

He slams the sash shut and hurries down the stairs.

Damn duty! Damn it to Hell!

And remembering he'd not taken his leave of Becky. *Damn her, too!*

At the bottom of the porch steps he looks back up at the window, sees a white face looking down. The sash is open, and the face calls: "You be careful, Sid Sawyer! And you come back!"

His anger dissolves. "With my shield, or on it, my lady!" he cries, and lifts his hand in salute. A sword would have been better, but he'd left his by that damned river.

"I didn't know you had a sweetheart," says Sharpe.

"Oh, she's not. Just an old friend from home. But she knows…"

"Knows this Huckleberry fellow? Well, that may be more trouble than it's worth, you know. But, say—" He swings down from his mount with the paper under his arm, hands the reins to an orderly, and unrolls the paper for Sid to see. "Have you ever seen this fellow?"

"Not that I know. Who is it?"

"You remember I said I had a man in Jackson's service? That's him. I wanted you to see what he looks like. And I didn't get it from Tom, if that's your concern. The fellow himself gave it to me, and it's a good likeness."

"Really? Looks young. Can I have it—for the time being? Huck will need to see it, you know."

"Sure. But remember: in the wrong hands, it's a man's death warrant."

"I know. I'll be careful. What's his name?"

"Jonathan Smith—at least that's what he calls himself. Remember it."

Now remembering the letter for Huck, which he'd stuffed into his blouse yesterday, Sid takes it out again. It's addressed to a "Corporal Huckleberry Thatcher," in care of the United States Territorial Command, and looks as if first postmarked in California at some mission in Santa Clara more than a year earlier—and since then presumably churning through the war-muddied mails. Sid thinks again about the girl looking for Huck in California. But why would Becky, who seems quite taken with Huck now, want to pass it on? Perhaps the other girl doesn't matter now? Well. He'll deliver it, he decides, if the chance comes, but certainly not till Huck, if and when found, can be tested for loyalty. And with that, he puts the letter back in his blouse and out of his mind.

24. When in Doubt, Build a Bridge

"Are you in command here, sir?"

The officer Sid addresses is looking ahead down the trail through a field glass. He turns in his saddle, lowers the glass, and beams at Sid. A loop of gold braid around his campaign hat has come loose, making a little pigtail in back of his head that swishes comically when he turns, like a price tag. "Why, yes, I am, Major. A splendid little business here! I don't believe I know you, sir."

"Sorry—Sid Sawyer, from General Butterfield's staff." Sid sticks out a gloved hand and the officer takes it, still grinning, and offers the field glass.

"Major Pennock Huey, sir—8th Pennsylvania Cavalry. My honor." He gestures ahead. "Observe, sir, that small building down this lane…toward the ford."

Sid takes the glass—from courtesy, really—and looks where he is bidden.

He has been in a sweat ever since leaving Becky. The day has brightened, but with Averell's cavalry still off somewhere up river, he can do little without hearing from Tom. Imagine depending on such a fellow! Having heard nothing more from Sharpe or Patrick, Sid has ridden down from Ely's to US Ford to help with the Second Corps crossing and be close to the telegraph. After yesterday's cross-country adventure, he has cautiously taken the road today, with the infantry columns. That has proved less cautious than it seemed, though. For one thing, High Bar, well rested now, wanted to gallop the whole way and was in constant danger of running down stragglers on the narrow road or getting tangled in wagon traces. For another, the south bank was not fully secure: there were still Confederates in the area, and if he took the wrong turn, he risked capture.

Moreover, the talk with Becky had first depressed, then infuriated him. My God! Men were dying for the Union by the thousands all over the country, leaving loved ones to grieve—with no more than some marginal advantage to show for it. But Huckleberry Finn, who could help strike a great blow for the

Cause—he has to be protected from hard choices! And why? Because Becky Thatcher, of all people, is infatuated with him. The worst complication imaginable.

Through the glass Sid sees what looks like a small, frame country schoolhouse. The schoolyard, if that's what it is—the building needs paint, and the yard needs some cleanup—is full of Rebel soldiers, seated and under guard, thirty or forty of them, three of whom look to be officers and none too pleased at their predicament.

"My flankers surprised them a little after dawn," says Huey. "They were all asleep in the schoolhouse. They had a lookout up at the ford, but none in this direction, and six or eight of my boys snuck around the place and hollered in that our whole regiment had them covered and to throw out their weapons or die. And sure enough, they did! You should've seen their faces when they saw how few of us they'd surrendered to. A whole company of the 12th Virginia, officers and all. Only the man up at the ford got away." The major beams at the magnitude of his victory. "There are a couple of nice side-arms, if you need something, Sawyer. Cigars, too. I can't stand 'em myself."

"No, thanks, Major. Your men earned the trophies, and I agree with you about cigars," says Sid, returning the glass. "But tell me, is it clear now down to the ford?"

"At least from this angle." Huey gestures down the road with the glass. "Though the rest of this 12th Virginia is spread out in the woods off to the right somewhere."

"How do you know that?"

"Oh, these prisoners told us. Didn't even have to ask! Figured that might scare us off, I guess. But with the whole IInd Corps ready to cross, they'll all be making tracks soon."

"I'd like to chat with the prisoners before I cross, if you don't mind, Major Huey."

"Certainly, Sawyer. But that's not the ford there. U.S. Ford is a mile downstream, if that's what you're looking for."

"But I thought I saw—"

"That's a breakwater of some kind. The locals call it Scott's Dam. Maybe it's for a mill race or something. But you could probably cross there if you wanted."

Sid learns little more from the prisoners, except that they were assigned to the area by General Mahone. Since Mahone's brigade is in Anderson's division, that corroborates Tom's map. Sid is impressed by the men's morale: they are in high spirits, even jaunty, in spite of being captured, and quick to disparage the blue cavalry. Although their clothing is a bit motley, some even wearing blue trousers probably stripped from federal casualties last winter (the three officers are a bit better dressed), they seem well enough equipped and their weapons are well tended. In short, they look and sound like part of an army that is used to winning and expects to win again. For some reason, this more than any direct intelligence convinces Sid that Lee—the Lee he knows—will follow his own script, not Hooker's.

Before heading up to the ford proper, Sid rides down to the dam. His eye takes in the flow, the placing of rock, the slope of ground on the other bank. It wouldn't take much to get something up here that heavy columns could use. And there's a road of some kind at the top of the opposite bank, with open ground below. Something to think about.

Back at U.S. Ford, he is impressed, even as a Regular, by the transformation there in twenty-four hours. The north bank has become the staging area for the campaign—a military city, with long rows of tents, wagon parks, stacked small arms and artillery tubes, huge dumps of coal and long ricks of fire wood, barrels of oil, carefully flagged privies and forge-wagons ready for blacksmithing, and stores of food and clothing and medicine, housed in tents and sheds and small buildings of the pre-fabricated sort that can be loaded onto trains and wagons, with numbered parts and everything needed to put them up right down to the last nail—and a few pre-existing barns and farm houses from which flags fly denoting their uses for headquarters, hospital, or telegraphy—as far as the eye can see. And men—men everywhere in organized motion, in columns, on horseback, driving teams, wielding hammers and axes, shouting orders—and building bridges. The pontoons and stringers are stacked at the ready as the last of an infantry brigade splashes up the south bank and out of the way of the builders. And there are depots even more impressive than this at Manassas Junction and at City Point and Falmouth and Arlington Heights, and on the lower Rappahannock, and a dozen other locations ringing just this one Rebel state.

It is, in its own way, as awesome and sobering a display as the morale of those Southern soldiers. Here, Sid knows, is a power that mere esprit cannot withstand. Ultimately, Lee will lose, overwhelmed by a tide of organized mass and energy. Ultimately. But how much better for all if the inevitable could be achieved quickly, and efficiently—with a decapitation.

"Quite a sight isn't it, Major?"

"It certainly is, General."

General Gouverneur Warren[12] is a man Sid is glad to have run into: a West Pointer and an engineer. (An engineer who has made general!) What is needed here is a bridge, and as the army's chief of engineering, though still in his early thirties, Warren gets right to work. Doesn't assign it to someone else, either.

"As soon as this brigade's over, we'll move the infantry crossing upstream out of our way."

"It's faster there," Sid notes.

"Yes, but it's fordable—at least by men and horses."

"How long will it take? How many do you have?"

"Well, Major, that's them down there cooking breakfast."

"An infantry regiment."

"Yes, but there's five hundred of them, and they're Vermonters. They can all wield an ax, I assure you."

Sid thinks about it.

"They can wield rifles, too. What about those prisoners we took up at Germanna, and all that bridging supply? They can work. Do you know where they are?"

"Why, no, probably with the provost back up the road here, but I doubt—"

"Major?" Sid turns to see a lieutenant saluting him. "If you're Major Sawyer, there's a telegraph for you, sir—up at the house."

At a long table in the parlor, Sid sees the terminal, a civilian telegrapher pecking furiously at a type-writer, and a disheveled-looking captain with his uniform coat unbuttoned frowning down at a paper. The captain waves him in without even rising or saluting. He looks up and thrusts the paper to Sid. "Well, Major, I don't know what to make of this. Maybe you do."

Sid looks at the paper:

MAJ SID SAWYER PER COL GEORGE SHARPE STOP THE KELLY'S FORD FAMILY WILL BE IN TOMORROW MORN STOP

ALL FAMILY MEMBERS MEET AT CHANC HOUSE 4PM TO PLAN REUNION STOP FROM GEN BUTTERFIELD END STOP

The major feels a jolt of excitement. The Kelly's Ford "family" is Averell's cavalry division—more than four thousand sabers. So now they'll be delayed till tomorrow morning. But at least it's a time, so Operation Reunion is still on. But Huck's appearance all depends on Tom—who are these other "members"? And what does Sid do till four? Cool his heels in the Rapidan?

"Thank you, Captain. Colonel Sharpe is not here?"

"Haven't seen him since this morning. Otherwise, I'd have given this to *him*, you know."

Sid ignores the sarcasm, picks up the message log and begins to write.

"I see. Well, please send this response to General Butterfield with my compliments, and keep a copy for Colonel Sharpe." He hands over the message:

TO: GENERAL BUTTERFIELD, PER COLONEL SHARPE, STOP. WILL BE HAPPY TO ATTEND REUNION, STOP. LOOK FORWARD TO LOCATING OUR BOY, STOP. RECOMMEND PLACING TELEGRAPH OFFICER UNDER ARREST FOR INSUBORDINATION AND CONDUCT UNBECOMING AN OFFICER. PLEASE ADVISE, STOP. RESPECTFULLY MAJ S SAWYER MILITARY INFORMATION. END STOP.

"And send it just that way, Captain." Without waiting for a reaction, he leaves the building.

Back at the ford he finds Warren instructing Vermonters in the joining of runners to floats. "General, if you have things under control here, I'd like to find those Rebel bridge-builders."

"Well, fine, Major. You're not under my command. Good luck, but I doubt we can use them here."

"Maybe not, but I know another good place for a bridge."

Sid finds the prisoners held in what was once a large livestock-holding pen attached to a dilapidated barn, to which has been added an ineffective-looking tin roof. Indeed there are now two hundred or so Rebel prisoners, including the unlucky Virginians captured by Huey this morning. They are now sullen and uncommunicative. Their ranking officer, a ramrod-straight, sandy-haired captain in his late thirties, has apparently demanded that none is to be questioned without his presence, and seems to have had that wish respected—at least by his own men, the captured bridge-builders. The stench in the pen is strong, likely in equal parts from unwashed prisoners and the prior animal tenants. Sawyer climbs onto a cracker box against the fence.

"You men are builders, I hear!" No answer, but he has their attention. "The Yankee engineers here think they can build bridges, too." A couple of snickers, but no other sound. "And they can, because they're led by West Pointers—like me and General Warren." Silence, waiting. "But that's not all they have. Look around you here, men!" Now there's some stirring and whispering: what's he up to? "Look around you. Look back toward the ford! Look!" Some turn to look. "They have that, too. Supplies. Mountains of it. And men. At this moment two hundred thousand are in training in New York state alone!"

"And we got Stonewall Jackson!" A voice from the prisoners, followed by a murmur of response. It's begun to work.

"Yes, you do. And so far he's whipped us every time." More murmurs. "But he can't whip *that*—not forever—not when there's none of *you* left." Silence, now. *They're wondering if I'm crazy.* "If you *are* that good, why not show the Yanks you can build a better bridge and a quicker one—a mile downstream. Beat General Warren and his crew, and I'll see to it you're paroled right away." Still *silent—well, this was a reach, but might as well.*"And if you don't. Who knows what will—"

"You don't have that authority, Major!" The Rebel captain. "This is improper. The laws of war don't allow you to force these men into labor."

Sid turns to the captain, who has stood up now. Even without sword or side-arm and unwashed for hours, he looks clipped and military—every inch a soldier.

"No—but *you* could. You're their ranking officer, Captain. And this *isn't* a war. It's an insurrection. We could put the lot of you in a chain gang. We *could* shoot you for treason." Silence. A woodpecker can be heard on the other side of the barn. "The bridge I want at Scott's Dam would let us bring some ambulance wagons across there—when you whip us again." He knows that doesn't make any sense, but he goes on—on a hunch. "And it would show your mettle—your mettle as a soldier—maybe even a West-Pointer."

"What makes you think I'm a West-Pointer?"

Sid, on his box, looks across the pen at the Rebel officer.

"I think I can tell that, Captain. What year?"

There is firing now off to the east. Sid, exhales, steps down, walks to High Bar and mounts, then calls out: "Well, men—think about it, will you? I'll get you some water anyhow. I like bridge-builders."

But as he turns his horse, the Rebel captain says evenly, over the silence: "Class of 'forty-seven."

Sid halts and turns, tries to read the man's face, but can't with the sun against him. He lifts his hat. "'Fifty-six here, Captain. My compliments."

"That was the damnedest thing I ever saw," says Sharpe, turning his horse to follow Sid along the switchback down to the Ford. "Wonder why we didn't think of that before—get the Rebs to help us by threatening to charge them with treason and offering better food."

"Well—appealing to their patriotism sure wasn't going to help."

"My favorite part was promising early parole. That man's right; you don't have such authority."

"No. But it wasn't a bluff. If they'd built something for us, I'd have found a way to help them. I like to keep my word."

"Well, so do I. You saw Butterfield's message?"

"Yes. And you saw my reply?"

Sharpe laughs. "Yes, and I share your opinion of telegraphers, though I don't think I'd have put it in a telegram—be careful, Sid, keep your head on straight." He takes a quick, critical look at the major. "But it's good news!"

"You mean about Averell."

"Yes. Although why it took this long is strange—orders from A to move as soon as word came from B, and orders from B to move as soon as A had confirmed...you know, that sort of thing. And then the line's down for a while. Why is *that* so hard to keep up?"

They watch as the first pontoons are shoved out into the water, lashed to the waiting buoys hanging from the ropes, and layered with planks and runners.

"Well," Sid responds. "It's fine if he's still at our disposal—"

"He is, he is. On the highest authority."

"You mean Hooker himself?"

"Higher than that. Or so I'm told. We'll find out soon enough, I suspect."

Sid looks back down at the work. "Well, let's hope tomorrow's not too late."

"Yes, let's. But why should it be? You don't think Bobby Lee will turn tail by then, do you?"

"No, I don't, Colonel." From below, there is a shout and a curse as a beam comes loose and washes away, pulling a stringer line dangerously askew. "I think he may attack."

"Attack?" Sharpe looks at him, smiles. "On our ground? Just what Old Joe wants. How convenient!"

"Maybe. But it would be a lot more convenient if we could find Huck."

"Well, as for that, there's hope there, too." Sharpe removes a glove, digs in his saddle bag, brings out a folded piece of note-paper and hands it to Sid.

Sid unfolds it and reads the familiar printing:

Our Boy is close by. Hope to locate soon, but rough country. Stay near ford tonight and tomorrow AM. Rebs have Mahone at Chancellorsville but pulling back to Anderson's line at Zoan Ch.

"Thank God! He's found him."

"Or 'Soon,' anyway," Sharpe notes.

"Yes, and by 'tomorrow AM' we may have a battle in progress."

"Maybe. But maybe that'll help. It'll bring the Head of the Family closer to the front."

Sid thinks about that. "And in the confusion a cavalry column might cut through—"

"That was my thinking."

"—And with a moon each night—does that help or hurt us, do you think?"

"Well—let's play 'em as they're dealt, Major. I'll see you at Chancellor's then. Meanwhile, I'll stay here and follow the cables." He sees Sid looking back away from the ford. "You're not still thinking about that girl, are you?"

"No. I was wondering about that Rebel West Pointer—why he's still just a captain."

Sharpe chuckles. "Maybe he's an engineer. They say promotion's slow in that line of work." Then, more seriously. "But I meant what I said about being careful, Sid."

"You mean about telegraphers?"

"And that girl. And Tom. And Huck if we find him. Just remember: it's a *military* operation."

Sid can feel his ears burning. He's not used to being rebuked. "I'm sorry, sir, if I—if I seemed—"

Sharpe waves it off. "Don't worry, Sid—you're still my man here. I'll see you at four. Where are you going now?"

"I'm going to help build a bridge." Sid turns High Bar down toward the riverbank where Warren and the Vermonters' Colonel are consulting. Sharpe cannot resist: "Watch where you step, Sidney! There might be water down there."

Part 4

"Your face in the cliff...your song in the trees..."

25. So of Course We Had to Charge Them

So morning brightens, and battle looms, and young Major Sawyer awaits events beyond his control by trying to build bridges.

And while he does so, I owe the reader some account of what Our Boy Huck has been up to in the war. What has his role been? Well, Tom's right; Huck is not far away. And ironically he may already have done a bit to neutralize Lee. Even Sid can see that Huck had extracted some kind of promise from Lee two years ago not to join the Confederate service right away, limiting himself to command of Virginia's mobilization. Did that promise save the Union from defeat in the first year of the war? Maybe not. Lee's first campaign, supervising Virginia troops west of the Blue Ridge, was not impressive. But it's tempting to wonder, isn't it, about the result if he *had* accepted that first Confederate offer?

But Huck has been up to more than that. He has a connection to one of those coincidences of war about which historians still argue—which, of course, makes it irresistible to me. Huck's still in the cavalry, but since his unit is often detached, records of its whereabouts are sketchy. When "1st U.S. Cav" appears on the order of battle, that may or may not include K Company (or K Troop, as mounted companies were often called[13]). Huck's career thus has that similarity to Sid's, which would also be difficult to trace, deliberately, after he leaves his engineer battalion to join the Bureau of Military Information.

But there the similarity ends. While Sid has spent the war mostly in the engineers and in staff work, Huck has fought in the ranks—even if most of it is in the mounted arm, not the infantry. True, old cavalrymen will remind you that mounted units were sometimes given virtually suicidal missions under both rifle and cannon fire. One thinks of Farnsworth's charge at Gettysburg, for example. And they were often required to fight on foot, with pistols and carbines, holding desperately to a position till infantry could arrive. But that begs the question, does it not? Who *was* expected, ultimately, to hold the position? The infantry. Look at any casualty list: that's where the big numbers are.

But, while letters home may not reveal much, journals and memoirs are often quite revealing. And Our Boy, at least during the war, was a diligent journalist. Is it full of longing for a certain Mexican girl? No, it's not, although references do crop up—and in the strangest contexts:

The lieutenant said he allowed the Rebs was no braver than Mexicans, which we "whipped right handy." Well, I says I couldn't speak for the men maybe, but I know a Mexican *girl* who could stand up to men twice her size, with rocks to their pitchforks. They asked if I think I'll ever see her again, and of course I says I don't *think*—I *know*. They ask how come, and I says because she's not just braver than men but smarter, too, and she'll find *me*. They judged I was joking then, and I guess maybe I was, but I do live in that hope and I do cherish the memories. Lots of women have cared for me and tried to help me do right, and I got to try to do my duty and be worthy. And if I'm going to do that, I got to look sharp and set out pickets tonight.

How ambiguous! There is certainly a tenderness toward the girl, but then he folds her in with the other women in his life who "cared" for him. But he has not forgotten her, no indeed, and he hopes—*knows*—he will see her again. *How* does he know? What has passed between them, besides fourteen years?

As for the war itself, the journal contains more than a hundred pages from the period, many of them "about battles." And nothing would delight me more than to present them all, with my usual expert commentary. But it would not advance our story much. If the reader was counting on it, I apologize. But here are the highlights:

1. Huck's squadron, detached from the 1st Cavalry, most of which is still in the West, participates in some initial forays along the Potomac, including a comically unsuccessful raid on a couple of Rebel gun emplacements, in which they run off the gunners, but have no way to drag away the guns and can't figure out how to set fuses to blow the things up, but do manage to set some hay on fire, scaring off their own horses.

2. Huck serves in the fall and winter campaigns of 1861, which help save West Virginia for the Union (opposing Lee and Jackson, though Huck doesn't

know it). Huck's missions mostly involve reconnaissance, because of his familiarity with the mountains west of Staunton. His memories of the severe winter of 1861-62—of surviving on moldy potatoes and feeding the peels to his poor horse—do put the lie to the idea that Federal troops were always well supplied.

3. During the Shenandoah Valley campaign of 1862 Huck takes sick, is left near death in Winchester, Virginia, captured by advancing Confederates under his old Lexington host, Thomas J. (now "Stonewall") Jackson, but then left behind again when the town is re-occupied by Union forces.

4. As part of a guard detail, he helps defend the immense federal supply depot at Manassas Junction in the summer of 1862, ultimately being chased off by Jackson's corps, which loots and burns the place.

5. He participates in the pursuit of Confederate cavalry (led by either J.E.B. Stuart or John Mosby—Huck is not sure which) whose raid, according to news accounts, nets a Union general and a Methodist chaplain. The Rebels later claim the minister is more valuable.

6. He fights—on foot—in a vicious skirmish at Catoctin Mountain in the preliminaries of the Antietam /Sharpsburg campaign in late summer 1862.

7. During and after the actual Battle of Antietam, Huck is in Frederick, Maryland, recovering from a wound—and under arrest! More about this anon.

8. Huck spends the winter of 1862-63, during and after the Fredericksburg campaign, with his regiment on picket duty up and down the Rappahannock River. Sometimes he knows where he is ("on the Mine Road near Culpeper") and sometimes he doesn't ("at a plank bridge over a small, icy run"). Huck is now in the newly organized Cavalry Corps, serving in the division of General Alfred Pleasonton, of whom Huck approves because he "has experience in the West."

This takes us up to the current campaign, but some of the episodes are worth a bit of detail. One of them, the brief layover in Winchester (see Number 3, above) wasn't a battle, but it is important. The town is as pretty a little village as you'll ever see, and it changed hands more times than any other town in the war without being burned down—but Our Boy is too sick to appreciate the charm. In fact, he is delirious with fever much of the time he is there.

I was out of my head a good bit, and had awful dreams—some of them about falling and being held under water by Pap, who was looking

down at me. When you're sick, somehow, the dreams get more real, and you wake up and discover you've been hollering out. When I woke up it was Sergeant Sam and the lieutenant looking down at me—for real. I was with my own company again now. Pretty soon after that I was still weak but able to travel.

I told Sam about that dream and he said it was a "humdinger." Then he said "Oh! Damnation, Huck! A Rebel officer give me something to give to you when you come to, and I plumb forgot about it—said 'twas a letter from home. Here, let me get it."

He scrounged around in his haversack and came out with a envelope. It was sealed, not addressed. There was a folded note in it, hand-writ:

Huckleberry:

If this should find you, and find you well, I am pleased and send you my blessing. In adversity, remember that it is the blessing of the Almighty that matters most and that all events are under His direction. My advice about prayer still stands, and if you can include in yours an old man who has disappointed you, I will be grateful. As a former comrade, please know that I wish you well, and that I know you are doing your duty.

Fondly, R. E. L.

PS: I have hurt my hand in a riding miss-hap, but learning that your unit may be nearby during the campaign, I have had Major Chilton write this for me and attempt to deliver it. You must be sure to destroy this: If found, it could damage us both.

Well, I was sure surprised! I don't know how General Lee got the note to me, but I have no doubt it's really from him, because it just sounds too much like him *not* to be. I guess I am fortunate to have such a great man care for me, even if he is on the wrong side. At least I hope it's not *me* that's in the wrong. I do wonder about that sometimes. And I guess my face must of showed it because Sam asked was it "bad news from home?" And I said not bad necessarily. I just wished we weren't so far apart.

"I know what you mean," he says, but of course he *doesn't* know, and I guess it's a good thing. I was afraid he'd ask me how come it got delivered through the other side, but he didn't. In any case, I resolve to guard my health from now on and be careful what water I drink. I'd rather take a bullet than go through that again.

Interesting. Lee cares enough for his former ward to leave messages under his pillow, like the Good Fairy. But, if he cares that much, why not just have him brought to Richmond when captured? That is, assuming Jackson, the commander at Winchester, *is* aware of Huck's presence. Does Lee's agent have instructions to keep Old Jack in the dark, fearing some outburst of righteous wrath against his old Lexington guest? At this time Lee doesn't know Jackson as well as he will later on. But if Jackson *is* in the dark, how does Lee himself find out about it, and why would Jackson leave behind a batch of disabled prisoners, at least a few of whom are officers? Did Lee himself spring the boy without Old Jack's knowledge?

Lee is such a straight arrow that this last seems unlikely. But the matter is really not so mysterious. Maybe Jackson knows, and maybe he doesn't, but I doubt if it matters. In the first place, sick and wounded prisoners are more a burden than anything else. And as for leaving *this* prisoner: well, that kind of thing was not unheard of, in this war between former comrades.

So there it is: a message left in the night—and left with someone else, potentially compromising the secrecy, but saving Huck from embarrassing questions later from his own superiors (although not entirely, as we'll see). Interesting.

And I simply cannot skip Huck's splendid description of the scrap over the Manassas supply depot during the Second Manassas campaign (see number 4 above) involving K Troop's heroic attack on a party of Confederate infantrymen who have just looted a loyal Union chicken pen:

When we first come at them the Rebs throwed rocks and eggs and ham bones at us instead of bullets. So we judged they must be short of ammunition, because we knew they wouldn't waste anything like that, so we mounted up and charged. While we run this bunch off, the birds themselves held their position, squawking valiantly, in spite of the missiles flying around. I said I reckoned they were all descended from

Colonel Lee's "soldier hens" in Texas, and Jack said somebody should cry "fowl." The boys all thought that was pretty funny.

Well, the Rebs come back with more infantry and live rounds and drove us off. They must of been mighty hungry because we weren't hardly across the road when they begun to stuff themselves and their packs. After a while they begun to torch the place and we had to move further off. I watched from the woods with the captain's field glass and I seen them fall in and march away with their belts, bedrolls, haversacks, and even hats and jacket-linings all stuffed full of cured hams, chicken parts, canned peaches, pickled herring, bars of soap, and one had a peck of coffee rolled up in his blanket and was leaking a brown trail as he marched off! There was many boxes of Bibles and tracts to be had, but I noticed that for a Christian folk they didn't seem much interested in those. No doubt they left them for our benefit, being concerned for our souls.

Number 6, the fight on the mountain, is less amusing. This is Huck's most serious combat, in the sense that would mean something to an infantryman. Lee has followed up the victory at Second Manassas by crossing the Potomac, throwing the North into a tizzy. The Federal commander, George McClellan, has instructed his cavalry to poke through Lee's screen of outposts in the Blue Ridge to find out where the Rebel infantry is. But the ground is so rough near the gap—too rough for horses—and so well defended by rifle pits manned by dismounted cavalry and miscellaneous foot soldiers (under Huck's old Lexington friend, Harvey Hill), plus a battery of horse artillery—that there is nothing for it but to form in a skirmish line and try to "root the Rebs out by hand." For this part of the effort, Huck's cavalry squadron—150 or so in strength—has been dismounted to fight beside a regiment of infantry. It takes only a few minutes of getting pot-shot from trees and hung-up in brambles to show that loose order isn't going to suffice, and that lines of battle are required. Now, I have to say that at this point the officer in charge should have requested reinforcements or a change in plans. Except in desperation, one does not send cavalry to charge dug-in infantry—even on foot. What a waste of a specialized asset!

Still, Huck's unit, like most cavalry on both sides, carries carbine rifles for such circumstances. Some in the squadron even have shotguns and long rifles because of the unit's particular scouting duties. All these can be loaded and fired more rapidly than infantry muskets, but the advantage lasts only till the lines meet. These are not weapons for taking and holding ground. Also, there have to be horse-holders—which further reduces effectiveness on foot. Here is how Huck describes the action:

We had to charge up hill over broken ground while the Rebel cannon swept the road, but we had to close on the road and guide on it, if we were to open it for use. It's just lucky the Rebel shot was mostly solid rounds and not exploding.[14] The damage was worst, sadly, among the horses and wagons below.

The musket fire was terrible enough, though. Sam went down right beside me with a thud and a grunt, laying where he fell, and looked dead as a rock. I bent to pull him back behind a tree when a leaf just by my head clipped off, and I guess that round would have done for me if I hadn't of bent over. The lieutenant hollered at me to "close up, close up," so I had to leave Sam, and I rushed back up even with the line, wondering how to "close" when the rocks and brush were causing so many gaps. I looked back to see what the lieutenant meant, but he was seated leaning against a rock, his sword across his knees, as if taking a nap, except for the blood draining from his mouth and ears. Soon anybody could see we couldn't stay there—every second or two there was another groan or yell or curse as someone was hit—so the major stood up in front of us waving his sword and yelling till his voice was hoarse that if we didn't charge them we'd all be dead anyway, and would we rather die cowards or heroes, and as if in answer a ball hit his sword—pang!—and knocked it out of his hand, but he cursed and grabbed it up and started running up the hill, so of course we had to charge after him. We couldn't let him be a braver fool than we were.

When we got to the top, the Rebs left their pits without firing a volley. We captured a few who didn't skedaddle quick enough. They had wheeled their guns back below the crest of the road and one of them had a busted axle, and we could have captured the lot, probably, but we were flanked on the right, so we had to hold to those pits while the infantry made a charge at them further up the ridge. We heard firing and cannonading up to the north and south till dark, and eventually an

Illinois regiment relieved us, and we were sent back down the road to report to General Pleasonton at Frederick.

Getting back up on Butterfly, I felt a pain in my foot and found my left boot full of blood. I don't know why I didn't feel it before. Two of the boys helped me get it off, and we found a ball or something had gone into my left boot and foot from the bottom, but I couldn't find a wound in the top—so I guess it's still in there. Shorty asked if I'd done anything to make the Devil mad enough to take a shot at me from below. The captain poured some turpentine over it and wrapped it up. He said I was lucky; it didn't look like a bone was crushed, and if I could ride, I should just carry my boot and not use the stirrup, and not say anything to the doctors because they would cut that foot right off. When we got back to Frederick, I tried not to let on I was hurt bad. I just hoped the ball, or whatever it was, wouldn't cause no trouble for a while. And luckily, too, I was given lighter duty for a few days.

26. I Will Hang You from the Highest Tree I Can Find!

At this point, Dear Reader, the cards turn up in a straight flush of magnificent coincidence, and I don't know what to say about it except that it surpasses the normal "lumpiness" of the universe. But we have Our Boy's honest-Injun word for it, and you can look up most of it. Here's what happens:

Huck, though gimpy from his wound and using a cane improvised from a cannon swab, has been promoted to sergeant (in Sam's place) and put on a detail helping to assign bivouac sites to Union regiments arriving on the Hagerstown Road near Frederick, Maryland, on the morning of 13 September, 1862, as McClellan concentrates his forces—still several days before the battle at Antietam Creek. The Twenty-Seventh Indiana Infantry, among the first to arrive, draws a meadow just outside town, along a fence line perfect for tent posts or firewood—a choice spot, except that a Confederate division had camped there a few days before. Prior tenants usually mean a lot of clean-up for the next occupants, and a chance for unpleasant—and unsanitary—surprises. But in this case, one of the surprises is pleasant.

I'd just showed Captain Kop where to put his camp, and he had a squad under a sergeant and corporal of F Company laying out the company street. I was leaning on my stick and talking to the captain while the men sized up fence rails for firewood or tent poles, and suddenly we hear a shout and there's a corporal waving a fistful of cigars in the air.

"Three of 'em!" he hollers. "Want one, Captain?" The captain smiled because that was a good sign. Cigars meant there'd likely been officers camped here, and they'd of been cleaner and maybe left even more valuable things behind. "And you oughta see what they're wrapped in!" hollers the corporal.

I started to limp over, but the captain says, "At ease, Sergeant. I'll go see what they've got."

He met the men and looked at the cigars, and smiled as he sniffed one to see how fresh it was. But then his face turned serious when he looked at the paper they were wrapped in. The men pointed to a spot next to the fence, and there was a bit of low talk I couldn't hear, and then the captain sends the two men off at a trot and comes back to where I was. He looked pretty serious now.

"Well, Sergeant, that *was* a find."

"You mean the cigars, sir?"

"No," he says. "I mean what was wrapped around them. It looked like marching orders from Lee himself—spells out who camps were and when, every unit in their whole blessed army. 'To General D.H. Hill,' it says. He must have been camped here. My God! What if it's the genuine article?"

"Does it look like the real thing?"

"Yes, it does. I suppose it *could* be a trick—left to send us on a goose-chase. Say, I should have showed it to you—since you were close to Lee before the war. Took his last name, even."

I said, "Well, I'm sure there are others that can check it, sir." But all I could think was: *Poor Harvey Hill.*

The captain looked off in the direction they'd gone and said, "Well, I've sent them to Colonel Cosgrove, and he'll probably send them on up the line."

Indeed he does. The good Colonel takes one look at the paper and goes straight to corps headquarters with the prize. And from corps it goes straight to McClellan, now in Frederick, and this is just what he needs to galvanize him. "Little Mac," as we know from Mexico, loves detail and procedure, and he sees this army—*his* army, after all, which *he* built—as a fine mechanism which it would be a shame to get banged up in a battle unless victory were more or less guaranteed. He thus has what Lincoln calls "the slows." He also has a credulous ear for reports of Rebel strength. Lee has 100,000, Jackson another 100,000. Stuart has 20,000 horse making for Baltimore….

But now, perhaps victory *is* guaranteed. Here, in these orders, he has the disposition of every major unit in the Rebel army—and Lee, however large his force, has split it several ways with utter temerity. Insulting temerity. As if McClellan, the Young Napoleon, were little danger to the great Lee. Well. He would see about that!

"Gibbon!" he exults, waving the paper at one of the XIIth Corps division chiefs, "Here is a paper with which, if I can't whip Bobby Lee now, I'll be willing to go home!"

This is his moment. Concentrated here at Frederick, he has caught the overconfident Lee in a mistake, spread out from the Pennsylvania border to Harper's Ferry. He is Napoleon at Castiglione, Washington at Trenton! Why, if the paper is genuine—what a stoke of luck, almost too good to be true!

Too good?

He strides to the door, calls out, "Thaddeus, get that damn telegraph working!" And, turning back, "Gibbon, go find Williams again. And get me a courier."

Later that evening, as the sun is setting, Our Boy and his company are preparing their own camp in a pasture on the other side of the road from Cosgrove's 27th Indiana and five or six other regiments arriving since. Just as Huck has about decided it is safe to use his improvised cane for roasting apples (but perhaps not safe to eat them—they seem a bit green yet, and he has not forgotten his illness in Winchester) three horsemen gallop up the road from town. In short order, Our Boy is on horseback, under guard, and on his way to army headquarters.

Huck is brought into what is likely the dining room of the house, with a nice table big enough to serve ten or twelve. The room is full of officers—at least two of whom are generals. Huck recognizes McClellan, of course, and John Pleasonton, the cavalry commander. There are maps spread out on the table and a good bit of smoke. A couple of the men have lit cigars, which, Huck notes with horror, they have been stubbing out on the cherry wood of the table and chairs. He remembers the Grangerfords' house and imagines the wrath such behavior would have invoked. Three cigars are in a neat row on the table, next to the found orders. Our Boy now knows why he is here.

"Well, Huckleberry, my boy! Do you recognize me? Good, good. At ease, man, at ease. It's been a while since Mexico, hasn't it? You're a sergeant, now. Done well, I hear."

"I guess so, yessir. Thank you."

"Gentlemen, I was this young man's lawyer once—when he was no more than fifteen." He was talking to the others, but he still was looking straight at me. "He'd got himself in quite a pickle, but I think we got him out of the worst of it. He's lucky he had a man like Robert Lee to look out for him, eh? Weren't you, Sergeant?"

"Yessir." I reckoned he was going to get around to asking me about the found orders and whether I thought they were genuine, but I tell you I was pretty surprised by the turn things took.

"Huckleberry, I'm afraid I must play the Devil's Advocate, this time." He reached down for the orders and held them up to me. "You recognize this paper, do you?"

I shook my head. "No sir." He looked surprised, so I said, "If that's the order that was found on the road today, I never saw it, sir. The captain told me about it. I remember the men held up some cigars—"

"These?"

"I don't know, sir. They never got close to me. The captain sent them off—"

"Bloss and Mitchell?"

"I don't know their names, sir."

"All right, but what do you remember about their being found?"

Well, he went on like this for a bit with me, and then the captain from the 27th. Then he questioned General Pleasonton. The whole business seemed to be about where exactly I was and what I'd been doing for the past four days.

Then he turned to me and said, "Sergeant, I'm going to have your foot un-wrapped. Yes—here and now. I'm sorry. We'll see that you get new dressings if needed—and cleaner ones."

So I sat down and a major took off the bandage, which was pretty dirty and caked with stale blood. It was stuck to the wound, and pulling on it hurt. I clamped my teeth and tried not to cry out. The wound looked pretty red and angry, but the foot wasn't swelled up as much as it was.

Finally, the general sort of harrumphed and said, "Well, Major, I guess we can eliminate that theory. There's no fakery here. Let's wash

and dress that thing. The young man has earned that at least. Now, Huckleberry—"

"Sir," the major put in, "he could have shot *himself* in the foot."

The general turned back to him. "From the *bottom*?" He laughed and so did the others. I didn't laugh. I just tried not to holler while the major doused the wound with spirits of camphor or something, but I'll tell you it hurt.

The general went on: "Sergeant, you are listed on the roster as a Lee. But in Mexico you were Huckleberry *Finn*. How comes this change? I understand you have reported yourself as a *kinsman* of the Rebel general."

"Yessir."

"Well, what is your relation?"

I took deep breath and says, "I'm his son, sir." Well, that caused a stir!

Then I told him how the general—he was just a major then—had adopted me not long after we left Mexico, and how it was a very fine thing he'd done since I didn't have no father of my own, you see, and it had helped me out of a bad spot. And I know he took it serious, too, even though I'd wrote him a letter saying I didn't want him to change his will or nothing.

Well, then McClellan leaned over to another officer and they whispered a bit. Then he said, "But you left the army. And then rejoined it again. Am I right?"

"Yes, sir. Early last year, when Colonel Lee took command of the First."

"But—did you ever live with him? As a son?"

"No, sir. I was never asked to."

It was quiet for a little bit while the general looked at me.

"Well, this is a strange tale, I have to say. Although what we've been able to check on—thanks to General Pleasonton here—looks true. Now, I would have said this Lee connection was fanciful, except for what I saw in Mexico. But I must ask you this, Sergeant: the general has a number of grown kinsmen—including sons—and every one of them, so far as I know, is in the Rebel service. Except for you. Why is that?"

Now I began to get a hint about what they were up to here. "Well—I really don't know, sir."

And I really didn't. And I guess I still don't. But I told the story about my last visit with Lee, about begging him to consider General Scott's offer and about the promises he made to me—to at least go see the general, and to not take the Rebel offer—and that led to some more whispering. I felt pretty strange, because I was sitting down and these officers were mostly standing up.

"And you've had no further communication with—with your father—since that day?"

"No, sir."

I said that right off—with no trouble—even though it was a lie. Maybe if your life is pretty much a lie like mine is, it gets to come easy. But as for the note I got—they *couldn't* know about it, with Sam dead, so why muddy the water?

But the general held the order up in front of me, for me to get a close look at now, and said, "Do you recognize the hand of this Major Chilton?"

I looked at the paper and my heart begun to beat hard. At the top it said "Headquarters, Army of Northern Virginia, Special Orders, No. 191" and it was addressed to "Major General D.H. Hill." That would be Professor Hill of Lexington, of course. The orders ended, "By command of Gen. R.E. Lee," and was signed by his adjutant, Major Chilton. And, of course, I recognized the hand very well because General Lee said Major Chilton had wrote the letter I got. I could see right away what they thought.

"Do you know the hand of this Major?" the general asked.

It was very quiet in the room.

"I never knew him, sir." (But of course I *did* know his hand. I couldn't admit that, though, because then I'd have to admit the letter, and I'd already denied *that*, so you see how one lie leads to another!) "But it sounds like General Lee. It's very clear and to the point."

"Yes, I had that same feeling. If it isn't by Lee, it's by someone who knows him very well." He stopped, then went on. "Now, Sergeant, I have to tell you that this find is a miraculous coincidence. Consider: the find occurs at the very spot where someone close to General Lee

happens to be on duty, with plenty of access to meadows and fence lines. You can see, I think, what someone might think. Can't you, Sergeant?"

"I guess," my heart really began to pound now, "they might think—that I'd wrote the order and put it there?"

"They might." The general nodded. "Or they might think you got the order elsewhere and left it where it was sure to *be* found. In fact, they might wonder why you didn't find it yourself, since you were up and down that fence line all morning. They might also wonder why that envelope—and those cigars—seem none the worse for being out in a field for three days. And, above all, they might wonder why a general like Lee, bold though he is, would cut his army into five little bunches so ripe for plucking that if we found out we'd move right in for the harvest." He looked up at the major as he finished. "They might wonder if it was a trap."

Then he paused again. The room was so quiet, you could hear a little shifting of boots, a cough, the tap of a man flicking cigar ashes into a cup. It was nothing like my "hearing" in Mexico, because there I never was really scared. Finally, I says, "Sir, I don't know if that order is real or not, but I swear I'm loyal to the Union, and I swear I never saw that paper before those men found it."

Then I took a deep breath and said what I knew I had to say: "But I—General, can I talk to you alone?" I don't know why I said *that*, because a dastardly thing done in a closet at midnight is as bad as one done in church on Sunday, as the widow used to say. And it wasn't really dastardly, I guess, but it felt bad, you know. Well, the general looked at me and raised his eyebrows and then said, "Gentlemen, that will be all. Leave a guard by the door." And the rest of them sort of shrugged and then walked out, one by one. The one he'd called Alpheus[15] said, as he left, "Save me one of them cigars, will you, George? My boys found 'em."

When we were alone, it really *was* quiet, and the general sat down across the table from me and waited. I pointed to the order lying on the table.

"General, what I said before is true, that I never knew this Major Chilton. But I *have* seen his hand. And that's it."

The general didn't seem surprised. He just looked at me and said "All right, Sergeant, tell us how." So I told him about being a prisoner for a while at Winchester and having the little note left for me. And I told him about who had wrote it.

Finally he nodded and said, "I guess you disposed of the letter. Or do you still have it?"

Well, I *should* have disposed of it. I was *told* to. But Heaven forbid I should ever do as I was told! "General," I says, "that's why I asked to talk to you by yourself. Because—well, I have the letter and I'll show it to you, but I wonder if you could promise me not to take it. You see, I feel rotten as it is. Like I've—I know it's my duty to show it, but—"

Well, he thought about that—and one thing I'll say for General McClellan is that he *does* think—and then he says. "Sergeant, I'll keep your secret as long as it does no harm to the Cause. My only purpose is to prove the order genuine. And time is not unlimited."

"Yes, sir." Of course I had it in my haversack along with my last one from Becky. He looked it over and then took up the order and placed it next to the note. Finally he looked back at me and pursed his lips, but still didn't say anything.

I started to get nervous, so I said, "So, you see, I do think it's the real thing, sir."

The general watched me for another second or two, and then he pushed General Lee's letter back across the table to me. As I took it, I couldn't help a sigh of relief. "Thank you, sir."

When he spoke again, he spoke very soft, almost to himself. "What a war this is." Then to me, still soft. "I'll tell you what *I* think, Huckleberry. I also think it's genuine. As it happens—here's another little miracle—on General Williams' staff there is a Major Pittman who happens to be an old Army friend of Chilton's, and he also recognizes the hand. There is now little doubt of that. The order could still be a trick, of course. We can't forget that. Now, I also believe you're a loyal man. Your record shows it, and so far everything you've said here has proven out—even the business about being captured and recaptured in Winchester. Yes, we know all about that. Still—I won't live by faith alone."

Then he stood up and straightened his blouse and spoke up louder. "You are under arrest, Sergeant, until this issue is resolved.

And it *will* be resolved, soon enough. If this order is genuine, young man, your—foster father, if that's what he is, has blundered, and we shall make him pay for it."

And then he raised his voice so it made me jump, and probably others out on the porch trying to listen in. "But if this *is* a trap, young man—if his troops are *not* where this order says they are—if this turns out to be a Rebel trick, and we suffer for it, and *you* had anything to do with it—I swear I will hang you from the highest tree I can find!"

And he brought his hand down on the table so hard the three cigars bounced in the air.

Well, the order does prove to be genuine, and even McClellan moves fast enough to give Lee a hard time. Lee gets his army back across the Potomac, but not before fighting to a bloody draw at Antietam. But Our Boy has little to do with it all, since he spends the next month under arrest in a loft in Frederick. True to his word, McClellan sends around a surgeon who allows that, yes, there is a ball or a piece of shell in his foot, he can feel it there—See? Just *there*—probably ricocheted off a rock, but they better not try to get it out now because it's so close to the joint, and since it looks to be healing up—maybe a cyst has formed around it—they'd best let it alone for now. After the war, if Huck survives, he should "come see me, and we'll give it a try." So Huck spends the time writing—and sketching the buildings he can see—till headquarters baggage is sent for and someone remembers him. By then, his foot is in good enough shape for duty, and he rejoins his regiment.

How the order got lost is still unknown. Hill goes to great lengths later to produce receipts for his own copy, which came straight from Jackson. Receipts can be forged, of course, and that is my theory: that the lost order *had* belonged to (as Huck put it) "poor Harvey Hill," and that after the war, with many eye-witnesses conveniently deceased, fakery became possible. But that's one mystery I'll let rest in peace.

Moreover, to this day, no one knows who smoked the cigars.

And that, Dear Reader, is what Huck Finn has done in the war—so far.

27. April 30: The Promise of a Right-Warm Time

Now let us return to the morning of April 30, 1863, with a riddle: What do you know that's lovely and inviting in season; full of pleasures quiet and unquiet, and also of dangers hidden and unhidden; and capable, in the right conditions, of bursting into ravenous flame?

Indeed, She is—but I am not talking about Woman. I am talking about the Wilderness.

The area along Scott's Run in Spotsylvania County, Virginia, in the spring, is not a true wilderness, of course, and it's not as hellish a setting for battle as you can imagine if you've been up the Amazon (or even the Dry Fork of the Brazos). But if you haven't, it'll do. Scott's Run rises just across the Orange Turnpike from Wilderness Church and runs right through the area. The name Wilderness is misleading: had the area really been untouched by the ax, it would have huge oaks, hickories, and poplars, with their canopy keeping underbrush to a minimum. You could see through those woods for fifty yards or more—shoot through them and march through them, at least in columns, and take shelter behind those trees. But this "wilderness"—more than a hundred square miles—has been cut over and burned and cut over again, to fuel nearby furnaces for low-grade metal and charcoal. So these woods are new and green, thick with second-growth pine, sumac, and black gum, and choked with honeysuckle and laurel and greenbrier near the streams. And by May any low areas are boggy and buggy, full of hungry young ticks and chiggers and snakes and poison ivy, thorn and thistle, and anything else hostile to human flesh. And stuffing those wool trousers into your wool socks won't help much—just make you hotter and give fleas and lice a place to lay eggs.

And lines of battle are nearly impossible, with officers and flags often out of sight, and once firing begins enemies and comrades may be visible only by rifle flash—and friendly flashes look just like unfriendly ones. But there's little real cover: the second growth stops you from seeing, but it doesn't stop shot and shell—which go right through saplings and into your groin, shattering your hip and sending you straight into shock, and when you fall, nobody knows where. Immobilized now, you may discover that these woods burn rather well. What with the late spring (two snows in April!), the trees are not yet in full leaf, but after two warm dry weeks, the winter brush has dried enough to kindle from powder flashes, and the young pines will explode into flame. And if you can't move when those flames lick their way into that caisson full of shells next to you or the cartridge box on your belt.... Believe me, if you *have* a loaded weapon within reach, you should blow your brains out first.

What's worse than such a Purgatory? Well, how's this: in spring it's beautiful. Bluebells and phlox and yellow jonquils and honeysuckle blooming where there's sun, and where there's less sun there is laurel, pink and white, and white cherries and lavender redbuds, and orchids and lilies here and there, and the fresh spring smell of soil and leaf. If Dante didn't say it, he should have: Beauty plus Irony equals Purgatory.

Walking these woods decades later, it's hard to believe what went on here, hard to believe that vine-covered hump there by the creek may be the remains of a cannon or caisson instead of a stump, that this half-buried hunk of metal in the stream bank is not a plow blade but an unexploded shell, and that that white stick pointing up from the earth isn't part of an old deer kill, but a human rib.... Hard to believe.

But, as it happens, Our Boy is right here—as the Union Bureau of Military Information sends operatives dashing up and down the by-ways looking for him—and he's writing away:

Well, it's the last day of April—and may *this* May be more promising to our Cause than the last! It's warm enough now that it's hard to believe there was snow on the ground three weeks ago. And the promise of a right warm time to come in other ways, by all the signs. We slept in our saddles last night, and some not at all, because of the Rebel cavalry pitching into us constant. I feel sorry for the poor horses and mules who've had just as little sleep. Some had to ride out on picket and eat with their feed bags on while they rode. But this afternoon we're relieved for a while, and we're here by Wilderness

Run [Scott's Run, probably][16], **so I've watered Butterfly and give her some oats and tied her up to graze on the grass by the stream bank. The new grass isn't good for them, but a little won't hurt and it's like a reward for being up all night. Meanwhile, to kill the varmints in my socks and trousers—all collected just this week!—I'm soaking them in thinned turpentine, which the surgeon gave me for my foot, and then rinsing them in the run, which is COLD, I can tell you, and doesn't work very well. Also I'm going to rewind my foot, and the cold water does help that. And then I'll try to get some shut-eye, in spite of the firing off to the left.**

He's an old trooper now: tenderfeet talk strategy, but veterans talk supply. And your horse comes first of all. A cavalry mount needs twelve pounds of grain a day during hard service, and the same amount of hay or forage, not to mention water—at least ten gallons, depending on weather—and where there are horses there must be forage, plus wagons full of feed and spare tack and horseshoes and blacksmiths with mobile smithies…Cavalry does not come cheap!

By now, those looking for Huck know what unit he's in and where it is, more or less. But "more or less" isn't good enough in this country. After crossing at Germanna, Huck's outfit spends most of the night of the 29th and the day of the 30th along Scott's Run, not heavily engaged, but getting little rest either, what with Fitz Lee's cavalry poking around, trying to find the infantry, maybe pick off a prisoner or two and find out what's up.

I tell you we're mighty surprised to hear reports of things being "pretty quiet" along the line—when every man of us has been ordered back and forth through the brush till we're all tired as sled mules. And we didn't know much more about *where* we were: some said Scott's Run was over there, and some that it was over the other way.

But in late afternoon a squadron from the 8th come in to relieve us, and we pulled back to the road for a two-hour rest before supper. It was our first rest in more than 24 hours and I tried to sleep, which I can usually do even in the saddle, but I couldn't somehow, so I'll catch up on this. Supper was fried beef, beans, and corn biscuits, our first cooked rations in a while, too, with a couple oranges thrown in—we

must be making headway down in Florida! We're not far from the inn, but we'll be strung out in the woods for pickets. The horses are held behind, though, because they need the rest even more than we do.

Well, I thought I might have more time to write, but before long we got reports of enemy in the woods and some firing broke out. Now I know, like as not, some of that's from us firing at each other. So I'm going to find a place to set up that's covered a bit from *both* directions!

Well, wouldn't you know, after not being able to sleep when it was peaceful earlier, now in the middle of all this wild firing I would go to sleep. It was dark now and quiet and getting a bit of a chill when I woke up, and I cussed myself for falling asleep—probably get busted back to corporal, and deserve it, too. I picked up the rifle and journal and snuck back toward the little shed my men was using as a picket post, but there wasn't anybody there now, and I worked on what my story would be when I got back to the line. But pretty soon I heard a rifle report from across the field and then a ball whines overhead, clipping leaves as it went. I dropped behind a stump in front of the shed and stuffed the journal in my jacket and felt to be sure it was in its pocket. We've all heard of balls being stopped by folded love letters and testaments and such. Well, I wasn't sure letters from Becky and Aunt Sally were that powerful, but I judged the journal was worth a try.

And just when I was about to turn for the shed, there came a voice behind me. "Sh!" it said, and I just about wet myself. When I turned, all I could see was a tall shadow in the doorway with the moonlight behind it. Then I heard the cock of a hammer, and the shadow said, "Just be still, Sergeant, and everything'll be fine." Well, when I heard that voice, I knew right enough things *wouldn't* be fine again, at least for a good while!"

"Jesus," I whispered. "Is that—"

"Well, shucks!" says the voice. "I guess if you recognize me it's no use being mysterious. Come on back here in the shed, Huck. And I guess you better pull in your gun, too, but don't raise it. You're covered."

Well, the face was even darker when we ducked into the shed.

"Tom Sawyer, what in Sam Hill are *you* doing here in the middle of a war?" I says.

The voice laughed. "Well, I might have asked you the same. But as it happens I'm *looking* for you."

"For me? Why, on earth? And why have you got a gun on me?"

He squatted, still between me and the moonlight leaking through the chinks in the shed, and struck a match to light a cigar. As he puffed it to life I could see that it was Tom, even with less hair on his top and more on his chin. He sat easy now, with his legs crossed Indian style, with a big double-barrel pistol on his knee, held easy but with both its "eyes" looking my way. It looked like a sawed-off shotgun with a pistol grip. I'd seen that kind of thing in the West, and it could cut you in half with one barrel, as they said, and dig your grave with the other.

"Nice piece, ain't it? Made from a sawed-off Enfield," he says.

I asked what he was about, since the captain was going to be checking the line any minute.

"You needn't worry about your captain, at least for a while. The Rebs will give him enough else to think about." And just like that there was firing out in the woods to our left and I could hear hollering and crashing in the brush. Tom put up his hand, cocked his head and nodded slightly as if admiring the sound.

"The Rebs?" I said. "What do you have to do with them?"

"Well, let's just say I get around. Covering the story, you might say." He blew a smoke ring to the side and looked at me, tilting his head as if considering me afresh. He held out the cigar a bit toward me and at first I thought he was offering me a smoke, but I guess he was just using it for the light. I wasn't really afraid of him, but somehow that gave me the fantods.

"Well," he said, "you're the same old Huck, I should judge. And you *are* a Sergeant, I see. Got respectable—Huckleberry *Lee*, of all things. I got to hand it to you, Huck. You don't have to take a back seat to *nobody* in spinning stories. It's just like old times, in a way," he said, and reached in his coat pocket and pulled out a big brown envelope, which he put down nice and gentle on the leaves in front of him without saying anything about it. "I mean it's a real war and all, this time. This ain't no Sunday school picnic, and we don't have to pretend to be a robber gang. We're real ones now." I asked what he meant by that, and he said, "That's all these armies are, you know. Just armed gangs crashing around the countryside. The folks in those pirate stories would feel right at home."

Well, this was strange talk, but it didn't surprise me that he would have a philosophical view of things. I asked him if he was in trouble, and he laughed: "Why, yes, I am, Huck! I'm in the same trouble you're in. I'm trying to save the Union."

"The Union! Well, I should of thought taking one of its soldiers prisoner like this was a strange way to go about it. But you're not in uniform. What are you, a sutler?"

"A sutler! Well, I've played the sales angle on occasion, Huck, but no, that's not what I'm about." He tapped the envelope with a finger of his cigar hand. "I'm about this."

"What's this?"

"This is news, Huck. I think when you look in this envelope, you'll see a couple of things—one, that there's somebody in authority around here that knows a bit about your past, and, two, that you can serve the Cause very well by getting up to Army Headquarters with me as quick as possible to talk to this person. You might also consider that a friend of yours will be in a mess of trouble if you don't." I said I couldn't go anywhere without orders, but he just pointed down and said, "Open the envelope, Huck."

Well, I did, and I saw two things, one a gold dollar with a "H" scratched on the back, like I'd done to my half of the gold Tom and me found. He'd put a "T" on his, and so I guessed he got mine now, too, and I wasn't much surprised. When I looked at it, Tom says, "I got it from somebody else in the family that wanted you to have it." Before I could ask who, he pointed at the other thing in the envelope, which was a post card, stamped "W. POINT NY," and that made my hair stand on end. The date was about the time I'd left. Then I read the message on the back.

"All right, Tom," I finally said. "Tell me what you want me to do."

28. Right Where We Want Him (April 30: 4 P.M.)

"Quite a view, eh?" says Sharpe, leaning to make himself heard over the whooping in the yard between the Chancellorsville Inn and the gate at the turnpike. Sid doesn't know if the colonel means the view of the fields beyond the turnpike, or the ruckus in the yard.

"It's got a nice porch," says Sid. They are sitting on one end of a rolled-up rug pulled out of the foyer to make it easier to carry crates in for an army headquarters. The noise in the yard comes from officers of the XIIth and Vth Corps and the general staff. They are in a fine mood: they have stolen a march on the famously swift Lee and Jackson, and self-congratulations are in order. "We're on Lee's flank, and he doesn't even know it!" They are, in fact, where Sid told Tom they would be by now: behind the rebel army (still mostly at Fredericksburg) with a huge force, already thirty thousand, soon to be fifty or sixty, with just as many opposite the town. Lee has only about sixty thousand altogether, though as usual he's doing what he can to create the impression of more ("deserters" stumbling into Union lines, for example, with tales of vast reinforcements).

Every now and then a white face is visible at one of the windows upstairs, from which the Chancellor women shout occasional insults at the Yankee Huns plundering their premises and, they feel sure, plotting against their virtue.

After a while, two generals tromp out onto the porch, letting a screen door slam behind them.

"But why here, Harry? This is only half way!"

Sid knows that voice: it's Meade. The other, then, would be Henry Slocum of the XIIth.

"Beats me, George. But you know my orders."

Meade waves off to the east. "So we're just going to wait here? We could take both roads—you take the plank and I'll take the turnpike or the other way around if you prefer, and we come up in his rear while Sedgwick comes across in his front. Damn it, they can't fight all of us at the same time. But if we sit and—"

"There they come!" shouts a voice from the yard. "Look!" And there's a commotion in the road as a cavalcade struggles through the clutter of wagon teams, stragglers, and orderlies. The color sergeant bearing the guidon of the army general staff is followed by thirty or forty horsemen and a couple of carriages.

Slocum shades his eyes and says, "Right when he said, too."

Sid pulls out his watch and notes the time: Five minutes past four.

"Time to meet the Family, I guess," Sharpe says, pulling down his jacket and brushing dust off. For a rainy morning, it has dried out considerably.

Out at the gate, an officer dismounts as two orderlies take his horse. He is short and a bit portly, but fit enough looking—clean-shaven on the chin, even a bit boyish in appearance but for the graying sideburns sprouting from under his wide-brimmed campaign hat. A cheer goes up from the men in the road. Returning salutes, he strides toward the house, smiles at Meade and Slocum waiting on the porch, then removes his gloves, turns, and waves at the yard, and at that a tremendous cheer goes up, along with a number of hats. "Hurrah for Old Joe!" and that sort of thing.

He turns back to the men on the porch and shakes their hands. "Congratulations, Slocum. Well, done. A fine march."

"The credit's yours, General. Excellent plan. Promising start."

Slocum squints off toward the southeast, and Meade adds: "Let's hope we finish just as well."

Hooker turns to him with a broad grin, hardly able to contain himself, and smacks Meade on the shoulder.

"Cheer up, George! We've got Bobby Lee right where we want him He has to run or come at us on our own ground. I tell you, he's the legitimate property of this army!"

Meade pulls his hat off, wipes his balding pate, and nods, but doesn't smile.

"Well, come on, men," says Hooker. "Couch will be here shortly. Let's go in and see if—" but Sid doesn't hear the rest, as Hooker, Meade, and Slocum go in followed by five or six others.

Sharpe leans back against the porch rail, lights a cigar. "Did you see Butterfield?"

"No. And *he* said four o'clock, too." *If he loses interest so will Hooker.*

Sharpe puffs impassively. Sid walks to the rail on the other side of the porch. Through the window he can see Hooker and his generals smoking and talking. Hooker seated at a table, pokes at a map. The mood looks good. In the yard, there are clinks and shouts where two lieutenants have driven bayonets in the ground and are pitching horseshoes. Horseshoes! As if they were at a clam-bake. As if the battle were over. He walks back past the window.

"You trust Tom, don't you, Colonel?"

Sharpe flicks ashes over the rail onto the rose bushes below. "Only so far. Too much of an adventurer. But I trust my man in Jackson's camp. And if he thinks Tom's gone wrong, he's got all he needs to get him hung—by either side." He looks at Sid, and winks. "In fact, Major, if it goes wrong enough, there's plenty enough majors—and colonels, too—that nobody'd miss—"

The door opens, and Hooker's generals emerge with a flurry of hat-donning and glove-pulling and a clanking of side-arms. Alone on the porch, the commander calls to one of the departing officers, "Strong works, now, *strong* ones, there's plenty of time till dark!" He waves his hat at the yard, gets another cheer, and then turns toward Sid and Colonel Sharpe. Still smiling. "Colonel...Major...please come inside, gentlemen."

The room is warm, stuffy with smoke and afternoon sun. Valises and maps and field glass cases are strewn on boxes and tables and overstuffed chairs along with the ubiquitous cigars. Hooker offers his hand.

"Major Sawyer, is it? I'm pleased. General Butterfield speaks very highly of—of you both! Well. Please." He gestures to a couple of straight-backed chairs next to an end-table where there are some maps and pencils and a compass. Hooker plops down on a nearby sofa.

"Don't worry about our nosey hostesses, men. They're well guarded upstairs." As if to confirm, boots are heard on the stairs, and General Marsena Patrick descends—neat as a banker now, except for the bandaged ear, black hair combed back, full moustache trimmed and waxed. He looks like an intelligence chief—in spite of what Sid gathers is Sharpe's mixed opinion of him. Sharpe considers Butterfield "Hooker's brains." Patrick leans silently against the banister, waiting for the commanding general to continue.

"Now, General. You and your people, please tell me again why I shouldn't push right down the road toward Fredericksburg this evening. Five miles would clear Banks' Ford. Why shouldn't I do that?"

"Well, as you know—George, brief the general on our status." The illusion of efficiency dies.

Sharpe clears his throat. "Because, General, we need to bring Lee out of town toward us, so we can get at him."

"You mean bring our forces to bear on his." Still smiling.

"Well, yes, sir, but I meant on him *personally*."

Hooker nods. This is not news to him.

"And where are we in this plan?"

"Well, sir, Stoneman and his cavalry are astride the Virginia Central, threatening Hanover Junction. Tomorrow they'll make for Telegraph Road and can receive messages from our…operatives."

"What messages? What operatives?"

"Well, sir, as you know, we have agents in the Rebel rail service and…some others within their lines nearby. We can signal Stoneman to move up behind Lee when our agents report him in the most advantageous position."

"Advantageous. For…"

"For targeting him, sir."

"Targeting."

"Yes, sir. For capture, hopefully."

Hooker nods, but the smile has pretty much wasted away. "And of course, if he tried to escape, you might have to shoot him."

"Well, yes, sir. But I should think he's more valuable as a prisoner."

Hooker leans back, his fingers drumming on the night stand by a full bottle of what looks to Sid like pretty good Scotch. He purses his lips.

"All right. And how would we know where our 'target' was? Your 'operatives,' I assume?"

"Yes, sir."

"So, they'd send word to you, and you'd send word to me…and we'd send word to agents in the RF&P to send the word to Stoneman, and he rides Hell for leather up to…wherever you happen to know Our Man is going to be. Is that it, Colonel?"

Sid sighs at the sound of the whole thing.

"Well, yes—" Sharpe nods, takes a puff on his cigar. "Except that we have Averell's cavalry a lot closer, upstream, where he can come in from the west. He'll be here tomorrow. And you *could* give us authority earlier and save some steps."

Hooker is silent.

"Look, General—even that way, I know it sounds like a long shot. And it is, but it kind of goes along with what you plan to do anyhow—forcing Lee into a risky move. Even if it doesn't work out, all it takes is waiting here twenty-four hours or so. If Lee comes out after us, we'll be dug in for him, just not as close to town. And you've got Sedgwick there to keep a lot of his strength pinned down. And just imagine what mischief a division or two of cavalry in their rear will cause, even if they don't bag Our Man."

Hooker nods, drums his fingers, then smiles. "And if they *do*? Jackson takes command. Just what we want!"

Sharpe pauses for another puff, then: "Unless we get Jackson, too."

Hooker blinks. "Well, now! You think they'll just ride around together, all bunched up for us?"

"Actually—yes, sir, we think that *is* what they will do. At least that's what we've seen. They have that kind of a bond—to our detriment. They may not sleep together," (a chuckle goes around) "but they'll not be far apart, at least at times."

"And you have agents close to both?"

"Yes, sir."

Hooker looks away, out the window, his fingers still now. Then, almost to himself he says, "If we have men that close to them…why not just shoot them both now, and save us the trouble?"

"Well," Sharpe sighs, "we do care about our agents' safety, sir. And—well, *they* might not be willing to go that far. Remember, they had to *be* pretty close to the men in question to *get* that close to them. Of course, lots could still go wrong."

Hooker looks back quickly. "Yes, it could. And all we'd lose is a lot of cavalry—and the initiative!" Sharpe is silent. "Well, what's the latest? From your agents?"

"Well—we expect an important report later tonight."

Hooker thinks about it. "All right, we wait till morning. But we'll need some results by then to wait any longer. And remember: we'd really like to *see* one or two of these 'operatives.'" (He turns to Patrick) "General—please see these men disposed for the evening close by, in one of these outbuildings, say. And set the watch for the Mayor. Be sure the passwords are clear."

The Mayor? Sid wonders as they leave the parlor. *Who in Hell is that?*

Says Sharpe, as if reading his mind: "Another officer, Sid. A ranking officer."

29. Honorable Mischief (1 May: 12:30 A.M.)

He wakes with a hand on his shoulder—too gentle to be the colonel, reminds him of his mother or his aunt waking him for school. He looks up to see the young Vth Corps courier, the one from Missouri.

"Major, sorry to wake you, but the general asked me to—"

"That's all right, Lieutenant, what time is it?" He gropes under the cot for his watch.

"A little after midnight, sir. The general said—"

"General Butterfield?"

"General Patrick, sir."

"Still no Butterfield, eh? I thought we'd get some rank here this time."

"There's plenty of rank, sir. If you'll come with me—"

The major is mostly dressed already, having expected to be roused—but as he picks his way after the lieutenant in the moonlight to the low stable-barn across the road from his bunk in the smokehouse, he feels un-presentable—rumpled, unwashed, and by now smelling like a rotten side of smoked pork. All is dark in the tavern's main house, and it's quiet except for the distant mournful sound of what seems to be—of all things—a bagpipe. But lanterns can be seen in the barn and several horses tied to a rail near the road or held by aides. In the moonlight Sid can see salutes and hear some low talk. A dark form near the road beckons.

"Hope you got a bit of sleep, because you may not get any more for a while."

It's Sharpe. A carriage is parked in an open stall—the two-horse kind, with brass appointments and coal-oil head-lamps. Did that mean—

"Tom's here? He said he just had a trap, but that thing sure beats—"

"That's not Tom's. Now here: look this over." Sharpe hands him a piece of ruled note-paper. Sid reads it while Sharpe fusses over him, pulling his blouse down and his belt around, brushing some straw off his shoulders—as if the major were a schoolboy about to address the class.

"But Colonel, this just says he has 'found Our Boy' and will be 'at the Family house by morning' he says. Why not now? Why not tonight?"

"I'm not sure, but he sent separate word to me that he and Huck had run into a bit of 'mischief' he said, and it might take a little while to 'get out of it'—whatever that means. But he assured me it wouldn't be any later than morning."

Sid just looks at him. *Morning!*

"Now, Sid, I know what you're thinking, but Tom'll come through. He may be in it for the adventure, but he's *in* it, I'd say. He's got *three* messages through to us, you know. Now come on and play nice with the rest of the Family. Up you go."

"We're not meeting here?"

"Nope. Not secure enough."

Sharpe drives, with Sid and the young lieutenant in the back.

A nice coach, Sid notes. Real springs, and a nice, matched team.... You could almost go back to sleep in it. When they turn down the U.S. Ford road, the destination is clear: back across the river. He hopes there's a bridge by now. There is. Pontoons solid as macadam.

Good for the Vermonters.

In the front room of the farm house several officers stand or sit—Hooker, Patrick, Pleasonton, a couple Sid doesn't recognize, and—finally—Butterfield, looking trim and dour, like a chief of staff. But no Tom. Seated on a couch with one leg propped up on a settee is an old man with a considerable paunch. A dark blue army duster covers the shoulder bars, if any, but a general's campaign hat is on the couch beside him. The white-whiskered face looks familiar, but Sid can't place it. The man looks at least seventy.

"This isn't Our Boy, is it?," rasps the old officer, pulling on a pair of spectacles and squinting at Sid. "I think I'd remember the fellow from Mexico." (*Mexico!*)

"No, sir," says Hooker, "this isn't the man, but—"

"But I understood he *was* to be here—otherwise I fail to see why my presence was—"

"Colonel Sharpe, perhaps you could fill in the general on what we expect."

"Yes, sir. General, may I introduce Major Sid Sawyer of the bureau of Military Information, whose work has done much to provide us this opportunity. Major, as you may know, General Scott is. . .an important official."

Sid's stomach does a flip flop. *Winfield* Scott? The U.S. Army's commanding general! So that's who the "Mayor" is! (Actually, the top general now is Henry Halleck, but Scott, though retired, is an important advisor, and many still think he's in charge—apparently including Sid.)

Scott questions Sid closely, mainly looking for confirmation that certain people are in fact who they purport to be.[17] He's less interested in the details. When the major gets to what he knows about the last meeting between Lee and his "son," Scott nods at Huck's guesses about offers of command. Sid is relieved when Scott doesn't ask him to produce Huck's letter—because of course he no longer has it.

"So they'll be delayed till morning, you say?" asks Scott.

"Yes, sir—but maybe not that long. Tom's nearby, in—"

"Surely a man in one of our units couldn't be that hard to find. I wonder if he and this other Sawyer—this half-brother of yours—are up to something." Then, turning to Hooker, "Will this not delay your campaign, General?"

"Why, I suppose we have to wait till dawn now anyhow. But not much longer—I'd like to get into more open country, you know. Still, I'd like to give it a while. I'll say, it surely would be a great blow for us, wouldn't it?"

"It surely would. The country would see it as a victory, almost by itself. Well, see here, gentlemen—" Scott says to Sid and Sharpe, wincing as he shifts his great weight. "Damn this leg—I don't know if it's the gout or the carriage. I'd forgot how bad the roads are in the South—but even if the two of you can vouch for Our Boy, this Tom fellow's word is all—" Just then there's a bit of commotion outside: a horse nickers, there are steps on the porch, and an aide sticks his head in, motions to Sharpe.

Outside, another carriage has pulled up in the lane next to the stable, just a covered trap, its panting horse being tied to the gate post as the driver leans down in the lantern light and tips his hat.

"Howdy, Gentlemen! Hope I'm in time for the family portrait?"

"But where's Huck, Tom? And what's this 'mischief' you—"

"*Honorable* mischief, Major. Perfectly honorable. And Huck's right here. But you'll have to help me with him. He's heavier than he looks."

Sid grabs a lantern from the gatepost and holds it up—and there in the rack behind the driver's seat is the recumbent form of—yes!—older of course, but indubitably Huck, and in uniform, too, Sergeant's stripes and all, but inert and deathly pale. *Deathly*—

"Tom, what's wrong with him? He's not—is he asleep?"

"Well, sort of—easy there! Just a bit of chloroform, boys. Enough to make him comfortable, you know—till I figured things out. Also the foot needed a little work. That *was* the plan, wasn't it?"

"How long till the man awakens?" It's a voice from inside the house, a deep, resonant voice Sid doesn't recognize, but it carries further than the others, and he doesn't hear the answer. Tom and a surgeon are re-bandaging Huck's foot—adding extra blood here and there—and that hurts enough that the patient is already beginning to respond.

"Looks like he's coming around." It's the deep voice again, and Sid looks up to see a tall figure in the doorway—one of the cloaked figures he had seen back against the wall.

"Major," (it's Butterfield this time) "the Mayor would like to speak to Sergeant Lee for a few minutes—alone. As soon as he's roused, you and the colonel are dismissed."

"General," says the deep voice, "please see the colonel and—and these other fine men—well bestowed close by. I shan't be long."

The only source for what happens next is (once again) the journal:

I was groggy and I retched once or twice. The only other time I felt this sick was when I woke up out of the fever at Winchester. I asked a question or two of Colonel Sharpe and Tom, but they said don't talk, just lay easy, and they picked up my blanket with me on it and carried me into the house.

When I saw all the officers I started to stand up, but I didn't when I found my foot was hurting again, and I had a start when I see *why.* Tom said don't worry, the blood was just for "realism." But he said I'd have a better chance to pass for wounded if I really *was.*

"You didn't shoot me again, did you?" I asked.

And he said, "No, but I had to make it look like I had. I never seen—"

Then one of the officers says, "Thank you all. Just leave the man here with me for a while alone."

And then the others all say yes, sir, and go on out, and the last one

out—Hooker, I think—says, "Please don't expose yourself needlessly, Mr. President. We'll be in the parlor if you need anything."

Well, I looked closer at the man under the hood to see if that "President" business wasn't just some kind of code, but when he turned back and held his hand down to me I got a good look at his face, and it sure did look like the pictures.

"Sergeant, let's see if you *can* stand." And I tried, but I was still pretty wobbly, and I set back down hard. When I started to get up again, he said "No, don't. Let me pull you out here onto the porch. We don't want any eavesdroppers, you see."

So he reached down and pulled my litter like a sled—I was surprised how strong he was—out onto the back porch, which faced east where the moon was well up now, and occasionally we could see a rifle flash way off south of the river and hear a report or two. He squatted down beside me and looked off in that direction. He kept the hood of the cape up, but I could see his chin whiskers from the side.

"How do you feel, young man? I mean the foot. Will it bear weight tomorrow?" I said I thought so, maybe not for a full day's march, but a mile or two is all I should need it for. Then he sat down with his legs over the edge of the porch. "Huckleberry, I did not need to come down here tonight. General Scott could attest to anything that needed verifying, and General Hooker and his staff are…quite capable. But I have made a number of such trips, often in secret, because…well, I like to get the feel of things, and I like to show my concern for those involved. Because I *am* concerned. Do you know who I am?"

"I think so, sir. They called you 'Mr. President.' And you do look like the pictures."

"You're observant. That's good. And you're right. I am the man who has sent thousands of brave fellows like yourself to their graves—men whose fathers and mothers loved them—and I'll keep doing it as long as I have to. You must understand that I am prepared to risk your life, Huckleberry. Are you?" He was a little higher, but I was propped up on my elbow now, so our faces weren't far away. I just nodded, and he went on, "You are willing to serve as a confidential agent—a spy—for what?"

"For the Union, sir."

"For the Union."

"Yessir." This reminded me of my "hearing" with General McClellan, and I was nervous, but somehow the president gave me confidence, almost like—come to think of it—like the way General Lee did.

"You were close to General Jackson in Lexington, weren't you? Lived with him, I hear."

"For a while, Yessir."

"He's on the other side now, Sergeant."

"I'm a soldier, sir. I know what that means."

He nodded. "And if you met him on the field of battle, you could shoot him down—without remorse?"

"Yessir—well, maybe with some remorse."

He smiled. "That's to your credit. Do you love him?"

"Sir?"

"You admire him, at least?"

"Well—yessir." I had to chuckle at that, even though it hurt my chest. "He had some strange habits. But I believe he was a good teacher. And he was very kind to me. I know General Lee thought very highly of him."

He paused for a moment. Then he looked away toward the river. "You've known General Lee for a long time, haven't you—Huckleberry, is it?"

"Yessir. Since Mexico. Almost fourteen years."

"Fourteen years!"

"Yessir."

"Does he love you?"

"Sir?" All this talk of love was making me nervous. "Well, I don't know, sir. I guess he cares about me. He adopted me, after all."

"Yes. So I hear. Tell me about the last time you saw General Lee."

So, I told him about going to see the colonel at Arlington and the promises he made to me before he went to see General Scott. He nodded as if he'd heard of that.

"Well! It's too bad you couldn't prevail upon him to accept our offer."

"I'm sorry, sir."

"No, no, it's not your fault these things are the way they are. But if he's the man I think he is, then he *still* loves you. And I'm sure you love him."

I was quiet for a minute. I didn't know why he was telling me all this. Maybe he's testing me, I thought, so I said, "Mr. President, almost the last thing Colonel Lee—General Lee—said to me was that I must always do my duty, no matter how hard it was. And this is hard, sir. This is very hard." He just looked at me, so I kept on going. "You see, sir, the Army took me in when I hadn't a home, so the Union is the only real family I ever had. The *last* thing the colonel said to me was that I should pray, but—Mr. President,"I pointed at the furled flag on the corner of the porch) "that flag there is all I got for a church. And the only prayer I know is to do the best I can for it—if that makes any sense."

He nodded. "Yes, it does, Huckleberry. It does. And now that I am satisfied that you are…who you are, let me ask if you…do you have a sweetheart, a mother, or…."

"No, sir, not really."

"Not really? No one?"

Well, I said I only had a sister back in Missouri, but no sweetheart except a girl I knew back in Mexico, and he asked me if I'd heard from her and knew where she was now, and I said I thought California, but I hadn't heard much, and he nodded like he expected it. Then I kind of took a chance and asked him, since he was the president and all, could he maybe help me get in touch with somebody like that, way out in the West, and he smiled again and said, "Well, even a president doesn't have a magic wand, but I'll promise you this, Sergeant. I will certainly use what resources I do have to help you, if we both—certainly when this conflict is over—I will do what I can."

"Thank you, sir."

"Wherever she is, son, I am certain she would want you to do your duty. And General Lee would, too, you know. And I believe in a way they would *both* be proud of you." Then he patted me on the knee and said,"Well, you must get some sleep tonight, Sergeant. I hope whatever other tests you face are easier than being quizzed like this by stern old men." Then he reached down and squeezed my hand.

"Good luck, Huckleberry. *My* prayers, for what they're worth, are with you."

I thanked him, and I couldn't help asking: "Did I pass the quiz, sir?"

He chuckled and said, "Yes, you did, son! With flags a-flying. Now let's get you back inside."

But as he drug me back in all I could think about was my Butterfly, and not the horse neither, and whether I'd ever see her again and hold her in my arms, and I wasn't thinking of the mission or nothing else for a while but only her and trying to picture her face, and if there was a boy what would that mean, and sleep sure wasn't in the cards, now that the sleeping salts was wearing off. But of course, sooner or later as I lay there waiting for morning I did think about what I had to do, and I said to myself: *I bet I'm the only fellow alive that's been called "son" by both Robert E. Lee and the President of the United States. And I'm a-going to have to make one or the other very sorry he ever done it.*

30. May 1: Just Like Old Times

"What're you looking at?"

There's a fog over the river as the bridge crew gets back to work. Even through binoculars, the shapes down below are dim and vague. But the sounds are strangely crisp—wood and metal, low commands, curses.

"See for yourself," says Major Sawyer, and he hands Huck the glasses.

"What are they doing?"

"Repairing a bridge."

"Yeah, but—" Huck hands back the glasses—"They crossed yesterday, didn't they? All three corps—the Vth, XIIth, IInd—or so I heard."

"You're a good listener."

"Don't worry, Sid." Grinning. "I'm on *your* side, remember?"

But to Sawyer it feels like West Point all over again: the winsome smile, masking…something. And having to work with the fellow, following the lesson, making sure he does his homework, but when push comes to shove, who knows? And he'd just been about to take the plunge, too, bring up that business at the Point, maybe apologize, and…*But he calls me 'Sid,' for God's sake! I'm a major!*

Huck reaches for a stalk of wild onion on the bank where they sit. "I made my choice in the West," he says. "For good." With a pen knife he makes a few quick slits. The tang of onion rises in the damp air. There's a high squeak as he sucks gently through it, then a lower tone as he breathes out. "Not as good as bamboo or willow." He wiggles the slits with his fingers and gets a bit of a tune going.

"You mean about the Union? That long ago—in Mexico?"

Huck laughs. "Not *that* long ago. I meant in Texas. By then any fool could see it coming."

"Did you get that horse in Mexico?"

"Butterfly? No, she's a Texas mustang. Lots better than those thoroughbreds they sent from Kentucky. I'll allow they did make a pretty picture. There was a different color mount for each troop, believe it or not. But they wouldn't even eat the grass in Texas. Honest to God, we had to ship oats in for 'em."

"She's big for a mustang. And that's a strange name. Does she chase after butterflies? Is she flighty or—?"

"No, no. I just named her after somebody. It was a long time ago. But she's worth it."

Sawyer wonders: *The girl or the horse?* And now he remembers the letter, but he wants to get to business first. "Well, look, Huck. She'll be fine—the horse, that is. I'll see to it. Now—are you sure you have it straight? Let's run through it again."

And so they do. But why not other topics? Here's this fellow Sid has known all his life, this fellow with whom the angelic Becky seems infatuated—and Sid doesn't want to talk about *that*?

Well, no—he doesn't. Men don't. This is something women have a hard time with. Two men, you see, can be after the same woman, and they can go build bridges or cut cane or sell real estate, or whatever, and then go out to a bar and get drunk and tell stories and stagger home with their arms over each other's shoulders, and The Subject just never comes up. Because it's just in a different category, you see: that's love, and this is business, or school, or war, and there's really nothing we two can do about that other thing anyway. The women will settle it somehow, in a manner mysterious to us, and we'll just play the hands we're dealt and then go hunt grouse. Although hunting accidents do occur.

So they run through it again. Finally, the major says, "All right, then, let me show you something. If you're up to riding. We'll take a courier just in case. Tom really did some convincing work on that foot of yours."

"I'll say! I'm convinced every time I put weight on it."

Soon they're above Scott's Dam and the sun is out now, sending the fog up in wisps and curls.

"There it is," says Sid.

"So you've got all that rock already there."

"Yes. We'd use that—wouldn't take as much wood—and there's plenty of sand, for cement."

"Would it hold?"

"Sure, anything. That's the beauty of rock."

"Unless you got a lot of rain."

"And then it would flood, yes. It wouldn't rise like pontoons. But it's a mile further down, and closer to the turnpike. If we needed to flank them, think how useful it'd be."

"But who've you got? I bet those Vermonters are already back with the corps."

"I'll show you."

By 9 A.M. Huck and the major are at the holding-pen watching the Alabama prisoners cook their first food since capture. Sawyer is describing the Rebel bridge-builders, and Huck points out an officer—the same one Sid had spoken to earlier, as it happens—whose empty holster and scabbard seem reversed. Is he a lefty? The fellow looks back at them, but before there can be any closer looks, a courier delivers a note from Sharpe: Huey's cavalry reports Rebel infantry pulling out of Fredericksburg, heading out on the turnpike, and—from Tom!—Jackson with them, Lee himself close behind.

"Come on, Huck," says Sid. "The reunion's on."

An hour later Sid is in a field east of the Chancellor house, watching Couch's men move ahead on the turnpike, with Meade's and Slocum's well off the road to the left and right—most of three corps against Lee's two lead divisions. All that Sharpe and Sawyer need now is a final message from Tom—and that is what they and a few signal corpsmen are out near the action with binoculars looking for.

When the first shell crashes into their clearing, the men dive for a nearby log pile. A couple more rounds land nearby, only one of which explodes. This time there are no casualties, except for a sprained ankle suffered by a signalman. Sharpe suggests the man consult Sid, who "knows all about boot problems." Sid ignores the jibe and looks at his watch: it's 10:00 A.M.

A Union battery opens up in response, from a log lunette, and the gunners are soon sweating in suspenders and shirt-sleeves, as the morning heats up. A cheer goes up from Couch's lead division, followed by a volley, and it's clear that both sides mean business. The smoke is soon so thick no one can see anything—even with binoculars. They back up a bit, but even near the Chancellor house the smoke looks high and thick.

"I'll watch the sky, Major. Why don't you go check on Our Boy."

Sid hands Sharpe the glasses. "All right, Colonel. Your turn."

The colonel chews on a cigar as he looks up into the smoke.

There's no horse-shoe playing in the yard now. Officers spread maps out on card-tables and cracker-boxes. Couriers gallop in on frothy horses, dash up the porch stairs, taking two at a time, even in riding boots, salute quickly, enter the house, dash out again, letting the door slam behind them, and cross the road to the stable where they change mounts and gallop back down the turnpike. Sid watches from the porch as wounded are beginning to come in, dragged into the yard or into the stable across the road. Eventually the hospital wagons there are hitched up and readied for a trip back to the Ford, leaking red like so many painters' carts.

Sid's mood is glum—not because of the beginning battle, which he actually welcomes for its weird combination of brisk manly physicality and a mystery that feels almost feminine—but because of the long odds against their sorry plan, *his* sorry plan, as it's rapidly becoming. Especially since Operation Reunion depends more and more on Tom Sawyer, a bounty-hunter at best, and Huck Finn, a time-server with seriously conflicted motives. Why, even now the fellow sits in the garden house at the inn trying to play a harmonica he has found, instead of concentrating on his Moment of Truth. As if the whole war might not depend on what he did in the next twenty-four hours.

And where in damnation is Averell?

A half hour later, Sid has just finished taking his turn with the glasses out near the turnpike, only a couple hundred yards behind the line of battle amid the chaos of galloping couriers, swearing officers, and staggering wounded, and he's got his map out again—have they misjudged the location? Maybe that Church isn't Zoan, but Zion?—when Sharpe lets out a whoop and holds out the glasses. Sid looks: nothing but smoke.

"Higher up, Major."

And there they are: two delicate little disks moving up over the smoke of battle. Two balloons.

"Both yellow!"

"You bet! Old Tom came through, didn't he? Now it's our turn!" and Sharpe claps him on the shoulder.

Sid finds it hard to share the joy. By now it's clear Stoneman's raiders are not going to cut the Rebels' communications, much less sweep into their rear to scoop up commanders. And yet—there are those two little balloons, with their dramatic news: Lee and Jackson, *both* of them, moving along a road to the south and east, coming within range. Sid shades his eyes till one of the balloons rises almost to the point of eclipse—an eerie double-sun effect through the rising smoke—and he has to look away.

"I'll go check on Our Boy," he says.

31. May 1, Midday: Huck Has *What?*

Huck has been resting his foot in a garden shed behind the inn—and under guard. For his own protection, of course. It isn't time yet to put him into position, but Sid feels the need to check. This is Huck Finn, after all. And then there's that business at the Point. Here's one more chance to bring it up and clear the air, a chance Sid keeps giving himself—*You know you won't! Oh, well, I just may!*—then avoiding. And then there's that letter.

"Corporal, I'd like to see Sergeant Lee."

"Yessir." The soldier ducks into the shed and a second later ducks back out, in apparent shock.

"Major, he's gone!"

"He's *what*?"

"I swear, sir, I never saw nor heard nothing. I been here constant, and there's only this one door."

"All right, let's have a look."

It's a small place, really, with nowhere to hide under the tools and seed bags, but pretty soon the flaw is revealed—a few pots cleared from a shelf, and above it a little skylight for letting in the morning sun when it serves as a green house. The pane has been neatly removed and left leaning against the brick wall.

"Damn! It sure seems like you'd have *heard* something."

"Sir, I swear!"

"All right, all right, help me look for some sign." But his heart sinks. *This is Huck Finn. You won't find him.* A circuit of the grounds shows nothing obviously fresh, and none of the other sentries remembers anything. He turns back toward the sound and smoke of battle and wonders what he'll say to the colonel.

"That'll be all for now, Corporal. But wait here in case he returns, or…or you receive further orders." *Like, for example, to arrest me for dereliction.*

"Huck has *what?*" Sharpe drops his field glass and turns, wipes the sweat from his eyes.

Sid has to yell to be heard: "Well, it's not as if we haven't had to find him before, Colonel!"

"No, that's right…but not when he was *trying* to get away from us! Where in Hell could he be?"

"I don't know, sir. But if his unit is still around, we should probably check there."

"Damn it!" Sharpe jerks the glass up by its strap and looks off, as if wondering where to throw it. "Tom's the only one who can find him, but he's way the Hell on the other side of—"

"Sir, how do we know Huck isn't there, too? *With* him? How do we know the Rebs didn't cook all this up to throw sand in our eyes—delay the advance?"

"Well—you're a suspicious son of a bitch, even for an intelligence officer." He is looking past Sid now, back toward the clot of wagons and orderlies near the inn. "But evidently I don't have to worry about that just yet." And he yells out,: "Where in blazes have *you* been, Sergeant?"

Sid turns and sees a familiar form limping toward them through the caissons, accompanied by a much-relieved sentry.

"Major, I'm sorry I give you the slip! I just wanted to go see an old friend without a 'honor guard' along." The dark blue jacket is gone now, and he wears only the cotton shirt, light blue trousers, and suspenders. He has a fresh-cut walking stick, and except for the cavalry breeches he could be a gardener coming back from his bean patch.

Sid is at once peeved and mightily relieved. "What friend?"

"One I knew in Mexico. He's in another troop of the 1st. I just—"

"Well, look here," says Sharpe, "all this camaraderie is fine, but you're both in harm's way here. We don't want to risk the sergeant's life to just any old piece of lead."

The only source for what Our Boy *was* "up to" is the journal:

While we chewed on some roasting ears Jack had saved from the night before—and *wasn't* I hungry!—I asked him a question I'd been worrying over, and not about the war. I asked him did he think a girl would wait for a man for ten years or more, supposing that she loved

him and all? He chewed for a second or two and then said, well, he didn't know, but *he* had waited ten years for a *woman*, so he figured it might work the other way around, too, though women folk *were* different.

But then he said: "Huck, whether she's waited or not, if she had strong feelings for you once, she still has. Then again, that *was* a long time ago, and women are different amongst theirselves, just like men are. The good ones want us to do what we think we have to do, or else they know we can't live with ourselves. If they didn't understand that, we couldn't go off to fight." He thought about that for a minute, then, "Though I expect some of us would anyway." Then he thought some more and says, "That'n'll wait for you. I guarantee it."

Course, he could of said that just because I wanted to hear it. Jack had been married three times—to a Mexican, a Indian, and a Creole. So he said he considered himself a international authority on marriage.

"Jack, you know who I'm talking about, I guess, don't you?"

"I think so, Huck."

"Well, if you ever run across her—you tell her I'll keep my promise?"

"I sure will, Huck. I sure will. Which promise, if I ain't being too nosey?"

"To find her," I said, and I said it as firm as I could. Then I said I had to get back, and he should take care of himself, and he said he would.

Sid, realizing the futility of a guard, leaves Huck alone this time and goes himself to check the fellow's story with his old unit. The story checks out. An hour later Sid returns, and then, according to Huck, Sharpe takes him and the major out to the stable to look at maps: where would it be best to lie in wait?

They finally settled on the furnace because it was the closest point on the road to us, though it wasn't the highest. Then all of a sudden, a hubbub went up and a flock of officers come out of the house onto the porch with a lot of door-slamming and hat-pulling, but I could hear some of their talk. General Hooker was saying something about "defensible positions," and one of the generals [*Meade, no doubt*] just

up and fired off, "Back? We're pulling *back* from that ridge? My God! If we can't hold the top of a hill, how in Hell are we going to hold the bottom of it?"

General Couch shook his head, and there was some talk I couldn't hear before they all mounted and rode off back to their men. Of course, I figured it was likely due to the job they had for me that they called off the advance.

[Not entirely. Out on the turnpike, Jackson is a wound-up spring of cold Calvinist will, as Anderson's brigades dig in. Good troops, well entrenched, they might hold against two-to-one odds. But holding is not the plan: Pack up your spades, Gentlemen, and pitch into them. And they do, and after Anderson, McLaws. Brigade after brigade lurches forward. And by the time Lee arrives Hooker has pulled in his horns.]

It was afternoon before Sid and me and a couple of corporals were pushing through the woods towards the furnace road, which wasn't easy leading the horses, though Butterfly was as good as could be in spite of the bugs following her. I was favoring my foot, of course, even though it didn't hurt much, because I wanted to stay practiced at it, but we weren't making much time anyway because of how thick and swampy it was. The major stepped into a slough once and swore wonderfully. It was the first time I'd heard him curse, and I was impressed. There was a sort of road from Fairview and Hazel Grove down to the furnace, but we didn't use it because we didn't want to risk being seen. Well, we didn't see any Rebs, though there'd been hard fighting in the area earlier.

[This puts the time after 4 P.M.—by which time Rebel brigades under Wright and Heth had swept through the area, only to be repulsed by Union cannon at Hazel Grove and Fairview. Still—why couldn't somebody look at a watch?]

We could see unburied men from both sides lying in the thickets. We run into a line of our own infantry, which was all right since we had the major with us. Sid just showed them the orders, even though they were kind of vague in case we got captured. When we got out near the

cavalry pickets we had to dodge around—because I can tell you cavalry tends to shoot first and worry later—though it was likely some of my own outfit [a term picked up in the West?]**.**

It was only a couple of miles, but took us near an hour before we struck the furnace road. We went along to the right, looking for the furnace, or another place where a wounded man might lay. Once we heard a clatter of horses coming from the west and dodged off the trail into a thicket, and sure enough, it was a bunch of Rebel cavalry, in a pretty big hurry, though I didn't see any that looked like generals, and they didn't notice us. Butterfly nickered once but not loud enough to be noticed. I begun to wish I hadn't brought her. It wasn't the first enemy cavalry I'd seen, but I judged they was the best dressed—with right gaudy cockades and regular gray uniforms, not the brown, which I'd seen a lot of that. [Maybe from Tom Munford's 2nd Virginia—an elite unit] **It was when I looked close at their mounts that I made up my mind not to keep Butterfly. These were the pitifulest, hungriest animals I'd seen since Texas, and some had bridles stitched together with rope and canvas. It must have been a hard winter for sure, and if they come across a mount like Butterfly, with good quality tack—why, they'd "enlist" her in a heartbeat!**

We came to the furnace soon, and the Rebs weren't to be seen, so Sid sent the two corporals off, one in each direction, for a lookout. We tied Butterfly and High Bar to a couple of rail posts, far enough apart so they wouldn't fight—they don't much like each other—and then we ducked into the spring house.

I could tell Sid was pretty nervous and trying not to show it, being a major and all, so I tried to put him at ease by saying something about old times, like Tom did.

"Old times," he said, looking out the door toward the road, which wasn't much more than a wide trail. "That was before the war, Sergeant. Things are very different now. I'm a *major*. You're a *sergeant*. We need to keep that straight," he says.

I was squatting on the ground, and Sid was sitting on a little wood-pile by the spring—though the ground was dry enough to sit on except where the spring flowed—and still looking out the door, stead of at me.

"All right, Major," I said. "We keep it straight." It didn't matter to me. I wasn't being ordered to do this. He asked me again if I didn't

want the other two men to stay with me in case whoever came along was well guarded, but I told him no, I'd rather be alone. It wasn't that I didn't trust the others, I told him, but a couple more wouldn't make no difference if there wasn't much of a guard. And if there *was*, two more wouldn't matter—it might *take* a regiment or more to get him out—and I wished he would just stop and let me get on with it. He nodded and thought about it. And while he did, *I* thought: does he want those others around to *check* on me?

"Maybe you're right," he finally said. "Anyhow, we'll have the regiment ready—or so we're *told*," and we both had to chuckle at that. "Let's just hope it's a high enough rank to make it worthwhile. A major general, or better."

Now I wondered how jackass-stupid he thought I was. "Look, Major—I know well enough it's General Jackson we're talking about." When he didn't say nothing, I went on. "I know right well the president of the United States didn't come down here to talk to a measly sergeant about any old major general. The Rebs have plenty of those. How many Jacksons do they have?"

But now *he* looked surprised. "The *president?*" he says. "So *that's* who the Mayor was!" Then he says, "Well, you're right, Huck—that's our hope. I should have known you'd figure it out. We picked you because you *can* figure things out...and of course you knew Jackson from Lexington."

And then he reached into his jacket and pulled out a rolled-up paper and said it was a picture of a Union agent I might meet along here, and I should memorize it because he was going to have to keep it, but it was a good likeness. I said it sure *was*, and I ought to know, because I painted it. It was Joe Taylor!

I shouldn't of been surprised. It explained a lot of things, like why he left the regiment a year ago, and how he could get close to Jackson: he used to live with him and wouldn't anybody raise a question.

But Sid was *mighty* surprised. He asked me did I trust him, and I said I did from what I'd seen in Lexington. Then I asked him how far he trusted *Tom*, and he said about as far as a noose from a tree limb, if I knew what he meant, and I said I did. He said he judged Tom was more on our side than not—and would stay that way unless it looked

like the South was fixing to win—and I allowed that was my view, too. But he said we had to be sure to warn "this fellow Smith or Taylor, or whatever he goes by," and he gave me a folded and sealed paper that said something like "A Soldier's Final Prayer" on it—I'd seen lots of such things—and said to give it to him privately if I got a chance. I said I would, but I said Joe probably already knows enough to take care of himself. But that made me think about that card he showed me, and I asked if he knew anything about Becky and whether she was all right.

He said he thought she was fine, and he said, "Don't worry. I'll leave word that she gets *both* of our pensions if things go wrong." Then he laughed and said, "Anyhow don't forget the passwords. I hear those Regulars are a bunch of cutthroats." Then he stuck his head outside, and reached back and helped me up out of the spring house. "We'll take your mount back. What'd you say her name was? Butterfly? I'll see *she's* safe, too."

Then he whistled for the two lookouts and swung up onto High Bar. "I think we'll ride back," he said. "I didn't see any fences." I'm not sure what he meant by that. Then he asked how the foot felt, and I said it felt so wonderful I was thinking of shooting the other one, too. He laughed at that.

"You are a brave man, Huckleberry Finn."

Then he thought of something and reached in his blouse and took out what looked like a letter, pretty beaten up, and another paper bundle tied with a string. He reached down to hand me the bundle. "I was asked to give you this," he says. "It's some personal effects of a man with your regiment who was killed out with the flankers a little while ago. I'm told just about the last thing he said was to give this to you. I don't even know the man's name. If you were...close, well, I'm sorry." I took the bundle, which didn't feel very heavy. "If you'd like to open it now, we'll wait. But I thought you might want to...be private, you know." I took it and said no thank you, I'd just wait, like he said. Then he looked at that other letter and put it back in his blouse. I asked him what that was, and he said it was just another piece of news he had to deliver and make somebody else miserable, if he ever got a chance.

Then the three of them rode back up into the woods. As soon as they was out of sight I unwrapped the bundle, my hands shaking a bit,

because I sort of guessed what it was, and there was a couple ivory finger-picks and a red bandana, and of course I knew whose they were, and I felt pretty bad. I stuffed them in my pocket and said to myself I'd try to be worthy of them. And for starters, I had to go to work and betray an old friend—Professor Thomas Jackson of Lexington.

Back at Hazel Grove, as the signalmen set up their post and a Federal battery unlimbers, Sid takes out the letter Becky had given him. The time to deliver it was there at the furnace, of course, and he'd thought about it, was just about to do it, but then thought: why further complicate the man's feelings, which were already complicated enough by the death of that friend of his? Maybe later. And shouldn't he himself have a look first? He *should* look, shouldn't he? As the officer in charge of this agent—it's really his *duty*, isn't it? So he opens it.

It seems to be some sort of funeral notice, in a dignified hand, signed by a Señor Hidalgo De Los Montes and announces, in stately but awkward English, the wish of the undersigned and his family to notify the addressee of the death of one Señora Maria Poseta De La Plata De Sangre De Cerdo, and provides an address to contact for information. The major sees, of course, a possible connection to the young Sister that Becky had mentioned, but the message seems ambiguous. The woman is called "Señora" for one thing—that means "Mrs." doesn't it? Of course, the major doesn't realize its true, stupendous significance. But now he has even less intention of passing it on, should he get another chance. For, if the deceased *was* that Mexican girl, and if Huck still had feelings for her, this news would seem to free the fellow for, among other things, the courtship of Becky Thatcher. Why make that even more likely than it already seems?

****

"This very important!" says the Chinaman.

He is standing on my porch, manuscript in hand. It is raining, and he has walked across my yard in his waterproof and slippers. He points to the part about the "Hidalgo" letter and jabs at it.

"How can Major Sawyer not tell his friend about this?" The rain drips from his hood onto his nose and moustache. "He have lots of duty.

One is to a comrade, who have this loss to face. Why he not do this duty to another man?"

I knew this would come up. Before answering, I look down the lane at the puddles in the road. The macadamized surface was supposed to prevent mud, but when it's wet, you get a sort of brownish paste in any low spot—especially where there are horses. Chiang's three little spruce trees—which he watered frantically all summer and sprayed with paraffin and other newfangled treatments to ward off the heat—look safe now, green and dripping.

"Sit down, Chiang. There's something in the house I need to show you. No, just wait here. It's not any warmer in there. I'm out of firewood."

When I return, he has sat in one of the porch rockers. I hand him a short roll of paper. "Unroll it, but be careful. That Sojourner fellow left the boy more than words of wisdom. He left him a letter from Her—from the real Butterfly."

"A letter! But why Huckleberry not say anything about this?"

"Because he didn't know about it till later. Remember the sketch Lee brought back from Double-Top? This is it."

"But how you get that?"

"The same way I got the journal." He looks at me. "Be patient. At any rate, I laid the picture on a bench in Hargrave's lab one day, and what do you think I saw next time I looked at the back? There was some lettering—I've forgotten what he said spilled there, but it brought out something."

"She use disappearing ink, for God's sake?"

"No, no—but some of the ink the natives use fades pretty quick unless treated with the right stuff—remember this Sojourner gave Huck some of it."

"What it say?"

I shake my head and point to the page. "It's hard to read. Something about **'My Fruit-Berry,'** *then* **'your face in the cliff, your song in—'** *something...* **'Big trees here in'**—*probably* **'California'**—*then* **'You must—'** *and then the rest is illegible. Hargrave wants to try ultraviolet on it."*

"He ruin it with that." He shakes his head.

"Whatever's the case, I'm sure Huck saw more than I saw. Anyhow, don't be too hard on the major. Don't judge him till the end."

He thinks about that for a moment. "All right, I wait for the end."

Then I think of something else. "There's also another trip I'd like you to make with me—out to that battlefield. It won't rain forever. You can take your car." He turns and looks down the street morosely. "You aren't afraid of driving with that blade are you?"

"Afraid?" He turns back and waves his spade-hand at me. "Remember, I dig train tunnel through mountains. No." (he sighs heavily) "I just thinking, now my trees may drown. I maybe water them too much. Sun Tsu probably say something about that."

"I thought Sun Tsu was a general, not a botanist."

"No difference in China—general, gardener, philosopher—all same. China gone now and good riddance." Then he faces me and smiles. "All right, I drive. Take students, too. Very educational. You sure you know way to that place? Roads change."

"Well, you're the motorist. Don't you have any maps?"

"Got lots of map. None from 1863."

Then he waves across the yard at the shed where his auto sits. "Only need to weld trace mounts in front and store bridle in back, you know." I look at him blankly. "For conversion, remember?"

Now I realize he is talking about the hardware he wants to attach to his auto. The idea is to allow it to be towed like a carriage by real horses on occasion—to climb a mountain, for example. There's still the issue of how to get the horses back over the mountain, but he has thought of that: progress will address it. He waves off toward the mountains. "Owner have stable on both side of mountain, and stable boys shuttle team back and forth—maybe not even need to, with traffic both ways. Work like charm, soon as somebody see market." Then he looks back at me. "Your wife ever drive car?"

"Not that I know. But she's pretty good with directions."

"Maybe we take her too."

Part 5

"It was your duty to do these things."

32. It Looks Like You're My Prisoner

There are important questions here. First, about that letter: if Sid's estimation of Huck is improving—and it certainly should be since Our Boy is showing the kind of loyalty and *sangfroid* that a soldier like Sid must respect—then why *not* show him the "Hidalgo" letter? Well—in spite of all that rationalizing about military duty—this is really about Becky. And when it comes to that, as a young cadet once put it: duty be damned.

But, second, why have these men still not leveled with each other about the mission itself? Why has no one told the principal agent the identity of his principal target, Robert E. Lee—unless we count those hints from the President? And Huck, for his part, has told Sid nothing at all about the Winchester message. Lee (and maybe Jackson, too) must *know* Huck is in the Union army. How can any masquerade be pulled off? Or does he have some other agenda?

Here's what I think: Huck just accepts the challenge. He likes to improvise. And maybe he's *not* going to pretend to be a Rebel, but only what he is: a wounded U.S. trooper. Whatever the case, Our Boy, too, can keep secrets, even in his journal.

And then I was by myself—for about another hour or two, long enough to get a fire going and write some of this. I got an oil cloth laid out behind the furnace with a ration of beef ready to put on a stick over the fire when I think it's time. I allow it won't be long before I have company of some kind, but I'm not planning to be found—leastwise, not till I need to be. But now here they come!

LATER:

Sure enough it was another troop of Rebels trotting up the road, this time from the east and a different regiment, most of them not near

as well dressed, but as usual some of the officers were quite well turned out. I figured the general I was laying for—Jackson, if that's who it was—would be the best dressed of the lot. But I'd studied the sleeves and collars for generals which Colonel Sharpe showed me, and I didn't see nothing like those. Only a colonel, maybe, and not worth the risk.

Of course, I don't look like much myself neither. Lots of the Rebs wear captured blue, especially britches, so I could be from either army—and I might have to be, before it's done.

At first I thought they were going to ride on by. But just as they were about past, an officer called a halt and sent a sergeant over to look at the furnace. He dismounted and stuck his head into the building, and I was in a sweat that he would find me, and I worked on what my story would be. But pretty quick he reported back to the officer, and then, to my surprise, the whole column dismounted and broke out carbines and loaded them and moved off into the woods on both sides of the road in skirmish order with every fourth man a horse holder, and the holders staked out the horses—all regular order. And while that was going on another troop come up the road and formed up in the same fashion back in the other direction. They looked like setting up to defend the spot. And one of them come up to the furnace and noticed the fire and got to work boiling water over it. So now I was cut off from my fire and my beef ration.

I laid still and quiet as I could in a laurel thicket next to the furnace and made sure my cheat-shooter was safe inside the pants seam...[This seems to have been a small two-barreled pistol, like a Derringer, and easily concealed—not very accurate, but deadly enough at "table range." The two barrels can be fired together or separately—two balls with one trigger. You can imagine less polite nicknames.] **Then I checked the sodium crystals in my pockets, and now all I have to do is wait, and try to keep a lookout back down the road to the east for whatever of interest might come by—like one college professor of my acquaintance!—and think about how to get back to my fire.**

And if I'd managed to *stay* awake, things might have gone different. But of course I couldn't, and by the time I came around it was late, near sunset and I heard voices.

"He's sure not dead," one of the voices was saying.

The other said: "But look at that foot."

When I opened my eyes I saw a white face and a black face. The white one was a Rebel sergeant, and the black one was Joe!

Well, after we seen who each other was, I managed to get out, "The rest...."

Joe cuts me off quick with, "Silence," which was the countersign, "if you knows what's good for you! You hurt bad, Mistah?" Now the sergeant who was with him starts asking who I am and why I'm here, what unit, which side, and all, but I didn't want to answer that kind of thing yet, so I pretended attacks of pain in my foot, which didn't require much pretending, I'll tell you, while Joe pitched in by offering to drag me down to the furnace where there's more light. "See, he ain't got no gun or nothing," and the sergeant says fine, but turn me over to the guard and report back pretty quick, because they're going to need all hands to make camp and water the horses.

That got us a couple minutes to slip into the coal room of the furnace, trying to whisper and not make noise. It turns out Joe isn't in the Army no more. Colonel Sharpe 'cruited him, he says, in Maryland from the Freedmen's League after he seen his record from Texas. I asked how he hooked up with the Confederates, and he said through Jim Lewis, a colored servant he knew from Lexington. I asked could Lewis be trusted, because I didn't remember much about him, but Joe didn't answer right off, then he said—picking his words more careful than I remember him doing, "Huck, Jim is...right fond of the general...right attached, you might say, and also to me, and that mixes things up—because you see I dasn't put *Jim* in danger."

"Well, then what *can* you do? The colonel calls you his man in Jackson's camp."

"Well—what I *has* been doing is to get news to him when I can through some messenger."

"Like Tom?"

"Yessuh, like Tom."

Then I thought, how much can he know about the plan? But even Tom seems to of guessed more than he was told.

And he went on as if he was reading my mind. "All I'z told about this business was to 'spect a agent—that's you, I guess—to meet me some'rs alongst the road here with 'futher instructions.'"

Well, my instructions sure set him back, all right!

"You sending a *regiment* through here to try an' bag the general?"

"That's the plan—or part of it. I have to signal first."

"Well, don't that beat all!" he said, and he didn't smile a bit. I could see his eyes wide in the dim light as he looked out the door and was trying to whisper. "You think these folks'll jus' let a regiment of cav'ry ride through here and scoop up Stonewall Jackson like a sack o' meal? What was the rest of the plan?"

"Well," I said, and I took a deep breath, knowing how wild and foolish it sounded, "The rest of the plan is for me to take him myself if I have to—or *us,* I guess."

He just shook his head, and then he said neither of us could do any such thing *yet*, certainly not by ourselves, and he had to get back to the trail to look lively and not raise suspicions, and the best thing for me to do was lay low and eat something or get some sleep while I could. The general was going to camp nearby, so there wasn't no rush, and it was too dark to signal by fire now anyhow—so the next chance wouldn't be till morning. Maybe by then the Rebs would forget all about me, and he'd try to get back to me before then. But now I got to worry about how *Joe* "thinks about things," as the major would say.

Then I remembered about the "Prayer" note Sid had give me for him and handed it over. I says better not open it till it's private and he can burn it.

I crawled through the woods till I could hear the Rebs giving orders and trying to be quiet while fires was lit for supper. The men laughed a bit once in a while and joked in low voices. On the whole I judged their army works a lot like ours, taking fun when they can, but everybody pretty businesslike when it come to business. I'm not sleepy now, at all, but what they're cooking smells like pork, and it makes me hungry. What I really do feel is small and pitiful and like the weight of the world is sitting under my hat. And I got time to wonder again how come Sid and the colonel didn't tell me from the start that it's Jackson, my old Professor, they were sending me after. Maybe they were afraid I would back out, but they must of figured when push come to shove I'd do my duty. But if they knew that, they know me better than I know myself. Like what if Joe gets in the way? How much of a soldier is *he?*

All I can do now is wait and hope for luck. More later…

I don't know the time, but pretty soon, before dark, there was a stir and some riders come down the road from the east and another bunch from the west and there was a lot of saluting and some hushed laughing. I couldn't see who it was, but when one of them saddled up—he had a bushy beard and one of those feathered campaign hats the Rebs like[18]—another one said to him something about "*all* the roads, General. Consult the citizens." And that sounded like Jackson, but I couldn't be sure without seeing the face.

[I have to say here that this need for a map is strange: Lee himself is an engineer, for goodness' sake, with an excellent map maker on his staff, Jed Hotchkiss, and now—with all winter to think about what might develop on this front—his men have to wander the roads guided by farmers? Sometimes that detachment of his looks less Olympian than oblivious!]

After guards were posted, most of the officers set down to eat, and some to sleep—just under blankets—they didn't set up any tents that I could see. It was getting to be pretty cool—I *wished* I had a fire now—and the bugs wasn't so bad. But I wasn't a bit sleepy.

But after dusk, there was some noise as some men moved up the hill nearly to where I was—till they were close enough to spit on if I'd wanted to, and I got ready to bolt. But it turned out they weren't looking for me, just wanted to get away private. They looked like officers, but they were between me and the light, so all I could see was shadows till they got close and got their fire going. One of them sat down on a cracker box and motioned the other one down and spread out a map between them on a box top. The one with the face toward me looked familiar, though he had a bit more of a beard now. When he talked there wasn't no doubt: it was Jackson.

He was pointing to the map and said, "Here and here. You see? And then he pulls back toward Chancellor's. It's a feint, no doubt—to draw us away from the town. He'll be gone by morning." Then he looks up and says "Do you not think so?"

The other shook his head—his back was to me—he was just a shadow now. And he answers: "No, General. I think he will be here. And if he is, he must not remain unmolested."

And every goose bump I already had grew a dozen more—that was General Lee.

Lee went on, bending over the map. "Now—how can we get at those people?"

Jackson said he wondered could Hooker be turned, and Lee asked what he knew about the roads, and then they both stood up as another officer got off his horse and walked up, and Jackson looked at a paper he held in his hand—a map I guess—and then the other man points off to the west and he and Jackson said some things I didn't hear, and then after a while the two generals came back to the map on the crackerbox and Jackson says, "General Stuart believes the enemy's flank is unprotected."

Well, they stood and talked for a while, and those working on the fire got it going pretty good—which I'd of appreciated except it made me easier to see. Finally the two generals come back and sat down again at the cracker boxes, and Lee asked, "Well, General, what do you propose then?"

Jackson put his finger down on the map and made a big circle. "Go around here."

Lee thought for a second—and while he did I moved my hand as slow as I could toward the seam in my pants where the gun was. Finally he looked up and asked: "With what will you make this movement?"

And Jackson answered, "With my whole corps."

I tugged a little at the thread and widened the seam a bit.

Lee nodded and looked up at him and said: "What will you leave me?"

And Jackson said, "The divisions of Anderson and McLaws," and then Lee was quiet again for a minute.

And I reached in and felt the cold steel against my fingers.

Now I couldn't see his face, but I could imagine it. I'd seen it on board a ship and on Cerro Gordo and in the Napoleon Room at the Point and under a tent flap on the Brazos and on the porch at Arlington House, and I imagined him thinking about a whole lot of things, about the battle, of course, and this general of his who was asking him to face at least three Union corps with whatever "Anderson and McLaws" might have—which I didn't know, but it had to be a lot less than what we had. He was

probably thinking about war and peace and rebellion and everything EXCEPT me—who was almost close enough to reach out and touch him—but if I did I'd probably have to shoot him, and how in blazes can I shoot a man like that in the back, let alone the face—? But *he* was pulling sense out of the night, I knew it, and it was a different kind of sense than I'd ever have, and then he said, just as calm as you please: "Well, go on then."

And I pulled that little gun out as slow as I could.

And then he asked about directions—did Jackson know anything about the roads, and Jackson said he'd had reports, but he called one of the guards and asked to send for Stuart, and I was calculating as best I could what *I* should do—besides cock this weapon, which I knew I should do, but if I did that, they'd hear it for sure—And then the two generals come a little back to where none of the other officers could hear, but VERY close to ME now, and if they'd looked right at me they'd of seen me, and General Lee asked Jackson if he thought he could destroy the enemy, and Jackson just give a nod, but that wasn't enough for Lee, I guess, because he went on—and I couldn't do nothing but listen.

"General, even a victory like Fredericksburg or Manassas Junction costs us thousands of good men, whom we can't replace. We can't afford many more such victories." Jackson still didn't say nothing, and Lee went on. "Soon we shall have to replace these valiant volunteers with conscripts, old men and boys—cadets—perhaps even..." And I wondered if he was about to say, "Perhaps even Negroes," but he stopped and put his hand on Jackson's sleeve, just lightly. "Thomas, we must not just compel Hooker to retreat. We must destroy his army, or a large part of it, and then take the war to the enemy's country. We must finish things. This year."

Then Jackson took General Lee's hand in his own and said, "General, I swear I will kill or capture every man in my front south of the river who doesn't run away. Or die in the attempt."

But maybe *that* wasn't what Lee wanted to hear, because he said, "Thomas—please do not expose yourself needlessly. You are my right arm."

And Jackson said, "We will need no arms, General, when the enemy is gone."

General Lee was quiet for a minute, then he said, "Well, in any event, God's will be done," and Jackson nodded and said, "Yes, yes. His will be done," and then Lee said he expected God would want them both to get a bit of sleep, but Jackson said, "Perhaps we should pray first, General?" And so they both bowed their heads right there, but what they said was so low I couldn't hear.

I didn't see any sign of Joe now, but there was two balls in my shooter, and I could put one in each of those two generals all by myself with my eyes closed—while *theirs* was closed, too, in prayer. And the war might be over in a month, and the Union saved! General Lee had *told* me to do my duty, and I knew quite well what that was, God's will or not. I tried to feel what kind of a heart I had—the heart of a murderer or the heart of a soldier—either one would do now. Hadn't the general himself talked about what he hoped would happen if he made the wrong choice?

Well, he *had*. And I knew it.

But I'd waited too long; they were folding the maps now, and others came to pick up the boxes, and the moment, if there ever was one, was gone.

Jackson moved back down to where his blanket was with his sword leaning up against a tree beside it, and was still talking to officers, and then Lee moved back up to where the men were picking up the boxes and maps, and this time one of them had a torch that lit up my laurel clump pretty good, and Lee pointed to where I was lying and said, "Drag that poor fellow out and see if he's one of ours." Well, I was going to play passed out or dead, but they grabbed me by the feet and it hurt so much I cried out. Lee took the torch and looked at me, and our eyes met, and he recognized me, but he didn't startle or nothing; he just give the torch back to the other and said to carry on, that he'd talk a minute to "this fellow"—meaning me—by himself.

There was a bit of both moon and fire light, and I could see his face, and I was struck by how old he looked—his hair was mostly all gray by now. He squatted down beside me and asked how I was doing. Not *what* in the ding-nation I was doing where I was, but *how* I was doing! So I said, "Not too bad, considering," trying to stall, you know, and he said: "But you're hurt—badly?"

"Not too bad. They just grabbed my foot wrong." He reached under my arms and lifted me up to lean against the tree next to where he'd sat with General Jackson.

"Long ago?"

"Yesterday evening."

"You're still with the First?"

"Yes, sir."

He nodded. "They're still in the area then?" I didn't say anything, and he nodded. "No, you're right not to answer. I had no right to ask that. Can you walk?"

"I think so—a little bit. I had a beef ration back at the furnace. I was hoping just to wait there till I could get back up—back up to—"

"I see. Well, that won't be possible now. Our troops are all over the woods in that direction—as I guess you've seen." Then he thought about that for a minute. "And as for what you may have heard—you were pretty close to us." I didn't say anything. But then for some reason he smiled. "Well—it looks like you're my prisoner, Sergeant." Then he turned and motioned to one of the officers on his staff and they talked quiet for a minute. And during that minute I thought about what the general had said to me. When it come right down to it, he had treated me kindly, but maybe just the way he would of treated any other "poor fellow" from either army that he'd found under a laurel bush. And he called me "Sergeant," not "son" or "Huckleberry." I was a soldier, and so was he, and he was doing his duty. And what would he expect of *me*?

When he came back up to where I was, I said, very quiet, "No, General, I'm afraid you're *my* prisoner."

And I pulled back both the hammers, one at a time.

33. This Mule Fart of a Plan

For Major Sawyer, it's a rough night—one more to spend waiting upon hopes that look ever more forlorn. So it turns out this agent of Sharpe's, this Joe Taylor, is an old friend of Huck's from Lexington—one *more* coincidence the Bureau has sprung on him. And now he's been left at Hazel Grove with some of the artillery reserve to watch the country to the southwest—while Sharpe himself has ridden back to Fairview, where he is close to Chancellor and can signal either way thanks to Hooker's balloon man, Professor Lowe. Sid has no balloons, just a sergeant and two corporals from the signal corps, but that's fine with him. His one trip aloft under one of those bubbles earlier in the spring had made him bountifully sick, to the vast amusement of the crew.

And then later in the evening there's smoke from near the furnace—no change in its color, though—and finally night comes, ending any chance to detect a color. And of course it could be a fire other than Huck's—from Rebel cavalry, or even Union skirmishers. So there on the high ground he waits, a silhouette under a full moon, till his sergeant respectfully suggests that the major can't do anything profitable by moonlight, but might well be *shot* by it, and ought to get some sleep.

But he sleeps little. The night is full of shouting artillerymen and farting mules and whinnying horses (every one of which High Bar has to answer) and false alarms of advancing Rebels, and reports of fires off to the south and rearrangements that bring a brigade of infantry into the area, part of a whole new corps, the III^{d}, with even more artillery sure to set up right where his tent is, as soon as there is daylight. And after all this, he will have to present himself this morning, not to Slocum, from whom he might expect help, but to the commander of this new corps, a General Dan Sickles—of whom he knows nothing except that he is a politician. Wonderful! And it's nearly sunrise now, and there is firing off to the east, and he can't signal Sharpe for advice on Sickles because there's no code for him, except in Morse, and the whole world could read that, and.... *And* he's probably about to get a good man killed, maybe several, for a plan that's not worth a mule fart. What had made him think he could send one cavalry sergeant through a hundred thousand armed men and bring down General Robert E. Lee? Because the man *used* to know him! *Used* to be highly regarded by him! Well, why not any one of a hundred other Union men who had also served with Lee and been close to him?

Because he's Huck; that's why. He gets through. He got to you, didn't he? He'll get to Lee.

Yes, but what'll he do when he gets there?

Well, his own duty, his *military* duty, is to wait till an hour after sunrise, long enough for any signal, then pack up and get out of the way—back to roads and rivers and bridges where he *may* do some good.

Finally: the sun is up. Good. Enough of this mule fart of a plan.

34. A Minister of the Gospel

I know Lee heard the hammers click, but he said nothing for a second or two, and I was hoping nobody else heard it. I couldn't see his face well on account of the moon was behind him, but he could see me, and I knew he could see the gun in my lap with my finger on the triggers. He took a deep breath and then out of the shadows he says, "So—once again there's more to you than meets the eye." And he chuckled. "Well, I see you have taken my words about duty to heart." He was still standing up, his hands straight by his side, near his belt, but I didn't see any weapon. "May I sit?" I didn't say anything, so he squatted slowly down to where he could talk quieter, and he almost whispered.

"Huckleberry, you could have shot me—probably you *should* have shot me—and General Jackson as well—did you know that was he? But now you have taken me prisoner. I am unarmed, and you cannot shoot me in cold blood. Nor can you march me back to your lines, if you can march yourself, though perhaps you can move better than we've been led to believe. We are entirely in control of this area now. No, I am afraid the odds are overwhelmingly against you, Sergeant. Mine is the stronger claim."

And he held out his hand for the gun.

But I didn't stir, and I shook my head. "General, I won't shoot you. I guess you know that. *Unless* you try to take this gun. I'll put a bullet through any man who does try. Maybe two."

He thought about that for a second. "Well, I can't leave you here long. And I haven't time now for discussion. In the morning I'll have you sent down to the trains at Todd's Tavern with the other prisoners. As for the gun—I'll let you keep it till morning, but you'll be well guarded, and I'll have to have it sooner or later. I also prefer not to shoot *you,* unless I have to. Do I have your word that—Ah, never mind, what's the worth of a forced promise? You will have to sleep some time."

He got up, but then he added, "There is much I would like to discuss with you, Huckleberry. Perhaps, soon, there will be a—a quiet day." Then he thought of something else. "By the way, did you receive my message at Winchester? I think you may legitimately tell me that."

"Yes, sir, I did. And I appreciated it. Thank you, sir."

He nodded. "I thought you would. I'm pleased."

If I'd of told him all the hullabaloo it got mixed up with in Maryland, he might *not* of been so pleased!

Just on a hunch, I mentioned I'd seen somebody with Jackson that looked like Joe Taylor, who I remembered from Lexington, and would he pay my regards. He said he'd mention that to Captain Smith[19]—assuming I was cooperative—and I was glad because I wanted to be sure Joe knew where I was going. I hoped he wouldn't think Joe was a spy, too. Then he turned and walked back down to the road and sent two men running up to guard me, and my second chance to shoot him—or third, depending on how you count—was over.

Now things are quiet again, with the generals asleep and the pickets watching (they don't seem interested in talking to me) and I've got my gun where they can see it, and I can hear horses nicker once in a while and whippoorwills call out, and I remember we used to think that meant somebody was dead, and there sure *are* plenty of dead now, and like to be more. The only other sound was the sound of something metal falling, and when I looked back toward Jackson's camp I noticed his sword that was propped against a tree had fallen down. That has to be a sign of something, for sure.

And of course I got time now to think about what a mess I made of my mission—better if I'd not tried at all! I *could* of waited till tomorrow and tried something then. But now I got my own personal guards, a private and a corporal, sitting nearby with carbines. I should pray, I guess, but instead I got this journal out and looked at my little flat butterfly, and tried to write a bit. I'm glad I learned to write without much light—and holding a gun at the same time!—because it helps keep me awake. And I'm glad I got to see Sergeant Jack. Some other folks are coming up now to change my guard, so I better look sharp and can't write any more now.

Next Day

Well, after all that worrying last night about duty—I leaned back against the tree, and in a little while, just as General Lee had figured, I was asleep!

I woke up sudden, with a hand under each arm, lifting me up and hustling me down out of the woods toward the Rebel camp. My foot felt better, but I put on a pretty good limp, till I was helped along smartly by my husky guards. The sun was up and the woods weren't dusky gray any more but bright green, and all around me was the smells of boiled coffee and oiled leather, and the sounds of marching foot soldiers—shouted orders and clanking canteens and bayonets. My guards made me stand by the side of the road for a bit, like they was waiting for something, so I watched the soldiers pass for a while. They looked even more tattered and ornery than the cavalry, with torn pants legs and button-less jackets, and a couple had baling twine for suspenders, and as usual there was more brown and butternut than gray, but they also looked very lively and pleased with theirselves, and not a bit interested in retreat.

Soon I saw General Jackson ride up to a bunch of officers, and one of them turned out to be General Lee. They had a few words, and Jackson nodded once or twice, and then Lee looked at his watch, and Jackson pointed off in the direction of march and then touched the brim of his cap and spurred his mount off to the west alongside the column. General Lee watched till he was out of sight and then reined his horse back in the other direction. And he never said a word more to me.

I only had one guard now—the corporal had sent the private off—but I soon figured out why: my gun was gone. I guess they took it while I slept. Well, soon a two-horse baggage wagon came along with two men in the seat. One of them, the passenger, was Joe Taylor, and wasn't I glad to see him! My guard shoved me up into the cargo space behind the shotgun seat, and got in after me. I sat down in the back as best I could amidst a pile of tents and kettles and blankets and a box of Bibles and hymnals, which I guess was all from Jackson's camp, and

I tried to get comfortable for the trip, which I reckon is off to prison. I expect I'll have plenty of time to write where I'm going.

LATER, SAME DAY:

Well, after a few minutes of waiting for the column to start, it finally looks like we're ready, and Joe leans down and says something to my guard, who hops up in back with me, and then Joe turns back and grins at me and says, "Good morning, Mistah Sergeant," and laughs and then turns to the other fellow, the driver, who turns to grin at me, too, and Joe says, "May I present the Reverend Mistah Thomas Sawyer—minister of the Gospel."

And before I could think what to say to *that*, I noticed a campfire still smoking right beside the road where we was stopped, and I cussed myself for nearly forgetting my orders. I asked my guard could I toss out some sugar I had in my pocket that was no good now and was going to draw ants, and he said all right, but let me see your hands first. I pulled out the crystals, which was pretty crumbled up by now, and let him see, and luckily there was a bug or two there, and he said all right, just toss them in the fire there—and that was *just* what I had in mind! When I tossed them in—first handful from the left pocket, next from the right—they sizzled a bit and went up in smoke. Soon after that, Joe said gee-up, and we moved off into the road. When I turned to look back at the fire, I could see it was making a different color smoke, just like the major said it would.

35. A Live Colonel or a Dead Hero (Morning, May 2)

Sid shoves his binoculars into their case. The sun's well up now, and nothing from Huck. Or Tom. Or this John/Joe /Smith/Taylor fellow. What *did* happen last night? Did neither Lee nor Jackson go past on the furnace Road? Was Huck captured? Or dead? Any conceivable report the major might write now, he knows, will amount to one long confession of incompetence. The signalmen's horses are weighted awkwardly with flags and camp gear. *We look like a band of gypsy peddlers*, Sawyer thinks as they wend their way toward Fairview, through the commotion of repositioning artillery and infantry.

At the bottom of the little swale below Hazel Grove, Sid takes a last look back and sees some waving arms. He waves back and turns to ride on.

It isn't long, though, before he hears some hoof-beats behind him and turns to see a bugler galloping toward him waving and yelling. He waits. The boy pulls up in the weeds, scattering up—somehow—both dust and dew.

"Captain says you should look at this, sir." Sid takes the glasses, looks to the south. "Further up, sir. You see the smoke where the road turns south?"

"Yes, yes, I do. Thank you, young man." He turns to his signalmen. "Sergeant, we have to go back up there. And bring the flags!"

Back on the high ground again, the sergeant signals to Fairview: Fire signal received. Family reunion last night. Family continues westerly.

It's all Sid can do to restrain a shout of triumph: If Huck has got it right, and Sid has read it right, both big *if*s—yellow and light, not yellow and dark—both generals are still out there on the furnace road, and there is still a chance! But now, like it or not, he has to find Sickles. Leaving his men in place, he takes High Bar back through the IIIrd Corps camps toward Fairview and the turnpike—only to be told that Sickles has gone off to ride the lines with Hooker and might not be back for hours. *Hours?* He spurs back to his post at Hazel Grove and sees an officer lying on his stomach by the gear Sid's men have piled on the ground. The fellow is propped on his elbows and looking toward the south with a field glass. It's Sharpe.

"Morning, Sid," he says, without lowering the glass.

"Morning, Colonel. Enjoying the view?"

"Indeed I am. And I bet the Rebs are, too. You're a nice target there. All you need is a moustache, and they might take you for somebody important." He turns and smiles pleasantly, still on his elbow. "I'm surprised they didn't use that circus tent of yours for target practice last night."

"You received my signal, then?"

"I did. Good work. But that's not what I'm looking at now—though I could use a smoke."

Sid reaches for his own glasses and looks off toward the furnace. "My God! How long is that column?"

"Well, I've been here thirty minutes, and there hasn't been a break. I've counted eight battle flags and a battery, and your man here says he's been watching it for an hour. That's four or five brigades—at least a division. Were they passing when you left?"

"No, sir. Or at least I don't think so." Sid feels his face reddening. "I think I would have—"

"Don't worry about it, Sid. Your job was looking for smoke." He grins. "You can do your penance by reporting to Sickles. He's in charge of this part of the line now, God help us." The grin vanishes. "The good news is he's Hooker's favorite corps commander, and that'll give him some clout if he wants to use it. But he's a loose cannon. He sure won't just sit on his arse. Meanwhile," he looks back toward Fairview, "I'm going to look for our promised horsemen. Keep your eyes peeled back that way for signals. And remember the codes: any Morse we use is just for confusion; if Sickles—Ah! Speak of the Devil and there he is! I'll leave you two to get acquainted. I really need that cigar now!" Sharpe springs to his feet, touches his hat, and starts downhill.

Sid watches as the colonel salutes an approaching cavalcade with a guidon showing the IIIrd Corps diamond and then gallops away over the fields toward Fairview.

The approaching officer turns out not to be Sickles, but General Birney, commanding his lead division, whom Sid sees as "competent" and a West Pointer, for which he puts up with some brusqueness. (He's right about the competence, but wrong about West Point. Birney is yet another lawyer. And a Mason, too, for what that's worth.)

"What have you to report, Major?"

Birney's sharp voice cuts through his full, brown beard. Sid hands up the glasses and repeats Sharpe's analysis. The general takes a look to the south, grunts, and hands them back. Without comment he turns and gallops back down the hill.

Twenty minutes later, almost nine o'clock, Sid is still wondering what Birney's grunt meant when another cavalcade approaches under the colors of the IIIrd Corps. This time it is Sickles. Bravely mustachioed indeed, he is all Sid had expected in a politician: short of stature, but long on self-importance and impatient with regular procedures. (So impatient that before the war he had shot and killed a man he'd caught having an affair with his wife, then pled not guilty by reason of temporary insanity and was acquitted!—supposedly the first successful use of that defense.) He bounds off his horse, offers a hand instead of returning Sid's salute, removes the cigar, spits impressively against the wheel of a caisson, re-inserts the cigar, takes Sid's field glasses, and looks off to the south while Sawyer watches the general's glob of spit hang by a tentacle from the wheel rim, a complex little universe, rich with nebulae.

"God damn," Sickles says, around his cigar.

"Sir, look for where the road turns."

"I see, Captain. I see. Look at those bastards!"

"*Major* Sid Sawyer, sir. I'm pleased to—"

"Oh yes—Major, I see. Sorry, son." Then he looks back toward the south. "How long has that column been moving like that?"

Sid repeats the estimates.

"You don't say. And there goes another battery, so I'd say that's well more than a division." Still looking off to the south, he hands the glasses backward. "Sure *looks* like they're pulling out—headed for Gordonsville. That's off that way, isn't it, Major? On the railroad?"

"Yes, sir." Then he decides to add: "Sir, Jackson's with them."

Sickles turns toward him. "And maybe Lee, sir."

"Lee!" He lowers the cigar.

"Yes, sir. He and Jackson were there at the furnace early this morning—together."

"This morning! *How* early? And how in blazes do we know all this, Major? But first let's get down off this target post here."

So they move down off the crest, and Sid tells him—pretty much everything, since his orders were to "cooperate"—while the Union batteries on Hazel Grove send rounds over the furnace Road, trying to calculate the range, and the IIIrd Corps staff cools its heals nervously a few yards away behind a clump of sumac in case Rebel gunners also begin calculating. Sickles, in spite of first impressions, listens closely, interrupting only when Sid gets to the business about the cavalry regiment.

"Cavalry, Hell! We can't do enough damage with that." He looks off, thinking. "They're up to something, Sawyer. They're pulling out from our front, that's sure, but they may be trying to flank us. Either way, those generals are out of range by now. Don't you think so?"

"Well—"

"I mean you saw this smoke signal, when? An hour ago? And it may have been there earlier."

"I guess so, sir. But they could still be at their bivouac spot."

"*Could* be."

"And a raiding party might—"

"Raiding party! Why do something half-assed?" He lowers the glass and looks back at Sid, the cigar between his teeth. "I'll send a whole division—maybe two."

"A division!"

"Sure. Birney's right here. Meagher!" A lieutenant spurs up from the group in the sumac. "Here, take this to General Hooker," and he tears off a half sheet of paper, scribbles a couple of sentences, hands it to the courier. "And be sure he answers it. Tell him I said this is his chance. He'll know what that means."

Then he turns back to Sid.

"You're a clever man, Sawyer. You've got us an opportunity here. What's needed now, son, is audacity!"

"Thank you, sir, but it will take at least an hour to get orders back from General Hooker."

"*Audacity*, Major. There's no harm in *preparing* for those orders when they arrive. We'll reconnoiter—in force—and if we're engaged, we'll defend ourselves." He turns. "Go fetch Birney!" And another aide rides off. Then, "Cheer up, Sawyer. We'll cut that column to pieces, and you'll be part of it. I'll give you a battalion of Berdan's men, and you can take 'em along the flank, go for their officers—generals, if they're there. It'll make your career, son. You'll be a live colonel or a dead hero!"

It's getting hard to hear, with both batteries in action now, and occasional cheers as the gunners get the range. And Sid is—well, *torn* is one word for it. On the one hand, Sickles' amateurish enthusiasm is refreshing—full of rough edges, maybe, but the man's not afraid to fight, to take risks. With the right leader, he might make a good executive officer, if not quite a Jackson. Sid hates that "son" business, but he likes the air of command. On the other hand, Sickles wants to send him crashing through the underbrush with some of Berdan's sharpshooters into God knows what, on foot, looking for generals to bushwhack—whatever Colonel Berdan himself might think about that. (Hiram Berdan, incidentally, was an engineer—a fact Sid did not know, but which certainly would have interested him!)

What to do, then? Well, Sid is a trained soldier, and he's been under fire, built *bridges* under fire, for God's sake, standing straight up giving orders while men dropped around him—notably at Fredericksburg, where his battalion lost fifty men in thirty minutes lashing pontoons together. So he's no coward. Still—under fire from a distant opponent while doing your job, taking your chances with the law of averages—that is one thing. But charging through the woods into close quarters with a desperate enemy—who may be surprised, or who may be ready to sweep you with canister and musketry, to take you with the bayonet and that hellish cry of theirs—and then, if you live, march you off to Libby Prison in Richmond or worse further south, where you'll starve or cough your lungs out with fevers....well that's another matter. But at the end of these images—in the gilt frame, as it were—is the word *duty*. What is his duty?

First, his orders from Sharpe were to stay here and watch for signals, and he's done that. And yes, several thousand infantry might well do some "damage," and the idea of sending the sharpshooters along is intriguing. Too bad they didn't think of that yesterday. But cavalry—speed!—that's still the ticket. Lee and Jackson may still be there, and they'd easily escape unmounted sharpshooters. For good or ill, he'll stick with the plan.

And just as he's telling Sickles about that, a Rebel shell screeches in and explodes right over the crest, killing or wounding nearly every man and horse in one gun crew and starting a fire in the grass near a caisson. There are screams and whinnies among the guns, and everybody who can dives to the ground except the mounted guidon-bearer and Sickles himself, who shouts,

"It's too late to drop *now*, you fools!" plus Sid, who somehow manages to say upright, immobilized by instinct and a caisson wheel next to him—rattled but unhurt. Sickles slaps him on the shoulder.

"Good nerve, Sawyer! You see, you'll be in as much danger here with us as you would be out there with Birney, so your career's safe! You've done well this morning."

"Thank you, sir." Then, though still shaken, he thinks of something. "And sir, if I may, remember that our agent may be dressed in a slouch hat and a white shirt without—"

"Don't worry, I'll pass the word. Cigar?"

"No thank you, sir."

Sawyer and his small party stand aside and watch as Birney's well-trained brigades double-time up over the crest in columns through the guns, and then to the edge of the woods where the lead regiments file off into lines of battle in the fields between Hazel Grove and Fairview, dress ranks, and pass into the trees while succeeding regiments follow, still in column. Well out on either flank in loose skirmish order are Berdan's two battalions, fading into the woods in their green jackets and black-plumed hats. And behind, a second division is deploying in support.

Sickles is serious. He *must* have Hooker's word then.

Musketry soon roars up from the woods around the furnace—nothing scattered about it. Sickles has his "engagement."

God—if you're up there, Sir—please, look out for Huck Finn.

Sid turns to the southeast to check the sky above Fairview. Union guns there are in action, too, firing in the other direction at the Southern guns beyond Chancellor's—which are firing back. Good thing there aren't rebel guns here at Hazel Grove, too, he thinks, or the Union batteries at Fairview would face…and then, in a flash, the truth comes to him, and its audacity is stunning.

Retreat, Hell. They're trying to surround us!

And this hill would be their fondest hope. And Dan Sickles is sending most of his corps *away* from it, into God knows what! Sid looks at his watch again: it is just after 12:30. Smoke thickens by the minute. How could a balloon even survive, let alone be seen? But here on the hill is the best spot, so he waits.

Major General Sickles, however, does not wait. Damage he's after, and damage he gets: Sid hears the lead division crash with a cheer into the clearing near the furnace. But even Sid knows most of Jackson's column must be past by now, with who-knows-what in the woods to the left, and before long even Sickles feels over-extended and pulls back with his trophies: a wagon or two, a couple of guns, and a few hundred disconsolate Georgians who'd been covering the furnace—and leaving behind an acceptable number of dead heroes.

At 2:30 Sawyer's sergeant shouts again and hands him the glasses. The balloons over Fairview are difficult to see at first, but they've been released, it seems, and are eventually high enough to clear the battle smoke. Their message seems contradictory, though: one says "cavalry underway," but the other says "consult local commander."

"What in blazes does that mean?" Sid mutters, his ears still ringing from that shell explosion.

"Consult Sickles, I reckon?" suggests his signal sergeant. Sid looks at the man—a bit older, thirty-something, originally from his own engineer company, a masonry contractor before the war.

"Hawkins," he asks, "if you could roll the dice and be a dead hero or a live lieutenant—twice the pay—would you take the chance?"

The man squints off into the smoke.

"An officer? No, thanks, Major. The war rolls those dice for us every minute, I think, anyways. No sense getting the devil involved."

Interesting—that the devil would have to be involved in such a choice. Sid can think of no answer to that line of thinking, though he admires the stoicism.

"Well—acknowledge it, then saddle up. I'd say we've already consulted 'the local commander,' and he didn't say anything about cavalry."

"Where we headed then?"

"Back to Fairview, I expect. And we need to hurry."

"You don't think much of Sickles, do you, sir?"

An impertinent question, Sid thinks, as he throws a leg over High Bar, but he answers it. "Actually I like him, Sergeant. He's got some genitals. But it seems he's got no cavalry. I'd check with the devil himself, if he had one regiment of horse."

36. We Know the Enemy Is in Retreat (Afternoon May 2)

Huck's normally neat, school-boyish print becomes more difficult after he's loaded into the wagon—fragmentary and hurried, occasionally obscured by stains, possibly blood—and requires some guesswork. I'd say what happens next is this: after the "crystals" go into the fire, the wagon rolls on for a little while but stops, for about ninety minutes, while some traffic gets unsnarled. The wagon is thus still close enough to the furnace crossroads to be affected by the consternation when Sickles attacks. Huck reports hearing heavy firing back to the northeast and sees couriers riding up and down the line. One of these is the "Powell Smith" Huck says Lee mentioned—who must be James *Power* Smith, a young captain on Jackson's staff and a Presbyterian minister (the staff seems full of those), whose horse has pulled up lame and who hops into Tom's wagon to keep up till another horse can be brought along.

At this point, what seems to happen is a misunderstanding about Huck's status:

When Captain Boswell[20] saw Joe and me knew [each other?] **from Lexington, he threw in a few questions about Jackson from those days and we had a** [laugh or 2?]. **He asked me was my foot any better, and since I wasn't sure if I wanted it to be or not, I said it was hard to tell because I hadn't put any weight on it since last night, and he said, well I might get the chance soon enough if we were attacked along the march. Smith put in that General Lee had told him to ask about my foot and to report about me to General Jackson. Then he said the general hoped to see me himself when there was time. I guess he meant General Jackson. But either way, he said it wasn't likely I'd need any other help and told my guard he was dismissed to his unit, and he'd** [take responsibility] **for me from here.**

Any other 'help,' he says. Can it be that Smith doesn't know Huck is a prisoner? His garb is rather neutral-looking. Could Smith think Huck is in the *Confederate* service? Tom and Joe could have helped the misunderstanding along, of course. In any event, Huck's cavalry guard would quickly defer to a staff officer. So, when the wagon reaches the Brock Road, instead of turning left toward Todd's Tavern with the wagons, or putting Huck off to walk there under guard with the other prisoners, Joe turns the little buckboard to the right, along with the infantry.

Huck now has some time to write, and also to look more closely at Tom:

He's got a pretty real-looking preacher collar under his jacket, so it's not a joke, I guess he's really playing it. Seems pretty risky. What if he runs into somebody amongst the Rebels that's knowed him as a reporter? But being as he's Tom, he'll have another story wrapped inside of this one, just like I would. "Oh, shucks, you found me out. Yes, I'm a Richmond reporter, just trying to get a good story on General Jackson. Didn't mean any harm, so how about helping a hard-working member of the press and tell me a good yarn or two? I'll put your name in. How'd you spell that?" I can just hear him!

Well, before long a trooper come back with Smith's new mount, and he got set to gallop ahead to catch up with the staff, but Tom said first, "Let's all say a prayer for the success of our arms under the direction of Providence," and he did pretty good. I had a hard time not laughing out loud. I'd of not been surprised if lightning struck out of the blue, and considering what I was up to myself, we were probably about as tempting a bank shot as the Lord ever gets on a Saturday morning. I'll write more later.

Late afternoon—the column come to a halt for a few minutes when we come to a crossroad [the Brock/ Plank Road crossing] **while there was some more riding up and down the lines. Captain Smith came down to tell Joe the column isn't turning on the plank Road but going to stay on the Brock till it strikes the turnpike, but Tom pulled us out of the line and hollered out that he thought "Maggie done pulled up lame and he needed to check on her," but when he got off he run back to the**

regiment behind us and I saw him hollering at the regiment's colonel and waving with his hat back our way and the colonel put his men in files of two to get by us till we pushed the cart off into the other road, and Tom went to looking at the horse's hoof. Under his breath he told us he'd convinced the colonel he had orders to wait here for Captain Boswell. He said that should be long enough to talk. Well, I knew we needed to talk and do it fast.

I told them what I heard the generals say the night before, and Joe says, "Law!" and Tom nods his head and says it sounded just like Lee and Jackson. They asked if I thought the Union generals had any idea what the Rebels was planning, and I says, well, they didn't yesterday when I left, but then I asked, what about those attacks today near the furnace? And Tom says, yes, but that was at the *end* of the Rebel line, which was headed *south* right there, and we hadn't seen no Union cavalry, so like as not they still thought the Rebs was retreating, and sure *didn't* know Jackson had turned up the Brock Road to flank them.

So we decided to risk a scout. We left the wagon well off the road, the team tied to a tree, and run up to some high ground where we could see down to the turnpike. We climbed up on top of a farmer's wagon stacked with sorghum barrels, and I tell you what we saw made our jaws drop: there along the turnpike less than a half mile away, was hundreds of Union troops, talking and smoking and getting supper ready, and some working on trenches and breastworks—but the works was facing *south*, towards us, not west, which is where Jackson will come at them—and all just as unaware as you please about what's coming. Now I can see why Jackson turned his men up the longer way: coming at our line down this road, he runs straight into it. But further on up to the west the line just peters out. Now, I see it whole: if Jackson *does* get around that flank—well, in heavy woods like these even a couple of regiments might set our whole line to skedaddling, and Jackson's bringing his whole corps down on it. "And if he gets *all* the way around it," I says, "Lord help us," and Tom says worse than that. Then I says, "Somebody got to get back soon to the column, or we'll be missed."

Now I'm not sure how far to trust Tom, but I come this far, so I'll *go* this far, and I says my orders are to signal Jackson's location, which I'd done, and if no Union raiding party comes along to help—and so far

it hasn't—I'm bound to try, along with any other available 'agents,' to take the general prisoner—or, if he resists, to shoot him. I kind of held my breath then, but Tom just nods.

Finally Joe speaks up. "Kill him?" he asks, and I says sure, he's a Rebel general. What would *anybody* do if a enemy refused to surrender?

Well, nobody said nothing to that, so then we thought about what to do: if we cut the wagon loose and taken the horses, we *might* be able to catch up to Jackson. And if we stick together maybe we can try something. Tom points out the Rebs ain't going to just let us gallop up to the front of the line on our own say-so. But I come back to what we'd seen and I said somebody's got to warn army headquarters. So, we decided Joe and me would stay and try to carry out the plan, and Tom would try and warn the army. Joe made me promise not to do any shooting if Jackson's boy Jim was in the way. Of course, I know I got to try *something*—Jim or no Jim—and not lose my nerve like I did last night! But I says before anybody does get hurt, what weapons do we have? And Joe takes my cheat-shooter out of his belt and hands it back to me. Tom grins and says, "Well, you've already seen mine, Huck," meaning that double-barrel monster he showed me the night before.

And Joe says there was two horse pistols and a carbine under the buckboard of the wagon. And he says, "That ought to be enough to shoot Lee and Jackson, and ourselves, too, if need be!

Meanwhile, Tom'll head on down this road toward the Pike and try and warn the Army. He needs the wagon for that, so Joe & me will be on foot and strike out up that other road we crossed [almost certainly the Germanna Plank Road]**, which maybe will take us back to Jackson's line of march.**

Then Tom says, "Now, once I've brought this bothersome news to our busy generals, I guess I'll trot back up the turnpike and find you boys. Where?"

And Joe says "What about that church over yonder?" [surely Wilderness Church]

"Yes, that'll do," says Tom. "Has a bit of a steeple, and I like churches, being a man of the cloth and all. So what will *your* story be?"

Well, Joe said when we found Jackson's column again, we could say Tom misunderstood the captain and took a wrong turn with the

wagon, and we couldn't talk him out of going on toward the turnpike from that direction. But I had to shake my head. I sure hope we don't have to use that story. Any fool can see the Union line straight ahead there. Besides, I'm blamed if I can see how Tom'll get back up the turnpike through the lines with a battle going on—which it's likely to be by then.

Tom says, yes, it'd be a challenge, but the traffic's like to be all in the *other* direction before long, and lickety-split, too. "If Jackson's whole corps is down on them," he says, "our boys won't be stopping to check passwords. And don't forget I'm well respected by both sides." Then he pointed at his collar and says, "Plus I have ecclesiastical immunity!" We give him a leg up onto the wagon, and he clucks to the team and heads on down the road toward the Union line. We saw him lift his hat once before he was out of sight.

Well, now there's Rebel infantry double-timing left and right off the road into the woods *behind* us—we hadn't figured on that—so I doubt it'll be long now before the attack comes, and *we* got to move on, too, so I doubt I can write any more of this till…

And the last two or three words are illegible.

Huck doesn't report times, but Major Sawyer does, and when next he looks at his watch it's just after 5:00 P.M. He and Sharpe have met back at the inn. They are on the veranda as aides come and go, or smoke and play cards, and Hooker sends off reassuring cables to Washington.

"He told you *what*?" Sharpe is saying. "But Sickles *does* have cavalry. He has most of Pleasonton's force at his beck and call!"

Sawyer is flabbergasted. Brigadier General Alfred Pleasonton has not a regiment but a whole *division*. Even a brigade would be more than fifteen hundred sabers—enough, you would think, to do some "damage."

"Well, sir," Sid splutters, "that's—that's sure not what he told me, and because of that we may have lost a great opportunity—especially since—"

"Especially since Congressman Sickles has pitched into Jackson's column with—God knows what consequences to *our* operation." Sharpe brings his hand down on the porch rail. "Damn it! Exposing our flank—our agents—"

"Well, what does Hooker think?"

A courier rides up in a cloud of dust, tramps up the steps, delivers his message to one of three aides lounging at the other end of the veranda. Hooker meets him on the porch, says "Thank you, Captain." To Sawyer Hooker looks paler—and somehow shorter—every time he appears. He opens the door and calls back in for Couch and Meade, then looks down again at the paper, motions to Sharpe and Sid. "Look at this, Sharpe. What do your agents know about this? Lee seems to be on the move southwest, and Howard's worried about being flanked."

"All we know, sir, is that long columns have been observed."

"Is he retreating?" says Couch, who is out on the porch now.

"Lee?" says Hooker sharply. "Without a fight? That's not his way." Then he looks up to the west. "But Sickles has been among his trains all afternoon. He *must* be in retreat now, with his communications cut, his trains in motion—and certainly, Colonel, if what you say is true, both Lee and Jackson out on the furnace Road, that looks like a full-scale shift of their base toward Gordonsville...maybe for defense...but we must still take precautions. At any rate I've told Howard to refuse his flank."

A pit opens in the major's stomach. *He's not thinking about the plan at all.*

Hooker turns and calls back into the doorway, "Captain, send a wire; tell Sedgwick[21] to make haste toward us from Fredericksburg. There can't be much force in his front there—that we know the enemy is retreating, trying to save his trains. We are confident of a strong position—something to that effect, and—the wagons have *what?*—well surely they can lay new wire." And then he is back in the house, along with Bill Candler, one of the aides.

The remaining aide, Captain Abner Danforth, looks off to the west.

"What do you think, Major? You were out there with Sickles. What *are* they up to? I can hear a bit of shelling, I think."

"I don't know, Captain. But Lee's not retreating; I'd bet on that."

Sid likes Danforth—another young aide trying to grow enough whiskers to look older than he is—but thoughtful and level-headed. Not a military man really, but a student of the classics, with an ironic wit and none of the foolish romanticism that led many of his ilk to volunteer. In quieter times, he'd be excellent company. Now the major is looking off to the west, squinting into the evening sun, and he's about to note that, except for the occasional clip-clopping of a courier's horse, it's strangely quiet out that way, considering all the Hell Sickles is raising—maybe it's the wind direction or something—when he sees a little cloud of dust over the turnpike, then what looks like a horse-drawn wagon coming at a trot, with a single driver, and hears some shouts and laughter from the pickets as the wagon pulls up at the gate. The driver smiles and waves to those on the porch.

"Good afternoon, brethren! Is this the headquarters of the Grand Army of the Republic?"

He wears a nondescript brown jacket, a bowler hat, and a clerical collar.

37. Huck Finn Must Die! (Evening, May 2)

"You got this from Our Boy himself?" asks Sharpe, as Tom pauses to light the offered cigar, then leans back in his chair. The only others there in the parlor are Hooker and Major Sawyer, plus Danforth in case a courier is needed.

"How else would I get it, George? The Rebs don't invite me to their war councils. I have to cultivate—"

"I understand that, but do you believe him?"

"I believe my eyes, Colonel. And here's what I see."

Tom leans over the map on the table and traces, with the little finger of his cigar hand, the line of march that will take Jackson to the Union right flank—the long, unprotected right flank—and at the end of it he taps the cigar, causing a little pile of ash to land on the very end of the Union line, where a few embers take root on the map and begin to burn.

Sharpe reaches over, brushes them off. "Well, we've been getting word of that."

"General Howard has been instructed to take precautions," says Hooker, who has listened quietly so far, except for his finger-drumming.

"Precautions?" says Tom.

"That's right, Sawyer—those that are necessary—send scouts, refuse his flank, fortify it—"

"Has he done that, General?" Tom looks up, lifts an eyebrow. "Have you checked?"

Sid is envious: only a civilian could get away with that!

"Well. What more could we do to prevent—"

"General, I'd say by now there's not much you can do, to *prevent* it. Jackson's already there. If I were you, I'd be trying to figure out how to save my army."

"*Save* it?" The drumming stops.

"That's what I said, General. What if he gets between you and the river? What if he gets his hands on all that truck you've got back at the fords? What if the army itself can't get back across? You going to defend Washington with acts of Congress?"

There's a moment of shocked silence.

"General," Sharpe interrupts, raising his hand, "if you'll allow me? Tom, we'll worry about the army and the Capital. But if there's not much time, let's get this straight. You say Our Boy overheard this from the generals themselves?"

"That's right."

"And he was—in a thicket not ten feet away?"

"'Spitting distance' was his term, I believe. Although he's a good spitter."

"And he was *armed*."

"I should say so! Why, I gave him a nice little two-barrel—"

"All right, so he stayed there all night—armed*?*"

"Well, he was captured, remember, and they took the gun. We've been through all this, George."

"Yes, but here's what I'm getting at: he had a chance to shoot both of them, or at least try to take them prisoner, and he *didn't?*"

"That appears to be correct."

"And now he and Smith—or whoever he is—are back in Jackson's column, and they say they're going to try again?"

"That is my understanding."

"And Our Boy now has, not only your personal weapon or one of them, but a journal where he's been scribbling the details of what he and the rest of us, including the Mayor, have been up to for—"

"For at least the last forty-eight hours, yes sir. It's interesting reading. The boy writes—"

But Hooker is alert again: "Mr. Sawyer—or Reverend, is it?—does this journal discuss meetings here, and back at U.S. Ford?"

"Why yes, though I haven't read it all, but the ones about the business with Lee are pretty fine, and the part about meeting the Commander-in-Chief is powerful, too. The man has a voice that—"

"All right. Captain Danforth, will you go out to the yard and see to Reverend Sawyer's horses? He may need fresh ones. See if that trap of his is still road-worthy." Then, turning to Sharpe, in a lower voice, "What do you think, Colonel? Whatever happens here, can we allow this Huckleberry fellow and his papers to fall into enemy hands?"

Sharpe looks at Sid, but Sid is focused on the plan itself and not fully alert to where this is going. Or at least that is how he later explains it to himself, and he is—to his eternal chagrin—silent.

Sharpe continues: "Not if we can avoid it. But I don't see how—"

"Well," continues the general, "this gentleman here—Reverend Sawyer—seems to be able to maneuver through the lines just fine. Has a charmed life, I must say, and perhaps as a man of the cloth—"

"He's not a real minister, sir."

"Well, that will make this easier for him. And he's not a soldier, either—that helps, too."

"You're saying—"

"I'm saying, Colonel, it sounds to me as if this fellow Huck Lee—or Huck Finn—is in a very hazardous position—as are all of us."

There is quiet in the room, although what sounds like cannon can be heard in the distance, but off to the west now, not the east. A bit of a breeze rustles the curtains. Hooker stands and looks out the door. "Where he is, gentlemen, I don't see how he *can* survive."

Hooker stands at the door, looking west. "Colonel," he says, "I think you know our mission now: we have to find Our Boy and bring him back—one way or another—and that journal of his. Major," this is to Sid, "maybe you can find General Pleasonton and launch that raiding party. Captain Danforth is at your disposal."

"Yes, sir."

Outside, Danforth is hitching Tom's wagon to a new pair of horses and says, "Let's hope the Rebs don't notice the switch."

"If they do, Reverend Sawyer may need to think fast."

"That, he can do," says Sid, then explains the new orders—find Pleasonton and then, against all odds, Huck and his journal, plus any accompanying generals. "What do you think of *those* orders, Abner? Or is it Abe? I myself detest—"

"Abner's fine, sir. I'd rather not be confused with the president. As for the orders, to me that all sounded sort of like, 'Who will rid me of this turbulent priest?' if you get the reference," but Sid doesn't get it, not yet.[22]

"Understood, Colonel!" Tom shouts back, as he comes down the steps to his wagon and hoists himself up—clearly favoring the old leg wound.

"Leg acting up, Tom?" Sharpe calls, as Tom picks up the reins.

"Not as bad as Huck's, I'll bet! Well, I'll see what I can do out to the west. Giddyap, boys!"

"And, Tom! Don't forget the passwords this time!"

"Got 'em, Colonel: Dead or alive! It's the Lord's work we do!"

He pulls out into the road with his little wagon full of Bibles and a white handkerchief fluttering from a stick raised over it—and soon becomes a little cloud of dust heading toward what appears to be another, bigger cloud on the horizon under the westering sun.

Sid pivots toward Sharpe. The light has dawned. "Dead or alive? What's—That's not a password."

Silence.

"*Huck* dead or alive?"

"Sid—"

"Because I'll have nothing to do with that, sir! That man is a soldier in this army and has sent very—*very* valuable information that—" Too angry to finish, he hurls his cap across the yard, where it lands improbably on a bayonet used for horseshoes.

"Sid, calm down, no one is asking you to—"

"No, not me! But *Tom*—he's not a soldier, so it's all right for *him* to just go kill one of our agents?"

"Sid, nothing like that has to happen. We do have to have those papers. Just think for a second what happens if that story gets out."

"What do you mean, 'gets out'?"

"Sid," his voice lower, "we're not the only ones with our necks out here. I expect higher-ups are worried about their *own* necks—maybe after the war, maybe hedging their bets, or—"

"*Hedging*?"

"Look, I expect us to win, Sid, but not everybody does, and—well, there could be folks trying to cover themselves."

"Sir, that sounds disloyal to me. And you're just going to allow—I can't believe I hear this." And then, illogically, "You ought to consider *yourself* under arrest! Danforth, fetch our horses!"

"What are you—"

"I'm going to find General Pleasonton. I understand *that* part of my orders anyhow! Danforth!"

There's a commotion out on the road now, fingers pointing off to the west. Tom's wagon is barely visible, but beyond it there's a growing cloud of dust—

much bigger than Tom's. Russell, on the veranda, raises his field glass and looks off down the road.

"Good God!" he says. "Here they come!"

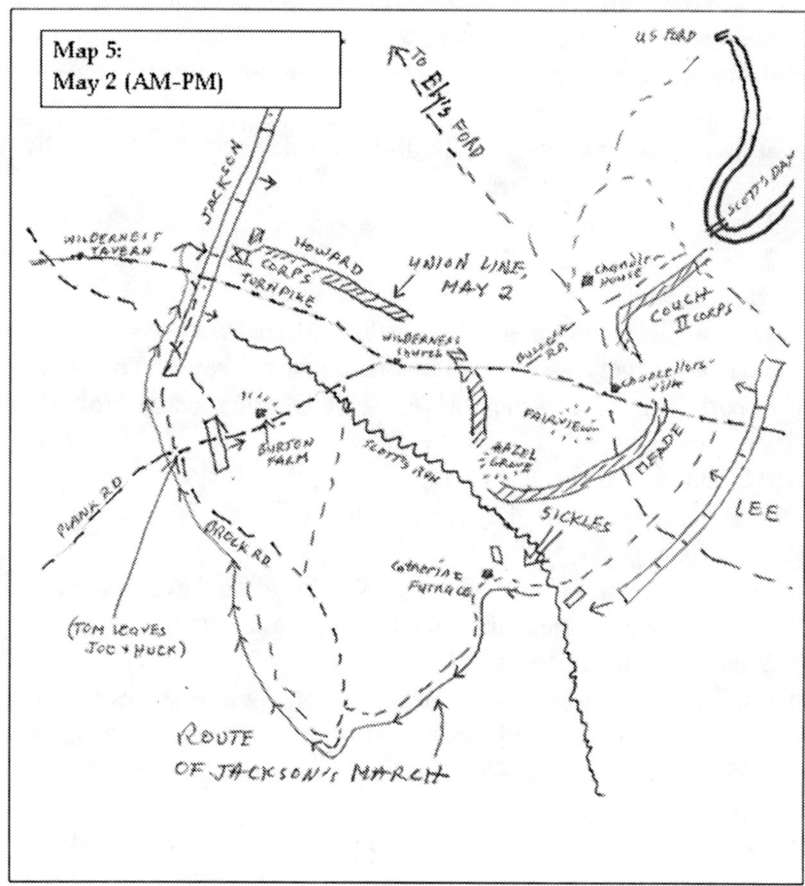

Sid raises his own glasses and sees coming toward them a dusty, panicky mass of men and equipment—foaming horses, some riderless, galloping aides, color bearers, shouting and swearing officers, jouncing field guns, caissons, and all manner of other wagons, one with a broken single-tree dragged along by a frantic, limping horse, and then sprinting foot-soldiers, some with weapons, some not, and all headed this way.

"Danforth, where are you?"

"Right here, Major. Here's your hat."

Hooker is out on the porch now, calling for his own hat and horse, his staff—whether he calls for his fiddlers three is not recorded. Sid yanks the cap on, mounts, and spurs High Bar into the road.

"What are you *doing*, Sid?" calls Sharpe.

"My duty, Colonel!"

"Fine, Major! But don't forget your *orders*!"

Sid spurs toward the approaching chaos. He dodges the first plunging, whinnying horses, foaming and riderless, and the pause allows Danforth to catch up.

"Look for Tom, Abner!"

"Why, Major?"

They pull off to the left to avoid a wave of galloping, hatless riders, and careening wagons—one with blood dripping from a dead driver slumped on its buckboard.

"Why? Because all that," Sid is shouting now to be heard, "all that sounded to me like 'Huck Finn must die'—*that's* why! I probably can't find him, let alone save him if I do, but I have to try, and that means catching up with Tom!" Danforth doesn't answer, but he spurs to catch up.

The flood is fully around them now, even foot-soldiers, many without hats, or much of anything else, and some have even torn off their unit insignia. Those that still have them bear the half-moon of the XIth Corps, which seems to have ceased to exist, except as a turbulent wave with occasional officers floating along, mounted and un-mounted, shouting, cursing, swinging swords. It's also like a herd, in that there's a kind of cohesiveness even in this rout. There are even some *actual* cattle, driven along as beef on the hoof and now loose, as well as deer and other game scared up out of the woods by the Rebel advance. And along with the rout, there's the smell—a strange brew of battle and supper: smoke, bacon, dust, horse sweat, gunpowder, coffee. And there's Howard himself, the corps commander, full-bearded and hatless, holding his colors under the stump of one arm, guiding his horse through the flood with the others, the flag flapping across his chest as he screams, pleads, weeps...

Within a mile the sounds of battle are clear—deflected earlier by some trick of wind or landscape—deep thuds and high flashes, an angry brown fog low over the road and woods. On the turnpike in the middle distance, between a field on one side and a country church on the other, Sid sees a Union battery sweep the road with canister.

"We must be getting close, sir!" Danforth shouts over the din.

They are. A shell bursts over one of the guns, silhouetting men and cannon against an orange flash and leaving several of one gun crew dead or writhing on the ground. The sound follows a second later, its percussive wave hitting Sawyer and Danforth like a hot blanket.

They are well off the road now to the left, dodging knots of panic and debris, leaping over axles and wagon traces and cannon prolonges and dead horses and looking for…what? They are past Fairview now, maybe past Hazel Grove, though the major isn't sure. South of the road, near a burning barn, in a field strangely empty for the moment, Sid pulls up to think.

"Have you seen Tom, Captain, or that wagon?"

"No, Major, and I've had my eyes peeled."

"Well, then, where's Pleasonton, do you think? The IIIrd Corps was off to the south here."

"He was with Sickles, but—"

"Hold it. Look!" Sid points to the left. At the edge of the hilltop clearing—and yes it *is* Hazel Grove, because there's that battery, and beyond them a body of horsemen—at least a few hundred—lounging in a field by their grazing mounts. "It's Huey!"

"Who, sir?"

"Pennock Huey! The 8th Pennsylvania. Come on!"

They meet Huey on foot halfway across the clearing.

"Evening, Sawyer!" Huey chirps. "I hear there's trouble out this way, but so far—"

"Oh, there is, Major! Lots of it. What are your orders?"

"General Pleasonton sent me, sir. My orders were to be at your service, or to stem a rout maybe, but I must say it's been a pleasant evening with—"

"Thank God! Well, Major, the time has come, and the rout is nearly here. Call your men to arms, and follow me!"

Huey turns to his bugler: "Boots and saddles, lad; let's hear it. Follow you where, Major?"

"To Hell, probably."

Huey mounts and the three officers spur through the rapidly forming columns to the edge of the woods where a card game has just broken up. The junior major, a big Irishman, is disappointed: "Damn it, Huey, that was a good game!"

"You must have a good hand, Pete," Huey laughs. "Leave them face down. You can turn them up on the way back. I'll give orders not to peek!"

Nobody seems very serious here, Sid thinks, as the regiment moves off jauntily into the woods between the hill and the turnpike, thick double columns—two battalions in column by squadron.

"Major, I must warn you, Jackson's corps has flanked Howard, and we are heading right for the enemy lines—I hope for their flank, but—"

"Well, so do I, Major. I enjoy flanks!"

There are flashes off in the woods to the left now, a rattle of wild fire.

"Major, rout or not, our mission is to break through, and if there's more than one line, to break through that one, too."

"I know of no other way to treat enemy lines, sir!"

A shell explodes in the woods ahead. A tree limb crashes.

"Then we must look—is that the plank Road ahead, Abner?" The Plank Road comes into the turnpike at an angle and would allow some chance to flank a Rebel force moving across their front—leaving their commanders vulnerable from the rear.

Maybe there's a chance after all...

"That's it, I think," says Danforth, holding one end of a map in his teeth, unrolling it with a hand.

And then, toward them, from the road to their front and the woods to their left, comes a body of blue foot-soldiers, jogging briskly to the rear in spite of their swearing officers. Huey, more sober now, orders his men to hold formation, letting the mob by. Then, out of the smoke, in the road and in the woods on either side of it, there they are: enemy skirmishers, coming at a trot. Behind these, Sid sees a mounted enemy officer, wheeling, sword in hand, shouting. And behind the officer, through the trees, he sees a mass of infantry, a red battle flag bobbing above it, hears commands go on down the enemy line...there's no time! Even he can see.

"No time to reform, my friend!" calls Huey. "We'll have to charge them! Double COLUMNS!"

"Major," It's Danforth. "This is my first time, really." For a terrible moment Sid thinks he's about to hear one of those last-minute premonitions. "If I don't return, Major, I'd be obliged if you'd read this for me." Danforth hands him a folded piece of paper.

"What's this?"

"Scripture!"

But there's no more time—Huey has spurred to the head of the second battalion—three squadrons, one after the other, a thick formation indeed—cups his hands and shouts over to the other column, led by 'Peter,' who nods vigorously, repeating the commands, and the columns launch forward with a cheer and a thundering of hooves, from the edge of the woods right into the road, then wheeling left as if on parade ground, down the road toward the enemy infantry.

Sid hears, "Pistols PORT! Draw SABERS! CHARGE!"

The Southern skirmishers are ridden over with a cheer and a quick rattle of wildfire. Sid had been with Huey, but now he and Danforth are just sort of, as Sid remembers it, "alongside the woods and probably in bad form."

Danforth draws his sword, but Sid had left his own against that tree two days ago. Well, he still has a pistol, but before he can get it out, they are through the Rebel skirmishers and there in front of them is the main mass of the enemy. Huey calls out a command he can't hear, but there's no time to react before several things happen almost at once.

Now Huey's cavalry has found, not the plank Road—which you can see from the map might have been one route to the south flank of Jackson's assault force—but the turnpike itself and has plowed head-on into the leading wave, probably parts of several regiments, at least a thousand rifles within close range of Huey's 350, plus a Rebel battery of six-inch field guns on the road trying to close up in support. The Rebel infantry are a bit of a mob themselves by this time, but a mob filled with the scent of the kill. It is amazing what that can do for young men who, let's recall, have marched more than twelve miles on pretty much empty stomachs. Issued three-days' rations twenty-four hours ago (not much in the first place) most have already cooked and consumed them in obedience to the veteran's rule that any food should be eaten as soon as possible; otherwise you have to carry it on the march, where a lot can happen to it, and besides you might come across legitimate plunder—remember Manassas Junction! Then they're deploying in the woods and dressing ranks, and then charging, screaming their heads off, and for an hour after that staying in nearly continuous forward motion, firing, loading and trotting forward, then firing again as the alternate companies reload, and taking casualties themselves as they meet resistance…and on top of all this they're supposed to stay in formation moving through woods?

Well, they don't. But they are still in command, more or less, whoever they're with, they're Lee's men, Jackson's men, and they're whipping the Yanks.... And now here comes Union cavalry charging through the skirmishers, right towards them....

Now, dear reader, this is a scene to which my poor pen is unequal. It requires a Dante—or a painter of the macabre. But I will try. And those of you with no interest in the details of what horrors otherwise decent men can inflict on each other may want to go for coffee and let a page or two turn without you.

At first the firing is scattered and surprised and Huey's men are slashing through on the road with pistol and saber, but then the Rebels' war cry swirls up from the woods on either side, and Sid hears a command to fire, sees a sheet of flame from first one side and then the other, hears two deafening crashes as if echoes of each other, hears lead thump into bodies and the screams of men and horses. The air moves and hums, as if with bees, tugs at his cap. His face is splattered with blood and bits of flesh from the back of the rider in front of him who bounces back off the rump of his horse, nearly knocking Sid off his own mount. Horses go down on either side of him, screaming, blood pumping from necks and chests, their riders crying out as shoulders and hips are blown apart or crushed. The lead squadrons have gone down as if hit by a scythe. A wounded captain staggers to his feet above the tangled mass of the first column, lifts his hand to his mouth to shout an order, but has his head whipped first one way, then the other by bullets from left and right, each of which takes part of the face, till he sinks to his knees, then falls in slow motion, face (or what's left of it) forward. With the second volley, followed in a split second by a blast of grapeshot from a battery further back on the road, the head of the right column is blown apart, literally, and in what is left of his own column Sid sees a man knocked from his horse, has a fleeting view of the man's heart pulsing through what's left of his rib cage as he dangles from his stirrup and his frantic mount rears in panic. Sawyer turns, calls for Danforth, doesn't see him, hears someone shout an order—is it Huey?—hears the retreat bugled back down the column. He has been on the left, in the part of the field next to the woods and not fully into the road, but gasps as his cheek is stung by something, feels blood on his tongue, pulls up, turns, sees what's left of the regiment galloping—crawling, bleeding—back down the turnpike...now he *is* exposed. As he moves toward the dubious safety of the woods, paralleling the main body of remaining horsemen, he comes upon the fallen form of Abner Danforth, next to his horse, which has stopped to graze incongruously on a patch of spring grass. He starts to dismount, but sees that the man is clearly dead, his lower body blasted apart, that what had seemed to be a belt or bridle tangled in one of the stirrups is in fact the man's entrails, and one side of his head is—

No more, no more! This is the stuff, not just of nightmare, but of Judgment and Perdition. What right or wrong is worth this? What duty? What Cause?

But Cause, of course, has little to do with it. That is not why men will face such a thing. They face it for their comrades, their leaders, their sense of who they are. Two years later, his line before Richmond crumbling, the Southern commander will need time to get his army out of its trenches and on the road. He fills a key fort with a battalion of artillery, all the ammunition he can find, and a few hundred colicky Mississippians (about the same number as at the Alamo), and says give me two hours. And for two hours they block that road, holding off most of a division—at more than twenty-to-one odds, till only a handful are left and the Federals are over the walls closing in on the guns, and a Rebel who's just rammed in a load of canister stands with his hand on the lanyard and fifty rifles leveled at him, and the attackers are shouting at him to surrender, and he screams, "Surrender and be damned!" and pulls the lanyard because that is what the Army of Northern Virginia does. And no one remembers his name, that I know of, and his sacrifice ultimately doesn't matter. But veterans still speak in hushed, respectful voices of the deed. And that of course is what *would* matter to him.

What rubbish! When the gods want to destroy us, they first make us brave.

Sid is on the turnpike now, moving back east with the rout and with what is left of the 8th, shells screaming over head, patrolling the hot, vibrant air and plowing the fresh-laid dead. High Bar seems strangely placid, doesn't want to run. Is he hurt? A hand is at his bridle. "Sir, can you dismount? I got her. Be careful with your hand, sir."

He dismounts. His left hand feels strangely warm, comforted. He looks down and sees blood dripping—from his arm? But what about the face?

"Take High Bar, Private. How is he?"

"He's limping, bleeding a bit. I can shoot him if—"

"No, don't. Tie him up when you can. I'll do it if it has to be done. Can you see my face, Private? Is it shot through? I feel like I cannot speak clearly—"

"Well, your face—excuse me, sir, but if you'll let me—I see some blood—just this scratch here. But I think your arm's shot through." Then he calls to someone. "Colonel! He's over here!" He looks in the direction the man has called, sees Huey coming across the field—it looks like Hazel Grove again Huey's braid once again dangling loose from his hat, his left hand bandaged, sword still in his right—not smiling any more. Sid feels faint.

"I feel a bit faint, Huey. I'll sit down if you don't mind."

And he falls back on the ground.

When he comes to, he finds himself on a stretcher born by two men into the yard of the Chancellor Inn, where there are many other casualties. It is still light, the sky still red in the west, and above the groans around him in the yard he can still hear firing, cannon and musketry both. His left arm hurts, and he remembers his condition. He looks at the arm and sees what looks like a tourniquet above the elbow, feels his heart leap in fear. Below the rolled up sleeve his lower arm is caked with blood, and there's little feeling. A man wearing the armband of a hospital orderly, leans down, offers him a canteen. It's not water but something alcoholic, and he splutters, but in his thirst he drinks it anyway. "Thank you, Private. Have they cut off—What's the condition of my arm?"

"Well, it ain't cut off, sir. Though I expect they will. That's mostly what they do when it's shot through like that. We can rewind the bandage. Yours is all soaked, and this other fellow ain't going to be needing his any more. Died before he bled much, y'see?"

The tourniquet is maintained with a horseshoe above the wound, a blood-caked hole in the lower arm. Sid turns it as best he can with the other hand, sees an exit wound. He winds the "new" bandage as tight as he can, then releases the tourniquet slowly, feels blood and sensation burn back in, holds his breath as he waits for the bleeding to begin again, and it does, but it's a smooth flow, not a spurt, thank God.

"Private, if I pass out again, don't let them—are you listening, Private? Where is Major Huey?"

"Well, Sawyer, that was quite a charge!"

Sid turns, tries to sit up. "Colonel! Were you there, too, with the 8th?"

"You put me under arrest, remember. What else could I do? I'll try to see they don't cut the arm off, unless it's the only way. Keep it clean if you can. I brought your cap. Thought you might want it as a souvenir." He holds it out. Sid rises unsteadily to his feet, supporting his left arm with the other, looks at the cap, and sees at least three holes. "Good thing you're not any taller, eh? Or fatter—there's at least three more in your jacket."

"Huey—Huey's all right?"

"So far as I can see, except for a cut hand—though I'm damned if I know how."

"Well," then, remembering, "I hope that other major got to go back and pick up his card hand."

"Pete Keenan?" Sharpe spies a cigar on the ground, picks it up, and feels in his pockets for matches, lights it, and puffs it to life. "In Heaven maybe, if they allow cards there. His body's over there in the wagon. They counted thirteen holes in him."

"Thirteen! And Danforth? Oh, God, it's all my fault, Colonel. I took him on a fool's errand. I took them *all* on a fool's errand."

"Major, just rest now. You did as well as anybody else around here, Lord knows—"

But Sid remembers, reaches into his blouse, pulls out Danforth's paper, tries to unfold it with one bloody hand, and hands it out to Sharpe.

"Abner said to read this for him, Colonel, and I—I can't see much. He said it was scripture. Maybe you could?"

Sharpe takes the paper and unfolds it, then removes the cigar and holds it with one hand, while holding the paper with the other, and reads out:

Fear no more the lightning-flash,
Nor the all-dreaded thunder-stone;
Fear not slander, censure rash;
Thou hast finish'd joy and moan...
The sceptre, learning, physic, must
All follow this, and come to dust.

—William Shakespeare

"Well—that's not the Bible. What kind of man calls that 'scripture'?"

"A thinking man, Colonel. Rest his soul. I wonder what it's from."[23]

Hearing renewed firing off to the west, Sid stoops for his pistol belt and, when he rises, feels faint again, then collapses. The colonel manages to catch him with one arm, quickly transferring his cigar to the other, and dropping the poem.

38. May 3: All Right, Then, I'll *Go* to Hell

Till dawn on the 3rd (Sunday, the Lord's Day) he tosses, dozes, wakes groggily—drunkenly maybe, since orderlies keep shoving "stimulants" at him whenever he wakes, as he's carried from the inn back over U.S. Ford, partly by wagon, partly by hand, and his left arm throbs with every jolt.

He sleeps, finally, for a few hours, and wakes with the sun in his eyes. And he's hungry. He hasn't eaten much of anything for two days, after all. He is on the porch of the main house—a prize spot, since the yard and outbuildings all look full of wounded. He has no idea what time it is, realizes his pocket watch is missing and feels more disoriented by that than anything else. He looks down at his arm: still there, though the sleeve's torn to make room for a bandage, the same one apparently.

"Don't pick at it, Major. We'll re-dress it when we can." Sid looks up to see Mary Carroll, whom he'd met at Ely's Ford Thursday evening—or was it Wednesday?—She smiles. Somehow she looks neat, despite an apron with pockets stuffed full of bandages and bloody surgical implements. "The arm's not as bad as I feared. How it missed the artery and both bones is a mystery."

"Oh, Miss Carroll, good morning—so they've abandoned Ely's then." He can hear guns in the distance. "Is Miss Thatcher here, too, then? Is she all right?"

"Why yes, she's here. As for all right—well—listen, she knows you're here and perhaps when there's time we can talk about it, but I'm needed now. Just wanted to reassure you about the arm: I believe we can let you keep it for now."

Sid shoves himself up with his right arm to where he can sit up against a porch column. He hears much firing in the distance, and—*What time is it?* He gingerly flexes the fingers of the left hand: they work, if painfully, but he can't flex the arm—he'll need a sling. His head aches and there's some dried blood on his cheek, a scrape and a knot above his ear, and…*I smell. How long since I've bathed*?

But he'll live. And—he has his badge of courage, does he not? A wounded arm. If things went wrong, no one could deny Major Sawyer had done well enough.

But well enough for what? After all, Sid knows he was not really *in* Huey's charge, and at the first sight of massed Southern infantry loading and leveling weapons, his first instinct was to move, not straight ahead after Huey, but to the left, not *exactly* away from the enemy—he was rather tightly pinned within the column after all—but when he heard the enemy command to fire he had nearly collapsed, and if it weren't for the momentum of the riders around him, he'd have spurred to the rear then and there, mission be damned. And what was that mission, in retrospect? A delusion! A fantasy! What had he expected? To find Stonewall Jackson at an unguarded campfire with a trio of Union agents? *Insane*!

Into this reverie intrudes a face approaching from the yard—a welcome face in spite of the gore on her apron and dress. She carries up the steps a basket of bloody towels and another of somewhat cleaner ones, pulls up a stool and leans toward him, avoiding his eyes. "Well," she says quietly, "let's see what we can do."

"Becky! Listen, I have news that I probably shouldn't divulge, but you have the right to know, I think—and it's about Huck. We sent him—"

"Huck's dead, Sid." She looks at him now, her face an open grave.

"Dead! But—how do you know?"

She looks down at the arm, pulls the dressing away, not gently. "This will hurt," she says (as if that *hadn't*), and pours whiskey over the entrance and exit wounds. The whiskey is new—something she learned in the West? Sid sucks the pain in with a breath, as she begins wrapping new dressing, and continues: "I know because Tom told me. Last night. He left this for you." She lifts the towels in the basket and pulls out a sheaf of papers sewn together between marbled paste-board, and tosses it on his lap. "It's Huck's notebook. That's what you wanted, isn't it?" She ties off the dressing, not gently, and rises. "And we hear that Jackson is dead, too—also part of your plan, I suppose. Congratulations. I'll send something around for you to eat."

"*Jackson's* dead?"

"So we hear—or at least badly wounded—and Tom says it's true." Her voice still toneless as a weather report. Sid tries to think.

"Becky, where's Tom now?"

"Who knows?" She looks back down at his arm. "He said he'd twisted his knee and was going to look in the ice house for something to put on it, and then said he had 'work to do,' and might even go 'fight for his country,' whatever *he* might mean by that. As we all may have to. The army has been routed, it seems, Jackson or no Jackson. Don't worry about me—I'm fine. And I really could not care less about Tom Sawyer."

She stands, turns, descends the steps, and Sid calls after her, "Maybe he's wrong, Becky! I'll go after him! I'll—"

"You can go to Hell, Major, for all I care." Without looking back, she crosses the walk toward the yard.

Sawyer stands and looks after her, cannot think, can hardly breathe, but he has to eat and drink, and when an orderly comes by with a handcart of provisions, he takes some powdered milk, mixes it with water and gulps it down, takes a couple of cold corn biscuits, and stuffs them into his mouth along with some dried pork. And never has such simple fare tasted so sweet, despite the taste of stale blood still in his mouth. He wipes his face on the sleeve of his good arm, lifts the journal, and, in the effort to stuff it one-handedly into his belt, something falls out: an insect specimen, gold and black, that had been pressed in a waxed envelope. He sits, looks at it: a butterfly? What in the—? Has the fellow become a naturalist? But there's no time for this now!

He shoves the specimen into the journal, the journal into his bedroll and springs to his feet. When you're young, you can do that—go hungry and sleepless for two days, lose a pint of blood, and, after a nap and a bite to eat, hop right up! But this is no affirmation of life, no indeed. The major knows what his duty is now. Becky Thatcher has just laid it out for him like a suit.

He buckles his belt—not so easy with a bad arm—grabs the cap with the holes in it, and says, to the world in general: "All right, then, I'll *go* to Hell!"

And what of Becky herself now? What might be on *her* mind? Having consigned the major to Perdition—she seems strong, so strong. No collapsing in grief. No sobbing on Sid's shoulder this time. How much does she know? She's desperately busy, and Huck's journal is almost two hundred pages. But she would have to look at it, wouldn't she? At least the final entry or two? And it's right there in the bedroll. But what could it prove, when Tom or Sid could easily have torn out anything incriminating?

But, strong or not, she has to talk to somebody. And eventually she does. Here is what Miss Carroll remembers:

I'd been in surgery all that morning and the night before, and I was beginning to make mistakes. So about mid-day I went to my cot in the loft to catch a nap and found Becky already there but not asleep, and she—well, she wasn't crying then, but she'd clearly been crying, and I asked her how Major Sawyer was doing and she said, "Who gives a bloody damn," or something like that, and I said something about war and difficult choices, and I trailed off realizing how stupid it sounded. I never knew Huck, of course, but I knew what he meant to her. I sat and tried to comfort her, put an arm around her, and she said, "You know, Mary, I once thought there were *some* men of honor left in the world, and I thought Sid Sawyer was one of them."

Well, what could I say? For all I knew then, she was right. At least *I* had met very few in the East. But I said we must all keep our faith in the Cause and our Lord—though I'm sure I didn't sound convincing. It seemed to help, though, for she said, "Yes, we must not despair. For despair is a sin, and we shall all meet again." And there was no irony in her voice. Her faith is really a rock for her, and I wish I were as devout. Well, then she wiped her face and I pointed out that Tom *could* be wrong. He'd *been* wrong before, after all, had he not? And she had to admit that was true. Then she said she was going back to work, for that was the best thing for it. And I was awake now, so I did, too, for a while. As we went back downstairs, I pushed my luck a bit too far, I think. "Whatever *is* the truth," I said, "you know Huck loved you."

She said, "Yes, he did. Everybody seems to love me." And then she just broke down and sobbed for ten minutes straight there at the foot of the stairs while I rocked her like a baby, and then she dried her eyes, and that's all she ever told me about it, then or later. I've no idea whether she looked at that journal, although later she did mention "a letter from that Señor something-or-other," which she said she regretted having given to "the intelligence people."

As for the letter, Becky might realize its connection to Mexico and the Sister who had been looking for Huck—but not its true, awful significance. *She* hadn't read it, naturally, because polite people don't read each other's mail.

So we shall leave Becky, who at least can ease her own pain by trying to ease the pain of others, and return to Major Sawyer, whose own anguish borders on madness. But there is some method in it. For he has remembered, from his scout along the river, that there *were* possible crossings above and below US Ford, or at least places easily bridged, and if the army were forced to make a stand up against the river and anchored, say, at US Ford, a flanking force might move across, upriver or down, undetected in the thick woods, and take the enemy in reverse.

Turn about is fair play! What a stroke *that* would be!

At the prisoner pen, he sees there are more now, but among them, still, are the sullen Alabamians and their blond captain.

He points out the man to a guard and asks to see him. "Major," says a nearby provost officer, "what's the business here? These are prisoners."

"I know what they are, Lieutenant. I have General Butterfield's permission to use them for an important mission." *Lies! Lies!* But he motions to the gray captain, who moves warily to the fence.

"How's the food?" Silence. "Remember what I said about helping me build a bridge? The offer stands."

The captain squints, looks haggard but not broken. Sid figures he himself looks just as bad, leaning on the fence with a bandaged left arm.

"You can't make any such offer."

"No? Well, how's this one?"

Sid raises his pistol, levels it at the man's forehead, and cocks it. The man doesn't move. There's a gasp from the prisoners, a shout from the provost. Another officer hurries over.

"Last chance, Captain," Sid announces loudly. "When you're dead, we'll go down the chain of command and see who *will* cooperate."

The man says nothing. His blue eyes look straight into Sid's. And then he bolts, leaps the fence, runs downhill for the bushes along the river, and the guard next to him lifts his rifle, but Sid knocks it away with his good arm, levels his pistol, and pulls the trigger. But there's only a click! He cocks again, pulls—another click!—and then he remembers: Tom had emptied the gun. *Damn!*

"I'm sorry, Lieutenant, I forgot myself there." As a guard detail begins to search along the river bank, Sid turns, sprints to catch up with an ordnance wagon while trying to keep his left arm from jostling, leaps aboard, and crosses the river again.

The wagon pulls up at the Chandler House. Works are going up in the yard, the tip of the new line as the Union salient around Chancellorsville collapses. It's a half mile short of the inn, which Sid can see up ahead between fields and wood lots and the low layers of smoke. He leaps off the wagon and calls to a mounted orderly, who gives him a hand up to ride the rest of the way behind him, and in the yard of the inn he dismounts, taking care with the arm, sees much commotion, hears much battle—west, south, and east (are they surrounded?)—sees the porch and yard full of aides, wounded, wagons, gesturing and cursing officers…clearly the enemy is much closer now. Shells are landing in the yard; one or two solid rounds have already hit the house. There are flames and explosions in the direction of Fairview. Artillery there must be having a rough time of it—he can't see for the smoke—have the Rebels taken Hazel Grove and put guns there, just as he'd feared?

He dismounts with the help of the orderly and improvises a sling from some loose bandaging, then calls to the nearest courier: "Captain!"

"Pardon, Major, I'm on my—"

"Wait a moment, Captain. I need to know—what's your name again?—Russell?—those guns way over there—that's Hazel Grove, isn't it? Are they ours, or—"

"They're the enemy's, sir. They drove us off there first thing this morning; must have put fifty guns up there, and they're giving us—"

"So the guns back on the Pike converge—"

"Fits, sir—yes, giving us fits. Usually our gunners get the best of them, but—"

"And out on the lines, man, are we dug in and—are we holding? Where's the pressure?"

The young fellow wipes his face with his sleeve, looks off to the west and then back at Sid. "I don't know, Major. Just about everywhere. We built works out there all night, but I've been running dispatches every which way all morning, and from the looks of things…well, the Rebs are taking casualties, but they're driving us. From both sides. I don't see how we can hold here."

"Well—who's leading them? I heard Jackson was killed."

"We heard that, too, Major, but listen, I have to *go* now."

"What about Lee? Anything about him?"

"Well, no, just that Stuart had taken command in our front but…"

"Stuart! Not Lee?" *Even their cavalrymen can whip us!*

"Major, I'm supposed to find Slocum out there, and I don't even know where to look. I suppose I could—"

"No. Listen: you go back and find Hooker. He'll need an aide with him. I'll take responsibility."

Then Sid remembers High Bar and trots across to the stables, his left arm jouncing painfully, and there he is, tied to a post—or is it a *she?* He realizes he's forgotten the horse's sex if he ever knew it. He checks: a gelding. "Well, I know how you feel, boy. Let's see what else you're missing." But he looks all right otherwise; has a cut on the flank and favors the foot a bit, but the hoof looks serviceable. No saddle, but there are plenty of empty ones around—*my fault, too!*

With an orderly's help, he mounts—painfully, his left arm aches and has resumed bleeding,—then he re-crosses the turnpike to the inn, sees a hole in the roof now, wonders if the family is still up there, and sees Hooker now on the porch, leaning against a column as if Rome were burning around him.

All he needs is a fiddle!

But just then a solid round hits that very column, shattering it and slamming a piece of it against the commander, who sprawls in the yard, motionless. Men rush over, try to rouse him. *Mother of God!* Sid watches them carry Hooker to a blanket—away from the inn, the obvious target. But he's not dead, seems to come around, is helped to his feet, shakes it off, waves an aide away, gestures for his horse, and just as he's moving away from the blanket, another shell explodes (this is true!) right on the blanket! High Bar shies, but Sid manages to hold him.

If there is a God, thinks Sid, *what better way to announce himself? Maybe He's going after Butterfield, too.*

And then the major gets the chance to do the duty Becky assigned him.

How it happens is this: General Couch—next in rank to Hooker—trots over to see about the commander, calls out that he's "just sent Berry in" and says something about needing to clear the field—a big field of stubble left from what looks like an early cutting of winter wheat. Sid trots closer and sees General Hiram Berry stub out a cigar on his saddle and stuff it carefully in a vest pocket as the lead brigade of his division simultaneously tries to form a line and allow routed units through. But the rout won't all cooperate. One panicked regiment clots along a rail fence at the edge of the field. The fence is more perpendicular to the enemy than parallel—little good for protection—but Berry's men will have to cross it to deploy. Sid's trained eye sees the facts right away: the regiment is doomed if it stays huddled along the fence, and whether it flees or withdraws Berry loses even more time. The only honorable direction is forward—a wheel to the left, a sweep across Berry's front, with at least their right flank exposed, into the woods where the enemy is likely massing to continue the assault, then a re-forming and withdrawal under fire to the other side of the field—by whoever is left—thus clearing the way and buying time for Berry. *They'll do. They'll do...*

"Captain!" Sid calls. "Are you their commanding officer?"

"No, Major! I don't think they have one!"

Sid spurs forward, starts to address the cowering mass against the fence, then hears what they say—and it sounds like German! "Doesn't anybody here speak the mother tongue?" he cries.

Confused, fear-filled Germanic faces stare up at him, and he realizes what a silly question *that* was. Then from one of their officers, a captain, he hears: "Major, ve haf lost our commandment! Ve haf no colonel, no major."

"Well, you have a goddamn major now! Ask them if they have any love for their *new* goddamn country or—where *are* they from? New York?"

Shells are slamming in regularly now and musketry, too, from the edge of the woods. It's not much of a fence, anyhow, and they're under fire down the length of it. The captain screams something at another officer, a first lieutenant with a garish, oriental-looking moustache, who passes along the order in yet other language, then flourishes his sword like some parody of a Samurai. Then the captain screams in German at his own men, some of whom scream back. Two are hit simultaneously and topple backward.

"Well, Captain, ask them if they have any balls, for God's sake!" And then Sid, atop High Bar, leans down with his good hand, grabs the regimental standard—which as luck would have it is right there against the fence. He lifts the colors as high as he can, and the oriental-looking lieutenant lifts his sword in salute—and Sid remembers what's missing. "Captain, I need a sword. Is there—"

"Here, vat you can use." The captain reaches up, offers his own sword. "Now you give me der colors and ve trade, py Gott!"

So he has his sword now, and he starts to shout something—pauses—then to the captain, "In God's name, what's *forward* in German?"

Bullets are whistling overhead, bringing sprinkles of leaves down from a tree on the fence line.

"Zey know zat one—*forvard!* Yust say *forvard*—und say *Vaterland*!"

So he screams that out, *Forward* and *Vaterland*, lifts his sword, spurs High Bar forward, trying to use his legs for control—still half hoping the Germans will move on their own without his actually having to lead them, but the horse springs ahead, leaps, takes the fence (quite a jump without much of a start and a bad foot in the bargain) and the major stays on somehow, and he's moving forward and waving the sword, and the German captain springs after him with the colors, and they are both trotting forward, and Sid is waiting now, waiting for the quick blow (thirteen of them maybe), the rip of pain, the welcome darkness—and he's midway across the field now and still holding his sword high, but now it's different. Now he's isolated, somehow, directionless and invulnerable, holy and transparent, and shot and shell are whizzing past, over and around and even through him if that's possible, and his senses are acute. He smells mown hay along with smoke, and there's woodsmoke in there, too, and flame at the edge of the woods, and then it comes.

High Bar is hit first, stumbles, and goes down, throwing Sid to the left, but not quite clear, his lower left leg taking the weight of the horse, and slamming his upper body and wounded left arm into the ground. Pain explodes through him, and he screams, nearly blacks out but then hears the captain standing over him, waving the flag and screaming in German, hears a scattered cheering in response and turns his head to see the regiment launching itself after them—not in a line, really, no complicated wheeling maneuver, but a sort of splattering of men across the field—but forward at least—and then passing over him, one man sprawling over High Bar, his head spilling its contents over the horse's quivering flank. Then they halt and dress ranks under the screams of their captain, and under steady fire now they lurch toward the woods, leaving a trail of dead and wounded.

Pinned under the struggling horse, Sid feels a growing numbness and lifts his sword, points it at the sky, cries "Vaterland!" once, twice, then his sword hand is hit, then his shoulder, then something else, an explosion behind his eyes, and then darkness. His last sensation is the smell of burning brush.

39. He Died Well

Mary soon knows Becky is all but disabled from worry—about Huck, certainly, but now this Major Sawyer, too, and, for all she knows, even Tom. And now there's the sound of battle ominously approaching—first the low thump of artillery and now crashes of musketry. Becky runs to every wagon from across the river, afraid of what she'll find. When a wounded Irish officer tells about a hopeless charge by a mostly German regiment in his brigade, led by "some major of engineers, just volunteered to lead 'em—had to borra' a sword, he did!—must've *embarrassed* 'em into it, y'see."

Mary tells her, "For God's sake go find him, Becky. You're no good to anybody here till you do."

"Oh, thank you, Mary! I'll go to the field and—"

"You'll do nothing of the sort. You'll go straight to headquarters and find the Intelligence people," a short laugh "if there still *is* any such thing in this army. Find that Colonel Sharpe. Don't do anything even more stupid!"

Becky stuffs an extra roll of dressing into her carpet bag with a couple of canteens of water, and leaps onto the next ambulance going back over the ford. Watching her go, an army surgeon says, "I'd say that's already pretty stupid, Miss Carroll. She's a woman, for God's sake. Supposing she goes out to the field and does find him, what will she do? Carry him back by herself?"

"If need be, Doctor. If need be."

By the time Becky appears at the "front," to the extent there is one, it is late afternoon, and the army has mostly fallen back to the Chandler house line, where there is frantic activity building works, shoving guns into lunettes, shuttling ammunition down the lines, and putting out abatis. Fairview seems to have been abandoned, as well as the inn.

(Actually, even now, if the Union command should suddenly rouse itself and take the initiative, Lee—assuming he's still alive and in charge—would be in a pickle, with the two halves of his army still separated and each less than half the force Hooker has on the field. But "Union command," at the moment, is a bit of a euphemism.)

Becky can plainly see flames shooting up over the road and trees ahead—is the inn on fire? And the woods, too? But then how will she—Crashes of musketry can be heard, and there is heavy smoke over the woods to the south and west. The air is sharp and sulfuric. Scores of dead and wounded are laid out on the ground in and around a ramshackle sawmill a few hundred yards behind the new works, which she can see down the road ahead and through the remaining trees on either side. Covered with dust, in addition to blood and sweat and flies, the casualties look almost gray. Some of them *are* in gray, of course, and some in butternut and some in nothing but bloody shirts and pants, which could be from either army, not that it matters to her. Bad as things were back at the ford, here they are worse. Some are not just wounded, but burned. And water is in short supply here. Two canteens are hardly enough.

There is no sign of a "headquarters," and the first officer she sees has heard Hooker is wounded and is not sure who is in command. But this is where they are bringing the wounded, so she looks among them—is there a German regiment nearby? From New York? But the needs of those around her are obvious, and so she moves among them doing what she can, mostly with a gulp of water here and a tightened tourniquet there or a mopped brow and a word of comfort. And if you think of wounded heroes lying in stoic gravity, think again: there is screaming, moaning, blubbering. There are dramatic pleas—for water, mother, the President, God, death—even one for a lawyer (these are Americans, after all). And there are the already dead, often frozen in some horribly comic pose. One corpse has a hand lifted as if offering a blessing or an accusation to the incompetent heavens.

Her back soon aches from stooping. Eventually the firing slackens, and it is nearly sunset when she hears a voice behind her: "Excuse, please, Miss."

She turns to see a first lieutenant of infantry. He removes his cap and bows slightly. He looks very young.

"You look for major of engineer?"

"Yes! His name is Sawyer. Do you know where he is?"

The officer—who looks oriental, not German—holds a cap out to her. "No, and don't know his name, but here is cap of major who led my regiment, Miss. You recognize maybe?"

Becky looks at the cap, sees the three holes, the engineer insignia.

"Oh, my God. This—this is Sid's, I think. I remember those holes." She looks up in fear. "Do you know where he is?"

"I am sorry, Miss, but I saw him go down; his horse go down."

"Then he was injured? I'll find him! Show me where. I'll search the field till—"

"No!" The lieutenant puts a gloved hand on her arm. "No, Miss! He was hit—two, three time—I see no movement. Woods now on fire. Field on fire. Fighting continue. You must resign yourself, please. He died well, yes? A hero."

"Lieutenant, let go of me! I will go through that field till—"

"No!" The man takes a breath, straightens his blouse. "No, if must be—then I find him. You go nowhere else." He releases her and turns, calls to another officer, a captain who is going down the line of wounded with a tin mug. The captain looks at Becky, then back at the lieutenant, barks something gruffly and points to a horse. The lieutenant salutes smartly and turns to Becky. "Wait here, Miss!" She watches him trot over to the horse, mount it, and ride off toward the new works and the smoke beyond. Then she turns to the captain, who himself has a bandaged arm, to see if he knows some English.

Two hours later, well after dark, she sits on a hay bale with her back against the brick wall of the mill trying to sleep in spite of the sounds around her—groans, whimpers, screams, the sound of bone saws. She closes her eyes. Why can't she sleep? And never wake up.

"Miss? Miss?" She looks up, sees the Oriental lieutenant picking his way through the wounded toward her. One hand is heavily bandaged. He leads a horse, which is limping badly and bleeding from the neck and withers. This time there's not much of a bow.

"Miss. I find horse, but not him. I find Russell from staff—others—all say he die on field, and maybe after battle we can…I am…so sorry. Horse may be saved, I think. Is hurt, though. You are Miss…"

Becky looks at the trembling horse, but says nothing.

"Well," the lieutenant touches his cap, "most sorry, and please to meet you." He turns to leave.

"Thatcher," she says without emotion. "Becky Thatcher."

He turns back. "Most sorry, Miss Thatcher. We keep looking for this man."

When he's gone, she says—to no one in particular, but loud enough for the German captain to hear, "Damn all you men! Damn you to Hell, every last one of you. And your horses, too!" She grabs the reins of the crippled High Bar. "Captain, where can I water this poor beast?"

40. May 5: Hell Does Come to Mind

The next hours—days?—are full of smoke, pain, unconsciousness, pain, nightmares, thirst, rough handling, more nightmares, gentler handling, then a wagon, more pain, then a barn or some place with hay, immense thirst, whiskey, feverish dreams, and when he is next jolted awake by pain into something like his right mind, he is on what seems to be a flat-bed wagon, in an open shed—an outbuilding at the ford?—or the inn?—is he a prisoner?—and his left leg is—He reaches down with his newly bandaged right hand to touch the leg, is relieved to find it's still there, though heavily splinted and there's a numbness—less pain there, really, than above it in his side and all the way to the chest and shoulder, which are also bandaged, and he's a bit sick to the stomach (from morphine?)—and he feels himself cold and shaking—but feverish at the same time?—is that possible? And as he continues to inventory himself, he notices a partner in the wagon, a sergeant. The fellow is also sweating and shaking, though not making a sound. The face is turned, and Sid croaks out, "Hawkins?"

"Over here, Major." Sawyer turns his head painfully, and sees the signalman on a stool beside the wagon. Hawkins smiles. "How do you feel?"

"What kind of damn-fool question is that?" he grunts. "Like Hell. How do I look?"

Hawkins winces. "Hell does come to mind, Major. You've got a good dent in your head, a couple new leaks in your arm and shoulder, a bad burn or two. Left leg's broke all to hell—that's the worst. You may lose that—but you may have to wait for your Eternal Reward."

"How did I get here? I remember nothing of…"

"Some lieutenant found you—a Chinaman, they say, if you can believe it. Don't know the regiment. Your horse had got hisself up somehow and limped off. You were out near the woods, past the pickets. It's a mystery how the fellow got you back by hisself in the dark. The woods was all afire."

"I wish I knew who he was."

How foolish he feels now as he remembers his behavior in the light of day at…"Where are we, Hawkins? And what are you doing here? You hurt, too?"

"We're at the ford, Major, and I'm here because the colonel said you was in a 'fragile state' and might need to be, 'looked after,' was how he put it. I guess he was right. 'Fragile' ain't the half of it. Also, I have a cable for you. It come yestidy."

"Just tell me what it says."

"It's about General Averell. He's at Ely's and 'awaits instructions,' he says, for your mission."

Sid drops his head back, wonders if it's possible to die from irony.

"Tell him his 'instructions' are to go straight to Hell. I don't give a rat's—"

"Oh, say—" says Hawkins. "Remember that question you asked me about the choice I'd make? Well, looky-here." And he holds out, in the palm of his hand, a second lieutenant's bars. "The colonel got 'em for me in case they made looking for you easier. But I never had a chance to sew 'em on yet."

"So you're a live officer after all!"

"He says I'm a brevet, whatever the Hell that is."

"It's good enough. Congratulations." Then he remembers. "How's the army, Hawkins? How bad was it?"

"Bad enough. We got back over the river. Sedgwick crossed at Banks' Ford—lucky to get back, I expect, after Lee concentrated on him yestidy at Salem Church—and the rest crossed here and at Scott's Dam. Remember where you was going to build that bridge? Good thing we had pontoons there. Maybe somewheres else, too. Maybe Warren remembered what you said: can't have too many bridges."

Then the major remembers something else. "Am I under arrest?"

"Not that I know. The colonel said *he* was under arrest—by *you*. He says once you're arrested, you're arrested forever until a judge says you're not. He sounds like a lawyer."

"He is."

But suddenly there is a sweep of linen by his face, and soft arms are around him, a soft face by his, and tears on his neck and face, and of course it's Becky, and Hawkins notes that the major is in good hands now and takes his leave, and then there's a good bit of what Huck would call, "sobbing and swabbing," and Thank God's and—no it wasn't his fault and he mustn't blame himself—and she'd heard he was dead and—no, no *he* was the one who was sorry, the sorriest man who ever lived—and so on.

And eventually Miss Carroll comes by. Sid notes they're calling her "Doctor Carroll" now—and informs him she thinks both arms will survive, and his skull seems intact, for what that's worth, but she doesn't know about the leg, it's broken badly in a couple of places, and she's done what she can for the moment and has given him some laudanum for the pain, but it'll have to be re-set soon, and he may still lose it, will probably never regain full use, and the thing to do now is prevent mortification and gangrene—she's learned a few tricks in the West. He will have to be moved soon, fighting could resume, and Becky should see that he doesn't try to eat or drink too much while the drug is at work, and now things are busy and she needs to get back to the other surgeons, but first will Becky please help move this poor fellow next to him on the wagon to a stretcher.

Becky returns with water, a bit of boiled pork, and a tin mug of coffee, "not too much, I hope." She sits, straightens her dress, apologizes for her appearance. To Sid she's an angel, of course, but he does notice that the dress, although rumpled, is not the blood-soaked butcher's smock she'd worn yesterday, or whenever that was.

"What day is this?"

"It's Tuesday."

"Tuesday." *What happened to Monday?*

He takes some water, but cannot eat. The pain in his left leg explodes with every pulse, the burns on his face and hands itch fiercely, and he can hardly breathe without a flame shooting from shoulder to pelvis—a cracked rib or two maybe? He tries to think what to say, to ask, but can't do much of either, and eventually he sleeps again. Close to nightfall—or is it dawn?—he wakes on a cot of some sort, in some other building, this time alone. All he can see is a hardwood floor, a rolled-up rug, a white-washed wall with a casement window, a pine-plank door with a rim-lock—pretty fancy for an outbuilding, if that's what it is—a parlor? A plantation office? But as clarity returns, so does memory—*Huck's dead, remember? And whose fault is that?*—and he calls for Becky. After a moment, there is a cool hand on his forehead.

"Hush, now, I'm here. You'll wake the children." *Children. Where the Hell are we?* He turns his head, sees Becky on a stool, a covered basket on her lap, a tin pitcher on the floor beside her—it's sweating a bit, so it must be cold—milk, maybe.

"Becky, I need to ask you—when you saw Tom—when he told you about Huck and gave you the journal and—"

"Oh, Sid—how can I forget about that business if you will not? Look, I brought you some—"

"No—please. If you've told Sharpe, that's fine, but I need to know, too." She is silent. "I'm going to keep at it, you know, until this is straight in my head."

She sighs. "Well, let's see, as I said it was late Saturday—the 2nd."

"How late? Was it after sunset?"

"Well—I think so, yes—and he'd come through pickets with the new passwords, he said—"

"Tom? And he already knew about Jackson?[24] Hmm! And he was going *back?*"

"Well, that's what he said, just as I told you: he had work to do—something from the colonel. And I don't know what he meant about that fighting for his country. For all I know, he sold us *all* out, not just—just Huck. Oh I'm sorry, I promised myself I wouldn't—"

"Becky, it's all right—I'm sorry, I just—so *you* knew Tom was—"

"Oh, of *course* Tom was in on it!" She laughs shortly, wipes her face on her sleeve. "This has Tom Sawyer's Gang stamped all over it." And then, holding his head up to the mug, "I know Jackson was the enemy and—now you *drink* this—and at least they had the decency not to send him after Lee." Sid notes that she must not have seen the parts of the journal Tom reported!

"And you haven't seen him since? Tom, I mean." He takes a sip—it is milk.

She shakes her head. He follows her gaze out the door, now open, across a porch and a field of stubble. "No." She turns back to him. "But listen, you need rest and—my goodness, your hands are cold, but your face is hot. Here, let me put this over your forehead."

"But—"

"Hold still now, you'll wet your dressings."

"But—Becky, I'm *not* guiltless. I—" He pushes the hand away. "You don't know how it pains me that—that I have hurt someone—"

"Sid, hush, don't say that." Her hand on his face again, smoothing, shushing.

"That I may have caused the death of the man —"

"Hush!"

"The man you loved."

"The man I—what do you mean? Of course I loved Huck. He was my brother."

"So what, Becky? So what if the Judge adopted him? That's a scrap of paper. Any fool can see you've been in love with Huck for years! It's in your eyes, your letters, your—"

"Oh, my God! Sid, Huck *is* Judge Thatcher's son—his *real* son. And he's my real brother!"

So, Sid now learns the rest of the story—first groggily, and then, after another night's sleep, with a bit more precision: the judge was a good man, a good father and a good husband, but he wasn't perfect, and after Becky's difficult birth her mother never really regained her health and—well, there was this river show with a beautiful young dancer, Sid probably wouldn't remember, but Becky thinks she does—light-skinned, but a Negress, she remembers, perhaps part Indian. She spoke a kind of French, Becky recalls. At any rate, Huck was born less than a year after Becky, and the judge knew, of course, and felt obligated, tried to see he was cared for, while trying to protect the family—at least the boy was rather light-colored, didn't even look Mulatto, only freckle-faced, you know—and after Mrs. Thatcher's death, naturally Becky had to find out when she took over the family's affairs and arranged the estate. The only problem was old Finn.

"Yes, how did Huck wind up with *him?*"

"Well, he married Huck's mother, Sid. She left him, of course, when she found out what a brute he was. I suppose he wasn't always so bad. He was determined to keep Huck, of course, because that was his way into Father's money. It must have been hard for her to leave Father, though—and Huck."

"But I thought Huck's money came from the gold he and Tom found—or was that just a ruse?"

"No, no, that was really found money. Very convenient, though. It solved the support problem without admitting anything. But even when he was sick—and old Finn was dead—Father *wanted* to go through with the adoption. I still don't know why Huck wanted to pull Lee into it. Father really wanted to leave everything above board, and I'm very proud of him." She smiles down at him. "And of you, too, Major Sawyer. You're a hero, you know."

But not *her* hero, he notices.

Still, Sid's not thinking about heroism now. He's thinking about the night of Saturday May 2: What really happened to Huck and Tom? This sorry life of his has to go on until he learns those answers.

41. I Seen Tom Act Out

And then there's this: what about Becky herself? Is she now fair game? Huck's parentage shouldn't surprise. It fits, in hindsight, with what Sid knows about the judge and his coddling of old Finn. But if Huck is dead now anyway. Can Sid himself dare to hope?

No. He knows this woman can never love him—except "in a way," that phrase a woman uses when she's about to crush your heart like a June bug, but doesn't want to "hurt you." No, he knows better than that, knows that his own spirit is too stiff, proud, mean, vengeful, even cowardly, in the deepest sense, to win such a woman. But it speaks well of him, doesn't it, that he would want to?

Short of that, what Sid wants is to talk to Tom. What does he know about Jackson's end—soon confirmed by the lachrymose Southern press? And how did Tom know of Huck's death? Granted, the journal—which Doctor Carroll tells him does bear bloodstains—provides some credibility, but still, this is Tom we're talking about. And if Huck—apparently not a rival now anyway—were *not* dead, and Sid could still somehow rescue him—? Well, that might give a wounded soul the will to live.

But Sid doesn't get to see Tom, or Sharpe, or anyone else in the bureau for weeks. To the major, it seems he's been dropped into a well. Hands are being washed of him. He is taken to Stafford Heights, then to City Point, then ultimately to a military hospital near Washington, and he's not even told exactly which. But he is not in one of the big wards. Instead, he has his own little room to himself upstairs in a staff dormitory—with a cot, a basin, a table, a small window—because ultimately, as he had feared, he is placed under arrest. Hawkins, now with the bureau, delivers the charges to him late in May, says there'll be a guard, eventually, but no one is much worried about his running away with such injuries. No dates have been set. The Army, as Lee and Huck could have informed him, takes its time in these matters.

The charges are:

(1) Insubordination—not to Sharpe, but to Patrick and, of all things, to Sickles!—

(2) Dereliction of duty, and

(3) Conduct unbecoming an officer.

The specifications boil down to these: that he disobeyed instructions to stay at Hazel Grove and cooperate with Sickles in the deployment of cavalry (his jaw drops when he reads that one!); failure to report for duty after "recovering" from his first wound and, instead, interfering with the authority of the provost over prisoners, allowing a captive officer to escape; and, finally, unbecoming conduct toward a fellow officer—a telegraph operator (oh, yes, he smiles to remember that one). And they're signed, not by Sickles or even the telegrapher, but by General Daniel Butterfield.

Well, some of these are false, all are arguable, or in any case excusable in the heat of battle. And they're not even the strongest. He *was* insubordinate, not to Sickles, but to Sharpe—threatening a superior with arrest! True, he *did* "interfere" with prisoners, but by threatening—and then attempting!—to kill one who didn't cooperate with his unlawful threats. And he *had* failed, failed miserably, to pursue his duty, however hopeless, to take that cavalry regiment through the Rebel lines and accomplish the mission, or die trying. Now that, as Huck might say, was at least one hanging, maybe two. It seems almost as if the Army wants to charge him with something, but dare not bring up the real case.

This idea is seconded by a visitor, who he had thought might be his appointed counsel, but turns out to be just an interested bystander: ex-General George B. McClellan. McClellan is on more or less permanent leave from the army now and in Washington politicking, when someone—he won't say who—sends him around to "look things over."

He arrives in civilian dress, looks at the charges, laughs, and says not to worry; this is what the Army does when it's about to cashier somebody it would rather hang, but hasn't the bowels to do it. Dereliction, after all, is not Desertion. If Sid really wants to make them squirm, says McClellan, he should call in a reporter from a Democratic newspaper and tell "the true story of the sorry debacle" or something of the sort. Little Mac offers to make the proper connections.

Sid thanks him, but says he will bide his time.

What he does do, as you know, is to write the memoir upon which so much of this is based. How important it is to leave a record, to get it right! And he wants to be ready in case he *does* need to take the "newspaper option." With so few credible sources loose in the world (how credible is Tom, after all?), Sid wonders who might do almost anything to silence him. Maybe not even try him, just send someone around to poison him. One hears about deaths every day in a hospital, after all, often of men who'd seemed out of danger the night before. Sid has taken to watching his food carefully, especially if it's some treat from an anonymous donor. A bit melodramatic, perhaps, but a man in such a grim place will have grim thoughts.

Of course, a more experienced officer than Sid might have wondered what he could possibly reveal that was worth silencing him in that way. That the Union had tried to kill Lee using a special agent? That Hooker had delayed his advance by a day, hoping for the plan's success? That, when it went wrong, the high command had tried to retrieve or eliminate the agent, apparently losing another agent or two in the process? A bit of wishful thinking here, some bungling and backstabbing there—embarrassing, to be sure, but what's new about any of that in this Army?

But how eager he is for mail, for news! Becky writes once, in early June, asking about him and describing her own hospital work—which is even worse *after* the battle, for a long time, as most civilians don't realize—still along the Rappahannock, in houses, barns, tents—and she has some guesses on the whereabouts of Huck's grave, plans to investigate if she can arrange safe passage. But there's nothing more about Tom.

The next week Dr. Carroll visits, keeping her promise to "try something else," complains that he was "hard work to find," clucks over the wounds, especially the leg. The shoulder, arm, hand, and head are coming along fine—though a couple of burns are still inflamed and look likely to leave scarring. She regrets having waited so long—has he had much pain? Well, yes, but nothing he doesn't deserve. She laughs, says we all deserve death, Major, and we'll all get it eventually, meanwhile let's not claim more than our share of credit. The cynical sort of thing Sharpe might have said. Then she puts him under chloroform, re-sets the leg, and when he wakes she's gone, and he finds a note from her pinned to his blanket, giving instructions for additional care.

Then he gets pneumonia.

He survives it, though. And then in late June the papers are full now, not of Jackson's death, which gave him some guilty satisfaction, but of Lee's new invasion: He's in Pennsylvania! He's marching on Philadelphia! The Rebel congress has put the Liberty Bell up for bid!

And just then there's another visitor, an older black man, fifty or so. There's something familiar about the man, and Sid looks closely, comparing him to his memory of the sketch Sharpe had shown him, but no, the man doesn't look like Joe Taylor, and he's much older than Joe should be. Hat in hand, quiet, well-dressed, and articulate, with a neatly trimmed, graying beard, he introduces himself as a Mr. Sojourner James. He asks gravely about Sid's health, nods, and says he has been sent by the Freedmen's League to express thanks for his service and to deliver a "letter from a well-wisher."

The name Sojourner gives Sid a start, at first, till he discovers that all the men in the League call themselves that, as an honorific like "Brother." The letter is in a large envelope—it feels like quite a document, ten or fifteen pages—and as the man hands it over he asks Sid to read it immediately and then destroy it. Then he leaves.

Sid looks for a salutation—there is none, nor a date—then flips through to the end, looking for a signature: *Mirabile.* That's all. It's Latin—"wonderful"? What could that mean? And there is no return address. But when he begins to read, there is no doubt of the author: it must be Joe Taylor.

The hand is graceful, almost feminine, as it could well be, of course—copied by someone else to disguise the author. Sid is standing, as he's been doing a good bit lately, with a cane and the good leg, by his window above the hospital courtyard when it's lit by the morning sun, as now. He's been warned by the doctors not to try the stairs *down* to the courtyard yet, though he still seems unguarded—but his bad leg has begun to throb now, as if in response to what he is about to read. So Sid sits in the chair in his shirt and suspenders, splinted leg up on the cot, and reads the letter—which begins where the journal left off, on the plank Road—and he sinks, in his mind, back into the smoke:

Here is what we done that I expect you don't know yet, though some of it is in the papers. We took our orders quite serious, and I hope the following will help the Cause.

After Tom left on Saturday eve [May 2], Huck and me watched from a hayloft as we could see lines of Rebel troops stop on the other side of the fence, dress ranks, and then move into the woods.[25] We could see to the turnpike, easy, almost to the end of the Union line. We knowed there was a big column of Rebs moving up around the Union right, and from where we was, we could see bayonets moving north of

the turnpike into the fields and woods, and they was still moving off there when we seen a puff of smoke a mile or more that direction and we heard a boom from a cannon. Then we heard some firing and then we heard something like the cry of a zillion ghosts all over sudden let loose which they calls the Rebel Yell, which even where we was so far away it raised every hair on our heads, and if you ever heard it, you know what it's like—and anybody say he heard it and *wasn't* scared, well I know he *ain't* heard it! Then we seen long sheets of flame and heard crashes of firing rolling long, and it was most like what I imagine the sound of a ocean wave, though I never seen it.

Sid sees Jackson in his mind—blue eyes bright in his Presbyterian gray, with a prayer from Lee and three ragged divisions poised over the carefree, arm-stacked and corn-frittering Union flank, waiting for the mystic moment—and he looks at his watch, and it's five o'clock, and he turns to Rodes—You may go forward, sir—and the gun booms, and the bugles ring, and the wave is launched, and the very first wave isn't even troops, but deer and rabbit and squirrel running like Hell from Hell itself, and then the yell rings out and the first volley, and the wave breaks over the poor sorry XIth Corps, and the flood is on. Sid remembers it now—riding into that wave with Danforth, Huey, and the ill-starred 8th....

Even from where they are, Joe reports, he and Huck can see and hear signs of a stampede on the turnpike and fear the worst. They'd like to get down there, but the wave is rolling from left to right, and if they just stay where they are, it may roll on by, leaving the way open to the Confederate rear. But they have identity problems: Joe is black and—at least until they find Jackson's staff—isn't going to get the benefit of any doubts. And Huck himself may be sought by either side.

So they watch a while longer, as the assault rolls down the Pike and across their front, and Huck writes and writes, and after an hour or more they move, as quickly as Huck's foot will allow, down the road they're on—almost certainly the plank Road—toward the turnpike. They have a few scrapes with Rebel flankers and Union shelling, and Joe gets a minor wound in the hand, but now, at least, says Joe:

We both had bloody bandages and figured if we could just get to the Pike nobody would bother us. Well, things was mixed up for certain there. We was behind the Rebel line now, and there was a church[26] up by the road being used for a hospital, and there was a good deal of wounded all over the grounds and by the road, many of them was Union, and a big batch of Union prisoners a setting in a ring of wagons in a yard behind the church, but without any guard at all that we could see. Huck says he wondered, "Had the whole Union Army just sat down and quit?"[27]

It was a-getting dark and look like the Rebs was in about as big a mess as the Union army, with men wandering all about the woods and fields, and officers shouting out orders to whoever might hear. Nobody round here knew who *we* was, and we hadn't been challenged yet. But our orders was to find Jackson, so we needed some kind of story, and I says it would help if Huck was more than a sergeant.

And Huck say, yes, it would, and it might help for me to play slave if I didn't mind. His foot was hurting so bad now that he had to do something besides walk, so we grabbed a horse tied up to a tree near some dead and wounded, mostly Union cav'ry. We didn't see no Union marks on the horse and tack, so we pulled him back in the trees where we could be more private. Then Huck pulls a jacket off one of the dead Rebs, which look like a officer's and won't too bloodied up. He 'llowed he'd go with his blue pants, which he'd seed lots of Rebs in those anyhow, even some officers, and then he say, "I wonder what rank I am." He say it warn't no general, which he'd studied up on those. Well, we finally allows he'll just wait and see what the others calls him. I say he ought to have a sword, so we fix one to his saddle, cav'ry style, but a pistol might be more use. He still had that little one, but we found him one for his belt—there was all sorts of truck in the woods, you know—then I hoist him up, being careful of his foot. As for me, I'd be his camp boy and help clear way for the horse.

When we come out on the road near the church, I ask Huck do he reckon Tom's near, and we heard a voice behint us, "Well, I allow he's pretty damn close." And who do you think it was, but Tom Sawyer his own self! And he say he lucky he picked the right church. I ask Tom how he made it through all the cannons and fighting and he just say,

"The Lord provides, you know." I didn't want to tell him much of our plans, such as they was, because of what you'd wrote me, but Huck knowed what need to be done and he telled Tom to wait alongst the road there—just as flat as if he *was* a real officer. I don't know if it was the uniform, but he did sound different. "Jackson'll come along it one way or t'other," he says; "you can rest assured of that. We'll go on up ahead, and you stay here, Tom, and keep a lookout back the other way. If you stay put, we can meet up again when Joe and I come back. Us two will have the best chance, I'spect, because if I know Jackson, he'll be as close to the front as he can get. And listen—If you do see him, don't try nothing by yourself, he'll be guarded, just keep track of him. Now everybody look sharp."

Well, Tom said that was fine, and he asked Huck was he still keeping a journal and said he admired Huck's jacket and said it made him sort of want to salute. Well, that made me think 'bout what you'd wrote, and when we got ahead a bit, I tole Huck I was a-feared of leaving Tom behind us—but I didn't say why, because you said not to tell him until I had to. Now I wished I had. Huck just look up the pike and says, "Tom's just confusion, that's all he is, and confusion'll help us as much as the enemy. Let's go on ahead—but stay out of the road."

I wish you could of seed old Huck, Major. He talked his way through two Rebel lines with the story that he have an important dispatch for General Jackson from General Stuart and could anyone direct him, and one officer says, "Well, Cap'n, you'll find him and Hill scouting up ahead there off the road, but there's mostly Yanks out there now, and if you're smart you'll leave your mount and your nigger back and go on foot." We should of took the advice about the horse, for the woods was most too thick to walk through, much less ride. But Huck says, "Joe, this probably *ain't* going to work. But we got to plan in case it does, and in that case we got to get away fast, and that means a horse—maybe two, if we got a prisoner. I just hope this'n's good. I wish I had Butterfly. Come on."

The moon was up now, and when we come to a little cross road [the Bullock Road?] **we could see a little bit either way. There was still firing and cannonading off to the right along the turnpike, but it was scattered now, and we could hear axes and trees falling up ahead. That was troops**

building works, and off that way it had to be Union troops, so we angled off to the left between that little road and the Pike, figuring that if Jackson was "scouting up ahead" that's where he'd be.

I don't know why we didn't think of how dangerous it'd be—but I guessed if Jackson was out there it warn't so bad. Before long we heard riders behind us, or a little to *our* left, and some shouting about, "What troops are these?" and then more firing, and then somebody hollers out, "General, is this the place for you?" or the like, and then somebody answers, "The danger is over; the enemy is routed! Tell General Hill to press on." And we both knowed that voice. That was Jackson.

I wondered where Jim Lewis was, but Huck said he blamed sure wouldn't be up with a scouting party, and I said no, that weren't likely, so we agreed to try to get in front of them and lay low till they come by, and if the general warn't so well guarded, we'd arrest him and walk him back toward the sound of those axes, or maybe tie him on the horse—or if we had to, said Huck, shoot him. Now, that was probably as flea-brained a idea as two grown men ever had. I guess Huck knowed that, because he leaned over close to me—he was still on the horse—and pulled a folded paper out of his blouse and unfolded and showed it to me. It warn't the picture of me that I'd give to the colonel, it was the picture he made of that Recorder fellow up on the mountain. He looked back behind us, and then he folded it up again and said I must see that it got back to you, sir, and that you'd keep it safe. And so you will find that with this letter.

That's all he said, and started to dismount, but before he done it we heard shouted orders and troops moving through the woods very close. Well, somebody called out, "That's Yankee Cavalry!" and then there was firing, and the party we heard with Jackson trotted towards us from the right, we seen them coming, and I dove off to the left away from them, and Huck draws his pistol out and charges off *towards* them and still on his horse, and I couldn't see what happen next, but it sounded pretty bad for anybody out there, general or private, man or beast.

(In his mind Sid sees Huck spurring ahead in the moonlight toward Jackson's party, tree branches whipping across his face as wild firing

breaks out again, and somebody rides forward from the right waving his arm—Is it Morrison, shouting, "Cease fire! You're shooting at your own men!"? and Huck dives off his horse and comes up with both pistols out and cocked, and he sees a man grab the reins of an officer's horse to pull him away—it must be Jackson's!—and he thinks about a hundred things and people all at once, as he levels his weapons, tries not to have the heart of a murderer, then hears a yell. "That's a damn lie, boys; that's Yankee cavalry! Pour it into 'em!" and the woods erupt with a thunderous flash.)

I laid low till I's sure the Rebel attack been called off and the wild firing pretty much stopped. Then careful as I could I snuck back alongst the north side of the turnpike to where I figured, best I could, that we'd turned off it. The moon was pretty high now—and I'm all ready to do my scared-nigger-looking-for-Marse-Tom act, which ain't that much of a act anyhow—but lucky for me pickets ain't posted yet from either side, and by the moon I can sure see enough damage from that volley laying around, and it warn't hard to home in on the spot, but I couldn't see no sign of Huck.

Well, as you know from the papers, I guess, the general warn't the only one kilt. There was Boswell and Smith[28] and others and horses too, all went down, and litter bearers still a-looking round amongst the trees, while trying not to get they own selves shot.

After awhile, when the moon come up good and I could hear axes and shovels up ahead again, I judged I'd resk a call or 2 alongst that little road, which I guess was the Bullocks Road.

Well, somebody heard me and call back. I hid behint a tree till I seed somebody limp out of the woods toward me in the moonlight, and when I seed it was Tom Sawyer, I shown myself and ask in a low voice was he hit, and he said no, he done wrenched his knee again digging a hole for—but he couldn't say it, he kind of choked a little and said now he didn't know what to do but tell me straight out—that Huck was kilt. He taken two balls right in the breast, and he couldn't hardly talk about it, and then he grabbed me and wrapped both his arms around me and just bawled like a baby and I reckon I did too, and I tell you I seen Tom act out, but this was different. Well, finally he said he couldn't of stood to leave him lay there for the foxes and buzzards, so when he see a

detail from the 3rd Michigan a-digging a pit for two of their own officers, he help them till they was done and then ask could he borrow the shovel to widen the hole a bit and put his friend in, too—but didn't tell them Huck was a *rebel,* of course—and so he was about to cover him up and mark it, too. But he ask me did I want to see first before he filled it in, and I says I guess I did, because I didn't want no tricks. So he took me back to where the bodies was.

The moon was high enough to see most of the trench was covered up, with two swords stuck up and pieces of paper tied to them. One end of the trench warn't filled in yet, and I knowed I had to look down. The moon was high now, and I could see him there curled up on his side, with the gray coat still on him dark and soaked, probably with blood—and those blue pants with the one foot bandaged and the other with no boot now, because Tom was going to put it over the sword hilt to mark the spot and put the hat a-top of it.

It warn't very deep, and Tom said no, we'd have to come back later and see it done right, and see what Becky wanted, and then he got down in the grave and straddled the body, and then he looked up and I could see his face from the side in the moonlight and his teeth clinched and unclenched and he was shaking but not making no sounds, and then he mumble some things, and then he says a bit louder, "I tried, Huck, Lord knows, and I failed the one thing I ever really wanted to do in my whole life—to put my own self down there 'stead o you," which I don't know what he meant by that, but then he leans down and touch his face, and finally he stood up and says, do I want to come in and pay my respects, but I don't want to get down in no grave. So I gives him a hand up and says, "Let's get him covered and make sure we remembers where it is."

I ask him if Huck died right off or had time to say nothing, and he says well, he was about dead when he found him, and his mouth was foaming blood, but he heard him mumble something that sounded Spanish, and then he seemed to see who was there and said clear enough to hear, to "tell his father he done his duty." Well, I don't know which father he's talking about, sir, so I'm a-telling you.

When we was done, Tom says he'll go back and give the shovel to the Michigan regiment and then try to get back to the ford and tell

Becky what happened, then maybe try to get back to me if there was time by morning—would Wilderness Church do? And I says fine, do he know the passwords, and he says yep, from both armies, and even some they probably didn't know yet theirselves.

But as I watches him go, the spell done wore off, I guess, and I draws my gun and levels it right at his back, because if you're right *he's* probably the one that kilt Huck, and I knowed he taken that journal. But I also knowed any more shooting wouldn't wake the dead, but it prob'ly would wake up the guns. And I knowed even if he didn't come back tonight he be back sometime, and *some* good might still come of it—cause I still had one card left to play.

I spent most of the night trying not to get shot myself, but 'long 'bout midnight there was considable firing off towards the south, and I goes back to my act, this time a-looking for Jackson's staff, but the Rebs was all jumpy and not interested in a lost nigger, but when I run into another camp boy, a darky like me, carrying a pail of water back "to de surgeon's at de church," he says, and says they's a-going to be needing it, because the Yankees done launch a *night* attack. I says, 'Good Lawd,' and ask what direction and he says, "Lawd knows," all he heard was a Yankee general name of Sickles[29] had a hand in it.

Now I was feeling awful bad about not showing Huck your message about Tom. So I follows the boy up to the church and falls asleep, and when I wakes up, it's just daylight, and there's no shooting yet, but no more sign of Tom, so I ask a sergeant who the commander is now and says I was Jackson's camp boy and had found a letter he ought to see, and when I shown him your message he took me to a officer who taken me to General Hill, who was Jackson's next in command and also was hurt, but not so bad—and he ask me where I got the note from, and I says I found it in the haversack of a dead Yankee I was searching for food and hadn't no idea who it's from.

Sid remembers well what he had written. He'd addressed it to an anonymous officer, so as not to implicate Joe:

Sir:

Thomas Sawyer is not to be trusted. There is clear evidence that he is in the Rebel service. Do not trust him alone with our agent. Use your best judgment about whether to inform our agent of this—he is already somewhat on guard, but may also have conflicted loyalties himself. I have reason to believe Sawyer considers it his mission to capture or kill our agent, which might please either side. If you value the Union Cause and our mutual friend, you may need to defend him yourself and expose Sawyer to the Rebels as a Union or even a DOUBLE agent. Much is in your hands.

Well, Gen. Hill had his hurt foot propped up on a cracker box, and looks at the letter and says Hm! and ask who this "agent" was, and I says all I seen was a Union cavalryman that was captured near the furnace and I thought he might of got loose or kilt the next day, but I says I thought General Lee knowed him cause they talked for a while, and then Gen. Hill says he reckons he'll report that to General Lee, who may want to know, and meantime he'll "see about Reverend Sawyer." And I guess he done so pretty quick, as you can see from the newspaper story I have put in. I warn't worried none about Huck, of course, since he was dead and couldn't anybody hurt him no more.

Well, this is all I know, sir. After the war, if asked I will be most glad to help you or your family to find the grave, as I believe I knows it well enough. I am no longer with the army but you can contact me through the Freedmen's League.

I hope my service have been valuable and I ask no reward but to be part of a Glorious Cause.

Signed: *Mirabile*

Sid waits a full minute before looking in the envelope for the "newspaper story." It's there: a short item, without a by-line, and clipped so that neither the paper's name nor page number is visible.

Yankee Spy Meets Just Deserts!
Man of Whole "Cloth" Fails
to Thwart Victory

***May 28*: The Provost of the Army of Northern Virginia reports that on Friday last, a FEDERAL SPY, using the name of Thomas J. Sawyer, and pretending to be a Presbyterian minister of the Gospel was convicted of gathering intelligence for Federal forces invading the Commonwealth and HUNG on the 26th instant at Orange Courthouse. It appears that Sawyer had operated for more than a year under various aliases and occupations. He was caught due to the alert work of a Negro camp aide to General Jackson who found incriminating papers upon him. Sawyer's origins and family are unclear, but he seems to have come from the West, and investigations are proceeding. The Provost wishes all citizens to know that General Lee himself urges the importance of keeping close watch and communicating any suspicious activities to the authorities.**

On the back of the clipping, there is a single sentence, penciled in a rather school-boyish hand:

I dasn't blame you one bit, never you fere Majer, and I am very proud for you to be in servis of our Cause—Your Old Fren, Jim.

Jim Lewis? But how could Jackson's man Lewis have…then it hits him: *that* Jim. Miss Watson's Jim. Good God. No wonder the man looked familiar.

Then, of course, he finds the Sojourner sketch also there in the envelope. He looks at the reverse side of this, too. But very little can be seen.

42. The Grave of Huckleberry Finn

So not only is Huck dead, but Tom, too. Or so it seems. But to Sid the story raises more questions than it answers: First, if "investigations are proceeding," how are they, if Tom is dead? Joe himself would not have stayed around long enough to be further questioned, but he surely would have been sought. Where is *he* now? Most important: *did* Tom kill Huck Finn? Joe seems to think so. But even if Joe really wrote the letter, some details still sound fishy.

Sid, of course, has read Huck's journal, and *it* has a ring of truth that's hard to fake. But even if it is genuine—right up to the dissolution of the threesome near the Burton Farm—after that, Joe asks us to believe Tom could get from Wilderness Church to U.S. Ford and *back* (with a detour to see Becky) between five P.M. and midnight during chaotic and nearly continuous fighting, armed only with a one-horse trap, a few passwords, and a clerical collar. Even for Tom, that's a tall order.

Still—why would Taylor lie? What could he gain? And Becky herself saw Tom and believed his report. Has she seen the report of *Tom's* death? Someone will have to contact her—Sid himself, no doubt. And then there's Jim's note: he "dasn't blame" Sid—presumably for either of these deaths. But that means...How widely *has* this business become known?

And the reader may wonder about Sid's message to Joe: Why betray Tom? Well, there, the major is convinced, he has the goods. First, there is Tom's magical ability to cross Rebel lines. Then there is this: on the evening of April 29 Tom had mentioned reports of Rebel reinforcements arriving on the railroad. Sid, because of Union agents on the RF&P, soon knew that those reports from "deserters" were false, likely planted, although they were taken seriously by Butterfield (mostly because one of the "deserters" was a New Yorker, like himself). But, crucially, the false reports were not actually received in Union lines till late on the 30th, at the earliest. Thus Tom could not have known about them on the 29th—*unless* he was part of the Rebels' disinformation plan. And as for Tom's brave warning of impending attack—well, it was a bit late, wasn't it?

No, about Tom Sid's conscience is clear: the man was a traitor—a charming and resourceful traitor, maybe, but a traitor nonetheless. He deserved what he'd got, for that alone. Quite aside from what he'd done to Becky. *I should have run him through—then and there!*

Then, in July, with the good news of Gettysburg and Vicksburg reverberating, Sid receives another visitor. It is a hot day, and the door is open to allow a breeze. He is sitting at the open window in his shirt sleeves with his leg propped, swatting flies away and watching a baseball game in the courtyard between the infantry and artillery (the gunners are winning 4-2) when there is a polite cough at the door.

"Don't get up, Major; I'll come to you. Be careful with that leg."

"Colonel Sharpe! I'm glad to see you, there's so much—"

"No doubt! But let's get this out of the way first. There is a change in your status. And I wanted to be the one to tell you." Sharpe sits on the edge of the bed next to Sid's propped up leg, opening a valise. "There's good and bad. I'll give you the bad first." Sid feels his chest tighten…tries to think.

Sharpe takes out a Richmond newspaper, and points out the article Joe had sent—about Tom. Sid nods, his heart pounding. *So…what does he know*? "This is true, then? I'd heard something."

"Well, we see no reason to doubt it. The source is good."

You thought Tom was a good source, too, Sid thinks. But he says nothing.

"Well, at any rate, I'm sorry to bear the news. He was your brother, after all."

"Half-brother, yes, and we weren't that close, but still—well, he knew the risks."

"Yes."

"Does Becky know, Colonel?"

"I don't know. I'll leave that to you, I guess. She'll likely be back from Pennsylvania soon."

Thank God Dr. Carroll is here for her, Sid thinks, as relief begins to trickle in: nothing about the note to Joe! And then Sharpe takes out a brown envelope and hands it over.

"Here's the good news, if you want to think of it that way." The envelope contains a short letter from the Army chief of staff about a transfer—and the shoulder straps of a lieutenant colonel. "They're just brevet, for now. Congress has to act, you know. You're up for a decoration, too."

"A decoration! But—I'm under arrest, for God's sake!"

"Not any more. All charges are dropped. *I* was under arrest, too, by the way. And not by you. I was blamed for the loss of Our Boy *and* your brother. But when they realized I was going to call Butterfield, Hooker, and Scott as witnesses, and, if I could drag it out till after the war, maybe the president himself—well, you can bet nobody wanted to see that happen. We'll both be getting new orders soon."

"Well. I'll have to be derelict and insubordinate more often. I expected to be cashiered. That's what McClellan said."

"McClellan! Well, he should know, shouldn't he? But no, when somebody gets himself almost killed charging across the field to glory—rallies a regiment under the eyes of the whole damned—"

"You mean that German regiment? How did they do, anyhow? I couldn't see much."

"Well, enough, I guess—cleared the field—drove on into the woods till both flanks were turned. Lost 105 killed and wounded. Saved their honor, though, if that counts."

"It counts. It counts." Sid thinks back. "That captain who carried the colors, I hope he survived?"

"He did, and he'll be decorated, too. Berry was killed."

"Yes, I heard. That's too bad. So, did they promote you, too?"

"No, but it doesn't matter to me; I'm not a career officer. Besides, I'd be a brigadier same as Patrick. That wouldn't do."

"Colonel, thank you. I know I owe this rescue of my fortunes to you."

Sharpe sticks out a hand, and Sid takes it. "We owe something to each other, I guess. There were too many majors anyway, remember?"

"Maybe now there are too many colonels?"

Sharpe laughs. "But I'm a *full* colonel, Sawyer, and don't you forget it."

This doesn't settle everything, of course. They talk a bit more about those questions Sid had been listing in his head, and it seems Sharpe wonders about them, too, but knows little more than Sid.

And so, for the time being, Sid keeps his secrets: Joe's letter and Huck's journal.

They can't help noting the good news from Gettysburg, of course, and wondering what would have happened had Jackson been there. Like Sid, Sharpe takes some satisfaction that they may have had a hand in preventing that.

Finally, Sid notes that it was quite a coincidence—"strange war" or not—for him to have been waiting in the fog that morning of April 29 for his own brother. Sharpe agrees it was quite a coincidence, but as he rises to leave, Sid asks him: "Colonel, I'm surprised that as good a sleuth as you *didn't* know about Tom and me—and Becky."

In the doorway, Sharpe smiles. "Who says I didn't?"

And that's the end of Sid's service under George Sharpe. As for whether or not Huck really did shoot Jackson—though there was certainly enough wild firing in the woods that night to account for it otherwise—the major is convinced Huck at least intended to. And later reports by Jackson's surgeon, Dr. Hunter McGuire, are even more provocative. Jackson did not actually die till Sunday May 10—and, according to McGuire, of pneumonia, not the wounds themselves—but the ball that did the most damage was *not* recovered. Interesting.

But what happened to Huck himself? Having read the journal, the major knows key evidence is missing. More than ever, he wants to have a look at that grave site.

As it turns out, he need not wait till after the war. In mid-November of the following year, when Sid has returned to duty in Washington, training a battalion of combat engineers—well after the battles in the Wilderness and at Spotsylvania Courthouse, after Grant's move south to besiege Richmond and Sheridan's victories in the Shenandoah Valley and the President's apparent re-election—Becky Thatcher appears in Sid's office, a document in hand. Her bonnet is still on.

"All right, Colonel, here it is." She holds out the document. "It seems they won't give an inch to your bureau now, but they'll let us at the commission do what we want."

"This is—"

"Permission. I can take an escort detail—that's you, I guess, and whoever you want to bring along—and a big enough wagon to bring back those two officers and...whoever's buried with them."

So Lieutenant Colonel Sawyer heads to the site—with Nurse Thatcher, a wagonload of orderlies, a local guide, and a white flag—though they meet no opposition. Sid's leg is better now, although, as the surgeon had foretold, not much use.

They cross the river at U.S. Ford on a single remaining strand of pontoons, past the littered remains of the huge Union supply depot—what memories these awaken!—and proceed thence to the Bullock Road, little more than a forest track, as Joe had described it. Fortunately, that year's fighting in the Wilderness was mostly elsewhere, and there's less foliage now, which also helps. It is thus not long till they find the three swords, rusted but upright. The hat is gone, but the tattered boot, chewed by animals, still covers one hilt. A local farmer is pleased to show them the site of Jackson's death—right there! Shot by his own men! How does he know? Oh, he got it straight from "the officers." Even then, it was not hard for Sawyer to imagine future tour guides making a living showing travelers around.

They dig it up, and there's nothing now at Huck's end but bones and some hair, and a bit of remnants from the jacket and trousers—plus the buttons and a buckle. And one more intriguing item: what looks like a badly stained but still intact clerical collar. What had preserved that? If for no other reason, this *has* to be the grave.

They put the remains in a plain box (for now), and then Sid—he's sorry, Becky, but this has to be done—examines the remains and the site carefully, by hand. How he wishes Miss Carroll were along! He takes care to preserve what's left of the uniform and bandaging, even the boot, and examines the soil around the corpse carefully, looking for munitions, weapons, pieces of shell casing and so on—but he can't find it, not what he's looking for. They unearth the two other inhabitants of the trench, box them, too, and return to Washington.

On the way back, though he says nothing yet to Becky about it, Sid mulls it over: he *may* have the answer, but he'd like Dr. Carroll's confirmation. So, while Huck's remains are still in the hospital morgue awaiting further arrangements, Sid asks the doctor to look at them. She acknowledges the logic of his theory, at least to a point. Everything matches Joe's account: the grave site, what's on it, what's in it, right down to the chest wound—one ball lodged in the front of the spine—easily fatal—and bone damage from a foot wound.

And the stains on what is left of the jacket *seem* to be blood; although in those days even a skilled investigator could not always distinguish human blood from, say, a pig's.

But even so—something is missing.

"Don't you agree?" he asks Dr. Carroll, as they stand in the coolness of the hospital morgue, amid the smell of preservatives.

"But how can you be *sure*? With that much dirt?"

"Well, I'm as sure as I can be without some sort of magic wand. I took a lot of care."

"Then you could be right." Then she glances up at him as she scrubs her hands and arms in the washtub. "But supposing you were right…how do you think that would make you feel?"

Sid thinks about it. How does one think about feelings? "Well…if it were true, I'd be very glad…for him." But he knows she means more than that. "I guess…I guess I wouldn't feel any better about myself, though."

"I was thinking of Becky. Will you tell her?"

"Do you think I should? I mean, if she's reconciled herself…"

"Sid—" She raises an eyebrow. "You have to. If you don't, I will." She flushes the sink, towels off her arms, rolls down her sleeves. "And there are other things you must tell her, too, you know. Important things—about your own feelings."

He feels his chest tighten.

"I know, Doctor. I know."

"Sid—please—it's Mary."

Sid does tell Becky about Tom right away, of course. She already knows, fortunately—she reads the papers, too—and is relieved, because *she's* been putting off telling *him*.

So what did happen to Our Boy? Sid's guess is that he faked it—the death, that is—that once again Huck Finn had "lit out"—just as he had once before when he needed to get away from civilization and from Pap, another father of whose judgment and retribution (though of a very different kind) he was afraid.

How difficult would it have been? God knows there were plenty of dead men of all descriptions in those woods that night—no pig's blood necessary!—and how much trouble would it be to add wounds as needed, say, in the foot?

True, he needed to look enough like Huck from the side in the moonlight that even a friend like Joe would be convinced. That's tougher, but remember it's only moonlight we're talking about, and Joe says he didn't get down in the grave. But Tom, now—Tom *buried* him. So Tom had to be in on it, even if Joe wasn't, which he could well have been.

And so maybe Tom didn't kill Huck, after all—whatever other mischief he was up to that night. And it could have been considerable: Why *did* Averell seem to misunderstand all his instructions? Why *did* the wires keep getting inexplicably cut between Stafford Heights and the fords? But at the end Tom did a pretty fine thing for his friend, didn't he? He helped him get free. Even the attempt on Jackson itself could have been fakery. And if anyone *could* have brought off such a thing, wasn't it Tom Sawyer and Huck Finn? Tom's histrionics at the grave site alone must have been worthy of the National Theater! So, from one point of view, Tom may have turned out all right in the end.

But there is another point of view: he betrayed his country. His higher duty was to the Union. And, for Sid, that sharp line cuts through any friendship, or even kinship—even what feelings Becky might still have had for him. Was he really hung as a spy? Becky is never able to recover a body. But Sid believes he was, if only because faking *that* would have required too much conspiracy. Also, for Sid, it would be too convenient. He knows *he* killed Tom, just as surely as if he'd put a gun to his head (loaded this time) and pulled the trigger.

I should have run him through.

Sid's responsibility for Huck, dead or not, is even more troubling. Year after year, May after May, by himself usually, he stands by the old grave site—not the new one in Missouri by the river, but that pit in the Virginia woods, now filled in and covered with leaves and honeysuckle—and argues with himself: why hadn't he done this, or that, or the other, and—

Oh, give it up, Sid, Give it up! If he's not dead, he's long gone.

But if he's not dead, where is he? Well, he could get as far as the railroad at Gordonsville with the walking wounded. But he wouldn't stop there, would he? He'd have to get clear, finally, of this corrupt and collapsing East. How would he go? Well, another thing Sid discovered soon after the battle is that—although the major had kept his promise to be sure Butterfly survived, had in fact sent her to the ford with the reserve staff mounts—she had disappeared without requisition.

So Sid sees Huck out on the Plains with Prescott's guitar strapped to his back, art supplies in his bedroll, riding west on Butterfly, but—alas!—without the real "butterfly" beside him. For, having read the "*Hidalgo*" letter, and now the journal, Sid knows that the deceased Maria Poseta must have been Mariposa. And, for keeping that news from Huck, Sid knows he deserves any perdition Becky might have wished for him.

But of course he *could* have missed something in that grave. Could well have.

He learns one small piece of the story much later at a reunion of West Point veterans—not so many by now! Sid is delivering the toast in the old Napoleon Room and remarks that he'd once had his career saved, in all likelihood, by having an unloaded pistol when he'd tried to shoot a prisoner in cold blood.

"Let us drink," he proposes, "to the wish that in moments of blind rage *all* our weapons may be unloaded." And to that wish they raise their glasses.

After dinner, as the plates are cleared, a distinguished-looking old gentleman introduces himself to Sid as the very captain whose brains Sid had once tried to blow out at the holding pen above US Ford. It turns out they are both now professors of mathematics and engineering, and Sid says he is very glad that the man's brains survived. When Sid asks the man—whose name is Lafollette—what was going through his mind as Sid cocked the revolver, Lafollette says, "I was hoping you *would* blow my brains out! I'd decided being a prisoner was a fate worse than death."

Lafollette also recalls he had gotten a clear enough look at Huck to recognize him from Mexico. Lafollette happened to be the "sandy-haired young lieutenant" you'll recall bursting into the Mexican chapel and placing Huck under arrest—the left-hander.

Had he escaped then, when Sid's revolver failed to discharge?

"Yes, I did. Had to throw off my coat and swim for it. First bath in a week."

(A *captain's* coat…interesting.)

When Sid asks what he would have done had he spotted Huck later behind Rebel lines, Lafollette thinks about it and says: "Well, you know, Sawyer, I might have shot him—or I might have just taken him out to the pickets and said, 'Get lost, man! Don't you ever learn not to make up stories?'"

High Bar lived a long time, too, by the way—till very old, and very lame. But aren't we all?

As for what happened to Joe, I have no idea since he did not keep his promise to be available through the Freedmen's League, but we'd like to imagine him out there in the West with Our Boy, wouldn't we? Did Lee "adopt" him, too? It is tempting to wonder if Joe and Huck are connected in some such way—in view of his depiction in the cactus-juice sketch with less than typical Negroid features and reminding some of the Indies. And Huck himself, of course, is his mother's son, "freckly-faced" or not. Were they both offspring of old Finn's beautiful half-breed?

No, there are enough coincidences here already; I'll leave that investigation for others. I'll let mine stand as it is, and let the reader judge. The real judgment is later, of course. From God, if there is one, or from Time in any case. Time is something that exists, relative though it is, and must be taken seriously. Because it may well be all we have. Because it gives us duty. Because without time, there is no pressure, and without pressure there is no reason to do things, to decide. And if there is no God? Doesn't matter: the thinking man must reason, and to reason he must have premises, and to have those...he must act *as if* there is a God.

As if.

That is our task then: to strive with all our might to see the logic in the universe, to recognize its premises, and deduce from it our duty. And at some point we must report.

This, then, is my report.

****

The knock is polite but firm, as the Chinaman's would be, but it's not the Chinaman.

"General!" I exclaim. "What a pleasant surprise! Surely you didn't come back just to report to me! Of course I'll pay your transportation—"

"You don't owe me a cent, Sid. I had other reasons to come back east. And I'll have none of this 'General' nonsense. We're not in the Army any more. You're going to have to call me George now, whether you like it or not." He sticks out his hand. "Sorry to just show up like this. You need a phone here. You got my wire?"

"Yes, thank you."

"You see, I've got a cane now, like you."

And very white hair. As we sit by the fireplace, I realize I must look just as changed.

"So you found nothing in California?"

"I said I didn't find them. I didn't say I found nothing." He grins under his white moustache and hoists an old leather valise—"Remember the last time I got you something out of this?"

"My lieutenant-colonelcy."

"Yes—Well, look at this." He opens the leather straps. "I talked to Grangerford and some others, as you know. But this I just dug out of the bin in a club car—just looking for something to read, no matter how old and out of date. It's old all right." He drops on the coffee table one of the old illustrated newspapers. "Look at the last column." I unfold it with care, trying not to crumble the yellowing newsprint—the old kind, an eight-column page with small print but a sketch somewhere in each column to grab attention.

*"'*The Cavalryman's Bride, *by Sawmill Thompson'? What's that?"*

"It's one of those Western yarns. This Thompson says he heard a sermon in some mining camp about a young lieutenant who got the blessing of his father, an American General, to marry an Indian 'princess,' whose own father was dying and—well, just look at this part." He points to the last column:

...And as the two young lovers kissed their vows into solemnity before the Lord and before the chief and the general—the old Indian, who had lain in deathly pallor, threw off his shroud and spoke with miraculous strength. And, as the setting sun passed its gold-banded benediction, the old chief said that the Lord had given him to understand a great and saving Truth: that he might survive, and his People also, if the bride and her young officer would separate, after one night, to fulfill separate destinies: the bride to the royalty to which she was born, and the lieutenant to a great destiny in battle...till after long lives they should reunite, at last joining themselves and their Peoples.

And the old man grasped both their hands, and they looked at each other and, with tears streaming freely, agreed to the compact. And with

the dawn the old Indian rose from his bed, cured of his illness, and the two lovers parted for the length of their lives. But out of their one night together, Brethren, I have heard, there came a child—whose own life would be the instrument through which the best of both races were conjoined....

Every hair on my neck stands up

"Interesting," he says, " isn't it?"

"Good God—yes, of course!"

"And look at this." He unfolds another page—also very old—which looks like a map of northern California. The title says: "New Gold Fields in the North."

"I thought this location would interest you." He points to a name in small print on the north coast. "Can you make it out?"

"It's Spanish. Looks like... 'Sangre de Cerdo Beach.'"

"It does, doesn't it? Does that mean what I think it means?"

43. Good Enough, at Our Age

The road from the new bridge at Ely's goes through the woods much as it did then, though a bit wider and harder now to accommodate motor cars.

"How far now?" says the Chinaman.

"Not far. Those mounds are all that's left of the old works. Now help me look for the pits. The swords won't be there any more—souvenir hunters, you know—but maybe the planks I put up."

"Okay, but we park this damn noise-buggy here. Only Americans go motoring through sacred battleground. Your excellent wife should teach you better manners for the dead. No, *not* take your cane. You stab dead with that, you be sorry."

"Too bad," I laugh. "They'll just have to post pickets and check passwords. Wait till they see what I *am* going to use on them!"

One of our students pushes the cart with the metal-detector and its battery, and another carries the digging tools. My wife waits behind with the second car. A surprising reluctance, I think, after all this time.

"But," Chiang asks as we walk, "why one bullet matter so much anyway?"

"Because the journal was so clear about it. I even looked up the surgeon who was on duty in Frederick, and he remembered him—yes, he said, there was certainly an unusual foot wound, and a ball or something lodged in there, did the man require—Well, he was sorry to hear that, and so on.... So, there *was* a piece of metal in that foot, Chiang. And nothing like it was found in that grave."

Chiang purses his lips at the machine waiting on the cart with its awkward wooden frame. "What make you think this thing will work?"

"Well, it worked for Bell. Remember the assassination?"

"Lincoln?"

"No, no! Garfield. In '81. Bell used an induction balance—an early version of this."

"And he find the bullet?"

"No, he didn't; he found bedsprings and such. But his paper shows it will work fine for our purposes."

Soon we are sitting on a ground cloth by the pit as our students deploy the detection device. A farmer nearby is burning brush from cleared land, and smoke drifts in the air. There's the sound of an axe.

"So, tell me, Chiang, what do you think of my theory?"

"About bullet?

"No, no—about the deception."

He nods. "I tell you story about deception. You know my family come to work on railroad."

"Yes, you said your father came in—"

"Father come to work, and die same year of fever, and three brothers also die working on railroad. Three sleepers fallen on them, one for each brother. They bury them in canyon, say prayer for my benefit, then we move on, and steam shovel come next day, dig them up, grind them for hog feed. Waste nothing, you Americans."

I feel sick.

"I'm sorry. You fought for our nation, and yet we treated you so badly."

"No! *Not* bad. Better than Canton. There *all* die. Here I survive, only lose this." He waves his stump at me. "Have good life, good school—mission school good as Andover! Go to university, have good family, friends like you." He smiles. I'm not sure how to take this. "Look—deception sometime honorable. You should know that, of all people."

"I see. Is that something Sun-Tsu said?"

"Ha! Pay no attention to Sun-Tsu. He say everything somewhere. He say big oak and little oak all have same size nuts. Ha! But then he say better be little oak than big oak in wind storm, and two page later he say better big oak than little oak in a fire." He throws a rock off into the woods. "But about deception now, what count is result." He thinks about that. "Many time, you must respect who you deceive." He waves his good hand around. "I see respect all around here. This grave. This sword, given you by a good man." He looks at me. "You are a good man, my friend. Your excellent wife not have you in her bed otherwise."

That's not something I want to discuss, so I change the subject. "How do your students think you really lost your hand?"

"Ha! They maybe think I lose it fighting Samurai or something." Then he changes the subject himself. "You ever talk to that reporter?" He looks at me and smiles.

"Chiang—just tell me who it was."

He smiles, but does not reply....and suddenly I suspect something! "There never *was* a reporter, was there? You made it up, didn't you?"

He continues to smile brightly. "I never lie, my friend."

"Then why could I never—no one ever came to my house or—"

"Reporter call me about something else—new automobile law. We talk about one thing another, I ask if he interested in whatever happen to Huck Finn and he say, sure, so I tell him talk to you."

"But—*why* did you do that?"

"Because that book rotting in your closet, and rotting in your head, is why. You need it out and buried—with ceremony, just like corpse of—"

There's a shout and a student sticks his head up from the grave. "Professor, we've found something. You think this is it?"

My stomach flip-flops. The thing looks like the wrong shape, but...I tap it with my cane, gently, to get the clay off.

"It's a nail, Peter."

"But they used nails in canister sometimes, didn't they?" We are all quiet for a moment. "Couldn't that cause a foot wound?"

Yes, it could. I scrape at it a bit. Finally, I breathe a sigh of relief.

"See the round head? They didn't use those till after the war."

"Well—then there's nothing else."

"All right then, let's fill it in, and pack up." Then to the Chinaman: "So what do you think? Am I right?" I can't help adding: "And I assure you none of *my* evidence is made up."

He sighs. Looking off into the woods now, he doesn't look inscrutable, or even oriental, just old. "Well—eighty percent, maybe. I guess eighty percent good enough at our age."

But eventually he asks me what I knew he would ask. What anyone would ask. "But what good is his life, you know, without his love—his Mariposa?"

"Ah, that's the best part, Chiang. Look, I know you haven't read the *Adventures*—but listen to this." I fetch the book from my pack. "This is the part where Huck escapes from Pap's cabin: **"I fetched the pig in and took him back nearly to the table and hacked into his throat with the axe, and—"**

"Yes, yes, you told me that," he says, tossing a stone over the pit. "He pretend his own death, use pig blood and his own hair on axe. Very clever, but what that have to do with *her?*"

"This! Here is the letter from that Señor—the one young Sid never delivered. Now listen:

February 30, 1862
To the Honorable Gentleman, Sergeant Huckleberry Thatcher,
C/O the United States Territorial Command, Their Honors, &c—

This is to advise to the addressee of the passing of Señora Maria Poseta De La Plata De Los Montes De Sangre De Cerdo. The Honorable Sergeant is advised that dedicationes of suitable shrine of the deceased will take place at La Plata De Los Montes on May 5, 1862. Donationes and Offering shall be made available through post box of the Hon. Undersigned at Santa Clara or this post.

All his faithful and Obedient Servant,
The Honorable Señor Hidalgo De Los Montes"

He looks at it, then at me. "Sound very dignified. Only few mistake. I might make more myself."

"Only a few!"

"Well, he is Mexican."

"And you are Chinese. But if you had to send such a formal letter, what would you do?"

He thinks about it, then smiles. "I would ask you to write it, my friend."

"Exactly! This is an important landlord. He would not send a letter like this with an extra *e* in 'donations'!"

"So you think somebody else write it?"

"I think *she* wrote it. Look at the names: 'De La Plata' and 'Los Montes.' All right, those are from her dead husband and uncle, probably. But look at the rest: 'De Sangre De Cerdo'—literally 'of the Blood of a Pig'!"

"Pig's blood? So you think that she has done something like Huckleberry, then?"

"I do! Look at the dates."

"February 30. There is no such day."

"That's right. And you know what May 5 is in Mexico, don't you?"

He throws a stone off into the woods, where it clips a branch or two before landing. "I would show this to somebody. There may really be some place by this name."

"Sangre de Cerdo? I already have, and there *is*. But not in Mexico. In California!" Now he looks at me. I pick up a rock and throw it after his. "She did the same thing Huck did. She 'killed' herself somehow. Took herself out of the old life—the estate, the convent, whatever held her, maybe with the help of that Sojourner fellow, whether or not he was her father. He certainly knew who she was. The letter was to tell Huck their time had come."

"But" (patiently, as if to a slow student), "he never *receive* this letter, my friend, and *you* know why."

"So what?" I wave up at the sky. "Huck pulls news out of the air, from smoke, from invisible ink, from the River itself! Surely he found her. Maybe they got as far as the ocean. I hope so. He would enjoy the ocean—the mother of all rivers." He says nothing. "And then there's this." I fish around in my pack, pull out the old magazine, and point.

He reads the title: "'Cavalryman's Bride,' by Sawmill Thompson—what is that?"

"A story. Just listen." And I read him the final paragraphs.

"Nonsense!" huffs the Chinaman. "Sentimental nonsense. There probably hundred such stories."

"Yes, but look how it fits: everyone's promoted—Mariposa to Princess, Huck to lieutenant, Lee to general, Sojourner to chief, if he wasn't already. The 'mountain,' of course, would be in the Ozarks."

"But how this Thompson fellow know about Our Boy?"

"Because 'Sawmill Thompson' was only a pen name. His real name was Sawyer—Tom Sawyer."

"Sawyer!" He thinks about it. "So—you think the child *was* Huck's?"

"Well, the one Buck saw is probably the Mexican lieutenant's, and I can't prove there was another. But *something* was settled there, among the two old men and—what? Are you smiling?"

He chuckles. "Yes, I smile! Is good story, true or not. What harm to believe it? And to think you find it out, and not Clemens! Have you told Becky this theory?"

"Of course. Eventually." The breeze has picked up, and it's getting cold. It is November, after all. "Don't worry about Becky. She's fine. She continues her work with Mary. The new nursing standards are largely their work, you know."

"And she forgive everything…all this?" Chiang waves his hand over the pit and the woods beyond.

"Well—'everything' is a big word. There are things we don't talk about."

I close the journal, then remember the butterfly and replace it in the book. The sound of the axe has stopped, its owner probably coming to see if we're on his property. There is still some smoke.

"Look, Chiang—I try not to deceive myself. I know I'm no hero—in spite of that medal. I killed my own half-brother, just as sure as if I'd tied the noose myself, and I sent a friend to kill his father, for God's sake, and maybe to his own death, not to mention Danforth—Huey's men—a hundred or so Germans."

"Yes, and others sent tens of thousand. It was your duty to do all that."

"Well, maybe. I've always tried to do that. I've followed the rules. I've worked hard, come home at night. I've—I've had no children of my own—Dr. Carroll and I married too late, I guess, but—"

"But you teach other people's children," he reminds me.

And then a voice behind us, "Yes, and he has much to do before Monday!" It's Mary. "I was afraid the two of you had fallen into a pit, and I would have to send these boys back after a winch. Come on!"

I take her hand, and she hands me my cane. As we walk to the cars, I think of a question of my own. "Where *did* you lose the hand, Chiang? Gettysburg? You had them both after Chancellorsville."

He laughs. "Long after war—set firework with blasting cap, to show students safe procedure."

"Oh," says Mary. "Speaking of mysteries—do you remember that closet-full of things you brought home from the Bureau, that I've been after you to go through?" (We are standing by the cars now. One of the boys is working the crank.) "Well, I finally looked through it, and do you know, there's a bundle of mail in there." I lean toward her to hear. "Yes. Now you listen: it goes back a long time, more than twenty years. Goodness knows why you didn't notice it. Nothing important, I hope."

I think about that. Twenty years!

"Throw it out," says Chiang. "Or burn it, even better. Not even look at it. You hear me—both of you?"

I sigh. "Maybe you're right."

"Well," says Mary, "can I help it if you men never clean up your own messes?"

The cars are idling fine now. Chiang waves at them, then turns back to me. "Come on. Modern students not wait till dark for old folk like us!"

****

Well, I'm tempted to say, as Our Boy once did, that now there isn't anything more to write, and I am rotten glad of it. Or if there is, as a result of this blasted map, which I half suspect Sharpe contrived as a joke—never mind the possibility of another child somewhere—someone else will have to write it. After all, as Mary noted, I do have a stack of scaled drawings to grade, and California is too far—even if the rails make it easier now.

Mary says I should cease my "obsession" with these matters and spend more time on something wholesome, like astronomy, which a colleague has gotten me interested in. Or paleontology—fossil hunting—as if that weren't what this has been all along! Paleontology is the Chinaman's suggestion. He says it would use my "passive strength."

All right. I shall. And perhaps someday when I shake that jar by the bed I'll see only snow, not the smoke of battle. Only trees, not the graves under them. And when I too light out (old Sam and I will probably check out together), I have no idea where I'll go, but I hope there are stars. Or dinosaurs.

As for Hell, it doesn't scare me. I've been there before.

The End

Notes

1. I have corrected Huck's spelling in the journal, while trying to preserve his voice. This led to tradeoffs: e.g., "correcting" *knoed* to *knowed*—as if there can be a standard spelling of a nonstandard usage!

2. Strategists take note: Sometimes coming straight at the enemy over forbidding terrain makes sense if it is what he does *not* expect. Lee doesn't forget this lesson either. But another young officer, Joseph Hooker, a bit of a rival of Lee's, was impressed by Cerro Gordo and is now convinced that another flank attack is the way to go. In fact, he is looking for a new route when the big frontal attack is launched. Hooker is livid and files charges against Scott. Hooker loses and eventually is exiled to California. Scott has a long memory. Thus, we see the truth of another, older lesson: if you strike at the king, you'd better topple him!

3. There is a rhythm to firing when it first begins: since it takes at least twenty seconds to reload a musket, the early fire comes in pulses, if not volleys, and often takes several minutes to reach a constant roar.

4. Much cooler than Becky Thatcher, who goes to pieces, you will recall, just from being in a cave with poor, hapless Tom Sawyer.

5. Yes, John Bell Hood. The one after whom all those little lanes are named in places like Atlanta, Georgia and Fredericksburg, Virginia. Cemeteries, too. A few years later his rash offensives will put nearly 30,000 southern boys into those graves. But in these days he is a charming lad with a sense of humor. And still has the arm and the leg he will later lose in battle.

6. The telegraph was a mixed blessing for armies, as new inventions often are. It promised instant control of distant forces without sending horsemen back and forth (for want of a shoe, and all that). Grant later will require telegraph posts at all corps HQs. Which is fine if you're running a siege, but a fluid campaign can be severely constricted. Important messages are lost because a line is down, and no one knows till it's too late. When a horseman

is sent, the message often is not timed and dated, so the recipient is unclear about the intent. There's that lesson again: *Dates! Times!* And *be precise!*

7. More than one, evidently. A Thomas Sawyer is listed (by another competent reporter, Walt Whitman) as a soldier and hospital orderly at the federal headquarters on Stafford Heights—unless Tom had even more identities. As the reader can well imagine, this has complicated my research!

8. Like many non-cavalrymen, including Sid, Sharpe tends to use the infantry term, "company," instead of "troop," the usual cavalry term.

9. No date, as usual, but it's likely April 19, 1861, because his trip to Arlington was probably on the 21st.

10. Custis Lee was actually out of school and on army duty in Washington, D.C. Lee had managed to get him a post there so that he could look after the estate in his father's absences.

11. Lee was then on leave to handle family affairs after the death of his father-in-law. He had to decide how to finance needed repairs to Arlington, as well as how to effect Mr. Custis's wish that his sixty-three slaves should be freed within five years. Lee himself owned no slaves and had no desire to be a slave-master—or trader—but the house was left to his wife and, since she was ailing, he had to put many of the "servants" to more work than they were used to in order to help repair the house and grounds.

12. Later, at Gettysburg, he has his moment of glory, noticing the importance and vulnerability of Little Round Top—and getting enough troops there just in time: notably the 20th Maine, under Joshua Chamberlain.

13. There was much moving back and forth between arms of the service and infantry officers moved to the cavalry (Sheridan, for example), often retained the more familiar terminology, using battalion for squadron, company for troop, etc.

14. It's possible they were supposed to explode, but did not. Confederate artillery shells were notorious for their high percentage of "duds."

15. Presumably Alpheus Williams, acting commander of the Twelfth Corps.

16. Lee's cartographer, the capable Jed Hotchkiss, calls it Lewis Run on his map for some reason, but everywhere else it's Scott's Run.

17. McClellan, of course, could have confirmed Huck's identity. It's interesting that Scott didn't know about that—or if he did, that he didn't consider it dispositive!

18. Could be General J.E.B. Stuart—Lee's cavalry chief. But if it is, Huck may be mixed up about the time, because Stuart himself, by other reports, doesn't arrive till later in the evening. Or it could be Fitz Lee or Tom Munford—the beard and the feathered hat were standard issue in the Rebel cavalry.

19. Power Smith, no doubt—a young minister and a captain on Jackson's staff.

20. Jackson's chief engineer.

21. Sedgwick commands the Union force left at Fredericksburg, 30,000 strong. His part of the grand strategy is to hold Lee in place while Hooker crosses the river upstream and moves down onto Lee's flank, or—if Lee moves west to face Hooker—Sedgwick can cross through the town and come up the turnpike in Lee's rear. Ambiguous messages and trouble with the wires have kept Sedgwick out of action thus far. Eventually he *does* drive off the small force Lee has left there under General Jubal Early and moves up the Pike toward Hooker. But victory depends on Lee's following Hooker's plan, and not one of his own—a dubious hope.

22. What King Henry II is supposed to have said about Thomas Beckett, Archbishop of Canterbury—a comment reported to have led to Beckett's assassination by a group of nobles.

23. *Cymbeline*.

24. Jackson, of course, actually took a few more days to die—not till May 10.

25. If so, it's unlikely they were as far forward as the Burton Farm, or they'd *not* have seen part of Jackson's assault force, Colquitt's and Ramseur's brigades, pass by, which they evidently *did*. There is some high ground at the edge of the woods behind the farm with good visibility from tree level. From there they'd *not* have seen Paxton's brigade (as they evidently did not) the extreme end of Jackson's line, waiting behind them on the plank Road. There is no building there now, but there could well have been at the time. Ramseur and Paxton, by the way, were kept out of the assault by Colquitt's delay—disobeying Jackson's instructions to plow ahead no matter what. For that, Colquitt was later relieved of command.

26. Wilderness Church, no doubt. Good for Joe: if you have no map, at least note the landmarks!

27. The Eleventh Corps ran so capably, in fact, that most avoided being either killed or captured, and when noses were counted in a day or two, most

were again available for duty—for what that was worth in their case. On the first day at Gettysburg, they will set new records in the sprint. After that, the corps is disbanded.

28. He's right about Keith Boswell, but wrong about James Power Smith: the young minister survived. He had heard the command given to fire and dove for the ground.

29. Who else? Dan Sickles—back at Hazel Grove now and worried about being cut off—had gotten permission to launch a night attack, which once again lit up the woods—ruling out peaceful burial details!

Sources and Acknowledgments

Many Thanks

The author thanks first his wife and family, whose encouragement and forbearance (for the time this took if for nothing else) were essential. The author also is grateful to a number of folk who lent their professional expertise and/or encouragement to this project: Robert K. Krick and Mac Wyckoff of the U.S. Park Service, Charles Bryan of the Virginia Historical Society, Sherri Oesterheld of the Commonwealth Governor's School. Ms. Oesterheld checked the math—not the author's area of expertise—and the others kindly prevented numerous unintentional factual mistakes. (As for the intentional kind, see below.) Finally the author wishes to thank a former student, Mike Taylor, and old friends John Gilstrap and Phil Edgren, whose critical insights were invaluable to a writer unused to fiction—Phil, especially, who saved me from an embarrassing slew of errors.

Source List (MLA-worshipers may wish to lie down first.)

Maps

These are (for better or worse) the author's own. Any mistakes in geography, especially with respect to Texas and Mexico, are probably deliberate: when something was unknown or unknowable, the author simply made it up. Truth, as old Sam knew, outranks accuracy any day.

Books

Ambrose, Stephen: *Duty, Honor, Country: A History of West Point.* Johns Hopkins U. Press, 1999. (Lots of useful minutiae. Contains Jimmy

Whistler's drawing of a sleeping cadet and the Civil War-period photograph of cadets, one of them in mourning.)

Bradford, Ned. ed. *Battles and Leaders of the Civil War* (one-volume edition), Fairfax Press, 1956.

The Editors of *Time-Life Books*: Several volumes from the *Time-Life Civil War* series (all useful, with excellent maps and many period photographs and drawings, including those of the marvelous snowball fight and of carrying the wounded out of the burning Wilderness).

The Bloodiest Day: The Battle of Antietam (Ronald H. Bailey & the Editors) 1984.

Decoying the Yanks: Jackson's Valley Campaign. (Champ Clark, et al.) 1984.

Pursuit to Appomattox: The Last Battles. (Jerry Korn, et al.), 1987.

Rebels Resurgent: Fredericksburg to Chancellorsville. (William Goolrick, et al.) 1985.

Spies, Scouts and Raiders: Irregular Operations. (By the Editors) 1985.

Freeman, Douglas Southall: *R.E. Lee: A Biography.* V.1-4. Scribner's, 1936. (An indispensable source, especially on the early Lee, but whose maps have, sad to say, glaring deficiencies.)

Frassanito, William A. *Grant and Lee: The Virginia Campaigns, 1864-65.* Scribner's, 1983. (A really good source of period photographs.)

Furgurson, Ernest B. *Chancellorsville 1863: The Souls of the Brave.* Alfred A. Knopf, 1992. (As good a one-volume treatment of the battle as there is.)

Linderman, Gerald F. *Embattled Courage: The Experience of Combat in the American Civil War.* The Free Press, 1987.

McPherson, James. *For Cause and Comrades: Why Men Fought in the Civil War.* Oxford University Press, 1997.

Robertson, James I., Jr. *Standing Like a Stone Wall: The Life of General Thomas J. Jackson.* Atheneum Books, 2001.

Royster, Charles. *The Destructive War: William Tecumseh Sherman, Stonewall Jackson, and the Americans.* Alfred A. Knopf, 1991.

Sears, Stephen W. *Landscape Turned Red: The Battle of Antietam.* Ticknor & Fields, 1983.

Wiley, Bell Irvin. *The Life of Johnny Reb: The Common Soldier of the Confederacy.* Louisiana State University Press, 1970. (Still the standard source—along with Wiley's companion volume, *The Life of Billy Yank*—on what soldiering was really like.)

Internet Sources

Association to Commemorate the Chinese Serving in the American Civil War (ACCSACW). Various authors: Weblog sponsored by ACCSACW, available at: http://hometown.aol.com/gordonkwok/accsacw.html

Robson, Rich. "The History of Kung Fu San Soo" *Jade Dragon Online.* 2006. Available at: http://www.jadedragon.com/archives/kfsansoo.html

Printed in the United States
115809LV00006B/133-162/A

9 781424 194766